Praise for Candace Calvert

"Fans of Dee Henderson and *Grey's Anatomy* will love this wonderfully sweet, healing story about finding one's way back to love after losing everything. Candace knows how to minister to her readers while keeping them on the edge of their seats—I'm adding this winner to my library of Candace Calvert bestsellers!"

—SUSAN MAY WARREN, RITA and Christy–Award winning author of the Christiansen Family series

"Candace Calvert is a master storyteller at the pinnacle of her career. Few authors can develop a novel surrounding loss and grief yet leave the reader with a smile on their face and a tremendous sense of hope. An author who can do that truly is a gifted wordsmith. Don't miss out on *Step by Step*."

—JORDYN REDWOOD, author of the Bloodline Trilogy

"Candace Calvert has delivered another feel-good prescription for a happy ending. *Step by Step* makes me want to volunteer as a crisis chaplain, adopt a pet from a shelter, and hug my best friend. Solid characters, real-life issues, and sweet romance . . . all administered with a hefty dose of hope."

—VARINA DENMAN, award-winning author of *Jaded* and *Justified*

"Candace Calvert launches the Crisis Team series, as she continues to reign as top inspirational medical-romance writer."

—*BOOKLIST* ON *BY YOUR SIDE*

step

by step

CANDACE CALVERT

TYNDALE HOUSE PUBLISHERS, INC. · CAROL STREAM, ILLINOIS

Visit Tyndale online at www.tyndale.com.

Visit Candace Calvert's website at www.candacecalvert.com.

TYNDALE and Tyndale's quill logo are registered trademarks of Tyndale House Publishers, Inc.

Step by Step

Cover designed by Tobias' Outerwear for Books

Edited by Sarah Mason Rische

Published in association with the literary agency of Natasha Kern Literary Agency, Inc., P.O. Box 1069, White Salmon, WA 98672.

Scripture quotations are taken from the *Holy Bible*, New Living Translation, copyright © 1996, 2004, 2007, 2013 by Tyndale House Foundation. Used by permission of Tyndale House Publishers, Inc., Carol Stream, Illinois 60188. All rights reserved.

Step by Step is a work of fiction. Where real people, events, establishments, organizations, or locales appear, they are used fictitiously. All other elements of the novel are drawn from the author's imagination.

Library of Congress Cataloging-in-Publication Data

Calvert, Candace, date, author.
  Step by step / Candace Calvert.
    pages cm— (Crisis Team)
Summary: Three years after a tragic accident left her a widow, ER nurse Taylor Cabot is determined to move on, checking off one item on her survival list after another. Her relationship with a handsome plastic surgeon even gives her hope for the last point-- "fall in love again." At least until crisis chaplain Seth Donovan steps back into her life, reawakening unanswered questions about her husband's death. While in San Diego to train community volunteers, Seth hopes to learn why Taylor is backing away from the crisis team and from their friendship. But nothing prepares him for the feelings that arise when he sees Taylor again . . . and sees her moving on with another man. When a community crisis hits home and puts lives at risk, emotions run high and buried truths are unearthed. Will hope make the survival list?
  ISBN 978-1-4143-9034-5 (sc : alk. paper)
  I. Title.
  PS3603.A4463S74 2016
  813'.6--dc23   2015028965

Printed in the United States of America

22   21   20   19   18   17   16
 7   6   5   4   3   2

For crisis volunteers, caring heroes who put their hearts on the line when tragedy strikes.

We can make our plans, but the LORD *determines our steps.*

PROVERBS 16:9

1

"YOU TOOK YOUR WEDDING RINGS OFF."

"I . . . did." Taylor Cabot glanced at her hand resting on the weathered boardwalk railing and found the small indentation on her third finger. She refused to accept her stomach's reflexive quiver. Her younger cousin Aimee Curran was right: the rings had finally come off, after migrating from her left to right hand in a painfully slow march through grief—like a turtle navigating broken glass. But two days ago she'd soaped her finger, twisted the rings off, and tucked them back into their original Grebitus & Sons box—along with a creased and well-worn love poem. The only poetry her firefighter husband ever attempted in his too-short life. *"My life . . . my wife . . . I love you more . . ."*

Taylor drew a deep breath of salty-cool March air, grateful there was no fresh stab of pain. Almost three years after the horrific accident that snuffed Greg's life, his death was a scar, not a tender scab now. All as it should be. She swept aside a breeze-tossed strand of her coppery hair and met her cousin's gaze. "It was time."

Aimee's eyes, nearly the exact Curran green as her own, held Taylor's for a moment. "I'm proud of you."

"Thanks. I'm . . ." Taylor raised her voice over the lively thrum from the busy boardwalk and beach below: music, loudspeakers, carnival rides, childish squeals, and the amazing syncopated flap-flutter of hundreds upon hundreds of colorful and wildly fanciful kites surfing the sea breeze—the annual Kidz Kite Festival in its full glory. She smiled, new certainty buoying her as well. "I'm kind of proud of myself, actually."

"You should be." Aimee returned her smile. "And I'm selfish enough to think that moving back home was a big part of that."

"It was."

In fact, it was at the top of the Survival List Taylor had drafted—edited, rewritten, lain awake night after night getting straight in her head and in her heart—during the last edgy, anxious months in Sacramento. Those long months she had been so frustrated with herself, uncomfortably angry, and completely sick of being a widow, an unwilling member of a select club no one ever wanted to belong to. Moving away had seemed like a good way to move on. It had been a tough decision, finally made easier when she was asked out on her first new-widow date—by the husband of a close friend. When Taylor's skin stopped crawling, and after she'd hurled her cell phone against the kitchen wall, she sat down and drafted her list.

She hadn't shared it with anyone, but accomplishing every

last item, regardless of how difficult, had become Taylor's biggest goal. She was determined to move forward, step by shaky step.

Transfer to a nursing position at San Diego Hope ER
Start jogging again
Lose the Krispy Kremes—and fifteen pounds
Find a good vet for Hooper
Take off wedding rings
Go through the last of Greg's things

And—
"So . . ." Aimee's brows rose a fraction. "Did the gorgeous Dr. Halston have anything to do with the timing?"

"Timing?"

"Taking off your rings. You know, that you've been seeing him?"

"Not exactly . . . maybe," Taylor conceded, unable to deny the confusing mix of feelings the surgeon managed to inspire. If you asked anyone at San Diego Hope hospital, they'd say Taylor Cabot and Rob Halston were a couple. Typical grapevine speculation. And not true. Though, lately, each step in Taylor's life did seem to be headed closer and closer to—"It's really more of a friendship thing."

Her cousin's lips quirked ever so slightly. "Always a good place to start."

"I guess." Taylor tried her best for a casual shrug. "I'm not sure I'm ready for anything more than that. Not quite yet."

It was the last item on her checklist: *Fall in love again.*

"I'm sorry." Aimee touched her arm. "I didn't mean to put you on the spot. It's so good to see you looking happier."

"I know." Taylor smiled at her cousin. "And I am. Really . . ."

Her gaze swept the vista beyond the railing, a long stretch of beach and tranquil green ocean dotted with palm trees and pastel clusters of beachfront bungalows. The sun shone on red clay roofs of far grander homes on the cliffs above. Today's cloudless blue sky boasted a joyful rainbow of kites. Like hope on a Southern California breeze. It was starting to feel that way now. She was back home, part of a skilled, tight-knit ER team at the same hospital where her favorite cousin worked in the dietary department. It wasn't perfect; Taylor didn't expect that. But it did seem promising, as if peace and healing were really possible. A new beginning. No more painful detours after unimaginable tragedy.

"Look." Aimee jabbed her finger toward the distance. "See? Between the big purple dragon and the SpongeBob that keeps going into a spin? It's a plane. I'm surprised they let the pilot fly in that close with all that's going on here. Maybe it belongs to a news team."

"Don't think so," Taylor said, locating the small plane. "There's a privately owned airstrip a few miles from here. Greg had a pilot friend who got permission to use it a couple of times when we flew in to visit the folks." She hesitated, prepared for a pang, but the memory came painlessly: Greg sitting beside his buddy at the controls of the rented plane, then turning back to grin at Taylor with boyish excitement on his handsome face—so full of life. The sun glittering like diamonds on the surface of the sea, that breathtaking view of Coronado Island from high above, and the roller-coaster dip in her stomach when the plane tilted into a turn . . .

"He'll probably be directed to another approach," Taylor guessed, buoyed once again by the certainty that removing her rings had been good timing. Not because of what might or might not be on the horizon with Rob Halston, or even that the rings had been looming large on her checklist, but because she really was past the worst now. She thought of what she'd said to her cousin, that the pilot would be directed to another approach. Maybe Taylor was being redirected too. A giddy laugh rose. She tapped Aimee's shoulder. "You know what we need?"

"Kettle corn?"

"No way. I've only logged 11,000 steps today." Taylor touched her activity-tracking bracelet. "It won't work in my calorie budget."

"That evil thing. I keep telling you: Curran women are born to be curvy. You're coming dangerously close to losing your membership." Aimee feigned a childish pout. "Okay, what *else* do we need?"

"Kites!" Taylor pointed down the crowded boardwalk. "Down there, past the face-painting booth, there's a tent where we can make our own. All different kinds of options: diamond kites, rollers, deltas, sleds. Crazy colors and even glitter. C'mon, we haven't flown one together since we were Girl Scouts."

"Wait, hold on." Aimee squinted, staring toward the ocean. "That plane . . . I swear its wing skimmed the water. Some kind of air show? But it seems too reckless even for that."

"Where?" Taylor turned to look at the same moment the crowd around them exploded with shouts.

"What's he doing?"

"Oh no, that plane's in trouble!"

"Pull up, dude!" a young man yelled. "Stop clowning—"

"There," a woman offered with breathless relief. "He's back up in the air again and turning toward—"

No.

Taylor's heart stuttered as the small plane banked erratically, dropped far too close to the water again, then hurtled, out of control, across the sand.

She grabbed her cousin's arm. "He's coming right at us!"

"Look out," someone shrieked. "He's gonna hit the board-walk! Run; get away from here!"

A tidal wave of screams was drowned by a deafening engine roar. Then a horrifying overhead shadow, a rush of wind that nearly knocked Taylor to her knees, the acrid and eye-watering scent of airplane fuel—and finally a thunderous, earth-jolting crash.

"Aimee!"

2

"... SMALL PLANE HIT the boardwalk, tore out the kite festival booths," Taylor reported, her voice huffing into the cell phone as she hustled toward the surreal swath of destruction just yards beyond. She'd dialed 911 and started running after the first tent collapsed. "I think the pilot crashed it onto the beach. I see some smoke out there now. There are so many children here," she added, battling a wave of queasiness. "Could be large numbers of serious injuries—a multi-casualty incident."

"Yes, ma'am. We have first responders en route." Sirens split the air, confirming the dispatcher's assurance. "Keep yourself a safe distance back and—"

"Yes, thanks," Taylor lied. *Stay back? Not happening.*

"C'mon, keep up with me." Taylor tugged at her cousin's

arm, raising her voice over the frantic chaos, shouts and screams of people running in every direction. "We need to go see what we can do."

"I can't. Oh, please . . ." Aimee pulled back and stopped walking, her eyes huge in her pale face and her whole body trembling. Her gaze swept the mangled tents and dozens of shell-shocked walking wounded, some with bleeding injuries. "I'm not good with this, Taylor. You know that. I'm a cook, not a nurse. I can't—"

"But I *have* to," Taylor interrupted, adrenaline making her tremble as well. She sucked in a breath tainted with a sickening mix of spilled beer, engine smoke, and panic-induced human sweat. "I need to go do what I can to help."

Her heart cramped as she met Aimee's gaze. "Here, sweetie." She took her cousin's clammy hand and led her to a low rock wall a few yards away. "Stay here." Taylor stripped off her lightweight hoodie and tucked it around Aimee's shoulders. "Give Lucas a call and tell him you're okay. I'll come back after I see what I can do to help. Someone needs to step up until the medics arrive. I'll meet you here. Right here. Okay?"

Aimee nodded, smiling weakly. "I'm sorry."

"No need." Taylor grimaced as a man strode by carrying a whimpering child in his arms. Someone shouted for help in the distance. Overhead, the loud thrum of rotor blades announced the arrival of a helicopter; she hoped it was a first responder and not media. She touched Aimee's arm. "Send up a few prayers."

"I will—be careful!"

Taylor took off at a jog, her eyes scanning the destruction in front of her. Flattened tents, upended tables, twisted metal canopy supports, broken glass . . . frothy puddles of soda, hot dog buns, and scattered mounds of merchandise: T-shirts, hats, hundreds of twisted kites. There were people kneeling on the ground and parents frantically calling names. A handful of other people, like Taylor, were scrambling to find some way to help.

"I'm an ER nurse," she announced, wading into the first clutch of survivors. A young adult sat on the ground holding a T-shirt against his bleeding thigh. Two sobbing children cowered in parents' arms—one with a wicked slice down her cheek. The child's mother pressed a bib against the wound as a compress.

"Thank you," the young woman said, tears shimmering in her eyes. "I think we're okay here for now, but . . ." She turned to look down the line of wrecked tents. "One of the women in the face-painting booth can't find her little boy, and someone said the man running the pretzel stand cut his arm really bad."

"Help!" A voice shouted again in the distance and then was joined by a chorus of other shouts. "We need help down here. Hurry!"

Taylor ran to the boardwalk railing and saw a crowd of twenty or more people surrounding the downed plane—a Cessna, it looked like, tipped on one wing with its nose buried in the sand. There was a thinning trail of smoke, no fire. People began waving their arms.

"It's the pilot," someone yelled. "We got him out, but it doesn't look like he's breathing. Get help!"

Taylor clambered over the low railing, then took off at a dead run across the sand, her brain checking off rescue protocols for cardiocerebral resuscitation: compressions first, get the blood circulating to mimic the victim's pulse. Her own heartbeat was blasting her eardrums with each footfall across the sand.

"Let me through," Taylor ordered, taking a gulping breath as she pushed through the anxious onlookers. "I'm a nurse. Where is the—?"

There.

The pilot was lying supine on the sand maybe ten yards from the wreckage; a furrow in the sand indicated he'd been dragged free. Taylor tried not to imagine the complications of that action if the man had a neck fracture, but then that might be the least of his problems. His face was gray, jaw slack, and his eyes had rolled back. She lurched forward in the sand and dropped to her knees beside the unconscious man. No palpable pulse, not breathing. Mercifully, sirens wailed in the distance as she positioned her hands over his sternum.

"He thought it was heartburn," a fiftyish woman, almost certainly the pilot's wife, sobbed as Taylor began compressions. "He was dripping sweat and dizzy. We were trying to make it to the airstrip."

Compress the sternum two inches . . . hundred times a minute . . .

"Please . . . please help my husband!"

Taylor rocked forward, elbows locked, pressing her weight against the man's sweat-soaked polo shirt, finding the rhythm and hearing it in her head, the way she'd taught it to new Hope medical employees. To the beat of an old disco tune, "Stayin' Alive"—"ah, ha, ha, ha, stayin' alive." The perfect cadence, though by the look of things here, she wasn't at all sure the lyrics fit the prognosis.

"Medics are coming!" someone shouted. "And the beach patrol. The hospital helicopter, too. Everybody's coming now!"

"Oh, thank you, God," the pilot's wife sobbed, sinking to her knees. "My Sandy . . . he can't die."

Taylor rocked her weight forward onto the man's chest again. *"Ah, ha, ha, ha, stayin' alive, stayin' alive . . ."*

She glanced at the pilot's vacant, glazed eyes and prayed that "everybody's coming" meant the community's crisis team too. Though San Diego's volunteers didn't call themselves "chaplains," as the Sacramento team did, they had the very same objective: to offer help and hope to survivors in crisis situations. And this woman was going to need them.

———

Crisis responder Seth Donovan braced his big palm against the console as the veteran police officer, his old friend, braked to a stop on the boardwalk. Walt squelched the siren, but countless others continued to wail, punctuated by the endless stuttering *thwoop* of helicopter blades. San Diego's kite festival had morphed into something akin to a battlefield.

"Victim's down on the sand," Walt explained, peering over his glasses at a paramedic crew unloading their gear. "The pilot. Wife told dispatch he was having chest pain and lost consciousness. She tried to set the plane down on the sand . . ."

"But it didn't work out that way." Seth grimaced, imagining the woman's fear, confusion, and panic. The events of today would have been nowhere in her plans. Neither would be the aftermath, for the pilot's wife and a large number of other people affected by this tragedy: victims, survivors, bystanders, and first responders. The perfect setup for traumatic stress. It was the very reason Seth was in this car.

"You going down there with me?" Walt asked, opening his door.

"For sure." Seth rubbed his knee—the old injury was always stiff after cramming his body into airplane seats, even for the short hop from Sacramento. He'd come to help with the training for new crisis volunteers. "I've been at this too long to expect disasters to wait until I've unpacked my suitcase and grabbed a nap. Or walked my dog on the beach." He smiled, thinking of the fox red Lab pup wedging her wriggling body into a cargo crate in her eagerness to accompany him. Lucy. Seven months old, cinnamon colored, with still-clumsy paws—she was the new and unexpected balm in his life. "You know, all that normal, everyday R & R stuff."

"You, kicking back? That'll be the day, Donovan. I've known you too long to buy that. I needed a playbook to follow you these last couple of years: that Sac County deputy shot by the freeway sniper, the warehouse explosion last fall . . ." Walt shook his head. "And don't tell me you're not already gearing up to hang with the families of every kid they pull out of the rivers this summer—God bless 'em."

"When tragedy strikes, we're there." Whoever wrote the California Crisis Care tagline had nailed it.

"Plus," Walt continued as they trotted after the paramedics headed to the beach, "rumor has it that you'll be tapped when the Crisis Care director position opens up in August."

It was fact, not rumor, and something Seth wanted but . . . "Nothing official yet. And I'm still dealing with a lot of things at the business."

"You'll be taking the helm at Donovan's Uniforms?"

"For now," Seth said simply, deciding not to share his struggle with that particular situation. Taking over permanently at all three store locations would be a full-time commitment, leaving little to no room for Seth's crisis work. Donovan's had been his father's business, a family legacy. He'd trusted Seth with it. And now there'd been an offer to buy the business outright.

No, Seth couldn't think about that now. Better to concentrate on the task at hand. He was glad to see what looked like an incident command site set up on the boardwalk. Plenty of first responders. No sign yet of the crisis team—easy to spot in their green jackets—but they'd be here soon; Seth had no doubt. They likely had a number of volunteers on call during this special event. From what he'd heard, there had been multiple injuries in this incident but no reported fatalities—yet.

"I was sorry to hear about your dad's passing," Walt added. "Emphysema's a long, tough battle. Even when you know the odds, it's still hard to face that loss. A man's father . . ."

"Yeah."

Even after five months, it still affected Seth more than he cared to admit, almost like someone jamming a Taser to his chest. When the opportunity came to spend these two weeks in San Diego, he'd accepted, hoping it would be a brief respite. Walt had offered his garage apartment, which had its own fenced yard—perfect for Lucy. Some beach time could be a good prescription.

"Oh, man." Walt gave a low whistle at the scene ahead. A crowd held back by law enforcement, two beach patrol vehicles, a fire rig, and a just-landed San Diego Hope helicopter, its blades still rotating. The blue-and-white single-engine

Cessna was pitched forward, tail up and canted sideways onto one wingtip.

"Lucky it didn't explode," Walt noted as they trotted closer.

"Yeah," Seth agreed, scanning the small group of people allowed to remain closest to the craft. Several police officers, a fire official, and a late-middle-aged woman. From her distraught body language, she was probably the pilot's wife. And there, lying on his back, was the pilot. Under CPR.

"Dispatch said an off-duty ER nurse started resuscitation," Walt explained as they came to a halt a few yards away. "Just happened to be at the festival."

"Good thing." Seth wasn't much on coincidence. "So it looks like a toss-up between the fire medics and the San Diego Hope flight team to take over from our Good Samaritan nurse?"

"Looks like it."

Seth glanced at the wife again; her blouse was torn and there was a smear of blood near one nostril. She probably didn't even realize she'd been injured. But Seth knew the bigger trauma would be to watch her husband packed into that waiting helicopter. No one here, no matter how seasoned a professional, was immune to the powerful emotional impact of tragedy. His gaze drifted to the woman doing cardiac compressions. A nurse, on her day off, kneeling in the sand to save the life of a stranger. She'd be affected too. "I think I'll mosey over there and introduce myself. See what I can do to help."

"Figured you would."

Seth had taken only a few steps when a paramedic moved in with his equipment, relieving the volunteer nurse of her duty. She stood and pressed her hands to her lower back as she watched the paramedics begin working. She looked to be youngish, modest height and slim, dressed in faded jeans and a white T-shirt. A sea breeze caught the nurse's shoulder-length red hair, and she swept a hand up to control it.

She turned, and Seth's heart hitched without warning. *Taylor Cabot?*

3

TAYLOR WOULD HAVE KNOWN Seth Donovan in an instant, even without the minor but telltale limp. Same rough-cut and careless good looks: dark, thick hair with hints of russet—always in need of a trim. Lopsided and engaging smile. Strong jaw. And that wide-bridged nose he often said was *"deservedly crooked, a reminder not to poke it into places it doesn't belong."* Seth's appearance, Taylor had often thought, was a mix of well-worn teddy bear and fearsome warrior. He looked the same as she remembered except that his bulky build seemed leaner, more muscular; he'd been working out. Odd that it had taken her the space of all these months to recognize how attractive this chaplain really was. She suspected the women in Sacramento weren't nearly as blind. And right now Taylor wished he'd stayed there with them.

"I wasn't sure it was you," Seth told her after glancing toward the pilot's wife, being assessed by a paramedic. His eyes, that familiar molten-chocolate brown, met Taylor's. "You've changed some things. Your hair . . . shorter?"

"It is," Taylor confirmed, knowing it was the least of the changes she'd been struggling to make. A haircut wasn't even on her list. But avoiding this man definitely should be. She'd only heard yesterday that he was on his way here. "It's been a while. Seven months since I left Sacramento." She dredged up a half smile. "But I knew it was you. You look good—healthy," she added quickly, realizing she'd been staring.

"Aiming for that. Turning forty felt real." His smile faded a little. "A wake-up call, I guess. Especially after losing Dad."

"Yes." Guilt crowded in. Taylor had sent a card, an e-mail too. But couldn't bring herself to call. Seth had been her mentor in crisis chaplaincy training and the rock she leaned on in her haze of grief. But it felt critically important to distance herself from all of that. "I'm so sorry, Seth."

"Thanks." His eyes held compassion. "I know you understand."

"I . . . Yes." *Because my husband died out on that road. Don't do it, Seth. Don't try to take me back there.*

Taylor stiffened, hating that this rumpled and easygoing chaplain might have the power to undo all she'd accomplished by moving away from Sacramento. Everything she'd managed through her checklist, the necessary steps to move forward with her life. She wasn't going to let him prompt any backsliding by resurrecting those still-unanswered questions surrounding Greg's death. After nearly three years, Taylor was done with it. She needed to be done with Seth Donovan, too.

"I should go," she told him after glancing up at what appeared to be at least three news helicopters hovering overhead. She lifted her cell phone from her pocket. Read the text preview. "I left my cousin back on the boardwalk."

"Aimee."

"Yes."

It wasn't true. The message said Lucas had come to get her. Aimee was in love for the very first time, still a starry-eyed believer in white knights and happy endings. Taylor wasn't that naive, but at least she'd learned how to protect herself. Getting away from here, now, was part of that. Besides, she should return Rob's text. He'd heard about the plane incident and was concerned.

"Well . . ." Seth glanced toward the boardwalk. "I'm going to find out what else I can do up there. And touch base with the crisis team dispatcher to see what's being set up for support of the victims."

Don't include me on that list. I'm not a victim anymore.

He met her gaze again. "It's good to see you. I'm glad we'll have a chance to catch up. I'll be working with the team for a couple of weeks, getting the new training session started. I saw that you volunteered to help with the practice scenarios."

"Right." Taylor felt another twinge of guilt. It had been too late to back out or she would have. At least it involved only classroom time, not actual fieldwork. Seth obviously didn't know she'd taken herself off the call list a few weeks back.

"It's good to get away for a while," Seth added. His eyes swept the seascape beyond them.

For a few merciful beats, there was a lull in the surrounding radio chatter and the sounds of first responders gathering their equipment. No discernible cries of anxiety and fear.

Simply a blending of the ocean waves and distant helicopter hums, with a few plaintive calls from gulls coasting on the breeze.

Seth's gaze moved to the man-shaped crevice in the sand inside a perimeter set up by law enforcement. The NTSB would arrive next. "It was good that you were here to help, Taylor."

"Mmm." She glanced down at her hands, remembering the feel of the man's breastbone under her palms. How she'd counted the cadence of that ridiculous song as his wife cried out to God. Right now the only thing Taylor wanted to count was her steps away from here.

"So . . ." The breeze ruffled Seth's hair. "You think the pilot will pull through?"

"No. I don't."

––––––––

"You're sort of a Jill-of-all-trades, then," Seth told the medical technician who'd offered him a cup of coffee while he waited to see the kite festival victims. He guessed the young woman to be in her early twenties, though she looked even younger. "Full-time ER staff, part-time waitress, college student, and new crisis volunteer."

"You can add bride-to-be to that list." Kasie Beckett waggled her ring finger.

"That's a plateful. You make me feel like a slacker."

"Right." The tech shook her head, tossing her dark ponytail across a shoulder of her scrubs. Her gaze took in the crisis team logo on the green jacket he'd donned for his visit to the hospital. "Coming from the mouth of a legend."

"Legend?" Seth grimaced. "Great. Now I really feel old."

Kasie laughed. "I can hardly wait to get more experience.

I'm trying to make myself available as much as possible. More than the required twenty hours a month. I'm learning a lot already, but there's so much more. . . ."

"And there always will be. I'm still learning too," Seth told her, struck by Kasie's eagerness. This young woman would be challenged in ways she never expected. Some of that would be painful. Stepping up in a crisis and giving of yourself always was. "Your service to your community will be much appreciated. I promise you that."

"I want to help. Do something that really matters." Kasie touched her fingers to a small silver cross nestled in the V-neck of her scrubs. "My father was a police officer."

"Ah . . ." *Was.*

Seth glanced down the hallway bustling with staff, some pushing ominous-looking equipment. Seth didn't much like hospitals. But he was fairly certain he'd seen Taylor walk by a few minutes earlier, still in street clothes. He wouldn't be surprised if she'd come in to check on "Sandy" Sandison, the pilot. The Taylor Cabot he knew, despite her dark response to his question about the man's prognosis, would need that follow-up. She might look different with her new haircut and the weight loss—too thin, if you asked him—but Taylor had always been a kindhearted and hopeful person despite all she'd been through. He wouldn't buy that a few months in a new zip code could change that.

"Looking for someone?" Kasie asked, following his gaze.

"Not really. I thought I saw one of our crisis team members a few minutes ago."

"Taylor Cabot?"

ER tech, rookie crisis responder, and clairvoyant. "Right. I thought I saw her walk by."

"Probably did." Kasie glanced toward the doors to the ER. "She came to check on Mr. Sandison. Taylor started CPR at the festival. But . . . she's not working with the crisis team much anymore. She asked me to pick up the rest of her shifts this month. She said she might be taking herself off the call list altogether, and—oh, boy, gotta go," Kasie said, glancing at her buzzing cell phone. "911 text. Mr. Sandison must be crashing again." She grimaced. "I mean they're coding him again."

"Got it—go."

Seth watched her sprint away, then took a sip of his luke-warm coffee. He thought of what the young woman had revealed about Taylor's plans to remove herself from the call list. It really wasn't a surprise; he'd suspected it when he saw her shifts disappear from San Diego's March schedule. He'd thought at first that it was a glitch in the computerized sched-uling system. Taylor was one of the most dedicated volunteers he'd ever worked with. The thought of her not being part of California Crisis Care was something he'd never wanted to imagine. When it was confirmed that she'd opted out of her shifts, he'd almost called her. But she'd seemed less com-municative recently. In fact, Taylor had given only minimal responses to text messages the last few weeks. Considering that, it had felt important to see her face-to-face in order to understand why she'd backed away. Then, out of the blue, the training opportunity in San Diego presented itself.

More than chance? Maybe.

Regardless, and whether Taylor liked it or not, she was a large part of the reason he was here.

4

"CHARGING TO THREE HUNDRED JOULES. Everybody clear!"

Taylor winced as Mr. Sandison's body jerked in response to the defibrillator jolt, one arm flopping over the edge of the gurney. The respiratory therapist moved back into place to administer breaths via an Ambu bag attached to the man's endotracheal tube. A ventilator was standing by, as was the cardiac cath team. Taylor glanced at the monitor showing a wide complex heart rhythm. Sadly, electrical activity didn't mean there was effective beating of—

"We've got a pulse with that!" Kasie reported to the ER physician, her face flushed by her own adrenaline rush.

Taylor read the hope in her young teammate's eyes. *But* . . .

The pilot's wife, Ava, had stopped Taylor in the corridor

to ask directions to the chapel. Taylor was relieved not to be recognized. It would have been painful and awkward. The odds were overwhelmingly against the pilot's survival even with CPR, defibrillation in the field, and the rapid transport to San Diego Hope.

"You want a set of scrubs?" Sloane Wilder glanced up at Taylor from where she sat at the trauma room computer. "Or are you just hanging around long enough to see if you earn a hero's badge?"

Hero? Taylor's lips tensed. She thought, not for the first time, that it wouldn't be a bad idea to add this nurse to her Survival List. *Don't let Wilder get under your skin.* All efforts to befriend the woman had ended in frustration. And confusion. What on earth was her issue? Sloane had been at San Diego Hope several months longer than Taylor and hadn't become buddies with anyone else, either. So it probably wasn't personal. Just incredibly aggravating.

"I don't think hero status is on the table," Taylor managed to answer. "Not with refractory V-fib untouched by an amiodarone drip. No decent blood pressure when we get a viable rhythm. And those changes on 12-lead EKG."

"The widow maker," Sloane confirmed, using a common name for the heart-rhythm pattern indicative of grave injury to the vital organ's left anterior descending artery. "Probably better if you'd never tried to resuscitate him," she added, her husky voice blending with the whoosh and beeps of monitoring equipment.

"We have to try. You know that."

"Yes, but . . ." Sloane's brittle smile crinkled the corners of her amazing eyes, a frosty shade of blue like ice on a northern California windshield. They were made more compelling in combination with inky lashes and porcelain-pale skin. Her hair was raven dark with burgundy highlights, worn in a short, spiky style. "Now you've gone and turned it into a Sacramento Hope reunion," she accused. "You, me, and Seth Donovan."

"I hadn't thought about it," Taylor hedged, though she'd muttered to herself about that sorry fact the whole way to the hospital. She was feeling too much like the cream filling in the Oreo version of her distressing past. When Sloane left her position as a flight nurse, she'd taken some shifts at Sacramento Hope, and she and Taylor had been thrown together. Nothing more than that—no real camaraderie. Which made it rankle even more that it had been this cynical nurse who first revealed to the San Diego ER staff that Taylor was a widow. So much for an attempt to start fresh with no pity-inducing labels. She wasn't sure how Sloane knew Seth. "He's only here now to support Mrs. Sandison," Taylor explained. "After Seth finishes with the crisis team training, he'll be going back to Sac."

"Ah . . ." Something that looked like relief flickered across Sloane's face. "Good, then."

They actually agreed on something?

"Pulseless V-tach," a staff nurse called out across the room. "Charging the paddles. Who's taking over compressions?"

"Here we go again." Sloane left the computer and started toward the gurney. Then she glanced back. "Looks like this bout's going to the widow maker. Better tell your chaplain to start praying."

Taylor stepped away before they hit the pilot with the paddles again. She couldn't watch any more. His body jerking. His wife waiting to hear. There was no point in explaining to the ever-mocking Sloane Wilder that Seth would have been praying for this man from the first moment he'd heard about the crisis. Or that Taylor had no intention of running into the good chaplain again today.

Except that he was waiting for her in the corridor.

———

"I heard they're resuscitating Mr. Sandison again," Seth began, noticing once more how different Taylor looked. The same wide-set green eyes, full lips, and straight nose. But her chin seemed sharper now, cheekbones more prominent. "It didn't sound good," he finished. "The overall prognosis."

"It isn't." Taylor swallowed, fingered a plastic bracelet on her left wrist. "He had a massive heart attack, but he's not stable enough for definitive treatment. Bypass surgery."

"I see."

Seth saw, too, that Taylor would like nothing better than to sprint away. He'd wonder if he had said something wrong, done something to offend her, but since they hadn't really spoken in months, it didn't seem possible. An important part of crisis care was looking after each other, watching for signs of stress and burnout, sort of taking an "emotional pulse." At the thought, Seth's gaze dropped to Taylor's wrists and hands. She'd removed her wedding rings.

"I should go," she said, glancing down the hallway. "There's really nothing more I can do."

Nothing? He'd almost said it out loud. *Since when . . . and why?*

"Mrs. Sandison is grateful for all you did for her husband out there on the beach," Seth prompted. "She was hoping she could meet—"

"I really need to go." Taylor tensed, twisting the plastic

bracelet again. "Maybe another time. Her family is probably coming."

"There isn't much other family, apparently. The hospital chaplain's with her now. I'll hang around and see how things go. And maybe touch base with the parents of the child whose face was cut so badly. I guess they had to call in a plastic surgeon."

"He's finishing her repair now," Taylor confirmed. "I peeked in. They gave her a little sedation. She's comfortable."

"Good." Seth hesitated, considering his options. He wanted a chance to talk with her. Really talk, like they used to. But he had a strong hunch this new Taylor wouldn't fall for his usual ploy to tempt her with chocolate cake, though she could use the calories. "I met your ER tech, Kasie."

Taylor smiled. He'd almost forgotten how pretty that was.

"I like her," she said, nodding. "Good person."

"And," Seth added, broaching the subject, "she's also a new crisis team volunteer."

"Oh, right." Taylor glanced at her watch. "I should get home. My dog's been having problems and—"

"She said you've given up some of your crisis shifts."

Taylor met his gaze. "I've had to cut back. Getting settled after the move, family . . . you know."

"She said you told her you might quit altogether."

Taylor took a slow breath. "I haven't made a final decision, but I'm considering several factors."

"Taylor . . ." Without thinking, Seth reached out and touched her arm. "I'm not trying to push. It's your decision. But you're such a good fit with the team. I . . . We would hate to lose you. I'll be here for a couple of weeks. We can talk about—"

"Taylor, there you are!" A man in scrubs and a white coat approached. Tall and lean, maybe mid- to late forties in age. Or at least old enough to have some gray at his hairline—the kind of clichéd good looks that hiked the ratings of TV medical shows. "I was afraid I'd missed you."

Taylor's face lit with a smile, this time clearly for the doctor. "Seth Donovan," she facilitated, glancing between them, "this is Dr. Robert Halston. He's the surgeon they called in for the kite festival victim. Rob . . ." The nickname seemed to come easily. "Seth is a Crisis Care chaplain from Sacramento. More than that, really. He's in a lead role there. And he's here to help with training for the new crisis team recruits." She nodded at Seth. "You're assisting the local trainers, right?"

"Right," he confirmed. It wasn't lost on him that the surgeon's hand came to rest briefly on Taylor's waist. "Good to meet you, Dr. Halston," he added, extending his hand.

"It's Robert. And a pleasure to meet you." The surgeon's grip was firm. "Taylor's told me quite a bit about the work you do. Stepping up like that in the wake of such rough situations takes a special dedication. I admire it. Though some of us are more comfortable doing our part in a more controlled environment." He smiled at Taylor, his hand brushing her waist again. He wore the same sort of plastic bracelet she did.

"I was there on the beach today," Seth said, trying not to analyze the expression on Taylor's face. "You treated the child injured by the tent post?"

"I did," Halston confirmed. "Nasty wound, temple to chin, with a lot of debris. The parents were really worried. But it came together nicely. In a year or so, no one will remember."

Seth met Taylor's gaze. *You don't believe that either.*

"I should get going," Taylor said again.

They said their good-byes, and Seth watched the surgeon walk Taylor down the corridor toward the parking lot. A muscle twitched along his jaw and he realized he'd been gritting his teeth. No need for that. Even if Seth had a strong sense Taylor's wounds hadn't "come together nicely," no matter how hard she was trying. He had a hunch, too, that the reason she was pulling back from the crisis team had little to do with getting settled in San Diego or family obligations. It was the same reason she'd finally shed her wedding rings: the man with the skills to put a new face on tragedy. Dr. Robert Halston.

5

"YOU'RE OKAY, THEN?" Taylor asked her cousin. She tapped the cell phone into speaker mode so she could fully devote both hands to the task of petting her elderly golden retriever. Hooper laid his big head on the carpet, his graying muzzle resting beside her iPad. Taylor's Survival List filled its screen.

"You're sure you're good with things now?" Taylor asked again.

"I'm fine," Aimee promised over the thunk-scrape of a wooden spoon against the inside of a mixing bowl. Cookie dough, she'd confessed. A long-standing family cure-all. A giant snickerdoodle could be the Curran family crest. "Especially after I heard on the news that no one died."

No one on the boardwalk, anyway . . .

"They mentioned you," Aimee continued, her voice taking

on an air of pride. "That you work at San Diego Hope and how you rushed out to start CPR on the pilot. They said you saved his life."

Taylor thought of Sloane Wilder's grim remark about the "widow maker." Her cousin didn't need to know about that.

"I saw it too," Taylor admitted. A reporter had caught Seth, asked him if he knew the nurse's identity, and he'd declined comment. Other issues aside, Taylor was grateful to him for that. She'd had enough media exposure to last a lifetime in the weeks after Greg's death. "You're on your way to your dad's place tonight, right?" she asked, determined to change the subject.

"Ten days' vacation. From work and classes." Aimee's slur was suspicious for speaking around a dollop of cookie dough. "Lucas is going to fly out and go with us when we take the kids to Disney World."

"Good." Taylor smiled. Her uncle had remarried after his wife's death and they'd adopted two boys from overseas—a second chance, a new family. He'd proved it was possible. "You'll have a great time."

"We will." Aimee's voice softened. "You'll be okay?"

"You mean without you to watch over me?" Taylor chuckled, traced her fingertip over Hooper's soft cheek.

"Your parents are on vacation too. So you'll be sort of alone."

Taylor was touched by her cousin's concern. "I have Hoop, a good seventy-five miles to log on my fitness tracker, a gallon of Sea Foam White paint for the—"

"I meant because of the date coming up."

March 26. The third anniversary of the night Greg had been struck and killed while coming to the aid of a driver with a flat tire.

Taylor took a slow breath. "I'll be fine."

"Call me if you need me."

"I will," Taylor promised, knowing it wouldn't happen. She had things under control. Finally.

They said good-bye and Taylor disconnected. She reached down to stroke Hooper again, then groaned. A puddle of dog slobber on her iPad screen. Slimed from *Lose the Krispy Kremes* to *Fall in love again*.

Grabbing a corner of the device, she slid it from under Hooper's head. Then glanced at the typed lines, marked with bullet points. Success, confirmed in black-and-white. She'd lost the donuts, putting it high on her list after a discussion at one of the few grief-counseling sessions she'd attended. Twenty women—and a lone elderly man accompanied by his sad-eyed beagle—admitting to chocolate binges, Doritos and ranch dip at 2 a.m., red wine in Solo cups, and Oreo crumbs in their bedsheets. *"Because when there's no one to answer to, cook for, no one to love us back, it's easy to fall into bad habits."* Taylor had decided then and there that she was stronger than that—capable of far more control. She'd lost the weight and was making steady progress down the rest of her list. Her goal, though unwritten and confided to no one on earth, was to complete this list by the twenty-sixth. Taylor's gaze swept over the last item, the word *love* magnified through a lens of dog saliva. Except for that one item. It was too fragile a reach—a someday hope.

"You and me, pal." Taylor smiled down at the twelve-year-old dog, so thin now that his ribs and hip bones protruded. The canine lymphoma had been diagnosed not long after they arrived in San Diego. Hooper had been in remission after chemotherapy, but now he'd developed a cough and his appetite had dwindled, prompting their vet to order a battery of blood work.

"You're my trouper," Taylor whispered, stroking a still-silky ear and reassuring herself that he always had been. Even with cataracts limiting his vision and a progressive arthritis that had thwarted his attempts to jump onto the couch for at least four years now. Or climb without help into Greg's truck . . .

A familiar ache filled Taylor's chest. Greg's dog had worn a path in the carpet, pacing to and from the front door of their Sacramento home, in the weeks following the accident. Staring out windows, checking maybe fifty times a day, whining, scratching the paint off the doors . . . and scattering the ragged remnants of Taylor's heart. When Hooper finally stopped pacing, he'd burrowed his nose into her lap, offering silent company as she cried. And he stood by, much later, as she finally began the painful process of boxing up the contents of his master's closet, dresser drawers. And desk.

She'd sold their Sacramento home, and now they were here. In a one-bedroom cottage, with easy access to a jogging trail, a roof-high bougainvillea trellis, a newly renovated glass tile–and–stainless steel kitchen, and a lease with a purchase option. The last box of Greg's belongings had been gone through.

Taylor glanced toward the breakfast bar. On it was the small stack of things she'd cleared from her husband's massive oak desk before giving it to his younger brother as a gift when he passed the California bar exam last fall. Greg's personal things had been sorted, culled, re-sorted, and pored over by Taylor—scrutinized far too many times in the past few years. His laptop, cell phone—with call records she'd obtained and printed out—and of course, the leather-bound handwritten planner Greg kept, despite all his electronic toys. A Franklin day planner with the jotted note she'd discovered only three weeks ago. That single, cryptic notation had kept her awake for too many nights since.

"We'll get it done," Taylor promised, dipping down to peer into the old dog's milky eyes. "By the twenty-sixth. We'll throw out those last things. We'll move on finally." Her throat tightened as she pressed a kiss onto the golden's forehead. "You and me, together. No sliding back, no giving up. I won't let anything or anybody get in our way."

———

"You've had a chance to make your phone calls?" Seth asked, trying not to show any reaction to the dramatic swelling and bruising of Ava Sandison's face. Fractures of her orbits, she'd been told—the bones around her eyes and upper cheeks. Broken capillaries in the whites of her eyes made them look like horror-show makeup. The injuries were a result of her face smashing into the Cessna's windshield as it hit the beach in her desperate attempt to land that doomed plane. "Everyone you needed to contact?"

"Yes. We don't have children, but there are neighbors. And old friends in Palo Alto." Ava ran a manicured finger inside the foam collar protecting her strained neck. "Sandy's brother flies for Delta. He's in Hong Kong. He'll get here as soon as he can." Her eyes shimmered with sudden tears; one slid down her face, pink with blood. "Do you think he'll make it in time?"

"I'm praying for that." Seth pushed down a memory of sitting at his dying wife's bedside. The best comfort for this woman would be to offer her a measure of control. "What have you learned from the doctors, Ava?"

"If they can get Sandy to surgery, it's his only chance." More pink tears spilled over. "It was a very bad heart attack. If that nurse on the beach, Miss Cabot, hadn't come to help, my husband wouldn't have had a chance at all. She's an angel."

"I agree." Seth nodded, remembering Taylor there, kneeling in the sand in the midst of so much chaos. He brought his focus back to the present, noticed the woman's lids drooping. "You should rest."

"I think I will." She reached out and grasped his hand briefly. "Thank you for being here."

"I'll be back," he promised. "Whatever you need, Ava, I'll do my best to help."

"Thank you."

Ten minutes later, Seth joined the hospital cafeteria line. A veggie patty, he'd decided, though every cell in his body screamed for a cheeseburger, loaded, with a side of onion rings. Last summer's chest pain scare, diagnosed as gastric in origin by the Sacramento Hope ER team, had set him straight. Taylor had been part of that.

"Typical," the woman in front of him was saying to someone in front of her. She swept her fingers through her short black-and-red hair. "Going for the hero badge, always. And the media spotlight. She loves it. Like in Sacramento after her husband was killed. Cabot needs all the attention. Sad, if you ask me."

What the—?

"Excuse me." Seth leaned forward to engage the woman. His jaw tensed and he told himself to chill, back off, but—"Are you talking about Taylor Cabot?"

The woman pivoted, ice-blue eyes meeting his. "And if I am?"

"Then you're dead wrong." He returned the woman's gaze with the persuasive force of the police batons his family had sold for decades. "Taylor is nothing like that."

"Well, whatever." Her lips tightened. "Believe what you want, I guess."

Seth hesitated. Was there something familiar about this woman? His gaze dropped to her name tag. *R. S. Wilder RN*. It didn't ring a bell, but . . . "Have we met before? Do I know you?"

"I . . ." There was a fleeting look of unease in the nurse's expression. "It's a small medical world." She jutted her chin. "Even if we've met, you definitely don't *know* me. Not at all. And I'd rather keep it that way." She grabbed her tray and stepped out of line. "But there's a Reuben sandwich calling my name over at the grill."

She was gone before Seth could say anything more, though he wasn't sure what that would be, anyway. He wouldn't apologize for defending Taylor. Even if he'd intruded on the woman's conversation and had probably been more confrontational than necessary. He frowned. Not probably—*definitely*. Seth's short fuse had brought nothing but trouble to his life. When he'd finally turned things around, he'd made a promise to do whatever he could to be a force for peace. Now if he could only remember that.

———

Taylor lifted the day planner from the stack and opened it to the calendar page: March 26, 2013. She read Greg's handwritten notation.

0800—Appt. with S. Donovan

An appointment . . . on the day he died.

She fought a wave of queasy discomfort, the same visceral response she'd experienced when she'd found this notation three weeks ago. She'd read it at least two dozen times since, all her questions and doubts rekindled anew. She kept telling herself to stop, that it had been almost three years. Dredging it all up again would only stall her progress in getting on with her life. The checklist said, *Go through the last of Greg's things.* Which meant disposing of anything that wasn't valuable, a special keepsake, or something to be passed on to his family.

She touched a fingertip to the inked notation in Greg's familiar half-cursive, half-printing—the same handwriting as the sweet poem now tucked into the jewelers' box with her rings. This old planner fit none of the requisite categories. And it threatened to disrupt the control Taylor had worked so long and hard to accomplish. She needed to put it back with the other useless things she'd salvaged from the desk and toss them all in the trash. But . . .

Taylor stared at the entry again. Her husband and Seth Donovan had been only casual acquaintances.

Why would Greg make a chaplain's appointment?

6

"Probably 150 calories," Taylor calculated, glancing from her smartphone app to her half-eaten bowl of hospital cereal, closer in consistency to wallpaper paste than oatmeal. She connected with Rob's gaze and recognized the look that was there more and more lately. A look that proved what he'd told her last week: he wanted them to spend much more time together. And he hoped their relationship might progress to . . . Her skin warmed despite a frisson of anxiety. "Plus forty-nine calories for the sliced strawberries—do you think that's half a cup?"

"I think . . ." Rob's smile crinkled the edges of his blue eyes. "I'm glad we could meet before your ER shift. And before I craft the movie-star nose that a grandmother of seven has dreamed of all her life. Seriously, she came to my office with a photo of Natalie Wood."

Taylor raised her brows. "Who?"

"*Aagh*. Ask your mother, kid."

Taylor chuckled. She had no doubt the woman would be happy with the result of her surgery; Rob was a very skilled surgeon. And it wasn't only nose jobs, eye lifts, and tummy tucks; in a few weeks he was being honored for his charitable services at Children's Hospital's burn center in San Francisco. Next summer he planned to extend that gift to children in India. If she'd tried to put together a perfect man—choosing all the best parts, like some widow's dream-date Mr. Potato Head—he couldn't have come out better than Robert Halston. And even though he'd admitted he wanted their friendship to evolve into more, he hadn't pressured her. He'd been amazingly empathetic about all she'd been dealing with.

"Any word from your vet on those lab tests? Your dog's progressing lymphoma?"

Taylor amended her thought about Rob's empathy. He'd been far more clinical than sensitive when it came to the situation with Hooper, recounting several stories regarding the need "to take necessary steps" with his own aging pets. He'd cautioned Taylor more than once to "be prepared for the inevitable."

"She didn't say it was the lymphoma, exactly," Taylor corrected, hating a nagging twinge of resentment that Rob didn't deserve. "Hooper was due for labs. Follow-up after the chemo," she clarified, remembering the veterinarian's kindness during their visit. The staff had put Hoop's dog treats in a to-go sack when he showed none of his usual interest. He'd hardly wagged his tail. So very different from the way he'd always looked at life: grateful, loving, eager. And he'd dropped several more pounds. "He's probably showing his age more than anything else."

"Ah," Rob acknowledged, offering a polite nod though the look in his eyes still warned, *"Be prepared . . ."*

"He seemed better this morning," Taylor finished, knowing the statement held as much truth as the vow she'd made to put Greg's planner into the garbage. She hadn't done it. And today was pickup day. Another week of self-imposed torture. Taylor had no doubt what Rob would think of that; procrastination was nowhere in his vocabulary.

"Glad to hear the old boy's hanging in there." Rob cut his toast into two perfect triangles, then scraped the butter from its surface like it would immediately become plaque in a major vessel. "I know it's been a real source of concern for you, Taylor."

"Yes." She watched as he took an impeccable bite from his toast, almost hoping some crumbs would linger. *Like Seth with a donut . . .* The unexpected thought brought an image of the laid-back chaplain with sprinkles on his chin. The two men couldn't be less alike. In appearance and in the way they handled things.

Seth Donovan flew by the seat of his pants, made notes on the backs of Starbucks receipts, kept a staggering schedule, and yet, miraculously, always found a way to be there for anyone who needed help—anywhere, anytime.

Rob Halston tackled each item on his fully digital task list like a scheduled mole removal: identify it, mark it, and then cut it out deep to the core. She'd never met anyone more methodical. It was he who'd recommended her step tracker, helped her link it with a specialized bathroom scale, and showed her how to log her food. He'd been using it for two years, his efficiency putting Taylor's meager efforts to shame. Monday through Friday Rob ran seven miles before breakfast. His hybrid car sent performance stats to his phone. He'd booked standing orders for his mother's and grandmother's birthday flowers. He even had the ability to change lawn sprinkler settings by phone, though his net zero energy home boasted artificial turf—the epitome of order and control.

It was more than a little intimidating, but Taylor envied the comfort that Rob's purposeful and preplanned existence must bring. If she had even a smidgen of that resolve, she'd power through her Survival List and not lie awake until nearly 3 a.m., second-guessing a simple calendar notation from almost three years ago.

"Hi. Hope I'm not interrupting."

Taylor blinked up at Seth, trying to find a smile. "Uh . . . no."

"Not at all," Rob said. "Join us?"

"Thanks, but I can't." Seth's dark eyes sought Taylor's. "I promised to relay a message to Taylor. From Mrs. Sandison."

"The woman from the kite festival incident? The pilot's wife?" Rob asked.

"That's right." Seth dragged his fingers through his hair, leaving a tuft standing. "But, I'm sorry to say, she's his widow now."

Taylor's heart squeezed.

"He died on the operating table late last night." There was sadness in the chaplain's eyes. He nodded at Taylor. "She's asked to see you."

"Oh, I . . ." Taylor glanced at her watch; she was due for her shift in thirty minutes. There was time, but the last thing she wanted to do was relive that beach disaster with a heartbroken and raw new widow.

"It won't take long," Seth prompted. "Ava's up on the fifth floor. I promised her I'd come along with you."

Taylor swallowed. There was no avoiding it. "Give me a couple of minutes to finish here?"

"For sure. I'll go grab a cup of coffee. Come get me when you're ready."

"Okay."

Rob watched as Seth walked away. His brows pinched very slightly, the only hint of discomfort in his unruffled expression. "I suppose the woman wants to thank you for what you tried to do for her husband."

"Probably," Taylor agreed, already dreading the encounter. The only thing harder than witnessing this poor woman's anguish was to be doing that alongside Seth. Especially now, when Taylor was trying so hard to distance herself from him.

"You've told Donovan you're rethinking your work with the crisis team?" Rob asked, dissecting the crust from his remaining toast triangle.

"We talked," Taylor hedged, setting her spoon down; her appetite was gone.

"Good. I had a feeling this visit upstairs had something to do with keeping you on the crisis volunteer call list." He shook his head. "It's a lot to ask of someone. Especially considering the rugged kind of work you do already. And what you've been through personally. Better to leave that work to someone else, Taylor."

She wished she'd never discussed it with Rob. He'd tried to understand her commitment to the much-needed, though sometimes gritty and gut-wrenching, community service. But until someone put on that uniform, walked in the shoes of a crisis volunteer, he couldn't appreciate what it meant. And required. Being on scene in the wake of tragedy to provide a hopeful presence for survivors wasn't like Taylor's work in the ER or Rob's in the OR—or even in a surgical suite in Mumbai. Much the same way it wasn't possible to compare the traumatic loss of her husband to Rob's unwelcome divorce. Though he continued to try.

"I'm the first one to give credit to volunteers," he added, after taking a quick glance at his phone. "We'd be hurting without them. But there are plenty of opportunities that don't require a person to show up at the scene of a drive-by shooting or after they pull some poor kid's body out of the river. Or—" he grimaced—"down from a rope strung over his bedroom door."

Taylor's stomach tensed; she wished it were an exaggeration.

Rob reached across the table, touched Taylor's hand. "There are gentler ways to be of service. And as meaningful." His thumb brushed her skin. "We could even do that together, if you like."

Together? Taylor imagined herself in a flowing linen pantsuit and long, gauzy scarf as she navigated a bustling city street in India. She could almost smell cumin, garlic, fennel, red chilies—

"Please don't think I'm trying to make your decision," Rob assured. "It's only that I see how troubled you are over this. The crisis team commitment and what's going on with your dog. I'd like to help make things easier, maybe lend a hand in putting all this worry behind you."

There was nothing but sincerity in Rob's expression. His touch—even this small, very public connection—made Taylor feel more alive than she had in far too long. She wanted to believe it could mark the end of grief and the beginning of joy she'd feared wasn't possible ever again, but . . .

Taylor glanced across the room and saw Seth Donovan

sitting at a table against a wall decorated with cardboard shamrocks. He was looking their way.

She slid her fingers from Rob's. Then pocketed her cell phone and gathered up the remains of her half-eaten breakfast. She wished she were as beautifully naive as her sweet young cousin. But essential stubborn truths tempered any real optimism: her dog was taking a turn for the worse, and a 2013 calendar on her breakfast bar threatened her sanity. Now there was a woman in a hospital bed upstairs who'd tried her mightiest to control the flight of a crashing airplane. And this new widow was waiting for the arrival of two caring volunteers. How could Taylor tell Seth that last night, after hours of insomnia, she'd finally added *Quit the crisis team* to her Survival List? She'd make it effective the first of April, but right now . . .

"I have to go," she told Rob with reluctance. "Seth is waiting."

"You should know," Seth told Taylor as they approached Ava Sandison's hospital room, "that she may have more to deal with than she even realizes."

"What do you mean?"

Seth frowned, remembering what he'd heard from Walt. "Liability issues related to the victims' injuries. And costly property destruction." He'd fully expected the pained look he saw on Taylor's face. "Rumor has it that lawyers are circling."

"She's not a pilot. They can't blame her personally."

"They could claim she accepted the responsibility when she took those controls. And steered the plane over the boardwalk."

"What was she supposed to do? A kamikaze dive into the ocean? She was trying to save her husband!"

"I hear you," Seth told her, relieved to see some spunk despite the situation. Whether she recognized it or not, Taylor was an advocate for what was good and just. He had no doubt they both would have done anything to save their spouses—his wife from ovarian cancer, and Taylor's husband from that car accident out on the rural highway.

"Has anyone said anything to her?" Taylor asked. "About blame?"

"Not that I know of. She's been spared so far. At least from that angle. But Ava's a trauma survivor, physically, emotionally, and spiritually, maybe. She's got to be asking herself those hard questions."

"Like . . ." Taylor's wince was barely perceptible. "'Why did it have to happen?'"

"Exactly." *The question you asked everyone, including me.* "We know the stages," Seth reminded her, referring to the Kübler-Ross model for the progression through grief and loss. "Shock and denial, then onward until—"

"Acceptance," Taylor finished, lifting her chin. Her gaze moved to the door of the patient room a few yards ahead of them. "Ava has a long way to go."

"And an angel to start her on that journey." He smiled. "That's what she calls you: an angel."

The look on Taylor's face, modest, sweet, and a little flattered, made Seth want to hold her close. He shook it off, surprised by the emotion. He was her mentor, a fellow crisis chaplain . . .

"So I guess we should go in there now." Taylor smoothed her scrub top over her hips. "She's waiting for us."

"Waiting for *you*," Seth corrected. "Ava asked to see you."

"You said you told her we'd come together."

"I stretched the truth."

"You didn't think I'd come alone."

"I . . . wanted to follow through. Because I know how much Ava needs to see you. You more than anyone else right now."

She held his gaze for a moment. "Because I'm a widow too."

"No. Because when that plane fell from the sky and Ava's life crashed with it, you ran *toward* her wreckage. And this good lady needs that kind of hope right now."

———

"Oh, you came."

"Of course," Taylor assured, not at all convinced that Seth's faith in her had merit. She might not have flinched at doing CPR on that beach, but this, now . . . "I'm so very sorry about your husband, Mrs. Sandison."

"Ava, please."

"Ava, then. And I'm Taylor."

"Yes, Seth told me."

Despite a raccoon mask of purple bruises and substantial swelling, the widow's eyes looked clear, blue as Saturday's sky when it was filled with a carefree rainbow of kites. She reached for her water glass, her hand trembling very slightly. There was a small, padded aluminum splint on her baby finger. Her manicure, amazingly, had survived the tragedy. She took a sip of water. "I had another visitor. From the hospital auxiliary."

"Ruthie Marks . . . I see that," Taylor said, noting the woman's card lying on the bedside table. A volunteer with a business card. Taylor felt the prickle of discomfort that always surrounded her encounters with the ever-present senior. She wasn't at all surprised Ruthie had found her way to this room. She had a sort of sixth sense.

"She came with the library cart," Ava continued, "but I think she mostly wanted to encourage me. Ruthie lost her husband too."

Eighteen years ago. And she still wore her wedding rings on a chain around her neck and had an endless repertoire of quirky "Roger always said" quotes. According to hospital staff, she'd also been known to pin a white rose to her volunteer uniform on her wedding anniversary. Ruthie Marks headed up the local Solace Share support group. Within two days of Sloane Wilder's unwelcome announcement that Taylor was a widow, she'd zeroed in. Pink uniform, cocker spaniel eyes, heart on her sleeve, and a jelly donut offering in her hand. Taylor had declined the invitation to Solace Share as graciously as she could, saying she'd keep Ruthie's card "just in case." The whole time, she'd bitten her lip to keep from saying that she was long past donuts, at no risk whatsoever for Chianti in a Solo cup or Oreo crumbs in her bedsheets, and that the saddest thing she could imagine was . . . *ending up like you, Ruthie. A woman defined by grief.* Taylor would never let that happen.

"Everyone's been very kind," Ava added. She exhaled in a halting sigh. "I wanted to thank you for what you did for Sandy."

Taylor stepped closer to the bed. "I wish it could have been more. That it had all turned out much differently."

"I do too." Ava raised her hands, stared at them. "I'd never done that before. Taken over the control yoke. Maybe for a few seconds in those early days when Sandy first started flying. He wanted me to know the thrill, I suppose." A smile tugged at her lips. "My husband is . . . was . . . so good about sharing." She splayed her fingers, and the stones in her wedding set glittered under the ceiling lights. An amethyst, it looked like, surrounded by tiny diamonds—vintage, maybe. Far beyond ordinary . . . a description that now fit everything in this woman's life, but in the very worst way.

"But I've never been mechanical or handy," Ava admitted. "Not one of those women who can change the oil in her car or install a ceiling fan. Are you?"

"No." Taylor's throat constricted as a memory rose: a new-widow moment when she sat half-crying, half-laughing, with a lap full of remote control devices and no clue which did what. And not sure if she really cared at all. "I'm not very handy either."

"I . . ." Ava's eyes closed; the creases of her lids were purple too. "I had to lean across Sandy to grab hold of the yoke. He was unconscious, making awful snoring noises. His shoulder was wedged against my ribs and he was wringing wet, clammy, and gurgling. We dropped into a nosedive and I pulled back as hard as I could. But Sandy kept sliding forward, blocking the yoke. I think his feet were jamming the pedals. I could hear the air traffic controllers on the radio. But I got so dizzy, and then there were kites wrapping around the windshield and the ocean rushing up at us. I pulled and pulled, tried to reach the throttle, to turn us away, but everything was so out of control."

Oh, God, please . . .

"Ava . . ." Taylor took hold of the woman's hands, her heart wedging into her throat. "I'm sorry. I'm so sorry this awful thing happened to you."

"I tried." Ava Sandison gripped hard, the metal splint cool against Taylor's fingers. "I tried to get the plane down and save my husband. I wouldn't ever want to hurt people. Not children, not *anybody.*"

Taylor's eyes brimmed with tears as the woman collapsed into her arms. She hugged Ava back despite a frantic, whispered warning to protect her own heart.

"Why?" the pilot's wife sobbed, her battered face burrowed against Taylor's shoulder. "Why did God let this happen?"

Taylor closed her eyes. "I don't know."

7

"I HAD A PLANNED AGENDA, of course," Seth told the crisis team assembled in a city administration meeting room. A few were certified trainers ready to begin classes for the new volunteers—a class of fourteen, all interviewed, background-cleared, and eager to start learning the ropes. The remaining folks were seasoned volunteers from a variety of backgrounds: retired military, teachers, salesclerks, college students—all willing to pitch in and do whatever they could to help when summoned by police and fire officials. One woman, incredibly, had recently celebrated her ninetieth birthday and continued to offer service to her community by way of crisis work. It always did Seth's heart good to see that level of selfless commitment. "But I agree that the kite festival incident warrants further discussion." He took a seat, nodding at the trainer opposite him.

"We had twelve team members on scene," the man reported. "Three of us made hospital visits to the injured."

Seth thought of Taylor's meeting with Ava Sandison. She'd exited the hospital room with tears in her eyes and blown past Seth, saying only that she was late to her ER shift.

"Would anyone who was on scene like to share an experience?" Seth asked, nudging the discussion. Though each volunteer received a debriefing by the crisis-trained dispatcher immediately following a call, at times confidential discussions like these allowed volunteers to further process their feelings regarding the incident. They fostered mutual support within the team and were an important means of watching each other for signs of stress, burnout. "Anybody?"

A young man raised his hand; he was dressed in the familiar blue polo shirt of the volunteers. Seth recognized him. A solar company employee whose wife was expecting their first baby any day. Seth pointed. "Go ahead, Evan."

"I was having breakfast down the boardwalk," he began, reaching up to touch his glasses. "Paige and I. It's sort of our Saturday thing. And Wednesday . . . if she gets a craving for chocolate chip waffles. Paige thought it would be fun to watch the kites, away from the crowd." Evan's smile faded. "She saw the plane before I did. We knew, by the sound of the engine, it was in trouble. Then it started to nose-dive."

Seth nodded, encouraging him to continue.

"I told Paige to stay put and asked the waitress to call 911. Then I took off running. I wasn't on call, and I didn't know what I could do, but I knew they'd need help."

"When tragedy strikes, we're there."

"Pretty chaotic," Evan recalled. "Kids everywhere. To tell you the truth, I didn't really want to see what might be under those crumpled tents. There was this girl, couldn't have been more than four, with a big slice on her face." He grimaced. "I did my best to help her mother stay calm. I told her that the sirens meant help was on the way. And I sent up a lot of prayers."

There was a murmur of understanding from the assembled volunteers. Though the crisis team had no religious affiliation and no proselytizing was permitted, Seth knew personal faith was a strong foundation for many volunteers. They saw it as a lifeline, a rescue rope. God in control despite the chaos.

"I saw that nurse there," Evan continued. "I didn't know she was a San Diego Hope employee at the time." He shook his head. "Just this little redhead tearing across the sand like she was charging the end zone. She wedged through that crowd of looky-loos, dropped down on her knees, and started CPR—never mind that there was a plane threatening to blow up right behind her. Takes *some* guts."

Seth nodded, the image still fresh in his mind.

"Must be hard for her now," Evan added, "knowing that the pilot went on to die."

And maybe even harder to meet widow-to-widow with the man's wife?

Seth thought again of the tears in Taylor's eyes when she left Ava Sandison's room. She might be determined to leave the crisis team, but he should touch base with her about that encounter. Even if she'd remained emotionally unscathed, it would have been a rough start to her day.

Taylor checked the trauma room wall clock. The p.m. staff was getting report now, and this shift couldn't end soon enough.

"Completely out of control," Sloane Wilder remarked, looking down at their critically ill patient. The young woman, a freshman at UC San Diego, lay semi-comatose on the gurney, eyes partially closed and sunken in appearance, lips and tongue markedly dry. Her respirations were deep and rapid, each exhaled breath reeking like overripe fruit. "No one explains the risk of ketoacidosis to insulin-dependent diabetics anymore?"

"Her roommate thought she had the flu," Taylor explained, hoping to deflect the nurse's impending diatribe; eight hours had been more than long enough to ride the Wilder train of negativity and sarcasm. "That whole group of friends had the stomach flu."

"Right. And we're treating that with NyQuil and Jell-O shots these days." Sloane rolled her eyes and reached out to adjust the oxygen cannula in their patient's nostrils. Her fingers lingered on the girl's hair, a fleeting expression of compassion on her face. It disappeared as quickly as it came, replaced by a smirk. "Exactly what a kid with a blood sugar of 1,200 needs. Where were her parents? Krypton?"

"Pahrump, Nevada."

Sloane snorted. "I rest my case."

Taylor decided not to mention that she'd talked with them and heard the panic in the mother's voice. They were booking the first flight out of Las Vegas. Fortunately, if things continued to progress the way they had been, their daughter would be well on her way to recovery in the ICU by the time they arrived. She'd received six liters of IV fluids, doses of bicarb, titrated potassium replacement, and a continuing insulin drip. All of it monitored by successive lab draws and blood gas values. The last results reflected considerable improvement.

"My turn," Taylor said, glancing down at the Foley bag filled to capacity with colorless urine. "I'll go dump it and then I'll finish up with the computer."

"I'll handle all that," Sloane offered. "And I'll give report to the p.m. shift so you can get out of here early."

Taylor stared.

"I'm not offering you a poison apple, Snow White. It's just . . ." Sloane frowned and glanced at the trauma room doorway. "There's somebody waiting for you."

Taylor turned.

Seth.

"Now do *me* a favor and get out of here," Sloane prodded. "Take the God squad with you."

———

Seth took one look at Taylor and was convinced he'd made the right move in coming to check on her. She looked exhausted— beyond that, worried.

"Tough case?" he asked. She'd shed her stethoscope and pulled on a uniform jacket. Green, like her scrubs. "That young girl I saw through the doorway?"

"Complicated, but we got things under control. It will be okay."

"Good." Seth knew better than to ask for details. Taylor would protect her patient's privacy. He expected the same from his crisis teams. He glanced back toward the ER. "That other nurse . . . I feel like I know her from somewhere."

"Sloane Wilder?"

"Right," Seth confirmed, remembering the woman's ID badge from their unpleasant encounter in the cafeteria. "Wilder. She looks familiar."

"She was a flight nurse in Sacramento. And then worked a few shifts at Sacramento Hope ER. Confused me at first, because she was going by the name 'Ronda' at the hospital. I guess Sloane's her middle name. Anyway, I had no idea she'd transferred here."

Something in Taylor's tone said it might have made her rethink her own move. Seth wasn't surprised, considering the harsh remarks her colleague had made about her.

"Sloane's ex-fiancé played with Greg's basketball group sometimes." Taylor met Seth's gaze. "Did you want something?"

"I was at a meeting with the crisis team, discussing the kite festival incident," Seth explained. "I thought I'd stop by, see you too."

"I don't need debriefing."

"I didn't say that," Seth assured her. *Even if I saw you on that beach. And those tears this morning.* "I only thought—"

"You could make a pitch for the crisis team?"

"No." He frowned, wondering why on earth things suddenly felt so adversarial between them. "I'm not here to do that either." He risked a smile despite her serious expression. "It's early for dinner, but I'm hungry. I thought you might be too."

"I don't know." Taylor glanced down the hospital corridor.

"I don't mean we'd eat here," Seth said quickly. "Somewhere with real food."

"Knowing you . . ." Taylor's teasing smile raised his pulse a notch. "That means fries. Or something wrapped in pie crust."

"No." He swiped a finger over his breast pocket. "Cross my heart, hope to pass a cholesterol test."

It looked for a moment like Taylor's wariness—this confusing new distance—would win out. But she finally let her shoulders relax. "Okay. Only because I checked on Hooper at lunchtime. And because I'm too tired to go to the store." Her nose wrinkled. "The only thing in my fridge is an iffy half can of black beans and a dried-up corn tortilla. So I'll come with you."

"I'm flattered." Seth laughed, glad Taylor couldn't know he'd toyed with the idea of simply hauling her off, regardless. Even if it meant going mano a mano with Dr. Face-Lift. "Your car or mine?"

"Yours." Taylor started walking. "I'm low on gas, too."

8

TAYLOR INSISTED THEY GET TAKEOUT. Hungry or not, she wasn't about to subject fellow diners to the ambience of eating next to someone in scrubs of dubious cleanliness. And she didn't want Seth to think this was anything more than two hungry people and Mexican takeout with separate checks. Not an invitation for a heart-to-heart across a dining table. Seth was fully equipped for that—and well utilized. His nickname in Sacramento was C2C, "chaplain to the chaplains." An official position for good reason. Seth was often sought out by volunteers here, too. Maybe it had to do with the fact that he'd been ordained as a minister, something he'd pursued to provide clergy confidentiality in his work with law enforcement families. But Seth rarely mentioned that, and Taylor suspected his role as a confidant and mentor sprang more from his accepting and empathetic manner. With his kind eyes and patient ear, he had a way of getting under a person's skin. Taylor's own on more than one occasion. But her skin was a year thicker now, so—

"What *is* that?" he asked, staring. "What are you doing there?"

Taylor raised her brows, plastic fork in midair. "Eating?"

"No." Seth shifted his position on one of the rocks she'd chosen as seating for their impromptu beach picnic. "That's not eating. That's trying your best *not* to eat."

"It's a salad." Taylor lifted two foam containers. "Dressing, lettuce . . . I'm eating it."

"You're eating the lettuce. And dipping the tips of the fork tines in the dressing once in a while."

"It's more efficient that way. There's more control . . . You know, fat and calories." She lowered the fork, resenting that he'd made her feel self-conscious. She started to explain her fitness-tracking bracelet, then decided against it. Seth didn't need to know about that any more than he needed to know about the Survival List. "I've been trying to get healthier," she explained. "Keeping a closer eye on food and exercise. That's all."

"Ah."

Seth's gaze shifted to the view, the sky turning golden pink as the sun dipped toward the ocean. When he turned back, his expression was softer. The waning sunshine backlit his tousled hair and warmed the rugged planes of his face. His dark eyes tried their best to skip past getting under Taylor's skin and instead make a direct grab for her heart. "We've missed you in Sacramento."

"My family's here," she managed. "La Jolla. I love Greg's parents, but I needed to be closer to home. It's better . . . *I'm* better here."

"And thinner." Seth chuckled. "I used to be able to woo you with molten lava brownies and sweet potato fries. No more."

Woo? He was kidding, of course. It had never been anything like that between them.

"Even with a sniper on the loose," Seth added, the last golden rays settling over his shoulders. "We've had some adventures together. Offered hope to a lot of hurting people."

Taylor tensed. He was going to make the pitch, make her feel guilty for reneging on the crisis team. Seth wouldn't understand that immersing herself in traumatic pain—like today, when she held the pilot's wife in her arms—dragged her back to the grief she was fighting so hard to leave behind. He knew how devastated she'd been by Greg's death. And the unexplained circumstances. She needed to let it all go but—

"Why didn't you tell me Greg had an appointment with you on the day he died?"

Seth coughed, set the remains of his fajita down.

"I found a note in his day planner."

"When?"

"Three weeks ago." A wave of confusing anger tried to choke her. She set her salad down, not caring that the fork fell onto the sand. "Why should it matter *when* I found it?"

"Because you've never mentioned it before."

His calmness was maddening. No hint in his expression that this was anything out of the ordinary.

"The note said *appointment*, like it was official," Taylor explained, crossing her arms. "I can't see him doing that. Even with all the problems going on within the fire department back then." There had been allegations that some of the fire-fighters were involved in illegal gambling. Greg's shift.

Seth nodded. "I was aware of those problems."

"I knew Greg was upset about being passed over for captain," Taylor added, her mind rerunning the scenarios that had kept her awake for three weeks now. "Everyone knew that. But he never once said anything about going for counseling. It wasn't like him." Her voice faltered despite the struggle to keep herself under control.

"Crisis chaplains don't counsel, Taylor. You know that. We're not therapists."

"I know. I meant that it wasn't like Greg to seek out a chaplain—talk with someone like that. I'm saying I can't make sense of it, Seth."

"It's still important to you that his death make sense somehow."

Don't. Taylor's stomach churned. "Don't try to wedge God into this. Make it something about my lack of faith or—"

"Hey, hey." Seth spanned the space between them, dropping to one knee in the sand in front of her. He took hold of her hand. "I'm not doing that. I'm only trying to understand."

"I don't need you to understand anything," she breathed, fingers trembling inside his. "I only want an explanation. Greg made an appointment with you. And then died out on some road to nowhere. Nobody can tell me why. And—" She squeezed her eyes shut, forbidding any tears to come.

"Taylor . . ."

"Did Greg have an appointment with you that day?"

"Yes." Seth exhaled softly, holding on to her hand. "But he didn't keep it."

"What do you mean?"

"He left a message about thirty minutes before, canceling."

"But . . ." Taylor's thoughts tumbled into confusion. "Did he say why he'd made the appoint—?"

Her phone buzzed, alerting her to a text. Taylor groaned as she read the message.

"Problem?"

"My vet." Taylor slid her hand from Seth's. "She wants me to call her and that never means good news. I should go home."

"Okay."

They gathered up their things and tracked down Taylor's barely touched dressing container, gone cartwheeling in the breeze.

"I'm sorry your dog's ill," Seth told her, kindness in his voice.

"Thanks." Taylor met his gaze. "I'm sorry it interrupted our dinner."

"No problem."

It was too dark to be certain, but Taylor thought she saw relief on the chaplain's face.

9

"I'm sick," Sloane groaned into her cell phone and struggled to sit upright on the edge of her bed. The motion hit her temples like a meat mallet against cheap steak, making her stomach lurch. "What time is it?" She squinted at the too-bright bedroom window.

"It's 8:28," Taylor answered. "We've been calling you since quarter after seven, Sloane. I was starting to worry. One of the PD officers offered to drive by."

"No need. I'm fine."

"You just said you were sick."

"I'm a little sick." Sloane fought an image of an empty shot glass . . . *glasses*. Tequila, even the good stuff, was not her friend. She knew better. "But I'll be there," she added, spotting her laptop on the bed and hoping she hadn't fired off any e-mails to her ex-fiancé. "I need to grab a shower. Look, tell everyone I'm sorry." It was miserable to be short staffed; Sloane knew that. "Really, Taylor. I am sorry."

"If you're sick, we could try to find someone—"

"I said I'll be there. Can't take this phone in the shower . . ."

"Drive safely."

"Always do."

Sloane jabbed the Disconnect button, let the phone drop onto the rumpled sheets. She pressed her fingertips hard against her gritty eyes. In truth, there were far worse things than the possibility of hitting the Send button on an e-mail to her ex. Like the man who'd bought her those drinks, an electrical engineer from Phoenix who'd teased her about her megawatt smile. What if she'd brought him home? It could easily have happened.

Sloane stood and the merciless mallet pounded again. She stepped over the pile of clothes she'd left beside the bed, shed in a tequila-sweat hurry to be done with an evening that had failed to soothe an ache gone deep as a bedsore. Boots, skirt, the figure-flattering tank top and trendy layered T-shirt—on top of the scrubs she'd dropped in an eager rush to dress for an evening out that might finally prove a hopeful balm.

In the end, Sloane had simply peeled off another layer of her self-respect. And more and more lately, there wasn't a lot of that to spare. To make matters worse, she'd run into Kasie Beckett in the ladies' room in the bar; apparently Kasie worked part-time in the adjacent restaurant. Great.

Sloane took a few more steps and winced—wicked blister from the new boots—then grabbed the printed ER staff schedule from her nightstand. Had she forgotten she was working today? She traced her finger across her column: Saturday, Sunday, Wednesday, and . . . She frowned, confused by a dense scribble of black. Felt pen, circling an upcoming date on the month's schedule, then obliterating it with cross-hatched layers of black. Her effort, but . . . *What the* . . . *?*

She traced the column to the top of the schedule and read the date she'd mangled on the printout.

Saturday, March 26

Sloane took a slow breath, stretched tall, and stepped over the pile of clothes.

Shower. Mouthwash. Visine. Neosporin and a Band-Aid on the blister. Fresh scrubs in the closet.

It was a workday. By the time she hit the doors of San Diego Hope, she'd have it together.

"He's so much better," Taylor told Rob, her throat tightening as she remembered Hooper's wagging tail when he followed her to the door this morning. Steady on his feet, a few solid mouthfuls of food in his stomach. She'd been beyond heartened. And when Taylor bent down to stroke his ears, he'd licked her face for the first time in weeks. She'd cried. "I'm glad I took him to the after-hours clinic."

"Cortisone miracle." Rob glanced away for a second as one of the staff doctors passed the ER nurses' station. "We're always glad to see that Lazarus effect, even if it's short-lived. I'm happy you're happy."

She hesitated, willing her edgy response to wane. She wasn't going to let Rob dilute her hope. Hooper had been better this morning; another remission was entirely possible. Lazarus had been raised from the dead, healed, but maybe Rob's casual faith didn't account for that. Taylor reminded herself that this man had been nothing but kind to her. Her dog had cancer. That's all he saw. She was wrong to judge Rob for his objective viewpoint.

"I'm hopeful," she told him simply. "If he's still feeling good tonight, we'll be going for a little walk down the cul-de-sac. Hooper has a crush on this mini schnauzer, Heidi." Taylor smiled, thinking of the duet of wagging, mismatched tails. "We'll probably take her a sweet potato dog biscuit."

"I could come with you." Rob gave her arm a gentle squeeze. "After I finish my last appointment, I'll swing by."

"I . . . No, that's okay," Taylor told him, the image refusing to gel in her mind. "There's only a small chance he'll be up to it. We used to spend hours in Balboa Park, up and down the hills, and I'd have to hold Hooper back from chasing after the squirrels." She breathed a sigh. "We haven't done much walking in a while. You shouldn't plan to come by."

"Okay." Rob's fingers lingered on her arm. "But I thought of something else today. I don't know why I didn't ask you before."

"About what?" Taylor asked, catching sight of Sloane's arrival in the department.

"The awards gala in San Francisco." Rob's blue eyes captured hers. "I know it's short notice, but I'd like you to come as my guest. I'd like us to attend together, Taylor."

Her breath snagged. Rob was being honored for his charitable work. He'd already told Taylor his family would be attending. There would be media exposure . . .

"Will you come with me?" He watched her evolving expressions, then smiled. "If you're worried about your schedule, I've already checked: you're off that weekend. I'll take care of the flight. And the overnight lodging. Separate rooms, of course. If you don't have an evening gown and want to go shopping, I'll be happy to—"

"I have a gown," Taylor broke in before her imagination could replay Julia Roberts's shopping spree in *Pretty Woman*. "It's not that. And it's an amazing idea, but . . ."

"But?"

"May I give you an answer later tonight?"

"Certainly." The look in Rob's eyes, his very slight inclination toward Taylor, hinted he'd like nothing more than to kiss her. Right here in the ER. For everyone to see. He chuckled instead. "Give me a call. Even if it's from your cell while you're feeding sweet potato biscuits to your dog's girlfriend." Rob squeezed her arm again. "Tell the old boy I understand that sentiment."

Taylor watched Rob walk away, then—

"I'm here now," Sloane announced, appearing from somewhere behind her. The frosty eyes, a hint of redness the only sign of her reported illness, glanced very obviously in the direction of Rob Halston's exit. "Not that you probably noticed. Considering."

Taylor stiffened, warning herself it was better to let it slide. But she couldn't. "What I notice," she said, meeting Sloane's gaze directly, "is your attitude. Just now. And over and over, no matter what I do or say to avoid it. I don't get it." Taylor's brows bunched. "What's your problem, Sloane?"

"My problem?"

"Let's get this settled," Taylor went on, already regretting the decision to confront Sloane. She wasn't good at it. But she was so sick of the innuendos and sniping. After the vague nonanswers she'd gotten from Seth regarding Greg's day planner, she needed to at least get one thing solved. Sloane Wilder would suffice. "Why are you always trying to push my buttons? What did I ever do to you?"

Sloane's lips twitched and she took a quick glance around the ER's main pod. "You haven't done anything—yet. Except not staying put in Sacramento."

"Oddly, I think I get that." It was the same way Taylor had felt about finding Sloane at San Diego Hope. And having Seth here now. "Something about trying to get away," she agreed, "and finding your past following you."

"Like a toilet paper tail dangling from the back of my skirt." Amusement tempered Sloane's brittle smile. "Don't forget I was here first, Cabot."

"You'll never let me."

"Count on that."

Taylor studied the nurse for a moment, hoping to catch a glimpse beneath that hard-edged beauty, maybe see something vulnerable and warm hiding there. "I didn't follow you here, Sloane. Trust me."

"I make it a point to never trust *anybody*." Sloane pressed her fingers to her temple for a moment, then offered Taylor what might have been a first genuine smile. It softened her icy eyes a little. "I'm not somebody for your friend list, Cabot. Not even close. We won't be going out for mani-pedis or sitting up all night together, pouring our hearts out over our rotten luck with love. So do yourself a favor and stop trying so hard, huh?"

Rotten luck with love. Maybe it was the one thing they had in common.

"You're right." Taylor glanced toward the nurses' desk, hearing the sounds of the base station radio keying for a call. "For the record, I wasn't really expecting us to be friends. I—"

"You wanted to smooth things over, get it all tidied up. And check me off some 'make nice' to-do list."

Taylor cleared her throat.

"That's who you are." Sloane shook her head. "But I'll give you this: you've got skills as a nurse. You know how to get it done. So I'll make you this offer. I'll bite my tongue. When I can. You swear you won't invite me to any department potlucks. We'll agree we don't like each other. But when something big goes down here, where it counts, we have each other's back." Her gaze flickered toward the desk, where a radio report now blared. "Deal?"

"I can live with it," Taylor agreed as sirens punctuated the paramedic report.

"Good. Because I think that radio call said—"

"Code 3 ambulances coming! ETA three minutes," a tech shouted. "Trauma. Two patients: one adult, one child. Multiple gunshot wounds."

Seth tried to catch a glimpse of Kasie Beckett's face as he followed her along the yellow crime scene tape. It was her first survivor support after a homicide—in this instance a murder-suicide. Not easy even for veteran crisis volunteers. As an ER tech, she'd seen more than her fair share of blood and tragedy. But this, today, was a completely different animal. A quiet, cookie-cutter suburban neighborhood turned upside down. There were helicopters overhead, police and fire vehicles parked on the lawn, an incessant squawk-crackle of emergency radios . . . and two men lying in separate, congealing pools of blood on the floor inside that house. A love triangle turned deadly.

There but for the grace of God . . .

Seth finally captured Kasie's gaze as they came to a halt a few yards from where detectives were questioning a tearful witness. "You okay?" he asked her.

"Yes . . . good." She managed a quick smile despite the obvious anxiety in her eyes. Her fingers reached for the small cross at the neckline of her volunteer shirt. Over the shirt, she wore the same green jacket as Seth, lettered in white with *Crisis Team.* Kasie glanced toward the distraught woman and the detectives. "I can't imagine how awful it would be to see something like that. Your family shot in front of your eyes. How can anybody get that angry?"

Seth wished he didn't know.

"We're not here to try to make sense of the tragedy," he reminded her. "We're here to support the survivors. Be a calm, compassionate presence in the midst of their nightmare. We can help them understand what to expect in the minutes, hours, weeks ahead. And—" he turned to look as a wail rose from the woman in the distance—"we *listen.*"

"Yes." Kasie reached into her pocket and pulled out a small package. "And we man the tissues."

"Absolutely." Seth smiled at the young volunteer. "Never run short of Kleenex. And always save an extra package for yourself."

"Right." The young woman's blue eyes met his. "Thank you for volunteering to be my mentor on this call; I know you didn't have to. You're here to set up training, not ride shotgun." She grimaced at her choice of words. "I'm going to need tissues and a big piece of duct tape for my mouth. Oh, man, I'm really, *really* glad you're here, Seth. I want to do this right. Make things better."

"You will," Seth assured, struck again by her sincerity. This young rookie had all the right stuff, even if she couldn't see it yet. He noted that the officers had taken the woman to an unmarked patrol car and gotten her as comfortable as possible in the backseat. "Do you remember what we were told about this survivor's situation?"

"It's her house. Her daughter and granddaughter moved in with her. The child's father—they're separated—heard there might be another man involved. And that he was over here at the house today. So . . ."

"The ex showed up on the porch," Seth continued, his stomach tensing, "then forced his way in."

"And killed himself—after shooting everyone." Kasie winced. "Except for the grandmother. Who saw it all happen." She looked toward the patrol car. "God help her."

"He will." Seth nodded. "And part of that is *us*. Right now."

10

"MY BABY . . ." The young woman, her ashen face beaded with sweat, struggled to lift her head from the trauma gurney. The oxygen tubing snagged on an IV pump, making the cannula slip from one nostril and stretch the other, already crowded because of a nasogastric tube. She didn't even notice. "Where is she? Lacey. Where—?"

"Easy. Here, let me fix your oxygen." Sloane pressed a hand against the woman's chest, encouraging her to lie back, and then adjusted the plastic prongs in her nose. The cardiac monitor alarmed: pulse rate 136. Panic and blood loss were bad bed partners. "Lacey's doing okay."

"Really?"

Sloane glanced toward the adjacent trauma cubicle, willing

the six-year-old not to scream again. Or whimper like a woodland creature caught in a trap. That had been even worse. Sloane could handle a lot of things, but not that. It brought back too many of her own memories. She was grateful Taylor was in there and she didn't have to be. Even with local anesthetic and IV sedation, the poor child continued to have pain. Picking buckshot from her little legs was a far cry from slapping triple antibiotic and a Band-Aid on a skinned knee. And now there was a question about a metal fragment seen on her abdominal X-ray. "She's okay. Don't worry."

"But it's my fault." A tear slid down the woman's face, pooling in a corner of her quivering lips. "If I'd stayed with him, tried to work it out somehow . . ." Her words disappeared in a primal groan. "It's all my fault."

No, don't . . .

Sloane made an attempt at a hand pat and then glanced away. She wasn't going to climb aboard this woman's emotional derailment. *Guilt.* There was always guilt. Cause and effect. Mistakes and consequences. When your life spun out of control . . .

Sloane told herself to focus on what she had to offer right now: skilled, clinical, save-your-life expertise, not touchy-feely emotional support. That was for priests and chaplains.

"Need any help?" Taylor asked, arriving at the bedside. "My patient . . ." She lowered her voice after glancing at Sloane's, dozing now that the last dose of morphine had kicked in. "We just rolled my little patient to the OR. So I can do whatever you need here."

"We're good." Sloane checked the monitoring equipment. "BP's been fairly stable after two liters of Ringer's, and the second unit of blood is almost complete." She glanced up at the smaller plastic bag hanging over the bed, its contents infusing in viscous, garnet-red droplets. "They'll send the next unit to the OR."

As if on cue, she heard an overhead page for one of the trauma surgeons.

Taylor frowned as the suction machine cycled and a large quantity of red-brown fluid sluiced up the nasogastric tube to spit into a collection container. "Still thinking bowel injury?"

"Yep."

"Awful thing," Taylor said, keeping her voice low. "Guns, jealousy—you don't want to get in the middle of that."

"Uh . . . right." Sloane's headache returned. Even if she'd agreed to a semi-truce with this nurse, it didn't mean she had to listen to any sanctimonious opinions. "I've got it handled here. Don't need you."

"Sure?"

"Hundred and ten percent."

"Okay then." Taylor took a last glance at the young mother. "The hospital chaplain's been here, right?"

"Haven't seen him." *Hope I don't.*

"I'll give him another page." Taylor's brows drew together. "I'm sure the crisis team is on scene at the shooting site. Maybe even Kasie. She was taking call today."

"I should have done something." The grandmother's eyes, still wide with horror, shifted from Kasie back to the house. The front door had been opened to facilitate the removal of the remaining victim, a second body bag on a second medical examiner's gurney. She shivered. "I should have helped."

Seth stopped himself from saying anything. Survivor's

guilt was expected. And this was Kasie's call—she was doing great.

"You activated 911," Kasie said gently, sliding a little closer to the survivor in the backseat of the patrol car. She adjusted a rescue blanket over the woman's shoulders. "You called for help."

"I still can't believe it." The woman hugged her arms around herself and began rocking forward and back. "He came through my door with that pistol shoved in his belt, waving the shotgun. Screaming profanity. I never saw Donny like that. So drunk and out-of-his-head jealous. Like some kind of wild animal."

Seth's gut twisted.

"I keep hearing those sounds," she continued, eyes wide in a thousand-yard stare. "The shotgun racking, my daughter's boyfriend shouting, my granddaughter begging Donny to stop, and then . . ." The woman turned to pluck at Kasie's jacket, staring into her eyes. "I ran to the kitchen." She clutched harder, with both hands, as tears streamed down her face. "He started firing that gun, and I *ran*. I should have stayed there, done something."

"I'm sorry," Kasie managed as the woman crumpled against her, sobbing. "We're going to do our best to help you. Any way we can. We're here. We won't leave you."

"That's right," Seth confirmed, slipping down to one knee beside the open door of the car. He shifted his weight and felt a jab of pain—a reminder of a day far too much like this one. He met Kasie's gaze over the top of the woman's head and gave her an encouraging nod. "Kasie is going to sit here with you while I talk with the officers for a few minutes. That way we can let you know what to expect. I'm also going to check on things regarding your daughter and Lacey," he added gently. "See what's happening with their care."

"They're . . ." The grandmother raised her head from Kasie's shoulder. "They're at San Diego Hope?"

"Yes, ma'am. In good hands."

Two of those are Taylor's.

11

"It sounds like the most magical place on earth really is." Taylor held the phone to her ear and stretched a bare leg off the couch to rub Hooper's belly with her toes. He closed his eyes, tongue lolling out in bliss. "I'm glad you're having such a great time, Aimee. You sound happy."

"I am and—" a crescendo of music mixed with childish squeals rose somewhere in the background—"Lucas is so great with those rascally little boys."

Aimee was referring to her adopted brothers, but Taylor had no problem reading between the lines. It couldn't be clearer if Aimee had written it in Magic Kingdom–colored markers: *Lucas would make a great father.* Her cousin had only known this young man a short while, but her heart was mapping a future with every beat. It had been that way with Taylor and Greg too, and she'd been so eager—desperate, that last year—to welcome children into their lives. But it hadn't happened.

"And how is Dr. Wonderful?" Aimee asked, a purr in her voice giving a clue that Lucas was by her side again. "Anything new?"

"Not really." Taylor's skin warmed. The feeling was paired with familiar nervousness. "He's asked me to be his date for that big charity gala in San Francisco."

Aimee's squeal rivaled her brothers'. "I can so imagine him in a tuxedo. You said yes, of course."

"Not yet."

Aimee was quiet for a long moment. No easy task. When she spoke again, her voice was gentle. "Maybe it's time, Taylor. Like you said about your rings. It's time to take that next step."

Accomplish the last item on her checklist: *Fall in love again.*

"Promise me you won't overthink it," Aimee added. "Like you do with your calorie budget and counting every step with that activity bracelet. When it comes to love, it should be natural . . . like 'breathing in and breathing out.' I read that in a little book of verses somewhere."

"Now you're quoting poetry?"

"Yes." There was a smile in Aimee's voice, as blissful as Hooper with a tummy rub. "It seems to fit. I want you to find your happy place too."

"I . . ." Taylor's voice choked and she swallowed against a sudden ache. The last thing she wanted was to worry her cousin. "I know that. And I am—I am heading that way. I promise."

They said good-bye and Taylor slid onto the carpet next to her dog, the best proof that things were happier. They'd had their walk. Molasses slow and stiff on his part, but they'd made the complete circuit of the cul-de-sac. And rung the mini schnauzer's doorbell so Hooper could get his kiss; his tail had wagged so fast that he'd nearly toppled sideways. "Lazarus effect" from cortisone or not, it had been the single bright spot in Taylor's day. A long, trauma-filled day that didn't end when she drove away from San Diego Hope.

Taylor lifted her iPad from the couch, frowning as an envelope slid to the floor, landing on her discarded running shoe. A lavender envelope from a card sent by the retired schoolteacher who ran Greg down. *"You remain in my prayers . . ."*

Three years, three cards.

No . . . Six cards. Taylor refreshed the iPad screen. An e-card this time. From the woman Greg had stopped to help that night. A single mother with a small child, stranded by a flat tire on that dark country road. *"Thinking of you . . ."*

The confusing anger rose again. What if Taylor didn't want to think of *them*? She'd forgiven them. Wasn't that enough? Was she not allowed to *forget* them now? Three years, six cards. Five envelopes addressed, stamped, dropped into the mail, timed to arrive by March 26. And now this e-card . . .

Taylor jabbed a finger at the Reply button on the tablet screen.

Please stop sending these. I've moved away. And moved on. There is no need to

She lifted her trembling fingers from the keys, squeezed her eyes shut for a moment. Then hit Cancel and slid the iPad from her lap. She'd do it later. Add it to her checklist to send notes to both women and put an end to it once and for all.

Taylor glanced toward the muted TV and reached for the remote. The news was showing a film clip from the shooting scene, taken earlier today. The camera panned past a group of officers, coming to rest on a patrol car at the curb. Taylor hit the button to raise the volume.

". . . two bodies removed from the house. Two victims, a young woman and a child, were reportedly taken to San Diego Hope hospital for treatment of gunshot wounds. And—" the camera lens zoomed in—"a remaining witness, the owner of this home, is currently being attended to by San Diego crisis volunteers."

Taylor caught sight of Kasie, dressed in a blue shirt and official jacket, sitting in the backseat of a squad car. Taylor's hunch had been right; she had been sent to the scene. Kasie's first callout for a homicide. Taylor grimaced. She hoped the new volunteer had a great partner and—

Oh.

A familiar bulk filled the camera. The second volunteer. He dropped to one knee beside the car to support his teammate and a woman whose world had been blasted apart.

Seth.

Of course he'd be there. That's who Seth was, who he'd always been, for Taylor too. Just because she was backing away from the crisis team didn't mean she couldn't appreciate his generous spirit and dedication. Tell him that. And check on Kasie . . .

Taylor grabbed her cell phone, tapped the speed dial entry . . . waited . . .

"Hey. What's up?" Seth's voice sounded breathless.

"Where are you?"

"Running." He drew in a harsh breath. "Trying to."

"Sorry. It's just that I saw you on the news. With Kasie."

There was a pause. "It's what I do, Taylor."

She decided not to read anything into it. Neither of their days had been spent in "the most magical place on earth." Not even close.

"Look, did you need something?" he asked.

"I left a message for Kasie earlier and didn't hear back," Taylor explained, thinking Seth's abruptness, winded or not, wasn't like him. "I thought she might have been called to the shooting scene, and I wanted to see how—"

"She did fine. We did our debriefing with dispatch. Kasie seemed good and . . . I need to run, Taylor."

"Okay, I—where are you?"

"On the beach."

"Where exactly?"

"Sunset Cliffs. Why?"

"Because I'm coming there." Taylor lifted the lavender envelope from one shoe, reached for the other. "I need to run too."

12

"No problem. Go on ahead," Seth told Taylor while wiping sweat from his neck with the T-shirt he'd stripped off and jammed into the waistband of his shorts. They'd jogged twenty minutes before Taylor joined them, him and his dog. Nearly twenty more since, and Seth needed a breather even if the young Labrador retriever and Energizer Bunny didn't. His knee, as usual, was calling him a fool. "I'll catch up, no worries."

"You're sure?" The flush, high on Taylor's cheeks, was nearly the same shade of pink as her running pants. "I can take a break."

"I'm sure. Go. That activity bracelet probably gives you a Taser jolt if you stop too long."

She laughed, reaching up to capture a handful of hair tossed by the sea breeze; it was the same burnished shade as his dog's. He was at the mercy of two determined redheads.

"I guess I shouldn't risk being Tasered," Taylor conceded. She glanced down at his dog and waggled her fingers. "Bye-bye, Miss Lucy. Drag him along if he dawdles, okay?"

"Gee, thanks for the vote of confidence."

Taylor laughed again. "Anytime."

Seth scrubbed his T-shirt over his chest, watching as she started off. He shook his head; he might be getting as much cardio this way. Even if Taylor had lost enough weight to sharpen her facial bones, there was nothing wrong with the way she filled out those running clothes. His resting heart rate was proof of that. Maybe it wasn't such a bad idea that she'd forced the issue about joining him here. He'd wanted some distance from the real world, a chance to clear his head after that shooting incident. But maybe a distraction was just as good. Better, even. He smiled, his gaze following the flash of pink down the beach. Especially with this view. Seth shook his head again—*Where is this coming from?* Beach jogging with a friend, nothing more.

He shoved the shirt back into his waistband, drew in a breath of salty air, and reached down to pat the young dog staring up at him. After all these miles, Lucy was still visibly eager to continue their run. At seven months, she was a far superior athlete; he was always cautious about her maturing joints, though she voted for no-holds-barred. He shortened the leash and they moved into a slow jog again.

With a chance to talk, he might be able to get a better handle on Taylor's decision to quit the crisis team. Talking could be good. As long as she didn't press him again about her husband's appointment. He didn't want to go there. Not at all.

Seth poured on the speed to catch Taylor and managed, despite his groaning knee and Lucy's occasional exuberant lunges toward the surf, to stay alongside her for another ten minutes. It was a quiet pairing for the most part. Arms pumping and feet dodging pieces of driftwood, disarticulated bits of marine life, and deserted sand castles. They took deep gulps of air and enjoyed the palm-lined panorama of cliffs and sandy beach as the sun began its descent toward the sea. It occurred to Seth, not for the first time by a long shot, that God must have taken particular delight in carving out the California coast. Lucy, slobbering, panting, and happy, would agree.

"Aaagh," Taylor huffed, shoes slapping the wet sand as she slowed to a walk at last. "I think that's it for me."

Bending over at the waist and gazing out at the blue sea, she added, "It's good, though. Really good." She rose back up, swept a hand across her forehead, freed a clinging length of hair. Her eyes, greener somehow in the late-afternoon light, met his. "Thank you for letting me share your beach. And your adventure-crazy dog. Walking Hooper around the cul-de-sac was nice, but I needed this."

"He's feeling better?"

"Yes." Taylor's brows pinched a little. "Hooper's blood tests aren't the greatest, but that tail's wagging and he can still make Heidi's heart go pitter-pat." She laughed at the look on his face. "Neighbor dog. Hooper's always had a way with the ladies."

"Good man. I'd like to meet him sometime." Seth pulled his T-shirt over his head, then glanced across the beach toward the palm trees and the red-tile roofs beyond. He reeled Lucy in, scratched her ear. "I know this sounds like a replay, but I'm hungry."

"Me too."

"I mean real food. Sitting down somewhere that doesn't involve big rocks."

"Sounds good. Though . . ." She glanced at her running clothes.

"Don't worry; I'm not going to inflict my sweaty self on anyone either. Lucy is finally worn-out; she'll sleep the rest of the evening. I can be showered, changed, and at your door in, say . . . an hour?"

"It's probably better timewise if we pick a central spot to eat and meet there."

"How about the Gaslamp Quarter? Tapas?"

"Mmm. Perfect."

"Good. But one more thing." Seth wondered why he'd never noticed the faint sprinkle of freckles across the bridge of her nose. Like cinnamon on a sugar cookie. "You have to promise me something."

"What?"

"None of that salad-dressing-fork-dip thing."

———

Taylor managed to get there, dressed and ready—khaki skirt with a sleeveless tie-front peach linen shirt—in less than the promised hour. Seth had already scored a patio table at Cafe Sevilla, a popular restaurant in the Gaslamp Quarter. A double miracle, she'd told him, since it was still within the limits of happy-hour pricing, gentler on a nurse's budget. Then Seth made it clear that dinner, a complete dinner, was on him. Taylor thought about arguing but was too famished to put up a decent struggle. Though if she were to be completely truthful, accepting this invitation wasn't only about hunger. She'd enjoyed Seth's company today and hadn't wanted it to end.

"Unbelievable," she repeated, having used the same word to describe the suit of vintage Spanish armor guarding the outside of the colorful, romantic, brick-embellished eatery. "I haven't had tapas or paella in ages," she added, raising her voice a little over the blend of flamenco guitar, tinkling glassware, and laugh-peppered snips of conversations between folks passing by on the sidewalk.

"And . . ." Taylor lifted a half-nibbled shrimp teased golden-red by sizzling garlicky oil and saffron. "I'm not going to even *try* to search the calorie counts and log them into my fitness app."

"Good." Seth smiled at her. "Score one for tempting you into food debauchery. I was afraid I'd lost my touch."

"Hardly."

Taylor met his gaze across the table, feeling her cheeks warm as if the fruity and delicious sangria he'd ordered weren't nonalcoholic. Minus that excuse, it must have been something to do with how Seth Donovan looked tonight. His skin sun-flushed and healthy after the beach run, the thick, rebellious hair damp from the shower . . . And then there was that washed-soft henley shirt. A sort of faded sea-glass blue, stretched snug across his broad shoulders and chest and worn unbuttoned at the top, with sleeves that hit mid-bicep. All of it a reminder of what Taylor had seen far more clearly on their run: this man was fit. She smiled, thinking of her impression of the chaplain as a mix of well-worn teddy bear and warrior. Right now she'd have to say he had far more in common with that suit of armor in front of this café.

"So what did you think of Lucy?" he asked.

"Wonderful," Taylor said quickly, hoping she hadn't been caught staring. She chuckled, remembering the gangly and eager red Lab leaving a trail of zigzag paw prints in the sand. Endearingly clumsy, with sweet, sweet eyes. "She's great. But puppies are a handful. I'm surprised you have the time."

"I probably don't. But the breeder was a good friend of Dad's, a retired deputy. Dad paid a deposit, picked Lucy out when she was only a few days old." Seth smiled. "I drove him over there to see her every week. He wasn't walking more than a few yards without resting even back then, so it made no sense that he'd take on the care of a dog, especially such a high-energy one. But I wasn't going to say anything. Figured I'd be doing the dog walking. Dad was waiting for Lucy to be weaned but . . ."

Taylor winced.

"I'd forgotten all about the pup until Dad's friend gave me a call a couple of weeks after the funeral. Said no problem, he had someone else interested and he'd return Dad's deposit."

"But you took her."

"Yeah. Dad was so excited about having a dog again. And he'd already named her."

"Why Lucy?" she asked gently.

"Because she's a redhead." Seth laughed at the confusion that must've shown on Taylor's face. "Lucy Ricardo. *I Love Lucy*, my parents' favorite TV show. Even after Mom's aneurysm, with all the brain damage, she'd still laugh at that show. I bought them DVD collections of the episodes." He shook his head. "Dad did a great impression of Ricky Ricardo. Knew all his best lines."

Taylor smiled. She could probably pass that trivia quiz herself.

"I think he couldn't get a grip on coming home to an empty house." There was sadness in Seth's voice. "So he joked that when he got the dog, he could come sweeping through the door after work and say in his best Ricky Ricardo voice—"

"*Lucy, I'm home!*" Taylor finished.

"Exactly."

Their eyes met; they both knew the lonely feeling of a too-quiet house. Taylor's heart lugged. "I'm glad you took her."

"Me too." Seth looked down at the two remaining Spanish tapas on his plate: a flamed Moorish chicken skewer and a cider-glazed, bacon-wrapped date stuffed with blue cheese. He sighed with obvious regret and reached for his sangria. "I think I may have overestimated what I can handle. Would you like—?"

"No way." Taylor tapped her fitness tracker, switched to an orange band to match her outfit. "Risk of Taser, remember? I earned some extra calories on that run, but I'm trying to keep it within the parameters of—"

"Why?"

"Why what?"

Seth met Taylor's gaze over the brim of his glass. "Why are you suddenly so intent on setting parameters for yourself?"

"I . . ." Taylor tensed. They'd been talking about his dog, and out of nowhere he'd taken the conversation in a completely different direction. Had she forgotten this man's ability to get under her skin? "I wanted to make some changes," she answered, trying to ignore a small prickle of irritation. "Good changes. Exercise, a better diet . . . I don't look healthy?"

Seth's smile was lopsided, slow. "You look *great*."

"Thanks." She glanced down at her plate. Even if she hadn't been fishing for a compliment, at least she'd managed to avert an inquisition. "Anyway, I made a promise to myself that I'd get back on track. Do the things that are good for me. And give up what isn't."

"Like the crisis team?"

13

"THAT'S NOT FAIR, SETH." Taylor leaned back in her chair and crossed her arms. The movement was underscored by a sudden, bold strumming of flamenco guitar. She wished she could laugh. "I took myself off the call list because of the move. It's taking a lot of time to get settled."

"It's been nearly nine months, Taylor. Do you have that many boxes to unpack?"

Only that one from Greg's desk, the Pandora's box I wish I'd never opened.

"I told you," Taylor said, forcing her hands to rest in her lap, "that I haven't made a final decision." She hated that the lie came so easily. Quitting the team was on her Survival List now. And that clock was ticking. "I've been considering several—"

"'Factors.'" Seth leaned forward in his chair. No guitar accompaniment. His expression was thoughtful, not accusatory. But undeniably intent. "When I asked you at the ER, the day I arrived—the day of the Sandisons' plane crash—you said you were 'considering several factors.'"

"I guess I did. I mean . . . I am."

"Factors and parameters. Pretty much the same, the way I see it." Seth's dark eyes held hers. "When I met your Dr. Halston that same day, he mentioned the crisis team work and said something about some of us being more comfortable in a 'controlled environment.'"

Your Dr. Halston"?

"Look . . ." The gentle compassion in Seth's expression spelled *chaplain* far better than reflective lettering on any Sacramento crisis vest. "I'm not trying to pressure you, Taylor. Halston is right. There's something to be said for a controlled situation, kind of like that body armor we sell at Donovan's. It's self-protective. In our particular community service, we're expected to be on board for scenarios that would make most sane folks run the other way. Gritty, messy, senseless tragedies . . . evil even. And painful. Almost always painful." He sighed. "I'm preachin' to the choir here. You know all this. And you showed up at that plane crash."

"As a nurse." Taylor clasped her hands in her lap to control a tremble. "I ran down there to see what I could do—as a nurse."

"Then you showed up at the hospital afterward."

And avoided the pilot's wife, until you forced me.

"All I'm saying is that I've known you for quite a while now, Taylor. Through some rugged times. Long enough to see that you have a heart for this work. A lot to offer. But you've heard me say it dozens of times to new volunteers and veterans alike: you've got to take care of yourself first. It's a big part of our training program and why we have debriefings." Seth's smile was gentle. "And why I kept an eye on you in Sacramento."

"A scab, not a scar . . . ," Taylor heard herself say aloud. "You always said there's a difference between a scab and a scar. That being involved in crisis work can open up personal wounds, if . . ." She lifted her chin. "I'm *fine* now, if that's what this is all about. I don't need you to take my emotional pulse. I'm perfectly fine. It's been three years. I've moved on, and I have things under—"

"Control. I see that."

"Good." Taylor battled queasiness. She should have ordered a small salad, not all this. She glanced at Seth and guilt prodded, doing nothing to help her stomach. "I'm sorry. I didn't mean to bark at you. I know you meant well."

"I did. I do." Seth pushed his plate away. "You don't owe me any explanations. Your decisions are your own business. I only hope it doesn't have anything to do with the way things are being run here in San Diego. Something I could help smooth over?"

"No." It was so like Seth to offer. She'd been wrong to jump down his throat. "Not anything like that. It's a great team."

"Okay, then. I'll back off." The lopsided smile reappeared. "Your emotional pulse is safe from me."

"Deal." Taylor returned Seth's smile with mixed relief. It made her think of her confrontation with Sloane Wilder in the ER this morning. Their precarious truce. She'd been relieved to have the conflict tempered to some degree but still had a strong sense it wasn't finished. It felt that way with Seth, too.

"We're closing in ten minutes, ma'am." The animal shelter volunteer, a UCSD undergraduate with an overbite and a Princess Leia hairdo, smiled at Sloane. "Unless you're ready to start an adoption? We've got plenty of time for that. No rush."

"No, I . . ." Sloane extended her freshly polished fingertip through the wire mesh, and the impossibly tiny kitten left his furry hillock of sleeping cage mates and wobbled toward her again. He was as soot black as the charcoal sludge she forced down the throats of overdose patients in the ER. One gray eye was runny and half-closed; his tiny tail quivered uncontrollably.

"Did you say he was abandoned?" Sloane asked as the kitten attempted a weak, raspy meow. It dissolved into a moist cough that threw him off-balance. One of the other kittens raised his head. "These three?"

"Um . . ." The girl glanced over her shoulder and then lowered her voice. "I'm not supposed to give details but—" her lips pressed against her teeth—"someone tried to drown them. Put them in a Save Mart bag, tied it with a shoelace, and tossed them off the Ocean Beach pier. Probably the night before the kite festival. And that plane crash."

The day Seth Donovan arrived.

"It must have been too dark to see that the tide was out," she continued. "They missed the water. The vendor setting up the kite-making booth found them just after dawn. One had died. Probably from hypothermia, our volunteer vet said." The young woman shook her head and one of her hair loops came loose. "I still don't get how people can be that heartless."

Sloane did. All too well. But this kid didn't need to hear that now.

"So there were four?"

"Six. The two calicoes were already adopted. I think some-one's interested in the orange one—maybe the spotted one, too. A lady who came in right before you. She has three chil-dren. And wanted to try to make everybody happy . . . You know how that goes."

Sloane didn't, actually. "Not this black one? She didn't want him?"

"She wasn't comfortable with how he looks. That cough started about an hour ago. It doesn't sound too bad but . . ." The volunteer's brows drew together. "We don't have the resources to treat these animals. If they come in sick or too young to eat solid food, they aren't adoptable. This litter passed the eating test. But now, with the cough, we'll probably have to separate that little guy from his siblings."

Add insult to injury—why not? Sloane's throat squeezed as the kitten pressed himself against her finger. "What's that mean?" she asked, pointing at the dates marked on a card on the cage.

"The date they arrived and . . ." The volunteer sighed.

"The kill date."

"I'm afraid so."

Sloane slid her finger from the cage, turned away.

"If you like him," the girl ventured, "we can fill out the paperwork. Then if he's better in the morning—"

"No. I can't. Really."

Sloane plucked at several white hairs stuck to her black knit top. She hadn't picked up any of the animals. She knew better; animals wormed their way into her heart far too easily. But she'd managed to get stray hairs on herself anyway. Not surprising since there was probably a pound of hair floating free, up and down these sad rows of cages and kennels. From dogs, cats, even a guinea pig and a lop-eared rabbit. The air reeked of disinfectant, soiled bedding, fear . . . and hopelessness. Not that different from a bad day in the ER.

"I'm sorry," Sloane finished. "I can't take him. My landlord requires a huge pet deposit. I work crazy shifts, and honestly, I'm not even sure I'll be in San Diego much longer."

"Too bad." Princess Leia offered a wistful smile. "You two seemed like a fit."

"Thanks for letting me look around."

"Sure."

Sloane dropped a twenty-dollar bill in the donation box as she left. It meant she'd have to find someone to charm if she wanted more than a second drink tonight. Not a problem. She knew for sure that she was "a fit" for something like that. Always had been. She pushed down a memory of one of countless beauty pageants: herself at six, in too much makeup, too-skimpy clothes, tasseled boots . . . Her mother's boyfriend giving her sips of *something to loosen you up, honey . . . Shake that sweet little booty and turn on the charm."*

Sloane slid into her car, picked several more hairs off her top. Then settled her boot on the brake and reached for the ignition button. She checked her rearview mirror and saw the volunteer locking the doors to the building.

Maybe the half-drowned kitten would get better. Well enough to turn on the charm and find himself a decent home. But if it didn't work out, at least he had the mercy of an end date: March 26.

14

"I SUSPECTED IT wouldn't take much to get you out here for a walk," Seth teased as he and Taylor made their way down the Fifth Avenue sidewalk in the direction of the ocean. He could already smell brine on the breeze. Blended, of course, with the pervasive restaurant aromas of grilled fish, fresh Mexican, Thai, Indian, Italian . . . "That slave driver bracelet on your wrist would demand you move."

"I could put it in my pocket if it makes you crazy." Taylor glanced sideways at him. Her lips quirked into a smile. "Though it can count steps through hip sway too."

"I should have guessed that," Seth told her, letting himself imagine tossing the stupid thing into the sea. Along with her "factors" and "parameters" and . . . Dr. Halston? The man with the matching bracelet. Was he the reason for all these changes? Including Taylor's decision to reconsider her crisis work? Seth had promised to back off about that but—

"I love what they've done down here." Taylor stopped, gazing at the downtown cityscape surrounding them. The Gaslamp Quarter's iconic lamps, white balloons against the darkening sky, cast a warm glow over her hair. "All these restored Victorian buildings. Along with—" her green eyes blinked up, up, at one of several high-rise, higher-rent, condominium complexes—"the steel, cement, and glass. It's such an exciting feel. Old and new, history and fresh starts."

"Yes," Seth agreed, certain Taylor must see her life that way too. Painful past and hopeful new start. It was healthy, good. Seth had been through it a couple of times himself. But moving on didn't mean you needed to leave *everything* behind.

"Won't be long," she continued, glancing east toward Seventh Avenue, "before the Padres start up at Petco Park. Rob has season tickets."

Matching bracelets and ball caps.

Seth frowned, grateful Taylor couldn't see it in the shadows. He was being an idiot. It had been a long day and a particularly tough crisis call. He was letting that color too many things. Taylor's company tonight was a natural extension of that therapeutic beach run, nothing more. Good to remember that. He took a breath and raised his voice over an explosion of laughter spilling from the doors of the Hard Rock Cafe. "Gotta love baseball."

"My dad would take me to the games sometimes. From way back to when I was like . . . seven, maybe." Taylor started walking again. "At first I was more excited about the hot dogs than anything. Those steamed-soft buns and so much sweet pickle relish that my hair would stick to my face. We'd always top it all off with a Fudgsicle." She sighed. "He doesn't get to many games now, but my dad's a huge baseball fan."

"Mine was too." Seth fielded a jab of pain. He heard his father's raspy voice, aided by a boost from a portable oxygen tank, rooting in a sports bar down the block from Donovan's Uniforms. "Giants. Always."

"Our fathers and baseball. I love that we have that in common, Seth."

The sweet sincerity in her voice made Seth's breath catch. It was who he knew Taylor Cabot was, sans this new need to control everything down to separate steps and calories. She'd spoken from her heart, no parameters. His whole day, the frustration and pain, might be worth it for that one thing.

"Me too," he told her. "I'm glad we have that together."

They walked on silently, threading their way through clutches of tourists and locals. The sixteen and a half blocks of the Gaslamp Quarter offered an incredible list of restaurants with names like Bang Bang, Funky Garcia's, China Too, Spike Africa's, Donovan's Steak and Chop House—Seth smiled at that—Escape Fish Bar, The Blind Burro, and The Tipsy Crow. As usual, the area was bustling with activity. All of it tempered by the timeless constant of the sea. That steadfast push-pull of waves, a compelling whisper to listen, learn . . .

"I've always loved that sign." Taylor gestured to the huge lit arc they'd passed under as they approached Harbor Drive. Blue-green and orange with a wedge of yellow stripes, vintage in design, it stretched from gaslamp to gaslamp across the intersection, proclaiming, *Gaslamp Quarter. Historic Heart of San Diego.* She gestured across the busy palm-lined intersection. "Next stop, the beach."

"You haven't had enough today?"

"I'm a Southern Californian. Is there ever enough beach time?"

He shook his head. "Probably not."

They stepped into the intersection, and Seth put his hand at her waist instinctively, keeping an eye out for traffic and trolley cars.

"One hundred steps to the top," Taylor said after they crossed the street. She pointed up at the immense glass-and-light San Diego Convention Center. "The grand staircase."

"Quite a hike." Seth slid his hand away, grateful Taylor hadn't seemed to notice his touch, and turned his attention to the building.

The structure never failed to impress him. With its huge Teflon roof sails and long stretches of tubular glass, he had to wonder if the design team had gone for a mix of Wonderland caterpillar and the *Jetsons'* Orbit City. That staircase, lit like a runway in the dark, seemed to rise endlessly upward. Seth's knee ached looking at it.

"I tried to jog it a couple weeks back," Taylor reported. "Made it to forty-seven. Barely. I can't believe some people use that climb as part of their regular workout."

"Me either," Seth agreed before she could give "some people" a name. He had no doubt one of them had season tickets for the Padres. "Let's follow Harbor Drive instead."

They walked down to the Marriott Marquis San Diego marina and stood for a while watching the highly varnished sailboats and big yachts bob and creak against their moorings, then gazed out at the lights on the dark ocean beyond. The breeze, salty and pristine, was a good reminder that simpler things were good for the soul. Sounds—gulls, distant boat horns, and the ceaseless lapping of the water—rearranged the restless score of Seth's day. Or maybe it was the saffron shrimp and sangria. He was grateful, regardless. His wish to put it all behind him had come true.

"It must have been tough—" Taylor's voice merged with the sea breeze—"to be there today, after those shootings. I took care of the child who caught the shotgun spray."

"Ah . . ." A muscle bunched along his jaw and he made himself take a slow breath. "It was bad. But I've seen worse."

"I'm sure you have."

Taylor studied the chaplain's face in the shadowy light; his expression said a lot more than he was letting on. Of course he'd seen worse. Seth Donovan made himself available in the aftermath of tragedies that challenged the equilibrium of the most experienced first responders. But something about today's call was eating at him. Only that would explain how curt he'd been on the phone when she'd called him today. And some reluctance to let her join him for the run? Probably. She'd sensed that, too.

"It was good of you to volunteer to go along with Kasie," she said. He'd turned away a little. "I know firsthand how grateful she must have been to have you there."

"She did fine." Seth pointed toward the road. "You want to try to find a way down to the beach?"

"Not really." *But you want to change the subject.*

"We should probably head back to the cars," she added. "I have to give Hooper his medicine and—"

"No problem." There couldn't have been more relief on Seth's face if she'd freed his leg from the jaws of a great white shark. "Let's go."

Somehow they managed to make it back to her car in less than half the time it had taken to get to the beach. There would, no doubt, be a serious Steps badge popping up on Taylor's fitness app. Ordinarily the thought would give her a rush of accomplishment. But right now . . .

"You're working tomorrow?" Seth watched as she searched her purse for her keys.

"Yes. Day shift. Ah, here they—oops." The keys slid from her grasp. Seth scooped them up before she could.

"Thanks," Taylor said, reaching out for them. "Too much fruit juice, I guess."

"Dangerous."

Her skin tingled as her fingers brushed Seth's. She remembered the warmth of his hand at the small of her back when they crossed Harbor Drive. "I had a good time. Thank you. For letting me squeeze in on your run, and for dinner—you didn't have to do that."

"I know I didn't." His eyes held hers for a moment. "I'm glad you came. It wasn't a great day before that. You helped make it better. Thanks." He turned, scanning the still-bustling Sixth Avenue. "Now I should go figure out where I parked my car."

At the sound of a phone buzz, they both reached for their pockets.

"Mine," he said, squinting at the screen. "Kasie. I should take it."

"Of course."

Seth moved a few steps away. The light from a nearby gaslamp cast a glow over his shoulders and the rugged planes of his face. He listened far more than he spoke. Nodding, pacing a little. Overall, an unmistakable picture of empathy.

Taylor's heart tugged. How many times had Seth done this? For how many people? *Including me* . . .

"Sorry." Seth returned to Taylor's side.

"Is she okay?"

"I think so." He scraped his fingers along his jaw, sighed. "First time with something like that. It's tough."

This good man knew way too much about "tough." He'd lost his wife to cancer, his mother, and then his father not even six months ago. But he was putting himself out there to help again, even after a day that had obviously taken a personal toll.

"All right then." He found a smile. "Drive safe. Have a good shift tomor—"

"Come meet Hooper."

"What?"

"My dog," Taylor explained, shifting her keys to the other hand. "You said you wanted to meet him, right?"

"I . . ."

It was possible Seth's expression hinted that she'd lost her mind. Didn't matter—for most of the last three years, Taylor had thought exactly the same thing.

"You mean now?" he asked.

"Sure. Get your car and follow me."

15

"I'D COME IN THERE AND HELP YOU," Seth called out to Taylor in the kitchen, "but—"

"Hooper has you trapped on the couch." Her laugh mingled with the whir of a grinder. An oily-rich aroma of roasted coffee beans filled the air. "I know his MO."

"I'll bet you do," Seth agreed, seeing that the retriever had managed to doze off, graying muzzle propped atop his knee. He stroked the old dog's head and heard his deep, vibrating sigh. His own lingering tension diffused. There was a good reason dogs were considered therapeutic. It was easy to imagine this old boy provided no small amount of that.

Seth glanced around, confirming his first impression of this space: meticulously planned, pristine and perfect. With more subtle variations of white than he'd ever imagined existed:

walls, woodwork, shaggy cream-colored area rug, pale leather chair and couch, and even chalk-colored pillows stamped with faint outlines of seashells. Artistic, Seth guessed, not that he knew the first thing about that. The Donovans' decor had run more toward hand-me-down practicality with colors and patterns that hid peanut butter smudges and furniture rugged enough to double as stadium seating and trampolines. Spaces that became—all too often—good-natured but rambunctious sparring rings. This was completely foreign.

His gaze moved to the mantel, a pale stretch of stucco topped with a single framed photo of Taylor and another redhead—her cousin Aimee, he assumed. It was a recent shot judging by Taylor's haircut and the new sharpness to her facial features. New . . . everything in this room looked new. No hint of the past. Except for this old dog.

Seth smiled as Hooper's eyes opened; he stroked the dog's head again. "You're it," he heard himself whisper. "You're all she's kept. Except for her Bible."

He glanced to where it lay along with a slim volume of devotionals. A well-worn, tabbed Bible lying on the coffee table, one of those glass-topped things designed to hold and display a person's special collections. Only this one was filled with a thin layer of white sand—smooth, like it had been scraped painstakingly with a carpenter's level—and one single, perfect shell. Planned, controlled, like a sterile sand castle constructed a safe distance from the sea.

"Getting settled after the move" had been Taylor's excuse for backing away from the crisis work. Seth had expected to find unpacked moving boxes, ladders, paint cans. Not this. There was nothing to settle because there was nothing left. He glanced toward Hooper's bed across the room, a rumpled

and faded camouflage-print flannel liberally sprinkled with the old retriever's shedding hair. It was the one thing in this room that didn't fit.

Besides me . . . Seth frowned, hating that he had no problem imagining the very smooth Rob Halston here.

"Here we go," Taylor announced, arriving with a tray. "Coffee, cream, sugar, and—" her nose wrinkled—"some Girl Scout cookies. It's all I had. And I'm afraid they're frozen. Two boxes, frozen solid."

"Because you didn't want to be tempted."

"I guess."

You guess?

Seth fought an irrational urge to pry open the coffee table, mess up the sand, and scatter it with Thin Mint cookies. And what? *Tempt her? Prove I can?* Yes. With cookies and then maybe with something kind of . . . romantic, like . . . He shook off the renegade thought, telling himself he'd moved from irrational to plain crazy. It had been a rough couple of days and he'd accepted this invitation because it would provide a distraction, keep him from thinking about—

"That call from Kasie tonight," Taylor said after settling beside him on the too-white couch. "I know it's confidential, but is there anything I can do to help her?"

Stay with the team? Seth had promised to back off from that subject. "Her fiancé," he explained, "had a problem with her being at a crime scene."

"Ah."

Seth read Taylor's expression. This conflict wasn't news to her; he'd bet Dr. Halston had voiced similar concerns. "Not everyone understands this work," he said. "I've learned that personal relationships can become an issue."

"The woman you're dating in Sacramento?" Taylor asked, blindsiding him. "The CSI staffer?"

"*Was* dating," Seth admitted, surprised she'd known about it. "Not anymore. And only partly because of the crisis work." He knew Taylor wouldn't ask him to enumerate the other parts, and he was glad. He hadn't entirely figured them out himself, even though he'd been the one to end it. He wasn't proud of that, but it had been an honest choice; he didn't want to make promises he couldn't keep. The relationship hadn't felt right. "I spent a lot of time with my father those last months."

"Of course." Taylor picked up a cookie, set it back down. Then peered at Seth over the rim of her coffee cup. "I think you said once that your father was a police officer for several years?"

"He was," Seth confirmed. Anyone who visited one of the three Donovan's Uniforms stores would find evidence of that. Framed and hanging behind the counters were a dozen or more photos of Mike Donovan in uniform. He'd never been more proud of any accomplishment. "Retired on medical disability after only six years. He lost three fingers in an on-duty accident."

"Oh, dear." Taylor's eyes met his. "I also heard that you'd planned to follow in his footsteps."

His stomach tensed.

"What changed your mind, Seth?"

———

The look on the chaplain's face said she'd asked exactly the wrong question. But before Taylor could backtrack from what was an obvious intrusion, he spoke.

"I applied to the sheriff's department, passed the initial exams, physical testing, and interviews. I had a slot in the academy, but . . . I did something stupid. So I went to jail instead."

Taylor forced her mouth to close. "I'm sorry. I shouldn't have—"

"It's okay," Seth said, cutting her apology short. "There's no reason you shouldn't know." He shrugged. "It doesn't make sense that I'm pushing everyone to be honest and open and still expect to dodge personal questions. I know better than that. Now." His expression was rueful. "Almost twenty years wiser, most of the time."

"I don't know what to say," Taylor told him honestly.

"You probably want to know what I did."

She did. And she didn't. Mostly Taylor wished she'd never brought the subject up in the first place. But . . . "I guess I do."

"I let my temper get the best of me." Seth shook his head. "A Donovan flaw. Add alcohol and you'd better call the bomb squad."

Taylor gasped. "Bomb?"

"Figuratively. I only meant there's a good reason I don't drink anymore. Temper and booze is a bad combination." Seth sighed. "The short version is that I was twenty-three and very full of myself. My girlfriend dumped me and moved in with some other guy. I couldn't deal with it. I got wasted, drove over to their place, and pounded on the door. My ex let me in and I tried to haul her out of there. . . ."

"And?"

"The guy had a shotgun."

16

"HE SHOT YOU?" Taylor asked, a mix of fear and horror on her face.

"My knee," Seth said, thinking she must have noticed the scar today at the beach. "Shattered patella, joint involvement, and vascular injury . . . A mess."

"Thank God it wasn't your chest."

"Thank God I left my handgun in the car." He grimaced against a wave of nausea, very like what he'd felt today at that murder-suicide scene. "It could have been far worse, Taylor."

She took a sip of her coffee, falling quiet for a while. When she met his gaze again, he saw no judgment in her eyes. Only concern. "He shot you. But you went to jail?"

"I did three months for simple assault; I was prepared to hurt him even if I didn't. He was defending himself. Her, too, maybe." That possibility still sickened him. "Technically, because my ex wouldn't press battery charges, I wasn't convicted of a felony. But the sheriff's department didn't want to risk putting a hothead on the streets."

"So you lost your chance at becoming a policeman."

"Yes." *And carrying out my father's dream.* Even if his father hadn't said it outright, Seth's washout had been a huge disappointment to Mike Donovan. "It was only a few months behind bars. But it gave me a lot of time to think and get squared away with God. I came out a better man."

"And started working at Donovan's Uniforms."

"After two years in the Army." It had been during a deployment that Seth had his first real contact with chaplains working in crisis situations. They were the definition of unsung heroes.

"Ah . . ." Taylor was looking at him as if they'd just met. It was true; there were a lot of things they hadn't learned about each other. "Then you became a volunteer chaplain and got married."

"Started college, then married first. Camille encouraged me to become a chaplain. And that helped . . . when I lost her."

Sudden tears shimmered in Taylor's eyes. "I'm so sorry, Seth. About all of that."

He gently squeezed her hand. "We've both had some tough times. But I have to believe they're taking us somewhere good." Seth glanced down at Taylor's Bible, lying atop that perfect, glass-encased beach. "That's the promise: hope and a future. Right?"

"Right." Her voice was small, hesitant. Her warm fingers moved beneath his but stayed where they were.

"And it's exactly what we're doing out there," Seth continued, deciding it had to be said, "when we put on those volunteer uniforms and show up for survivors. Whether it's a drowning, a death notification, a homicide . . . or a plane crash. We're offering hope."

"You're good at it," Taylor said. Her closeness, coupled with the feel of her hand in his, affected Seth more than it should. "People feel comfortable with you. They seek you out."

He had to stop himself from tracing his fingers along Taylor's cheek. This warm, lovely woman in a colorless room. Beauty against a blank canvas. He'd never noticed it before, but her green eyes were flecked with copper, the same color as her hair. After all these years, it was like he was seeing her for the first time, and he wanted—

"I think that's why Greg made that appointment," Taylor said softly.

There, she'd said it out loud. Had to. She'd invited Seth here because he'd seemed distressed by the events of the day. And now, after what he'd revealed, Taylor could understand that. The murder-suicide scene had been far too much a reminder of his past. She felt awful about what he'd endured and admired him even more for how he'd grown as a result. She hadn't planned to broach the subject of Greg, but . . . "I think he felt comfortable with you," she explained.

Seth lifted his hand from hers, his expression hinting he wasn't good with this turn in conversation. "I hope I do make folks feel that way. I try to."

Taylor wasn't going to settle for a generic answer. "I meant

Greg, specifically. That appointment he made to meet with you on the day he died."

"The appointment he didn't keep. I told you that, Taylor."

"And I told you that it wasn't like Greg to seek out advice and share things that might have been troubling him." Taylor read the immediate pinch of Seth's brows. "I'm not going to ask you to reveal any confidences," she assured him. "I've been thinking about it, though. Why he'd make that appointment and not say anything to me." *Gone quiet for weeks . . . distant.* "There was talk that the reason he was passed over for captain had something to do with those off-duty poker games, the illegal gambling. That some of his shift mates may have been involved.

"He didn't give me details," she continued, "but I know Greg was upset. He thought he didn't make captain because he refused to point a finger, offer information he didn't have. It makes sense that he'd want to talk about it. You'd just become the liaison to law enforcement and fire. I've been thinking about the timing." *All day and night for weeks, since the moment I found that planner.*

Seth was quiet for a moment, then nodded. "I suspect Greg felt stressed; there was a lot of that throughout the department. The volunteers right on up to top brass. I facilitated some meetings, but . . ."

"You can't say anything because of confidentiality. I get that, Seth. I understand." She blinked against a rush of tears. "Even if Greg didn't keep that appointment, I'm still grateful. It means a lot to know that he felt safe coming to you." She struggled to control the quaver in her voice. "I think I'm done with this now. Really done. No more looking back or making myself crazy trying to understand why Greg was on that road, way out—"

"I don't know that. I don't know why."

"You told me that three years ago. Everyone did." Taylor brushed at a tear. "I think I stalked half of Sacramento, badgering people with that question. But I'm not going to do it anymore. I'm done. I'm moving on with my life." She reached out, grasped his hand. "Thank you, Seth."

———

"Me?" Seth asked, very aware of Taylor's touch. "Why?"

"You've stood by me from the beginning. After I lost Greg, then through my volunteer training and my first crisis activations—and those awful days with the freeway sniper." A residue of tears only made her eyes more beautiful. "And you were supportive when I decided to leave Sacramento and transfer to San Diego Hope."

One of the stupidest things I've ever done.

"Thank you," Taylor repeated, surprising Seth with an unexpected hug. She twined her arms around him, resting her head against his shoulder. Her breath warmed his neck. "I don't know how I could have gotten through all of this without you."

"I . . . You're welcome," Seth managed, despite the fact that his heart had crawled up his throat. He breathed in Taylor's scent: clean and sweet—vanilla maybe, and a trace of the coffee beans she'd ground for him. Suddenly, like a kid at his first middle school dance, he didn't know what to do with his arms, didn't know where to put them that didn't risk giving in to an overwhelming urge to bury his hands in that kitten-soft tousle of red hair, look into her eyes, capture her sweet face between his palms, and—

"This plan for moving on with your life," he heard himself say. "Does it involve that doctor?"

Taylor slid her arms down, drew away. "Rob?"

"Forget it. I shouldn't have asked. None of my business."

"No. It's okay." She swept a length of hair behind her ear. "I asked you about your CSI girlfriend. So—"

Taylor laughed as Hooper rose from the floor and propped his head on Seth's knee again.

So . . . ? Seth realized he was holding his breath.

"I guess so. Maybe." Taylor's expression looked wistful, little-girl vulnerable. "I'm taking things slowly."

"And I . . . should take myself out of here." He scratched the old dog's ear, then got to his feet. "Let you and Hoops get some sleep."

"That's probably a good idea."

Taylor thanked him again, then offered a thawed box of Thin Mints and another hug. Seth took the cookies, dodged the embrace—it was too risky. He'd begun to rethink his motive for coming to San Diego, beyond the crisis team training. It wasn't only to discover Taylor's reasons for backing away from her crisis work. That was a good excuse, absolutely. But something else was happening here.

———

Taylor turned slowly in front of her bedroom's full-length mirror. Overhead lighting caught the metallic threads in the long, sleeveless gown, making it shimmer. Against the backdrop of the room's Dune White walls, it looked new-penny bright. But it wasn't new. And it hung on her now, at least a full size too big.

"I have a gown." Her response to Rob's invitation.

Taylor pressed her fingers against the waist of the dress, imagining Greg's palm there. Guiding her across the dance floor at the Firefighters' Ball. Clowning, pretending they were contestants on *Dancing with the Stars*. Then dropping his hand low to give her backside a covert pat . . . Would his fingerprints be there still? Did fingerprints remain on fabric?

Taylor's throat tightened as a bigger question intruded. *Would he care if I danced again?*

It had been strangely difficult to buy new clothes since Greg's death. Anything beyond scrubs, running shorts, and a pair of new jeans. Everything else, anything feminine, trendy, silly-fun, or marginally slinky, felt like a huge betrayal. Because Greg wouldn't see her in it. It wouldn't be for her husband. Feeling attractive seemed wrong. But now . . . Taylor grabbed at the seams of the gown and stretched it taut enough to give a modest boost to her newly thin figure. Now it was time to give herself permission to shop again.

"I'm moving on with my life."

She was surprised by a flush at the memory of how it had felt to hug Seth. Warm . . . stirring. A reaction worthy of a teenager. These three years, hugging her dog and saying her nightly, "Good night, Hooper"—complete with a kiss on his head—had provided her only tender, loving interlude. Clearly Taylor needed to give herself permission for a bit more than shopping. Seth had asked about Rob, and she'd said maybe. It had been an honest answer; she really wasn't sure how she felt.

Taylor glanced down at her fitness bracelet, a plastic mismatch to her glamorous if baggy evening gown. She tapped it and saw the tiny blinking lights that tracked her daily fitness effort. There should be a special light for truly big steps. Like dating again. *Can I actually do this?*

She looked across the room to where Hooper slept on the bed she'd moved from the living room. Next to him was a white wicker wastebasket. After Seth left, she'd put Greg's day planner into a plastic Target sack, then pulled it back out long enough to shred the page with the notation of his appointment. It was gone. All of it. Her questions and her doubts. She had it under control at last. And now—

Her cell phone rang where it lay on the fluffy white comforter. She grabbed fistfuls of her shimmery gown and hurried to grab it. Her stomach tensed: Rob, responding to her text.

"What's up?" he asked.

"I told you I'd give you an answer about the awards gala."

"You did. I'm holding my breath. Picture me going dangerously cyanotic."

"We can't have that." She smiled despite the fact that she'd begun to tremble. "I'm sorry it took me so long but—"

Taylor whirled around at an ominous gargling noise across the room.

"Oh no . . . Hooper!"

She dropped the phone and rushed to her convulsing dog.

17

KASIE GLANCED UP from the nurses' station computer, her forehead creasing with concern. "Hooper's never had a seizure before?"

"No. It's related to his lymphoma." Taylor's heart lugged. The young vet, "Dr. Wendy" to her clients, had handled the emergency with both skill and kindness.

I'm afraid the cancer has reached this sweet boy's brain, Taylor.

"It must have been hard to deal with that all by yourself. At the house, when it happened."

It had been. Fortunately the drive to the vet's office—they offered an after-hours emergency clinic—was less than a mile. But even with Hooper's weight loss, it had been a struggle to get him into the car. She'd kicked off her heels but couldn't take the time to change her clothes. She'd finally pulled Hooper onto her comforter and dragged it out to the garage. "He didn't stop having tremors until they gave him the IV Valium."

"And now?" Kasie asked, lowering her voice as Sloane walked up to another computer. "Can they stop it from happening again? Control the seizures?"

"They kept Hooper overnight. He's had a loading dose of phenobarbital and it looks like I'll continue that with pills."

Rob had been blunt in his opinion when he phoned her at the vet hospital: *"You need to take care of this now, Taylor. Do the right thing and put him down. It's time."*

She'd made an excuse and disconnected, not trusting that she wouldn't burst into tears. Or scream at him. She was glad he'd gone to San Francisco for a surgical consult today.

Taylor sighed. "I'm picking him up on my way home. He'll still be pretty groggy. One of the vet techs lives a few blocks from us. She'll be going off shift then and offered to help me get him into the house."

"It sounds like you found a great veterinary group."

"Absolutely."

It was a blessing. And had been one of the first items on her Survival List. She hadn't known back then that it meant Hooper's survival too. Taylor shook her head, remembering how the veterinary staff teased her about overdressing for an office visit. First client ever to show up in formal wear.

The gala. She'd never given Rob her answer. . . .

Kasie excused herself as one of the other techs called to her for help.

Taylor checked the assignment board. She still had labs pending on—

"Ambulance coming." Sloane stepped up beside Taylor, her

eyes noticeably bloodshot, apparently the norm these days. She'd been late again too. Only ten minutes, but people were complaining.

"Fifty-eight-year-old female," she continued. "Report said difficulty breathing, but her lungs are clear and there's no history of pulmonary disease. Monitor looks good. Breathing fast and observably anxious, according to the medics. I'm betting on a panic attack." Sloane's gaze swept Taylor's face. "You don't look so good either. Your dog has seizures?"

Taylor tensed. The last thing she needed was to be double-teamed by Sloane and Rob on the subject of euthanasia.

"Ambulance!" someone announced in the distance.

"On my way," Taylor signaled.

Grateful to get away from Sloane, she directed the medics as they wheeled their stretcher in. The head of it was raised, a portable monitor in place. A firefighter walked alongside, obviously trying to reassure their patient. A blondish woman, well dressed and sitting bolt upright, with eyes wide and hands pressed to her chest.

It was Ava Sandison.

———

"It's important," Seth told the small group of crisis team trainers, "that volunteers understand the concepts of critical stress management. To guide them in dealing with survivors of tragedy, but also to recognize the symptoms of stress, acute and cumulative, in themselves and in their teammates."

"It's the reason we have debriefings after our callouts," one of the attendees, a veteran responder, offered. He scraped his fingers over his close-cropped gray beard. "And a reason we lose team members. Stress takes its toll. It's not easy out there."

"Exactly," Seth agreed, reminded of the time he'd accompanied Taylor to the door of a fellow chaplain in Sacramento. They'd had to inform her that her son had been shot in the line of duty. A chaplain delivering horrifying news to a fellow chaplain. Thank God it didn't happen too often. "But we aren't promised 'easy' when we volunteer for this gig. We step up because we feel a calling. In the process we learn how to offer a lifeline to others—and to grab hold ourselves. Then take care of each other too."

An image of Taylor's face rose, her tears when he'd shared the story of what had led him to his faith. He still hadn't sorted out these new feelings he was having for her. . . .

"Okay," Seth said, forcing himself to concentrate on the task at hand, "who can give me a quick five symptoms of acute traumatic stress?" He pointed to a fortysomething woman with wavy, graying hair who wore the San Diego volunteers' uniform.

"Upsetting memories of the traumatic event," she began, counting on her fingers. "Flashbacks—feeling like the event is happening again." She touched a third finger. "Nightmares. Feelings of intense distress when reminded of the incident."

Seth ignored the sudden unprovoked aching in his scarred knee; he had long ago accepted it for what it was. "That's four," he told the crisis team trainer. "Give me one more."

"Intense physical reactions to reminders of the trauma," she offered. "Nausea, tense muscles, sweating . . . pounding heart. And rapid breathing."

———

"I can move my fingers now," Ava told Taylor. She flexed them to prove it. "And my lips . . ." Her dry tongue snagged across her lower lip. "They don't feel so numb anymore." She fumbled a reassuring smile. "My heart is still trying to pop the buttons off my cardigan. Thank goodness Chico's is good about returns." Then Ava's eyes filled with sudden tears. "Thank you for being here. Now, and on that beach too."

"I'm glad I was . . . *am*," Taylor told her. Though she wasn't entirely sure about it. The most important thing in her life right now was to move past widowhood, and this dear lady seemed determined to drape her in black again. She thought of Ruthie Marks with her wedding-ring necklace and jelly donut. "I'm glad you're feeling better now. We're still going to run those tests, but the doctor thinks your symptoms came from hyperventilation."

"Overbreathing. Too fast." Ava made an observable effort to exhale slowly.

"Yes. Too much oxygen, not enough carbon dioxide. It causes that tingling you experienced and the cramps in your hands and feet. It's usually a response to stress and anxiety."

"The symptoms will go away completely?" Ava glanced down at her trembling fingers. "If I keep my breathing under control?"

If only it were that simple: a Breathe Right strip for life-altering loss. "How has your appetite been?"

"The neighbors have been bringing food."

Which you aren't eating . . .

"Trouble sleeping?"

Ava closed her eyes. "I keep dreaming I'm in that plane. I feel the yoke in my hands. I hear Sandy's breathing."

Taylor's throat tightened. How many times had she lain awake imagining that car slamming into Greg? How long had it taken to remember his face without seeing it battered, gray, and lifeless on that UCD trauma gurney? Ava needed sleep.

"We had a fight," the woman whispered, grasping Taylor's hand. Her eyes were filled with pain. "That day, right before we got in the plane. It wasn't about anything important. It was trivial, stupid. But I was so angry with him. Completely unforgiving." Ava's fingers tightened on Taylor's. "Sandy was upset. Because of me. This, all of it, was *my fault*."

"Ava . . ." Taylor slid her arm around the woman's shoulders, wanting to comfort her—and to run away too. *I can't do this*.

"I was praying out loud as the plane went down. I kept telling Sandy I was sorry. I kept saying, 'I love you. I love you. . . . I'm sorry. . . .'" She met Taylor's gaze, her expression desperate. "Do you think he heard me?"

"Yes." Taylor blinked against tears. "I'm sure of it."

"There. That's better, isn't it, big guy?" Taylor sat down on the living room floor next to Hooper's old bed. A patch of his once-golden hair, dry and dull now, had fallen onto the white area rug. Autumn leaves giving way to snow. "Your pillow bed, a Happy Meal . . . and home." He'd eaten only a small bite of his favorite treat. And he looked far too still on that bed.

Dr. Wendy had given Taylor the phenobarbital pills and instructions, saying the best medicine now was love and kindness. She'd said, too, that she'd be available if and when Taylor wanted to discuss other options. The best guess was that they were talking weeks, not months.

Taylor lifted the old photo pulled from a box she'd tucked away months ago: Hooper, a fat and happy puppy, on the couch—wrapped in Greg's arms. Who could have known then that the dog would outlive the man?

Only God.

Taylor thought of her encounter with the pilot's widow. *"I was praying out loud as the plane went down. I kept telling Sandy I was sorry. . . ."*

Ava thought her husband's death was her fault. She thought she might have been able to prevent it.

Taylor closed her eyes.

Greg had phoned her the night of his accident. She let the call go to voice mail because she'd been walking Hooper and didn't want to haul the phone out of her pocket, juggle things in the dark. Hooper had been rambunctious and eager to get out. And Taylor needed some fresh air to clear her head. Truthfully, she'd been relieved when Greg got the call to go help a friend—a request Taylor had never been able to track down. But that night it had felt like a reprieve; things had been strained between them that day. In truth, for months. She'd felt the space would be good for both of them.

He called and she didn't answer.

Taylor had replayed the phone message countless times afterward. So many times she had it memorized. It still hurt to remember, still confused her. It had been so unlike Greg.

"I guess you aren't there . . . or you don't want to talk to me. I don't blame you." He'd sighed. *"I don't like the way things have felt between us, Taylor. I want it to be different. I had this sort of crazy idea. Remember how we always said we'd go to Europe someday? Take a few weeks off, backpack around, see Paris? I think we should do that. Not someday. Now. I think we should go. I just . . ."* There had been pain in his voice. *"I love you, Taylor. I need you to know that. And . . . I'm coming home now. We'll talk then."*

Of course, that didn't happen. According to eyewitnesses,

the accident occurred barely ten minutes later. She'd never know if talking to him then, taking that call, could have changed anything. Or everything.

Taylor stretched out on the rug, slipped an arm around her dog's thin body, and rested her face against his side the way she'd done every night for years. The old retriever's heart thudded beneath her ear, his rib cage rising and falling in a contented sigh.

"Good night, Hooper," she breathed, finding comfort in the familiar ritual. "I love you," she added, her voice choking. "I hope you know that."

18

"I'M . . . SURPRISED," Taylor told Rob, wishing he had said he was in her driveway when he called. Now there was no time to make herself look like she hadn't slept on the floor next to a dog bed. He'd never been to her place before, and she wasn't sure she liked him coming uninvited. "Don't you have to be in surgery this morning?"

"My blepharoplasty canceled because of the stomach flu, and the first of my three liposuctions doesn't start until ten o'clock." His smile crinkled the edges of the blue eyes she'd heard at least half a dozen nurses sigh over. "Are you going to invite me in?" He raised a paper sack. "I'm bearing breakfast."

"I guess," she said, offering a small smile. "But if you mentioned liposuction and brought donuts, that would be wrong on *so* many levels."

"You know me better than that."

She did. And in a few minutes they'd topped the living room coffee table with a modest plate of fresh fruit, buckwheat muffins, and a single tofu-scramble burrito to share. Rob was vegan and these choices reflected that. For some reason it made Taylor think of Seth. She had no doubt he'd bring what he liked to call, in a ridiculous British accent, a "rasher" of bacon and then feed half of it to Hooper. Rob had simply made a polite, disinterested acknowledgment of the sleeping dog. Taylor was relieved. She wasn't up to a mix of tofu and talk of euthanasia. She had told Seth about the seizures when he'd stopped by the ER yesterday. As she had expected, he'd been concerned and asked for details.

"It's a great space," Rob said, taking a second look around the living room. "In fact, it's a lot like mine. Clean, uncluttered, minimalist." His spreading smile unleashed a single dimple, a boyish departure from his sophisticated good looks. "That was a direct quote from my decorator. I can't take credit for the majority of it. Except the stainless-steel and chrome accents. She hinted it had everything to do with my proclivity for surgical instruments. But this . . ." He glanced down at the glass coffee table with its brushed sand and single white shell. "It's what I'd expect of you, Taylor. I'm impressed once more."

Hooper made a small yelping noise in his sleep, legs paddling. Taylor tensed, then smiled. "Chasing dream rabbits."

"Dogs can be a big comfort." Rob glanced toward Hooper, then returned his gaze to Taylor as she topped his cup from the insulated carafe. "I understand how hard the loss would be. On top of what you've already endured." There was a gentleness in his expression she'd never seen before. He blotted his fingers on his napkin and rested his hand over hers. "I don't think I've expressed it well enough. But I want you to know if there's anything I can do to help, make things easier for you, I will. I'm here."

"I appreciate that, Rob. It is hard. I'm dealing with it the best I can."

"I'm sure you are. I can relate, actually." Rob flinched slightly, a second expression Taylor had never witnessed. It pointed out that she knew very little about him beyond the hospital, a few coffee dates, and exercise-related meetups. "I had a spectacular saltwater aquarium built into the wall of my last house," he explained. "Over twelve hundred gallons. A unique, carefully balanced marine community. It couldn't have been a more perfect extension of that ocean view. I conferred with experts at the Monterey Bay Aquarium before acquiring some of the fish. Each one required specific care. I hired people to do that. Supervised them myself." Rob sighed. "Clarion angelfish, Australian flathead perch, and a male Neptune grouper worth more than six thousand dollars. He was a beautiful example of the species . . . a joy to own."

Taylor glanced at Hooper, grateful for fur not fins. There was no way she could get what Rob was saying. You couldn't snuggle up to a saltwater fish all night.

"My ex-wife went for the jugular in the divorce," Rob continued, his tone growing edgy. "She wouldn't let me have that tank. Refused to even consider it. Arianna had no heart for fish. No concept of what it takes to keep a marine ecosphere in perfect balance, under careful control. Everything *died*. Every fish. Every crustacean. All the coral. Even the snails. And my grouper, of course—it was pure cruelty."

Cruelty? Taylor thought of Hooper, his body stiffening in the throes of that never-ending seizure, lips drawn back over his teeth and terror in his eyes. Rob was making a fish comparison?

"So," she said, eager to change the subject, "did you get in late from San Francisco?"

"Around eleven." Rob's expression was still tense. He took a slow, measured breath that he'd probably learned from his oft-mentioned yoga instructor. It occurred to Taylor that this man had a fleet of people at his disposal. "I stopped by Deep Blue for one of their beet salads. The kitchen was closing, but—" his smile returned—"one of the kids I treated pro bono belongs to the chef's church. Nice family. Great salad."

"Deep Blue Grill?"

"Right. You know it?"

"Only that Kasie works there sometimes. To help out," Taylor explained. "Her brother-in-law owns it."

"Small world. I didn't see her, but when I was leaving, I saw one of your other friends."

Taylor raised her brows.

"Sloane Wilder."

"I'm not sure I'd call her a friend, exactly," Taylor admitted. "You talked with her?"

"No. I just caught a glimpse. She was in the bar. Therapy after surviving the trenches of ER, I suspect. Looked like she was having a good time—I hope she wasn't driving."

Taylor frowned. The reason for the late arrivals to work?

"The gala," Rob said, capturing Taylor's gaze. "What have you decided?"

"What did you mean by that?" Sloane asked the girl's step-father, unable to soften the barb in her tone. He should feel lucky she hadn't hurled something at his head. "Were you say-ing she *deserved* to be assaulted?"

The man, a pest company employee according to the dead-rat logo on his shirt, glanced toward the exam room where the fifteen-year-old, battered and very likely drugged, was being interviewed by a female officer from San Diego PD. He met Sloane's gaze, narrowed his eyes. "I don't believe I was saying anything to *you*. Now if you'll excuse me—"

"There *is* no excuse for people like you." Sloane's words hissed through her teeth; there was no way to tamp this down. She couldn't care less that several staff members and patients were listening. Or that Seth Donovan passed by. This guy shouldn't be able to get away with—"You called her a tramp. You said any girl who dresses like that is asking for it. I heard you say it to the triage nurse."

"Look, lady, this is none of your business."

"And that's what you count on, right?" The anger swirled, making Sloane tequila-shot dizzy. "That people won't ask questions. And little girls won't tell. You count on it that her mother is too scared or too drunk to defend her child."

"What the—?" The man's face contorted. "You're accusing me of something?"

"Sloane, hey," Kasie said gently, stepping close. "Let's—"

"Butt out, Beckett!"

"Sloane, that's enough," the ER doctor ordered, jogging forward. "You're out of line. Take a break—*now*."

Sloane shot the stepfather one last look, then shoved her

hands in the pockets of her scrub jacket and whirled away. She hated that tears threatened. "This whole lousy world is out of line."

———

"I heard the coffee's fresh in here."

"And I was told I could find a few minutes of peace." Sloane glanced around the dimly lit hospital chapel, then met Seth's gaze. Her blue eyes were glacier cold. She held up her coffee cup. "It's disgusting. Looks like we both got lied to. Figures."

Seth was struck again by the nurse's looks. Classic. Like a young Elizabeth Taylor, his father would have insisted. Beautiful, guarded—and very wounded, from what Seth had seen in her caustic exchange with the assault victim's stepfather. He gestured toward the coffeemaker. "Think I'll get some anyway."

"I hoped you wouldn't."

"I guessed that."

Seth moved slowly toward the coffee, the way he would if she were an injured animal, expecting her to bolt. She'd pulled out her phone, then set it down and closed her eyes. He doubted she was praying. This was as good an invitation as he was going to get. He glanced at the chapel's simple stained-glass window as he snagged some coffee: the Good Shepherd carrying the lost lamb. Then he took a seat a few chairs down from Sloane. Heard her irritated sigh.

"You're right," he told her after risking the coffee. "Tastes like burnt rubber."

The blue eyes regarded him for a moment. "You're wasting your time. The only reason I haven't walked out on you yet is that the clinical coordinator's waiting for me. Along with the department director, no doubt."

Seth sipped his coffee.

"You're not fooling me." Sloane shook her head.

"About what?"

"Anything. I'm not stupid enough to think you came here for coffee. Or that you aren't itching to give me some of your great, life-changing advice." She jabbed her finger toward the altar. "Maybe sling me around your neck like I'm a stray animal who got separated from the flock. Or wound up in a stinking shelter cage." There was the smallest tremble in her chin. "I know the agenda . . . *Chaplain*."

"You're right," he told her, glancing down at his cup. *Help me, Lord. . . .* "I didn't come for the coffee. But I have no intention of slinging anyone around my neck." He offered a rueful smile. "Too old, bad knee. And I don't give advice unless I'm asked." Seth paused. "But I'm a good listener."

"And you think I'd talk?"

"I think you were really angry back there. And you got hushed up pretty fast. Probably had a lot more to say." He glanced around the chapel. "You said you came here looking for peace. Maybe having someone really listen would help."

"Help?" Sloane stood up so fast that she knocked her coffee cup to the floor; her jaw clenched, face reddening. "*You?* You'd be the last person on earth I'd turn to for help." She pressed her hands to her forehead, uttered a sound that was half groan, half laugh—and pure pain. "I can't believe you're pulling this, Donovan."

What?

"Hold on." Seth stood, at a complete loss. "I don't know what you mean. Tell me—"

"I'll tell you this: Stay away. Stay out of my life. I'm not going to let you screw it up again."

19

"THE TAG CALLED the color 'indigo,'" Taylor told her cousin over the phone. "A really dark, dark blue." She'd had to carry the dress to a Macy's store window for enough light to be sure it wasn't black. She'd spent too many painful hours in black. "It's knit, a wrap style, sort of close-fitting, but not too—hits me at the knee. I bought new shoes, too."

With sparkles—Taylor had to fight a lingering sense of betrayal over the shoe sparkles. Greg had always teased that her love of glitter came from lost gypsy blood. But this wasn't about Greg anymore. It couldn't be. "It's nice . . . It feels good."

Aimee's sigh was like a hug. "It sounds beautiful. *You* are beautiful, Taylor. And brave. This gala with Dr. Halston is your first real date. A huge step."

"Yes."

She wasn't going to confess that changing her Facebook status from married to single—it sounded so ridiculously shallow and superficial a task—had felt far more profound. She'd done it barely an hour ago, hovering her cursor over the word for an agonizing few minutes before she finally clicked the change. She'd had to "combat breathe," a skill she'd learned in crisis training, to ease her anxiety: close eyes, inhale through the nose while counting slowly to seven, breathe out through the mouth for another count of seven . . . It was a technique used by soldiers to calm themselves when facing hostile fire. But comparing a Facebook status change to combat? Insane, especially since Taylor's account had strong privacy options and fewer than three hundred "friends," most of them family, church members, and coworkers. It wasn't like she was taking out a tacky personal ad. Still, "single" meant "available" in social terms. Taylor's stomach nose-dived. *Dear Lord, are you with me here?*

"I love that your first date is with a man who is being honored for his charitable work. It says so much. It fits with who you are."

"I guess." Taylor tried to banish the idea of Rob battling with his ex-wife over a six-thousand-dollar fish. She preferred to think of what he'd said about her situation with Hooper. *"I want you to know if there's anything I can do to help, make things easier for you, I will."* That unexpected display of kindness had prompted her to agree to the date.

"Did you tell your mom?"

"Yes. She and Dad called just as I got home from church." Taylor smiled. "I heard the cruise staff calling bingo in the background. Mom seemed happy about the gala."

Relieved, probably. And a little worried, too, knowing her parents. In truth, Taylor was glad their vacation spanned the anniversary of Greg's death. Her mother's carefully casual, "just saying hi" call on March 26 had become something Taylor dreaded. Especially this year, when she was determined to complete her Survival List. According to her parents' travel itinerary, they would be far from a port that day and the chance of placing a call would be slim. "They'll be home on the twenty-ninth," she added.

"Do they know about Hooper?"

"I didn't want to worry them. They love him too." Taylor glanced at the old dog, sitting up, tongue lolling, and content to watch her. "Besides, he's feeling so much better after the IV fluids. Not as groggy now either, and I'm . . ." She had started to say she was hopeful. *Please, God, don't take him. Not yet.* "I'm glad these were my regular days off."

"You're back tomorrow?"

"Yes, though I could have worked an extra shift today. The staffing office called." Taylor frowned. "One of the nurses was suspended."

Sloane Wilder.

———

"I was looking for a kitten. . . ."

The shelter volunteer with the *Star Wars* hair chuckled. "Kittens we got. Lots and lots. Kitten smorgasbord. Take a look around and—"

"The black kitten someone tried to drown," Sloane interrupted. "In the Save Mart bag."

"Oh." The young woman grimaced. "I remember you now. You look different."

Jeans, hoodie, sunglasses . . . and an ugly hangover. "Is he still here?"

"Last cage on your right. No more cough. The rest of that litter was adopted," the volunteer said, following Sloane past the double-decker rows of cages. There were a number of plaintive mews, the occasional hiss, and a few paws reaching through the cage bars. "Black kittens have like a 50 percent less chance of being adopted."

Sloane stopped in the aisle. "Why?"

"No one knows for sure. Maybe because black doesn't photograph well on a rescue poster. Or stripes are *so* Cheshire cat or . . . stupid superstition?" Her lips quirked. "I always counter the last one with a quote from that ancient comedian, Groucho Marx: 'A black cat crossing your path signifies it's going somewhere.'"

Sloane rolled her eyes. "How does that work for you?"

"We have three black ones—no takers. Yet."

The kitten wobbled to the bars, eyes bright and tiny nose smudged with food. Sloane's heart squeezed. *Hey, Marty.* She'd started to think of him that way, a name inspired by the Save Mart bag.

"You're going to take him?" the volunteer asked.

"I can't. My situation is still the same." That was a lie—except for the hangover. Otherwise Sloane's situation was much worse than when she'd been here last. She'd been suspended for two days. From what she saw on their faces when she left, the ER staff was probably still singing "Ding-Dong! The Witch Is Dead." She stopped herself from poking a finger through the cage bars. Then spoke the truth this time: "I'll probably be moving away."

"Cats travel. I could find you a freebie crate." Princess Leia lowered her voice to a whisper. "And a big sack of kitten chow. If you promise not to tell."

Saving the empire—and black kittens, one at a time. Sloane could like this gutsy college student.

"I'm not really that good with animals," she hedged.

"You had me fooled."

"Well . . . I'll ask around." She didn't risk another look at Marty. "Maybe one of my friends can take him." *The Munchkins or Glinda the Good Widow.*

"I hope so." The volunteer glanced at the card on the cage. "He's only here until the twenty-sixth."

"Your first day," Seth began. "I can't tell you how good it feels to be standing where I am, looking out at all of you." His gaze swept the small group assembled in the meeting room. Fourteen volunteers, newly recruited and eager to start the necessary training to become part of California Crisis Care. "And I've got to think it's a lot better than sitting out there looking up here, at me. Don't panic—this limp and the new gray hairs aren't from my crisis work."

Seth used the few seconds of laughter to move closer to the recruits; he'd never been a fan of stages and podiums, preferring to share what he knew in a casual, friendly way, even when he was talking about police Tasers at Donovan's Uniforms. He thought, once again, that there was no comparison. This was where his heart lived. With these teams, this work. It was a reminder, too, that he had a tough decision to make; Seth couldn't avoid it much longer. He nodded at one of the trainers. They'd been doing a great job today. "That's better. I never liked the nosebleed seats."

Then he told the group, "I'd like to read something to you. A short note from a survivor to a chaplain on our Sacramento team. A rookie, as a matter of fact. Not that many months ahead of where you are right now." Seth glanced at the note, remembering the incident. And the survivor. "This note was written by the daughter of a search-and-rescue volunteer. Her father gave countless hours to those heroic efforts. Saved lives, trained new volunteers. And then he was killed in a freak accident on a hunting trip."

There were empathetic murmurs.

Seth raised the paper and read the note of gratitude sent to the crisis chaplain:

"She saw me unravel and didn't judge, only cared.
I'm still trying to understand what happened with my
father. But there is HOPE and a profound feeling that
I am not alone in this. How do you get through a life-
altering crisis? With an angel by your side."

Seth set the paper down. "I'd guess that none of us finds it easy to imagine ourselves as divine—I'm not sure they make halos in my size." He smiled. "But I want to assure you that we are absolutely offering hope to these survivors. We step in when their world is spinning out of control, when they feel most alone and their lives have been unimaginably altered. Tragedy and trauma leave an indelible mark. And . . ." Seth paused briefly. "We must never forget that when we make that connection with a survivor, *we* forever become part of the event too. Part of the pain and, God willing, a first step in the healing as well."

He saw nods in the crowd.

Seth spoke for only a few minutes more; he'd said what he'd come to say by reading that letter. He'd told them the truth. So many times he'd been recognized, even years later, by someone he'd helped. Almost without exception there would be a mix of emotions on the survivor's face. A reflection of the pain along with a look of relief that here was someone who understood what they were living with. Even if no words were spoken, it was there. Though sometimes a survivor wouldn't move on to healing and instead would wrap himself in the trauma and hold bitter feelings toward all involved.

Seth frowned, shifting in the chair he'd taken at the back of the room as the other trainers continued. He was still troubled by that conversation with Sloane Wilder. It wasn't surprising that she'd be abrasive and resist his offer of help. He'd seen enough to suspect it was her usual way of dealing with things. A reprimand—suspension, from what he'd heard today— wouldn't improve her disposition. But her parting shots in the chapel had sounded personal.

How had she put it exactly? *"Stay out of my life. I'm not going to let you screw it up again."*

Personal as the scar on his knee. But . . . *why?* The fact that she'd looked vaguely familiar when he saw her at San Diego Hope had been explained by Taylor. Sloane had been a flight nurse. She'd worked some shifts at Sacramento Hope. Seth had experience with a number of medical and rescue personnel, at the uniform store and at trauma scenes as a chaplain. But nothing stood out, no specific memory of working with her—or ticking her off. He certainly had never dated her. So . . .

Was she a trauma survivor? Had he had an impact on her life in that way? It was rare he didn't recall something like that, and the nurse's face, glaring or not, was definitely memorable. But Seth was drawing a total blank when it came to Sloane Wilder. He shook his head. Asking her directly would be like throwing gasoline on a fire.

Besides, it was enough of a challenge trying to keep his mind off Taylor. He'd called her this morning before attending services with Walt and his wife. He'd wanted to ask about her dog, but her phone had gone to voice mail. When she called back, she said Hooper was doing much better and that she'd gone out shopping for a dress. And shoes. Seth didn't ask, but it was a fairly good guess she wasn't buying new clothes to impress her dog.

20

"Um . . ." Kasie tried not to squirm; she'd never had a one-on-one conversation with Sloane Wilder. She was grateful for that. As a tech, Kasie was far down the pecking order from this registered nurse. And frankly, the hard-edged woman made her nervous. She'd cornered Kasie at the nurses' station.

"I love kittens," Kasie began. "I'd have one in a heartbeat, except my fiancé is super allergic. He'd take one step into my apartment and start wheezing."

"You're engaged?"

"Yes."

Sloane stared.

Kasie's pulse kicked up a notch. "Like I said, he's aller—"

"First of all," Sloane interrupted, "Benadryl is over-the-counter. He probably has an inhaler. Several inhalers. And secondly . . ." Her lips twitched. "You don't live together?"

"I . . ." Kasie lifted her chin, battling a telltale flush. "That's really not an appropriate question."

"Oh, right." Sloane raised her hands and feigned a shudder. "Don't want to get in trouble again."

If they'd polled the staff, Kasie was certain a large majority would rather see Sloane fired. Kasie wasn't sure where she stood on that. Sloane had probably viewed the unprofessional rant as an attempt to defend that assault victim. It wasn't the first time Kasie had witnessed something beneath the nurse's gruff exterior that hinted at—

"This kitten was shoved into a grocery sack and dumped off a pier. Like so much garbage."

Kasie winced. "That's awful. I really wish I could help but . . ."

"But we don't want anyone to sneeze." Sloane narrowed her eyes. "No problem. I totally get that."

She strode away before Kasie could say anything else, though she didn't know what else she could add. Sneezes weren't the half of it; adopting a kitten would probably be the final blow to her relationship with Daniel.

She frowned, remembering his angry parting words in their phone conversation last night. *"You're stretching yourself too thin. School, work, filling in at the Grill, and running out—anywhere, anytime—to volunteer for that crisis thing. You're obsessed with it. It matters more than anything now. More than us—that's obvious. You've got plenty of time for total strangers. But nothing for me. What do I get? What's in this for me?"*

Kasie twisted her engagement ring. It wasn't the first time they'd had this discussion. She was sure it wouldn't be the last. They loved each other, but they were very different. Daniel was an IT guy. Computers, spreadsheets—order, systematic analysis, and solutions that didn't require a post-incident debriefing. How could Kasie expect him to understand this calling? She was still figuring it out herself. Yet she'd never had such a feeling of being exactly where she belonged.

She'd smooth things over with Daniel. Tonight.

Except she was on call. . . .

———

"Don't worry," Sloane told Taylor. "I'm not going to hit you up about the kitten. You've got your hands full with your dog's situation."

And you've been eavesdropping.

Sloane's smile was rueful. "I feel like I'm hawking one of those anticellulite scams. Everyone scatters like cockroaches when I get close."

Taylor was surprised by a twinge of sympathy. This woman didn't even realize that people scattered because she'd made no true attempt to befriend anybody. Taylor didn't want to imagine the loneliness in that. Even self-imposed.

Sloane's eyes captured Taylor's. "His kill date is the twenty-sixth."

Taylor's throat closed. There was no way Sloane could know the visceral impact of her words.

"Pass it around," Sloane added, glancing away as a patient called out for a bedpan.

"I . . . Okay," Taylor managed. "Maybe I'll ask Seth. I'm going to see him this evening. At a funeral."

It was impossible to tell if Sloane's grimace was a reaction to the suggestion of Seth as a kitten adopter or the mention of a funeral.

"Memorial service, really," Taylor explained, feeling once again how much she dreaded it. "For Ava Sandison's husband, the pilot from the kite festival incident."

"You're a glutton for punishment."

"I promised."

"Yes, well . . ." Something in Sloane's expression hinted at vulnerability. It was instantly eclipsed by a smirk. "There's always a way to weasel out of a promise."

Taylor watched Sloane walk away and then headed for the ER assignment board. Her patient with abdominal pain was still in ultrasound; the asthmatic had found relief after a second round of albuterol treatments; they were waiting for a psych consult on the woman in—

"Hey there." Rob appeared by Taylor's side, dressed in OR scrubs. She didn't care that the other ER staff were watching. She'd accepted his invitation to the awards gala. People would know they were dating. His smile made her skin warm. "I've got this itch for Thai food," he told her. "Plumeria in University Heights has an amazing yellow curry with mock duck."

"It does?"

Rob's smile spread. "It was an invitation, not a food review. Seven o'clock reservation?"

Her regret was real. "I'm sorry, but I can't. I'm going to a memorial service."

"Family?"

"A patient."

"Ah." Rob's lips compressed. "I've found it's better for

everyone concerned to set limits on that connection. They need to move on. And so do we."

Taylor couldn't argue with that, considering how determined she was to complete her Survival List. "I'm going to the service with Seth. We were both invited."

"I see." His expression said he'd rather not. "Well then, maybe I'll get takeout."

"I'm sorry."

"Not a problem. Hey, how's the dog?"

"Much better," Taylor said, knowing it was petty to be irritated that he hadn't called Hooper by name. "We walked down to see his little Heidi again last night."

Rob's slight brow raise said he hadn't a clue what she was talking about, didn't remember Hooper's schnauzer neighbor. He nodded. "Good—great news."

"It is." Catching a glimpse of a gurney coming their way, Taylor told him, "I should go. That's my patient coming back from ultrasound."

"And I'd better go say hello to my tummy tuck." He touched her arm. "We'll talk later, when you get back from the service."

"Sure." Taylor smiled.

"Hey . . ." Rob's eyes met hers. "Donovan's not using this as a way of influencing your decision about the crisis work, is he?"

"Not at all." She took a breath, made herself say it: "I'm finished with that, starting the first of the month."

"That's my girl." There was relief in his eyes . . . and satisfaction too?

Taylor watched him walk away, sensed the staff watching. And maybe even enjoyed it a little. She smiled, adjusted the stethoscope around her neck, and started off toward—

"Taylor?"

She turned and saw Kasie walking her way.

"I need to ask you a favor." The tech's expression showed uncharacteristic distress. "I know I said I'd take call for you tonight with the crisis team. But I'm having sort of an issue with Daniel. I need to take care of it. It's important. Can you take the call? I'm down for 1900 to 0700. But I could take over again after midnight if you want. I know you work tomorrow."

"I . . ." Taylor wanted, with every fiber of her being, to say she wouldn't—couldn't. But she looked at Kasie's face and thought of all the "issues" with Greg that would never be taken care of. "Sure," she heard herself say. "I can do the whole twelve hours. Don't worry."

"Thank you. You're the best." Kasie sighed with relief. "I owe you."

"You don't owe me anything," Taylor assured her. "But get things right with Daniel—it matters."

"I will."

She watched the tech walk away, thinking of her night ahead. A funeral that could be interrupted by more tragedy. No better reminder of the need to get life back under control.

21

"I'M . . . SO . . . GLAD YOU'RE BOTH . . ."

Ava Sandison forced out the words, her voice as wooden as the boardwalk at the kite festival. The widow's red-rimmed eyes scanned the small chapel, then returned to Seth. Her dazed stare could be a textbook depiction of shell shock. "Thank you for . . ."

"Ava," Seth began, stepping closer.

Taylor took the woman's hands before he could, though she appeared to be struggling against tears herself. It had been a moving memorial service, complete with a poignant family photo collage and a small display of Mr. Sandison's flight memorabilia. His brother, a pilot himself, read from a framed copy of John Gillespie Magee Jr.'s famous poem, "High Flight." The man's voice had choked on its final line: "*Put out my hand and touched the face of God.*"

"We wanted to be here, Ava," Taylor murmured, meeting Seth's gaze over the widow's shoulder as the two women hugged. The ache in her eyes grabbed his heart. "If you need anything . . ." She glanced toward the flower-laden altar, her face suddenly far too pale.

"Taylor . . ."

Before Seth could say anything more, a trio of Sandison neighbors swept in and whisked Ava away, saying something gently persuasive about food and a gathering of close family and friends.

Seth touched Taylor's arm. "You okay?"

"Fine." It was more of a chirp than an answer. Her immediate sigh said she knew better than to try to fool the chaplain to the chaplains. "I really need to get out of here, Seth."

"Me too. C'mon."

He took her hand, led her outside. They were met instantly by a cool sea breeze; the tiny chapel, its modest grounds laden with neon-pink ice plants and a profusion of wildflowers, perched on a rocky coastal cliff. Every inch of its staggering view was made even richer by the setting sun. God's garden by the sea. Seth breathed in the salty air, amazed by the natural feel of this woman's hand in his. "Is this better?"

"Much." Taylor inhaled, sliding her hand from his. "I think it was the scent of all those floral bouquets and how close the room was."

"And this was your first memorial service since Greg's."

"I don't know how I managed to avoid it for three years."

Seth did. Only the fact that he was an ordained minister and sometimes asked to officiate had forced him to attend services after Camille's death. It had taken all his strength—and a hundred prayers—not to break down that first time. It hurt beyond belief. Thankfully, Taylor and Greg had a pastor who'd officiated at his funeral; Seth wouldn't want to be a reminder of that day. More and more lately, it seemed important that this woman see him for who he was, not only the roles he embraced. He cleared his throat. "It was a nice service."

"It was." Taylor checked her phone, then hugged her arms around herself. "Except for that ugly moment when Ava went ballistic over the program."

"Yeah, that." The woman had fumed, cried, and then threatened to sue the printer. The program contained several typos and, sadly, a substantial error regarding the number of years Ava and Sandy had been married. Seth doubted a single person in the chapel had missed her near meltdown. "She needed that measure of control—and a safe target for her anger."

Taylor hugged herself a little tighter as she gazed toward the sea. "Those grief stages," she said at last, her voice soft against the breeze. "You've got to check them all off."

"Or stall out and punch walls for a while." He rubbed his knuckles, managed a grim smile. Taylor hadn't jousted with anger as publicly as he had—as Ava just did—from anything Seth had seen. It didn't come naturally to her. He wasn't sure if that was such a good thing. Knuckles healed; walls could be patched and repainted. But hearts . . .

"I remember reading something about that once," he continued. "Written by Max Lucado. Stuck with me. He said something like 'Anger lives in sorrow's house.' Because in grief, we have to deal with more than memories; we're battling disappointment . . . our unlived tomorrows. None of it feels fair, so we get angry at the doctor or the battalion commander or the bartender who let that guy on the road. But mostly we get angry at God."

Her eyes met his. "You think what we saw in the chapel was Ava mad at God?"

"I think she's asking herself those questions: 'Why him? Why us? Why did this have to happen?'" Seth took a breath. "Only God knows the answers. It takes a whole lot of faith to trust that God is good in times like that. It's a lot easier to come unglued over printing errors or slam your fist into a wall."

She held his gaze a few seconds longer, then turned back toward the sea. "I guess so."

Seth heard the last of the cars leave the chapel parking lot behind them. He watched the ember-orange sun extinguish itself in the sea, fully expecting that any minute Taylor would say she had to—

"Hey," Seth heard himself say. "Walt, the PD officer I'm bunking with, offered me his motorcycle tonight. I thought I'd take a short ride up the coast, breathe in more of this air before I have to go back to the valley." She turned to look at him and he took the risk. "There's an extra helmet. Want to come?"

"I . . ." Taylor's brows drew together. "I probably shouldn't."

"Hooper?"

"No. He's doing all right. I have something I promised to do tonight." She raised her phone. "And Rob texted. He wants to bring Thai food."

"No problem." Seth feigned a casual shrug. "Thai sounds good."

And suddenly, so did punching another wall.

Taylor scraped the remains of the mock duck into the garbage. She'd never liked tofu. Or duck. And she also didn't like that Rob had shown up with the Thai food despite the fact that she'd begged off with a fictional headache. He'd arrived on her porch with a disarming grin and his diagnosis that her headache was from hunger: "Too many steps, not enough protein." Frankly, it had given Taylor a real headache. And made her want to run to the fridge for a handful of frozen Girl Scout cookies. She stabbed a piece of eggplant with the duck skewer and flung it into the plastic-lined pail. It landed with a satisfying splat. For some awful reason, it made her think of Ava Sandison, ripping that funeral program to bits.

"'*Anger lives in sorrow's house.*'" Donovan quoting Lucado. Of course he would.

Taylor closed the under-sink cupboard and padded barefoot back to the living room to join Hooper, eager to put an end to this day. She drew her legs up on the couch, glanced at the wall clock. Only 9 p.m. She was on call with the crisis team until seven in the morning.

She hadn't told Rob because there was no need to have that conversation again.

She hadn't told Seth, either, because she didn't want to see hope in his eyes. In a few days, he'd read her letter of resignation. She didn't want to have to explain her decision; he'd promised to back off about that. And she didn't want to start analyzing it again herself. She was starting her life afresh. She'd tucked her wedding rings back in the box, not hung them around her neck. And tonight, being on call for Kasie for another few hours would mark the end of her commitment to the crisis team. She'd tell Hooper good night, get him settled, and then crawl into bed and read.

Taylor's gaze moved to the collection of papers in front of her, lying on the glass of her peaceful sand-and-shell display. There was a notepad with the numbers Rob had recited: calories in the Thai food—she'd subtract the jettisoned mock duck—a final draft of her resignation letter, and the "Thinking of You" card from the retired teacher. Taylor reached for the card, feeling the strange irritation it had prompted this year.

She stared at the back of the card and read its small-font quote:

> "You no longer have yesterday. You do not yet have tomorrow. You have only today. This is the day the Lord has made. Live in it."
> —Max Lucado

Taylor set the card down, accepting that a second quote from the same writer was mere coincidence, but the angry prickle grew.

"You do not yet have tomorrow. . . ."

There was nothing wrong with planning her future, getting a good grip on it after all these years of feeling she had no real control. Taylor wasn't going to be made to feel faithless for letting her past go, actively embracing what would come. To have "only today" felt stifling, inert . . . *hopeless*. She grimaced, thinking of the funeral this afternoon, the sad mix of confusion and pain on the new widow's face. It had hurt to see her that way, but it made Taylor even more determined to take all the necessary steps to put that part of her life behind her.

She lifted her iPad from where it lay on the couch, letting

her gaze scroll down the nearly completed Survival List. The twenty-sixth was only a few days away. She was as on track there as she was on her calorie and step count. By determination and willpower, she was making it happen. It was something to be proud of.

She was sorry if Ava Sandison was mad at God, but Taylor was finished dwelling on the unanswered whys of Greg's accident. Seth had put her mind at ease about that chaplain appointment. It made sense that it had to do with the problems within the fire department. And she wasn't going to spend any more time questioning where Greg died, why he was on that highway. As Seth reminded her, only God had all the answers. She'd have to trust him with that one. Taylor didn't have any more questions. But she had a future . . . and sparkly new shoes.

She'd toss the teacher's card in with the tofu, delete the e-mail from the young mother, and . . . She checked the clock again. San Diego's crisis calls averaged fewer than two per day. There was no full moon tonight, no heat wave, and no major holiday, which, sadly, often triggered suicides. All signs pointed toward her favor to Kasie being accomplished without a crisis. For anyone.

"Good night, Hooper," Taylor said, gently taking her dog's face in her hands. She pressed a kiss on his forehead. His milky eyes met hers, and his tail thumped against the snowy rug. Taylor's heart cramped. "We're going to be okay, pal. You and me. We're going to beat the odds."

"You're not listening," Sloane hissed into her cell phone. "I don't gamble. Ever. I'll spell that: *e-v-e-r*. Not with money, anyway." She glanced at the overeager man sitting on the barstool next to her. She didn't gamble; she only let dubious strangers buy her tequila. "Besides, my chances at winning anything are about as good . . . as a black cat's of being adopted from the city pound."

"Right, honey. You're breaking my heart." The too-familiar voice—coarse and Eastern European, she guessed—gave a guttural laugh. "We don't care about cats. We care about money. We care that you don't pay."

"I keep telling you that I have nothing to do with those gambling loans," Sloane told him, fear warring with the numbing effects of alcohol. "It was my ex."

"Where is he?"

"I don't know," Sloane insisted, wishing it were completely true. She didn't know exactly where Paul was. Only that the last time she'd heard, he was somewhere in Mexico. "And I don't have any money. I can barely pay my rent. So stop calling me."

The ugly laugh chilled her. "Watch your pretty back, sweetheart. There are other ways of paying."

"You don't scare me," Sloane lied, gripping the edge of the bar as her stomach roiled. "Do the world a favor and crawl back under your rock."

"Funny girl. I see you're still driving that heap-of-trash Jetta."

Sloane's throat closed. She jabbed the Disconnect button, then blocked the wandering hand of the man beside her, getting far too friendly for the price of a watered-down drink.

"Hey, darlin'," he murmured, leaning close enough that Sloane saw the patchy evidence of transplants at his hairline. "Anyone ever tell you that you could be a model . . . or a beauty queen?"

"Shake that sweet little booty and turn on the charm."

Sloane stiffened. "I've got to go."

"Hey, that's not fair."

She shot him a look. "Life isn't fair, buddy. Get used to it."

She pulled out her keys, fisted the martial arts Kubotan attached to them, and started for the door. She'd go home to her apartment, lock the doors, and hunker down. Hope that slimy guy didn't have the smarts to find her address. He was probably bluffing about spotting her car. If he'd checked Paul's credit, and public records, the Jetta could have been mentioned any number of places. It made more sense that he was calling from Sacramento, but . . . she'd better look into trading in the car. And find a new place to live.

Sloane winced, imagining Marty in his lonely cage at the shelter. No real home, dwindling chances of ever feeling safe. She knew how that felt.

———

"No problem," Seth said, managing to wedge his cell phone close to his ear despite the helmet. The idling bike's engine rumbled against the sound of the sea. He'd pulled over when the phone buzzed inside his jacket, hoping it might mean Taylor had changed her mind. "What do you need, Evan?"

"I wouldn't ask," the crisis volunteer assured him, "but you said if anyone had a problem with a shift this week, you'd be glad to help. And . . ." It sounded like he gulped a breath. "We think we're starting labor. The baby's not due for ten more days, but this doesn't feel like those 'practice' contractions we've had before."

"No problem," Seth repeated, smiling at his use of *we*. He had no doubt Evan felt every cramp. "I'd be happy to help you out—all three of you. You're on the call until 0700?"

"Yes, sir."

"Consider yourself relieved of duty. I'll let dispatch know."

The young man's exhaled breath was Lamaze-worthy. "I owe you, Seth."

"Just text me a picture of that baby."

"For sure. Oh, another contraction—gotta go."

"I'll be praying, buddy."

Seth tucked the phone back inside his jacket. He glanced at the ocean and sighed, glad he could help the father-to-be, but still sorry this evening hadn't been spent with Taylor.

Thai food and Plastic Man.

Seth had indulged his temper for a few minutes after Taylor left, then told himself to practice what he preached. After all these years—the hard knocks, the wake-up calls—he knew better than to play the angry blame game. Sometimes things didn't work out.

He put the bike in gear, revved the engine, and merged back onto the coast highway. It was nearly nine thirty. Walt said things had been quiet out on the streets. Seth might get some sleep despite being on call. Maybe the only drama tonight would be the best kind: Evan and Paige welcoming their newborn.

The callout text came at 11:05.

22

"I HAVEN'T DONE THIS KIND OF CALL," Taylor told Seth, grateful he was here with her, even if she'd had to admit she'd withheld her own call status earlier. It didn't matter; she needed Seth's experience. "A SIDS. It's going to be awful."

"I've never seen it otherwise." Seth turned to look toward the doors leading into the near-empty ER lobby of Oceanside Hospital, lights dimmed this time of the night. It was an hour that should offer merciful sleep for exhausted young parents . . . or a rocking chair and mother's milk for their hungry infant.

An ache rose in Taylor's throat. "Did you get any information from the paramedics?" she asked.

"First baby. A boy, James—they call him Jamie. Eleven

weeks. Healthy. Parents are James Sr. and Robin." Seth's face was lightly stubbled with beard growth. The lights of a remaining police car flickered, red and blue, over his crisis jacket. "Mom fed the baby at four thirty and expected he'd be hungry again before nine. She fell asleep waiting. Woke up at ten and found him blue. Dad started CPR."

Taylor swallowed against the ache, imagining the desperate scene. "How long did they work in the ER?"

"Around thirty minutes, I think. There was no response at all."

"And now?"

"Jamie's parents are holding him." Seth met her gaze. "And waiting for us."

———

Kasie tucked her legs beneath her on the old sofa and squinted in the darkness to read the crisis dispatcher's message on her phone for a third time. A call for crisis response to Oceanside Hospital for a SIDS case. Sudden infant death syndrome. Parents, or maybe a single parent, grieving the most unspeakable of losses. She'd seen it before in the ER—the desperate attempt by staff to save the baby, tears in the eyes of even the most veteran emergency department staffers. And then— after resuscitation efforts finally ended—there would be what felt like an endless wait for a pastor, social worker, or chaplain. Someone who would be a different kind of hero in that vital moment. Someone to offer what the emergency team, obligated to move on with care for others, couldn't: ongoing comfort, support, a listening ear for as long as needed.

Tonight that person would be a crisis volunteer and . . .

It should be me.

Kasie glanced down at her engagement ring. She'd solved nothing with Daniel this evening. Even with a dinner that had required an Internet search, driving all over town, and a big chunk of her hospital paycheck. She'd followed it with a wedge of Daniel's favorite chocolate cheesecake and a speech she'd rehearsed in front of her bathroom mirror. A plea for the man she loved to understand that her crisis work felt more important than anything she'd ever done. As if, she'd confessed with tears welling, it had been God's whisper all along. She'd tried the best she could to explain what it was like to work alongside people with the same dedication. And how amazing it felt to step in and offer a lifeline in the wake of terrible tragedy, be the one person a survivor could count on.

Daniel had pushed his dessert plate away and gone quiet. Kasie prayed she'd finally reached him but . . .

"This 'important work' is more important to you than I am? You don't care if our relationship survives? Does God ever whisper anything about that, Kasie?"

She'd planned to invite Daniel to the next crisis team meeting.

He told her he'd made an appointment for couples counseling.

Seth watched as Taylor spoke to the young mother still holding the blanket-wrapped infant. Now and then the woman would rock in the chair, her hand patting the bundle in her arms. Each time it looked as if Taylor's heart would break.

Beyond the closed door of the quiet room, an overhead stat page for respiratory therapy sounded. Continuing crises on the heels of tragedy. And, Seth hoped, another chance to win

one. He lowered his eyes. *Please, Lord, be present there . . .
and here, now.*

"We're here to help you in any way we can, Robin," Taylor
continued, leaning forward in the chair she'd pulled close.
The baby's father, sitting next to Seth, hadn't taken his eyes
off his cell phone in several minutes, though Seth doubted he
could comprehend a single word. "There will be things that
need to be taken care of," Taylor gently advised. "It can feel
confusing. Seth and I will help explain and be here with you
and your husband during all of that. So—"

"He asked us if the baby cried a lot," the father broke in,
turning to Seth. "He wanted to know if Jamie was a colicky
baby . . . fussed a lot."

"Who?" Seth knew the answer and hated the pain that the
question inflicted on these grieving parents, no matter how
carefully asked. And necessary. "Who asked you about that?"

"One of the police officers." James glanced toward the
bundle in his wife's arms, agonizing disbelief etched on his
face. "The ER doctor, too. She said she was sorry to ask, but
they needed to know if we'd ever shaken him."

Lord . . .

Seth kept his voice gentle. "I'm sure the doctor was sorry.
And I am too, James. I'm sorry for *all* of this. There's no way
to make what's happened easier. It's not possible. But I can
promise you that we'll do everything we can to help you get
through this. One thing at a time."

"Jamie . . . isn't . . . wasn't a fussy baby." Robin's voice was
raw and halting. "Everyone said we were blessed that way. He
had this little routine. We'd joke that it was his internal baby
app. Eat, sleep, and—" Her voice broke. "I should have set
an alarm. I never lie down before his evening feeding, but I'd

only slept a few hours the night before." Tears splashed onto the blanket as she hugged her baby close. "I should have set an alarm. Held him longer . . . kissed him more . . ."

"Robin, don't . . ." In an instant, James was kneeling beside her chair, both of them bending over their child, both crying. His deep sobs underscored her keening moan.

Taylor rose from her chair, blinking against tears.

"Taylor . . ." Seth drew her to his side, slipping an arm around her shoulders. She'd given so unselfishly to this grieving mother—her heart on her sleeve. She'd always been that way, and Seth had kept an eye on her because of it, because her heart was so fragile after her husband's death. But her transparent compassion had always touched him, soul-deep.

"They'll need to send the baby to the medical examiner," Taylor whispered to Seth, her nursing experience injecting procedural reality into the painful moment.

"Yes. And we'll help them when that happens. But right now they need to be a family . . . saying good-bye."

Taylor nodded, her shoulders rising and sinking with a sigh.

They kept a silent vigil until the family pastor arrived, a short, balding man with kind eyes who'd baptized Jamie only weeks before. He made no attempt to hide his tears as he blessed the baby and offered a prayer of comfort.

"And even in our heartbreak, Lord, parted for now from this sweet baby, we know that you keep Jamie safe, with you . . . where we all belong."

More family arrived, standing by as the couple at last surrendered their baby to the hospital staff. Robin's aunt, a retired pediatric nurse from Imperial Beach, came prepared to accompany them home and stay as long as she was needed.

Within minutes, Seth and Taylor found themselves alone

in the quiet room—always a sad vacuum. Taylor seemed intent on filling it with activity: rearranging the chairs, tidying resource brochures, and it appeared, organizing the Kleenex boxes by weight.

Ah, Taylor . . . "Here, let me help."

"Got it, no problem. I'll finish up," she insisted. "You can go on home, if—"

"Hey." Seth touched Taylor's jacket sleeve, saw the pain in her eyes. "Thank you for being here, Taylor. You were a blessing to those parents. Even if it was your tenth SIDS call, it wouldn't have felt different. It's hard. We all—"

"Don't," Taylor interrupted, her expression suddenly tense, perhaps even angry. "We both know I wouldn't be here if Kasie could. I don't need you to talk me down from an emotional cliff. I don't need two debriefings. I'll report in to dispatch, but the only thing I really need . . ." She glanced toward the doorway. "Do you still have that motorcycle?"

"Five minutes from here." Seth's heart stalled; he was a fool to hope. It was after midnight, and Taylor wouldn't—

"Take me for a ride, Seth. I need some ocean air."

23

TAYLOR BURROWED CLOSER against the back of Seth's jacket, trying to stretch enough to link her hands across his broad chest. It wasn't happening. She settled for grabbing fistfuls of the soft leather as they sped along the lit stretch of the Coronado Bay Bridge, a high-rise, curving ribbon surrounded by miles of ocean. She turned her head to gaze at the glittering San Diego skyline beyond and was immediately buffeted by chilly, salt-scented wind. She was grateful for the fleece-lined Levi's jacket. Seth's hosts, the PD officer and his wife who'd just celebrated their fortieth wedding anniversary, not only had an extra helmet but also an assortment of women's jackets. Left by their daughter's visiting girlfriends over the years. "The crazy bunch," the wife called them affectionately, and Taylor suspected her current situation might very well fit into that description too: midnight, roaring down State Highway 75 toward Coronado Island.

"Whoa . . ." She clutched tighter, keeping herself balanced as Seth downshifted and they exited the bridge. They came to a stop, sounds of traffic rumbling around them.

Seth turned to glance at her. "Where to?"

Anywhere but where we were. And how awful that felt.

"Wherever . . . air and ocean," Taylor told him. "You choose."

The bike roared to life again and she spread her palms over Seth's chest as he steered left onto Orange Avenue, content to let the sounds and jostling replace the memory of that young couple beginning their journey through grief. And distract her from the fact that there were six more hours in this unwelcome volunteer shift.

Mercifully, in minutes, they pulled up to a view that provided the perfect distraction. Taylor never grew tired of seeing it: the Hotel del Coronado.

An immense, elegant 1880s Victorian mansion, it boasted huge red-tiled towers, grand porches and verandas, white railings, formal gardens and lawns, palms and lavish pools. All of it offering staggeringly beautiful views of the city, ocean, and bay. At this hour, white lights outlined the steep, multi-level gabled roofs, making the hotel look like a child's fairy-tale castle. Its rich history included visits by a host of notable celebrities, presidents, and movie companies eager to use the setting. An inspiration, too, for novelists . . .

"*Somewhere in Time*," Taylor said as Seth pulled off his helmet. He glanced back as she unbuckled hers. "That old sad movie with Christopher Reeve and Jane Seymour. The novel it was based on was set here at the Del. They filmed it out in Michigan, but I'm always reminded when I see this place."

"I remember that film. And the music—hard to forget that." Seth smiled. "Stop me if I start humming Rachmaninoff."

"That was my aunt's favorite movie," Taylor said, thinking of the romantic time-travel fantasy. Lovers from different eras finding, then losing, each other and finally reunited only in death. "A 'soggy-popcorn movie,' Aimee calls them—those heartbreaking, hopeless love stories." A ridiculous lump rose in her throat. She swallowed it down. "Because you cry in your popcorn . . ."

"Right." The hotel lights reflected in Seth's eyes. "Still preferable to my musical offerings." He looked toward the road. "So . . . a little more ocean air before we head back? Silver Strand State Beach isn't far."

"I'm sure it's closed by now."

"Hard to close up a beach. And besides . . ." Seth patted the SDPD sticker on his borrowed helmet. "I know a lot of the patrol folks." His grin crinkled the edges of his eyes. "We'll risk it."

"I'm seeing the renegade side of you," Taylor teased as Seth stoked the embers they'd found still smoldering in the fire ring. "I think beach fires aren't allowed until summer."

"I think you're right." He cocked a brow, noticing how pretty she looked in the faded jean jacket and the glow of the new flames. "So it's a good thing we came down here to check on this situation—as a public service."

"See? Definite renegade." Taylor sank down to sit on the

sand. Then gazed out at the dark sea. She tipped her head back and drew in a deep breath.

"Getting enough ocean air?" Seth asked, sitting beside her. He thought of how she'd looked back there after their SIDS call. That mix of pain and anger. He wasn't going to press her but . . . "Better now?"

"Yes. Thank you for this." She turned to look at him, and the breeze sifted her hair, as golden in places as the fire. "I'm sorry I was so defensive at the hospital, Seth."

He shrugged. *Your flak jacket against hurt. I get that.*

"I was hoping I wouldn't get a call," Taylor admitted.

"I was too. If we get a call, it means someone's in trouble."

"I meant that selfishly. I didn't want to be there." Taylor traced her finger in the sand. The only sound was the push-pull of the waves in the distance.

Seth wanted to tell her she couldn't be selfish if she tried. And the way she'd handled things with the grieving parents only proved what a natural she was as a crisis volunteer. But clearly she was having serious doubts. For reasons important to her. There was a fine line between speaking to Taylor chaplain-to-chaplain and overstepping that privilege by moving into personal—

"You and Camille didn't have children."

"No, we . . ." Seth hesitated. After nearly seven years, he still thought about that when he saw a mother holding her newborn. Even tonight, with Robin and Jamie. "We were only married a few years when she was diagnosed with the cancer. We'd talked about children, but Camille . . ." He shook his head, stoked the fire again.

"She couldn't?" Taylor asked, then immediately apologized. "I'm sorry. That's personal. Forget I—"

"It wasn't that she couldn't," Seth found himself explaining. "Camille wasn't sure she wanted children. I knew that from the start. Her mother was abusive, and Camille had a lot of unresolved issues around that. Fears, probably." He read the question in Taylor's eyes. "Yes, I wanted kids . . . very much. I guess I thought she'd change her mind, be secure enough in our marriage and her faith that it would be a natural progression at some point. In fact, I thought it had happened. She'd started to talk about going off the pill, but then . . ."

"She got sick."

"She'd gone to her sister's in Portland," Seth began. He'd told few people about that time. The complete story to no one. But there was something about Taylor . . . "For a visit, a girls' getaway, they called it. They did that a couple of times a year. Then her sister called and asked me to come. She said Camille was having some 'routine' tests done and they'd found a problem. It sounded serious. I got the first flight out."

"Routine tests?" Taylor's brows pinched. "Her doctor was in Oregon?"

"No."

The old ache returned, duller after the years, but still there. Seth breathed in, let it go. "She'd arranged to have a tubal ligation. To prevent her from ever getting pregnant. That was the real reason for the visit with her sister. I found out when the oncologist mentioned it in passing. Camille hadn't planned to tell me."

Taylor touched Seth's arm, sympathy in her expression.

"Don't worry." He managed a smile, buoyed by a surprising eddy of relief. "I'm not going to start humming Rachmaninoff."

———

Taylor looked toward the fire as it crackled and launched a shower of glimmering sparks. "I guess we think everyone else has it together better than we do. Those times we're not kidding ourselves that it's the other way round."

Seth's leather jacket creaked as he shifted on the sand beside her, but he stayed silent.

Taylor sighed. Hearing Seth's story, knowing that he trusted her enough to share it, touched her more than she could say. He'd be leaving in a few days, and then their chaplain connection would end. Maybe it was that, or all the ocean air she'd breathed in, but for whatever reason it felt safe to—

"Those last months with Greg," she began, "I was desperate to start a family. We'd been trying for more than a year without luck. All he could think about was getting promoted to captain, doing whatever it took to make that happen. All the while I was hopping up onto specialists' exam tables, enduring fertility tests. . . ."

Seth looked at her with kindness in his eyes. The firelight picked out tufts of dark hair left boyishly awry by the motorcycle helmet. "That had to have been a tough time."

She nodded, her throat tightening. "It got worse when I was told that there was no problem with my ability to get pregnant. I was fine. Which meant . . ."

Seth's flinch was almost imperceptible.

"I wanted Greg to start the testing as soon as possible. He said it was a bad time. They'd uncovered those problems with the illegal gambling. There were rumors it was tied to the Russian mafia—crazy probably, but everyone was pointing fingers and looking over their shoulders. Greg was consumed with trying to distance himself and prove he wasn't involved in any way. He said he didn't have time for doctors and tests."

Actually, he'd said much more than that: *"Great. You're saying it's me? That there's something wrong with me? That's all I need right now, Taylor. . . . Thanks a lot. I appreciate your support. What a wife."*

"Things were pretty tense," Taylor added, not sure she'd had enough ocean air after all.

"And then he got passed over for the promotion."

"I reminded him that we both had good incomes, a home, supportive families, and good friends. I talked about God's timing. I tried to make Greg understand that it didn't matter to me if he was captain. It didn't. Not at all."

"But it mattered to him," Seth said with a knowing look.

"More than anything, I think." *As much as a baby mattered to me.*

"Those last weeks before the accident," Taylor continued, "Greg managed to be gone a lot. Overtime, classes, basketball. I kept telling myself he needed that space. But I did try to arrange for counseling. I'd found somebody through our church."

Seth raised his brows.

"Greg said no. He'd found excuses to stop attending services and definitely wasn't interested in seeing a Christian counselor. That's why I was surprised when I saw that note about an appointment with you."

Seth glanced toward the fire.

"The evening of the accident he'd been moody, tense. And . . ." Taylor took a breath. "I was relieved when he finally said he was going out." She felt Seth's eyes on her. "It's the truth. I wish it weren't, but it is."

Seth's hand found hers. "It's too easy, afterward, to tell ourselves what we should have said or done."

"The day we treated Ava Sandison in the ER for her panic attack," Taylor recalled, "she told me something. I can tell you, chaplain-to-chaplain." She smiled ruefully, knowing it was probably the last time that would be true. "She said she argued with her husband before the flight. About nothing, but she'd been unforgiving and he'd been upset. Ava blamed herself. She . . ." Taylor blinked against sudden tears. "All the while she was trying to get control of that plane, she kept telling her husband she was sorry. That she loved him. I know how that felt."

———

Seth slipped his arm around Taylor's shoulder, feeling her relax and lean into him. He breathed in the scent of her hair as they watched the flames dying to embers for a second time. That they'd both responded to the SIDS call and ended up here, sharing long-buried experiences, couldn't be coincidence. God had a hand in this moment.

"Greg left me a message that night," Taylor told him, not moving away. "Not long before he was killed. I'll never know what prompted it or why he was out there on that road. I've accepted that now."

Seth tightened his arm around Taylor and closed his eyes. He told himself not to ask or offer anything.

"He said he loved me. That he wanted things to be different . . . better between us."

Seth exhaled. Felt his heart thud. *Thank you, Lord.*

"Having that last message and knowing now that Greg wasn't coming to you because of doubts about our marriage . . ."

Taylor nodded, her soft hair brushing Seth's chin. "It makes a difference. I'm still working on getting things under full control. But you've helped me finally move on with my life."

"I'm glad," Seth murmured against her hair. It wasn't completely true; he was glad Taylor was finding peace, but he had a strong sense that moving on meant moving away from him. Because she didn't need him anymore, if she ever really had. And because her feelings for him were nothing like what he'd begun to feel for her.

"I'm grateful." Taylor leaned away enough to look into Seth's eyes. The sweetness in her expression made his heart ache.

"You don't need to say—"

"But I do," Taylor interrupted. "I'm not leaving anything unsaid anymore. I've learned that much. I need you to know that I've never had anyone be as good and loyal a friend to me as you have been, Seth."

"Hey." His voice was trying to choke. "Let's not make that sound like some kind of farewell. I'm not going anywhere."

"But you are. Back to Sacramento. I'll be here but . . ."

He'd known it, but it didn't make this moment any easier. "You're not going to continue with the crisis team."

"No." Taylor swallowed. "I'll still help you with the training scenarios this week. I'll keep that commitment. But I wrote my letter of resignation, effective the first of April. I've covered the remaining shifts this month—tonight was a fluke."

It wasn't a fluke or a coincidence. Why couldn't Taylor see that?

"I know that's part of the reason you came here," she continued. "To check up on me, because you saw that call list. You were worried."

"No, I—"

"Don't even try to deny it." Taylor rested her palm against his cheek. "I know you too well. Chaplain to the chaplains, man who is kind to old dogs, not-so-secret fan of fudge brownies, and . . ." She smiled, and her thumb caressed the stubble on his jaw. "Incorrigible renegade. You came here to be sure I'm okay."

Taylor touched her lips to Seth's cheek, warm and soft, and so close to the corner of his mouth that his heart stalled. It took everything he had not to gather her into his arms and kiss her. He wanted to. Maybe more than he'd ever wanted anything before. And for the first time, he wasn't confused by or sorry for that outrageous thought.

"I suppose we should head back," Taylor said, reaching for her helmet. "I'm the fool who's going to need a caffeine double shot before I even get close to those ER doors in the morning. And you're in the classroom, right?"

"I am," he confirmed, finding his voice. And his helmet. "But I should deal with that fire first."

Someone had left an old plastic sand pail near the fire ring, and Seth jogged down to the water to fill it for dousing the flames. He hoped the time and space—and a dose of cold surf—would similarly extinguish what he'd felt when Taylor kissed him. It didn't work.

When he walked back to the bike, Taylor was helmeted, zipped, and looking intently at her phone. Chuckling, she turned the screen so Seth could see.

"What is that?" he asked, trying to make sense of what appeared to be a video with no movement. "I can't tell what—"

"It's Hooper. Asleep beside my bed." She smiled. "Nanny cam streaming to my phone. I'd bought one but didn't have a clue how to install it. Rob hooked it up in a couple of minutes when he stopped by tonight. He's amazing with that stuff."

"Right." *Dr. Amazing.*

Seth buckled his helmet and started the engine. Taylor nestled close against his back, wrapping her arms tightly around him. The crazy new warmth spread. He'd be taking the longer route home.

"I meant it, Seth." Taylor's voice rose over the engine roar. "I'm grateful you came to San Diego to check on me."

"No problem. Hang on."

He revved the engine and took off down the highway, glad the traffic had thinned. It was hard enough to concentrate with that memory replaying endlessly in his head: the feel of Taylor's lips near the corner of his mouth. How close—yet maddeningly far—it had been to a real kiss. And the sweetness in her expression when she touched his face and thanked him . . .

Seth smiled, enjoying Taylor's weight against him as they leaned into a highway curve. She was wrong, of course. About the reason he'd come to San Diego. In fairness, though, he'd only figured it out for himself a few minutes ago. Maybe renegades were slow on the uptake.

But regardless of Taylor Cabot's determination to move on, never mind about the surgeon with Thai food, Padres tickets, and amazing tech expertise, Seth hadn't come to San Diego to check on this woman chaplain-to-chaplain. Or even because she'd been his good friend for a long time now. That was all valid, but this was far, far different. Seth was here in this coastal zip code, on this borrowed bike, right here, right *now*, because . . .

I'm in love with her.

24

"Suit yourself," Sloane told Kasie after the tech asked to join her at the cafeteria table. Even at eleven thirty the place was packed to the gills with a lunch crowd; clearly Kasie was desperate. "I won't be here much longer anyway."

"Thanks." Kasie set her tray down, pulled up a chair, and reached for her coffee like it was a matter of life and death.

"Too bad they don't offer it Irish." Sloane smiled at the confusion on the girl's face. "Shot of whiskey—double shot from the way you look."

"I don't drink."

"Why am I not surprised?" Sloane watched as Kasie unconsciously twisted her engagement ring; she'd been doing that since she arrived this morning. At this rate, she'd either drop the minuscule stone into her coffee cup or saw off her finger. "You and Cabot both look like you slept standing up."

Kasie glanced toward where Seth Donovan sat, talking with a hospital chaplain. "I'm fine. Taylor didn't get a lot of sleep. She and Seth went out on a crisis call."

"You make it sound like war, without pay and commissary privileges. Don't you see enough trauma and misery right here in this place?" Sloane watched Kasie saw at her finger again. "I'd think you'd want to spend your time collecting fluffy wedding ideas on Pinterest."

"It's . . . different out there, working with the crisis team. Sometimes it does feel like a war zone. But we're there to offer comfort. And hope."

Sloane thought of the day Donovan had followed her into the chapel. Then suggested she might benefit by talking with him. Her lips tensed. That would happen when hell froze over.

"People sometimes think we're cops or social workers—or maybe we're out there to quote Scripture and sign folks up for church," Kasie continued. "None of that is true. I'd say most of us feel motivated spiritually, but there's no preaching allowed. We're not therapists, either. I guess we're more like emotional paramedics. We go through the training and make ourselves available to our community . . . because we care."

"Unlike the rest of us, who don't?"

"I didn't mean that," Kasie insisted too quickly. "Really."

Sloane frowned. All she needed was a self-righteous spiel from a kid who didn't have the heart to rescue a lousy kitten.

"I only meant it takes a different kind of commitment," the tech explained. "In the ER, when it's a critical case, we— *you*, way more than I—are knocking ourselves out to stop a tragedy from happening. But crisis volunteers show up afterward, when there's nothing left to do for the victims. No way to save them. We're there for the *survivors*. Like last night, for the parents who lost their baby to SIDS. Or when I sat with that woman after the shooting in her home. Sometimes we're asked to do death notifications or—"

"Okay." Sloane raised her palm. "I don't need a list. I get it."

She didn't, but she had no interest in going down the path this conversation was taking. The only thing Sloane cared about was putting one foot in front of the other to propel herself out of the black hole that had somehow swallowed her own life. Lately, that escape looked pretty iffy.

"Look, kid," she said finally. "If wearing that volunteer uniform and letting your heart bleed at ungodly hours does it for you, who am I to argue?" She shook her head, wondering if she'd ever in her life believed in anything that deeply. Anything . . . or anybody. She wasn't sure but was dead certain it wouldn't happen now. "Knock yourself out, Beckett." She glanced toward Seth Donovan, alone now at his table. "But promise me one thing."

Kasie stopped her sandwich halfway to her mouth. "Promise you what?"

"That you won't come peddling hope to me—ever."

"Truthfully . . ." Kasie's eyes met Sloane's. "I can't even imagine that."

"Good." Sloane rose from her chair. "But I'd still recommend that other thing."

Kasie raised her brows.

"Irish whiskey. Double shot."

"Can't imagine that either."

"Give yourself a decade." *Or the last few years in my shoes.*

Sloane tossed her napkin onto her lunch tray, lifted it from the table. "See ya."

"I'll be there in twenty."

As Sloane turned away, she caught a glimpse of Dr. Rob Halston taking a seat opposite Donovan. Even if she'd never believed in anything altruistic, her cynical intuition was spot-on. That unlikely connection could only be about one thing: Taylor Cabot.

Sloane wasn't going to waste any time speculating. What she had to do now was keep a low profile, hold on to her job long enough to put aside some overtime cash, and figure out a way to keep herself safe. Moving was still on the table, though there hadn't been another phone call or—

"Hey, Sloane." One of the ER clerks, her ample chest dotted with service pins, stepped off the elevator as Sloane approached. "Did your brother ever find you?"

"What?"

"He called the ER. Said he's been trying to reach you on your cell because he just arrived in town."

No. Sloane's heart slammed hard against her ribs. "When was that?"

"Right after you left for lunch. Is something wrong?"

"Nah . . . it's nothing."

Except . . . *I don't have a brother.*

———

"Sure," Seth told the surgeon, "grab a chair."

Halston switched his phone to the other hand as he slid the chair out and settled onto it. He'd traded the activity tracker bracelet for a variety that clipped to the neck of his scrub top. "Thanks."

"No problem." *But I'm guessing you have one with me?*

"I hope I'm not interrupting anything." Halston pointed to the back of the cafeteria flyer Seth had been scratching notes on. He tapped the slim stylus attached to his smartphone and smiled. "Pencil and paper, almost a lost art."

"You're not interrupting," Seth assured him, not quite sure if the surgeon's expression was smug or amused; he decided to cut the man some slack and go with the latter. "I was picking the hospital chaplain's brain about a few things. And trying to ignore that dessert display whispering my name."

"Ah." Smug smile, 100 percent.

Seth took a drink of his coffee, waiting. He'd learned a fair amount from the detectives who frequented the uniform shop—and from the impulsive act that landed him behind bars. Patience was indeed a virtue, and if you waited long enough . . .

"Your classes for the crisis team recruits are held downtown," Halston said, meeting Seth's gaze. "I'm surprised to see you here."

"I'm not the primary instructor. I'm here to assist the trainers and lend a hand if needed," Seth explained, getting a sense of where this was headed. It was about territory. The hospital, overtly, but maybe also . . . "I'll be going back this afternoon," he added, then decided to test his suspicion. "But I wanted to come by and see how Taylor's doing. Last night's callout went late and was emotionally rugged."

"Callout?"

"A crisis call." *Taylor didn't tell him?* "We responded to a request for the crisis team. I can't give any details because of confidentiality but—"

"You managed to drag her out there again."

"She took a shift for a friend," Seth explained, determined

to keep the edge out of his voice, even if Halston hadn't. "I ended up doing the same thing. We were both surprised to find each other there."

The surgeon's smile was as tight as a tummy tuck. "Ah."

"Taylor was amazing," Seth told him, thinking of Robin holding her baby. "She always is."

"She's resigning."

Seth wrestled his anger, remembered the scar on his knee. "She told me."

"Good . . . that's good." The plastic surgeon took a deep breath, his tanned collarbone rising enough to nudge the activity tracker pinned to his neckline. "She needs to step away from all that. Not dwell on tragedy and loss. It's not easy to start over. I understand all about that from my divorce."

Divorce?

Seth thought of Camille's last hours. At least he'd been able to say good-bye; Taylor hadn't. Halston's marital demise wasn't even close to comparable. *Wait . . . wait . . . Don't lose it with this man.*

"I keep telling her the same thing about the dog," the surgeon continued, wiping his fingers on his napkin, though he hadn't touched the chickpea-topped enchilada on his tray. "Dragging out the inevitable isn't healthy. It hurts, I understand that, but it can also be empowering to take control of the process. Sign the papers, pack your bags . . . flush the fish that's sinking to the bottom of the tank."

Seth stared at him.

"A metaphor." Halston's lips compressed. He picked up his utensils and made a deft incision through the tortilla. Tofu oozed out. "I'm sure that volunteering as a crisis chaplain filled a certain void after Taylor's husband was killed. I agree that she has a heart for service. I can see her in the role of a charity spokesperson. With her intelligence, passion, and attractive looks, Taylor would be a natural. I'm on the boards of several organizations. Including the overseas ministry at my church. There are plenty of opportunities to introduce Taylor around, make strategic connections. I have to admit it's a big part of the reason I'm taking her to the Hands for Hope benefit gala."

The dress shopping. And another warning about territory. Halston lifted a forkful of enchilada.

Seth reminded himself that nothing would be gained by making an enemy of this man. And that he, personally, had no relationship with Taylor to defend, beyond friendship. It was best to ignore a territorial challenge, no matter how it irritated him. "If there's one thing I've learned, it's that grief is personal. As individual as a fingerprint—everybody does it differently. On God's timeline. Nobody has the right to say they understand someone else's journey through it." He met the doctor's gaze directly. "Or oversee the process by suggesting the survivor take control. Like it's simply a matter of avoiding the dessert tray, logging enough exercise, checking items off a master list . . . or disposing of the dog on the bottom of the tank."

A muscle bunched along Halston's jaw, far beyond what was needed to chew his soybean curd. "I think you've misunderstood me, Donovan."

Seth wished that were true.

"I care about Taylor," the surgeon said, sincerity replacing the challenge in his tone. "Very much. I only want to see her happy."

Seth nodded, remembering the warmth of Taylor's lips on his cheek. "Then we agree completely on that."

―――――

"First molar, first fever . . . new mom," Taylor told Seth, cuddling the chubby, naked, and dripping-wet baby girl against her scrub top. They'd been sponging her to bring her body temperature down. "I told the mother to go grab herself some juice. The lab's going to draw a blood sample and—"

"You wanted to spare her that," Seth finished, the warmth in his knowing smile causing Taylor's stomach to quiver unexpectedly. Probably because of all they'd shared with each other on that beach. About how they'd both wanted children, but tragedy had intervened. She took a breath, half-expecting to catch the scent of the leather jacket he'd worn last night. The baby burrowed her damp face into Taylor's shoulder. "Poor thing, she's so tired."

Seth leaned against the exam room doorway, studying Taylor's face. "You must be too. You probably got five hours of sleep."

"I'll live."

She'd slept less than three; her brain had refused to shut down. It had run in an endless sensory loop: the heartbreaking image of the young couple cradling their dead infant, the chill whipping of salty air as Seth's motorcycle sped over the bridge toward Coronado Island, the feel of gritty-soft sand and the scent of woodsmoke as they sat side by side on the beach . . . the sparks rising from the fire, and even strains of Rachmaninoff's rhapsody. It had all melded somehow into an ache, even a yearning, that confused Taylor.

"Why are you here?" she asked, shifting the baby in her arms. "I thought you were busy at the training site today."

"I was. And I'm going back but . . ."

Seth's dark eyes met hers, an instant reminder of the

scratchy-warm feel of his cheek against her lips. It had been another curious curve in the endless loop of memories that kept her awake.

"I thought I should stop by and see how you were," Seth continued. His brows pinched. "No. That sounded like a debriefing. It's not like that at all. What I meant was I wanted to see you because I—"

"Lab here. Excuse me. Have to get by, sir," a tech interrupted, sliding into the doorway beside Seth. Dwarfed by his height, she angled her head backward to squint up at him through her glasses. "Are you Dad?"

"No, no." Seth shot Taylor a sheepish look. "I'm—"

"He's a chaplain," Taylor explained.

"Oh, dear." The tech's eyes shifted to the sleeping child. "Is she . . . ?"

"She's fine," Taylor said quickly, understanding the anxious assumption. A chaplain's presence could signify a number of things, some worrisome. "Seth's not here officially." She met his gaze as the tech stepped inside the room and began to assemble her equipment with a hollow tinkle of glass tubes. "He's . . ."

"On my way out—we'll catch up later."

———

"I have it on my calendar," Kasie promised, having moved to the ambulance bay for some privacy during her phone call with Daniel. She glanced down the hospital sidewalk, saw Sloane walking the perimeter of the building; her arms were folded and she kept looking over her shoulder across the parking lot. "I'll be off work at four o'clock Thursday. I won't miss the appointment."

"Marissa and Allen saw this same counselor," Daniel offered. "Allen says she's very good and we'll like her."

Great. Kasie bit her lip to keep from groaning aloud. "You told him about us?"

"A little. He completely understands. Marissa had this thing about spin classes—bicycling—and was going to the gym like six days a week. In the evenings, their only time together. It was becoming a real problem."

Kasie stiffened. "You're comparing my work with the crisis team to gym classes?"

Daniel made no attempt to disguise his sneer. "How can I do that? Marissa doesn't volunteer to ride exercise bicycles in the middle of the night, in the company of police officers and dead people. Lucky me. I win hands down with that one."

Kasie's stomach plunged. "What do you want me to say?"

Daniel was quiet for a moment. "That you'll be at our appointment. I'm sorry. I shouldn't have said that, Kasie. I should keep my big mouth shut. It's only that I love you and I want us to work more than I want anything in this world."

Kasie twisted her ring, letting her gaze wander back toward where Sloane had been standing. She was gone, and Kasie should be too. There was a splint to put on in ortho room 2. Plaster, sheet wadding, and an Ace wrap. Crutch teaching. No adrenaline rush, no heroics. It wasn't like crisis work. But it was still important, a valued skill. . . .

"Kasie?"

"I'll be at the appointment, Daniel. I promise."

25

"IN SCHOOL," SETH MUSED, walking a few steps and looking out at the assembled trainees, "were you that kid who sat in the front row frantically waving your hand and nearly bursting to give the answer?" He chuckled as several in the group shook their heads in the firm negative. "Me neither. I was the kid hunkered down in the back row, wondering how I could fake crippling laryngitis if the teacher called on me—I got pretty *goooood*," he rasped, choking out the last few words. "Some of us don't like to be put on the spot to come up with an answer."

He walked a few steps the other way, made eye contact with one of the students, a middle-aged man who'd been furiously taking notes. "But suppose it has nothing to do with school. What if it's a friend, a neighbor, your spouse . . . your child? What if something's happened to put them in trouble and cause them pain? How many of you would step up then?"

Hands rose around the room.

"And what if it was a stranger who was desperately in need of help?" Seth nodded as the hands stayed aloft. "I would expect that of this group. You're not here because the pay's good. Or because you look sexy in a green jacket. You're here for the same reason I came that very first time, years back. You're fixers. You want to help. Maybe you feel sincerely called. Or maybe, like me, it's because you wouldn't be where you are today if someone hadn't helped *you* in your desperate time of need." He flexed his knee, feeling the proof. "Anybody?" Seth read affirmation in the eyes of more than one. "I thought so. So now that we've established you're the kind of folks who are willing to step up and help, what next?"

"You teach us how to do that," a young man offered.

"Right," Seth agreed, recalling that the trainee worked as a maintenance supervisor for a local school district. "I give you a sort of crisis tool belt, with everything you need to help get things back under control and bring peace to survivors in the wake of tragedy. All the right things to do and say to fix it."

"Works for me." The young man smiled.

"Except that it doesn't work. Because there *is* no fix." Seth swept his gaze across the group. "There are no magic words to erase the overwhelming pain of someone who's experienced a life-altering loss. For the teenager who's the sole survivor in a crash that killed four of his best friends, or the elderly woman whose husband went golfing and never came back, or the young mother who found her baby cold and still in his crib . . ." He took a slow breath. "We can't give you the fix-it tool belt. It doesn't come with the crisis team jacket. But there *is* a tool that can help. A very effective one. We call it skilled listening. Because in large part, crisis volunteers serve in a 'ministry of presence.' Meaning that the concern conveyed by our very presence benefits survivors."

Seth made eye contact with a senior-age woman in the front row, a retired teacher. "How does that relate to the concept of skilled listening, Marion? From your reading."

"Survivors talk. Share their pain, disbelief . . . confusion." She cleared her throat. "And anger sometimes. We sit and listen, giving them our full attention."

"That's right." Seth smiled at her and then addressed the group again. "We listen, without offering platitudes, opinions, or even the hard-earned wisdom of our own experiences. It runs counter to all our urges as fixers. But it's the first step. All healing, all consolation for a survivor of tragedy, begins there: with simply being heard. *You* will be their first hopeful step." He nodded at the eager faces gone sober, unsure. "And now we're going to teach you how to do that."

―――――――

"A new class. I envy them," Kasie said, peeking in at the trainees taking a break in the meeting room. Seth saw a hint of nervousness in her expression. Her casual visit was for a definite reason, he would bet. "I remember that feeling," she added. "Being new and scared and excited, all at the same time."

"Now you're out there. Making a difference."

"I'm trying. I make myself available for every shift I can. But last night . . ."

"Your life took priority." Seth thought of what she'd said about her fiancé's concerns regarding her crisis team service. "I hope you're not here to apologize, Kasie."

"I . . ." She hesitated. "Taylor was so good to take my hours. I did get a text of the call. I know about the SIDS. I wish I'd been there to help."

"We did all right."

Kasie's face flushed. "I didn't mean that I thought you couldn't handle it. You and Taylor . . . you're both seasoned. I haven't even done a death notification yet. You're light-years ahead of me in experience."

"That may be true. But it isn't only the number of calls or years as a volunteer. Sometimes it's what a volunteer brings to the mix from their own life experience. Their ability to offer genuine, nonjudgmental support for people very different from themselves. And in situations that may seem foreign . . . or even frightening. Taylor has that ability. And from what I've seen and heard, you do too, Kasie."

Her eyes widened. "I hope so. I really do want to do this well. Nothing's felt more important."

Seth thought of the example he'd opened with in class today: the student waving from the front row, bursting with eagerness to be called upon. Kasie Beckett was all that, in spades. She wanted to make a difference. He knew that feeling.

"I think I told you," Kasie said softly, "that my father was a police officer. With the LAPD. He was shot and killed when he walked in on a convenience store robbery back in 2001. The owners were an elderly couple, new to the area, and he'd stopped by to check on them. September 17 . . ." She swallowed. "On the Officer Down Memorial Page, they call the date 'end of watch,' just like what they call the end of each duty shift, when an officer goes home to his family. Back then, everybody was focused on the Twin Towers. Flags were at half-mast and people all over the country were wearing black ribbons. I was eight. I know now that it was unrealistic, selfish even, but I wanted there to be flags *only* for him. The most important person in my life . . . didn't come home."

Seth's throat tightened.

"I'm okay," Kasie said, finding a smile that made her look ten years old at best. "Really. I only said all that because I think I'm finally doing something that would make him proud. I'll go on to finish college, but this . . . the crisis work, it feels good. My father would want that for me."

"I have no doubt at all." He held her gaze. "And that personal issue you were taking care of last night—better there?"

She took a big breath, sighed. "Working on it."

"Remember that self-care is part of this. Take care of you, too."

"I will." Kasie turned to look as the trainees began to take their seats again. "I came by to ask if you needed any help running the practice scenarios. I could do that."

Seth smiled, imagining her waving her hand again—like it was her father's flag. "Got it covered. But thanks."

"No problem. Oh, and . . ." Kasie half shrugged, making Seth think she was about to reveal the real cause of her visit. "Did Taylor happen to say anything about wanting to pick up the rest of her shifts this month—go back on the call list?"

"No," Seth told her, remembering Taylor's face in the light of the campfire. Her words about moving on that sounded far too much like she was telling him good-bye. "Taylor won't want those shifts back. They're yours, Kasie."

"Great. I mean, I'm happy to help wherever I can."

"I know you are."

Seth said good-bye to Kasie and was heading back into the

classroom when his phone rang. The lawyer in Sacramento, Randall Ayers.

"Hadn't heard back from you," the attorney told him, something in his voice hinting that he was speaking around one of his ever-present cigars. "This offer's not going to age like a fine wine, Seth. Our buyers won't wait much longer. They're already talking about another business in Fresno. This is a good deal. It would set you and your siblings up nicely. Pay for your nieces' and nephews' education—your own kids' when you have them someday. I remind you that the buyers are willing to retain the Donovan's name, which goes a long way toward satisfying any lingering emotional issues. So I think we should—"

"Stop," Seth told him, trying not to think of the number of times this man had accompanied his father to ball games, eaten his mother's pot roast, gathered with Seth's brother and sisters when they were dealing with the debilitating complications of their mother's cerebral aneurysm. *"Any lingering emotional issues"?* Like the fact that Mike Donovan had asked about the uniform stores in his last struggling breaths? Seth ground his teeth. Ayers knew as well as Seth did how much the business meant to his father and how he'd feel if—"I'm not selling," he heard himself say. "No deal."

"What? But your brother and—"

"I'll work it out with them. Tell the buyer I'm out. And now I have to go. If you need anything signed, I'll be back in Sacramento in a few days."

Seth disconnected, closed his eyes for a moment against a brewing headache. He thought of what Kasie said about her father's "end of watch" date. If Seth was going to run three stores, there was no way he could act as California Crisis Care director. Or function as fire and police liaison, "chaplain to the chaplains," oversee training . . . or volunteer for much in the way of callouts. He'd be moving on much the same way that Taylor was. Even if it had tasted like a surprise when he'd blurted, "No deal" to the attorney, Seth had known it all along; he'd been fooling himself that coming to San Diego was a respite, time to think and consider. There wasn't any other answer. He wasn't going to disappoint his father again.

He looked at the assembled trainees in the distance, hearing the eagerness in their voices that spoke of their commitment to this new journey. He thought of Kasie's words, *"Nothing has felt more important."* The young rookie had mirrored his own feelings exactly. And right now, nothing felt more important than doing all he could to prepare these new volunteers for what awaited them. If this was to be Seth's "end of watch," he couldn't think of a better way to meet it.

26

"THERE," TAYLOR TOLD THE STILL-ANXIOUS CHILD, "that's better, Mandy. Keep your lips around the mouthpiece like it's a juice box straw. You don't have to suck on it, though; just breathe normally and the mist will still come in." Taylor stroked the girl's dark curls. She let her gaze sweep over the long pink scar on her cheek, the wound she'd sustained from the tent collapse on the boardwalk. The stitches had been taken out, another step toward healing. "You're doing great, sweetie."

"She is," the child's mother agreed, visibly relaxing as her daughter closed her eyes and leaned back against the pillows. "I can't tell you how much I appreciate your help today," she continued, lowering her voice. "She's getting better. But we've had challenges since the accident. These asthma flares and some bad dreams. Kites turning into planes and . . . We're very grateful for all the help. Our church family has been wonderful."

"I'm glad to hear that."

"And there's Dr. Halston," the mother added. "I can't say enough good things about him. He was so gentle with Mandy, from that first day. Patient and kind. I still can't believe he took her case pro bono. And it's not only that . . ." She glanced at her daughter, dozing now with the treatment mouthpiece still between her lips. "He has a small aquarium in his office waiting room, and I guess some of the guppies had babies—dozens of teeny fish darting around the plants and rocks. Mandy was completely fascinated. One of the office girls asked if she would please help name one of them. Mandy chose 'Lego' and said that she's saving her money to go to Legoland." She sighed. "I've wanted to take her, but I'm a single mom and things are always tight. It was at the top of my someday list."

Lists. Taylor understood that, for sure.

"Anyway, I think the office clerk must have told Dr. Halston what Mandy said, because—" the woman's face lit with a smile—"on our last visit, he surprised Mandy with tickets to Legoland. Tickets for both of us. Can you believe it?"

"I . . . That's wonderful," Taylor managed, deeply touched. Her lingering discomfort regarding Rob's fish-related divorce issue drowned in a flood of new respect—and an enjoyable eddy of warmth. "Dr. Halston is a good guy."

"He's not hard on the eyes, either," the mother added quickly, a dimple joining her smile.

Taylor laughed, deciding it was best to leave it at that.

"The crisis volunteers were a godsend," the mother said, her expression sobering again. "Especially Mr. Donovan."

Taylor nodded. Seth had headed up an intervention for children affected by the kite festival incident. Offering tips for coping with related stress and information regarding community resources. *A godsend.* Taylor would agree absolutely; it wasn't the first time she'd wondered if Seth's unexpected arrival at times of need was more than coincidence. But she wasn't going to believe he'd been sent on a divine mission to bring her back to the crisis team. Tonight she'd help with the training scenarios, and that would mark the end of her commitment. Mandy was healing, and so was Taylor.

"You don't sound all that sure to me." Walt wrestled the sodden piece of driftwood from his black Lab's mouth, hurled it toward the sunlit surf again. Lucy yipped and bolted forward to try to keep up with her new friend. He turned to Seth, the sea breeze lifting a shock of gray from his thinning hairline. "About running the uniform stores full-time."

"I'm sure." Seth squinted, watching as their dogs raced across the sand toward their goal. "It's the right thing."

"Because you think it's what your father wanted."

"It's what I *know* he wanted—expected from me. With his dying breath." Seth swallowed.

"He said it?"

Seth shoved his hands in his pockets, tired of his cop friend's well-intentioned interrogation. "He didn't have to say it, Walt. You've got kids; you think they don't know what you expect of them?"

"Right." Walt gave a short laugh. "It doesn't mean it happens that way. If I need odds-on certainty of obedient follow-through—" he tugged the piece of wood from his wiggly-eager dog again—"I'd do better to pitch this stick. Into the waves, up the seawall, or down the beach as far as I can throw it without blowing out another shoulder joint. Sadie's going to go for it. Eyes on nothing else. I can count on that; it's about as much control as I have over anything." He shook his head, then met Seth's gaze again. "I can expect things from my kids, give them my best advice, but what I *want* for them is to throw themselves into what makes them happy and satisfied. Like what I see in you. As a chaplain."

Seth drew in a breath, deciding he'd said enough. Walt didn't know about his washout from a law enforcement career. He'd already racked up a big one in the paternal disappointment tally.

Sadie barked and Walt hurled the stick again. "I'm only saying that if one of my kids was as passionate about something as you are about crisis work—"

"I get what you're saying," Seth interrupted, hoping he hadn't really heard that edge in his voice. Walt didn't deserve it. "Even if I'm turning down the directorship, I'll still stay involved with the crisis team. Time permitting."

"'Involved'? That's like me holding on to Sadie's collar and telling her to watch me throw that stick."

Seth pinned him with a look. "You done, Master Yoda?"

"Mostly." Walt's half smile didn't erase the concerned look in his eyes. "Except for Cindy's plug."

"Your wife?"

"Yeah." Walt nodded. "She said to tell you she liked Taylor Cabot and that you shouldn't run back to the valley and leave her behind."

Seth's chest constricted. "Taylor's great. But I don't think she'd be on board with Cindy's expectations." He managed a wry smile. "I'd be better off chasing a stick there, too."

"It's a fitness program," Taylor explained, not proud of an urge to leave her lunch and bolt from the cafeteria. Ruthie Marks's cocker spaniel eyes were already making her uncomfortable. Ridiculous, since the volunteer hadn't said one thing about her grief support work. Maybe she'd stopped drawing a bead on Taylor. "I wear this bracelet and it tracks every step I take, then communicates with my phone app. I log the calorie count of meals . . ." Taylor watched as Ruthie bit into her donut. "Anyway. I find it helpful. I guess I like the feeling of accomplishment."

"I understand that." Ruthie's smile revealed a crimson dab of jelly on her front tooth. "Sewing and needlework are like that for me." She slid a length of fabric from the huge tote she'd set on the table. "Comforting, too."

"That's pretty," Taylor told her, noting all the mismatched patchwork squares: plaids, stripes, tropical prints. She was relieved by the benign conversation. She'd get out unscathed this time. "A quilt?"

"A memory quilt."

Taylor's stomach sank.

"I'm helping a friend with it," Ruthie explained, touching a finger to a flowered square. "This is from the shirt she bought her husband on their Hawaiian cruise. And that's from his Otis Elevator uniform. The plaid is a hunting flannel—she thinks she can still smell his cigar on it. This was his high school football jersey. . . . That's the dress shirt from their daughter's wedding and . . ."

"Nice." Taylor battled a wave of queasiness. *Don't ask me—*

"I could help you with one, if you like," Ruthie offered. "I usually embroider special dates on some of the—"

"No," Taylor said, cutting her off again. "I mean, that's good of you to offer, Ruthie. But . . ." Must she explain that she'd given away Greg's clothes? And that the one last remnant of memorable fabric was a faded and fur-littered camouflage cover on his dog's bed? This woman would never understand that the only "special date" Taylor cared about now was the date she completed her Survival List. The very last thing she wanted was to wrap herself, literally, in a painful patchwork of memories.

"Hello." Rob stopped at the table, giving a warm smile to Ruthie as well. Taylor could have kissed him.

"I should go," the volunteer said after returning Rob's smile.

"I don't mean to chase you off," he told her, sincerity etched on his handsome face.

"You're not," the woman assured him, pushing decades of memories back into her tote bag. "I still have to unload the library cart." She nodded at Taylor. "Thank you for the company, dear. I hope the rest of your day goes well."

"I think it will."

After a round of polite replies, Rob settled onto the chair opposite Taylor. His blue eyes warmed with obvious pleasure and surprise as she reached across the table and took hold of his hand. "I'm liking this already. What did I do right?"

"It's just good to see you," Taylor told him, meaning every word. "And a little bird told me you did something lovely for our girl from the kite festival incident. Legoland tickets?"

"Not so big a deal," he said, modesty in his offhand tone. His fingers were warm against Taylor's.

"A very big deal to a very little girl." She met his gaze, grateful once again that she'd heard the story. And that he'd saved her from Ruthie. "You have a good heart, Dr. Halston."

He smiled, tracing his thumb over the back of her hand. "Which could segue nicely into the reason I came over here. I don't want to wait until the charity gala for our first official date. Will you let me take you out to dinner?"

"I . . ." Taylor wasn't surprised by a small flutter in her stomach. She was slipping into a new life, not wrapping herself in a lonely cloak of memories. The fabric of her life was crisp and new. "I'd love that."

27

SETH CONVENED THE CLASS, introduced Taylor, and then took a seat with two other trainers at the front of the room. He shuffled some papers but stayed stone silent. His teaching team did exactly the same, despite the confused and inquisitive stares from fourteen pairs of students' eyes.

Silence.

The moments ticked on. Seth glanced at Taylor, then down at his papers again. He heard a few people in the audience clear their throats, shift on their folding chairs. Someone's stomach rumbled in the front row. Someone else whispered to the person next to him.

Finally one of the students raised a pencil and expressed concern. "Excuse me, Mr. Donovan; is everything okay?"

Seth nodded in the affirmative and looked back down at his papers.

After another few moments, the same student spoke up again. "Um, excuse me, sir, but . . . you said we were going to start class, and you're not doing anything."

Taylor shot Seth a knowing smile.

"And how hard was that for you?" Seth asked, hearing relieved murmurs among the group that he'd broken the silence at last. There were a few "aha" expressions. Light was dawning or at least peeking through the window shades. "How uncomfortable was it to sit there, even for a few minutes, and not fill that silence with something . . . anything?"

"Ah . . ." The student, one of the class's most eager hand wavers, nodded. A humble grin began to spread. "Would *excruciating* give you a clue?"

Seth laughed. "I hear you, friend. You're looking at a Grammy contender in finger drumming. The fact is, most of us feel a strong need to fill awkward silence. Which points right back to what we've said before: crisis volunteers serve in a ministry of presence. Meaning that the care and concern conveyed by our very presence benefits survivors. Speech is optional. The overwhelming majority of a responder's time should be spent *listening*." He smiled. "And we're in good company with that. A quote often attributed to Saint Francis of Assisi says, 'Spread the good news. If necessary, use words.'"

The class chuckled. Seth stole a glance at Taylor, and her lovely and encouraging smile smacked at his heart. It felt so very right to be here, doing this . . . *with you*.

"We call it 'sacred silence,'" Seth continued, "and it's an extension of what we've already learned in our skillful listening module. Bottom line, if you can't improve on silence, then don't try. Because if you are talking, the survivors *aren't*." He reached toward the table and tapped the PowerPoint slide on his laptop. "Let's go over the key concepts of sacred silence. After our break, we'll use these in our role play of death notifications."

———

Taylor told herself she was fine with this. She'd signed on to help with role-playing, not sure what exactly she'd be asked to do. There was no reason to make it personal; she'd do what she could for these students and get through it the way she had everything else.

"You're okay with this?" Seth asked.

"Of course." Taylor hoped her voice hadn't sounded as chirpy-thin to him as it had to her. "I'm glad to do whatever I can to help . . . with this training." *Only this. And for the last time.*

Seth's expression said he'd read between the lines. "We're ahead of schedule. Death notification was supposed to be the next class."

"Doesn't matter." Great, she was morphing from chirpy to angry bird—she was letting Seth's concern get to her. *Because I don't need you to watch over me anymore.*

"Then let's do it," he said as the students began filing into the classroom again.

Taylor settled onto the chair next to Seth, admiring his ability to connect with the students. It wasn't really that long ago that she'd been sitting in his classroom. And now . . . *I'm walking away.*

"Among the unique aspects of death notifications," he began, "is that in this one instance, it is the crisis responder's actions that are the proximate cause of a survivor's trauma. *We are their trauma.*"

There were murmurs among the students, and someone whispered, "Ouch."

"Exactly." Seth nodded. "We are walking into an ordinary day, bearing news no one wants to hear. It will forever change lives." He let his words sink in, then continued. "So we need to do that with heart and skill. And then give them tools to help themselves. Which includes a copy of the Survivor's Emotional Bill of Rights. Taylor's going to share that with us."

"I . . . Yes," Taylor said, moving to start the PowerPoint. She was grateful she wasn't holding a sheaf of papers; her mouth had gone dry and her fingers were trembling. It made no sense since she'd taught dozens of paramedic and community CPR classes. "I believe you all have a handout, too."

She saw nods in the affirmative.

"Good." Taylor sucked in a breath and reminded herself this wasn't personal. "One of the volunteer's key tasks is to teach survivors how to care for themselves in the weeks and months ahead. Often, in addition to the trauma itself, survivors suffer from unrealistic expectations imposed upon them by themselves and by other people." She glanced toward the list projected on the screen. "Crisis responders can help by providing a copy of the survivor's bill of rights just before leaving the scene. Survivors might not actually turn to resources until days or weeks after the trauma, but at least it will be there when they are ready."

Did I ever read it . . . after Greg?

"I think," Seth offered, glancing Taylor's way, "it might be a good idea to go around the room, having folks read these out loud as written. Then maybe we'll have some of you take a stab at paraphrasing the bill of rights in your own words. Good idea, Taylor?" he asked, his voice gentle.

"Sounds . . . great." *I'm okay. Back off.* Taylor reached for her water bottle.

"'Grieve in your own way without comparing yourself to others,'" a balding man in the first row began, reading the first numeral.

"'Be very gentle and don't criticize yourself,'" a woman followed.

"'Permit yourself to think and feel what comes naturally.'"

Taylor took a slow breath, counted to seven.

"'Confusion, numbness, guilt, anger are normal,'" someone else read.

"'Expect frequent and repetitive attacks of grief and waves of sentimentality,'" a young woman continued.

"'Cherish your memories.'"

Taylor closed her eyes, trying to blot out the image of Ruthie's sad quilt.

"'Lean on others without feeling guilty, shameful, or weak.'"

No. Taylor was finished leaning. *Done.*

"'Seek out friends to keep you talking, rather than keeping it bottled in,'" another person added as the students continued to take turns around the room.

"'Embrace and express your spirituality, even if you feel angry with God.'"

Like Ava . . . poor Ava. An awful way to feel . . .

"'Use rituals to acknowledge your loss, express your grief, and connect with others who have suffered.'"

The Oreos and wine-in-a-Solo-cup groups?

"'Search for ways to bring good out of tragedy, even if this search goes on the rest of your life,'" a man's voice boomed from the rear of the room.

The rest of my life?

Taylor stiffened. Who wrote this document? She was sure now that she'd never read it—probably left it on the floor beside the trauma gurney where Greg's body lay. And she must've skimmed over it during her crisis training or blotted it out for good reason. She'd never really read it, studied it, though she'd dutifully passed it along at death notifications and in the aftermath of homicides and suicides.

"Taylor?"

She blinked, realized Seth had called her name. Her mouth was cotton dry and her pulse ticked in her ears. "I'm sorry. Could you repeat that question, please?"

"Sure." Seth's smile was as comforting as the soul-soothing sweet potato fries they'd shared in another lifetime. "We're paraphrasing the Survivor's Emotional Bill of Rights, starting from the bottom. Can you read the first one and give your own take on it?"

"Absolutely," Taylor managed, trying her best to unstick her tongue from the roof of her mouth. She'd promised this much to Seth. A farewell to the crisis team. She'd do it. No problem. "Which . . . ?"

"Number twelve," Seth said gently, glancing toward the list projected on the classroom screen. "Read it aloud and then give us your take?"

"Sure." Taylor smiled, read the survivor's right aloud. "Number twelve: 'Don't get stuck in one emotional place. Although your old life passed away with your loved one, that does not mean your new life cannot eventually become as healthy, joyful, and fulfilling.'"

Her throat closed; she wasn't sure she could breathe.

Seth's brow furrowed. The room was quiet.

Lord . . . I know you're with me on this. . . .

"Yes," Taylor rasped. She took a deeper breath and lifted her chin. Crying wasn't an option. She'd do this and be proud. "I think this one is the best of the list. Important beyond everything else. It means go on and survive, no matter what. Take control of your life—step by step. Count on yourself. It's up to you." She cleared her throat, closing her eyes for a moment. Then she stretched up tall. "I lost my husband in an accident, three years ago this week. My life is moving on. . . . I've survived. I'm proof of survival."

Oh, Lord . . .

Taylor wasn't sure if she heard applause or if it was simply her heart banging that merciless drum in her ears; she stepped away from Seth's touch, focusing only on the door out of the room. She hoped she was imagining the tears streaming down her cheeks. But it no longer mattered. She had to get out of here. She'd come back in a few minutes, finish her commitment to the crisis team. Then check it off her list and be done with it.

"I'll be back in a few, but I need to—"

"Go," Seth whispered.

Taylor nodded at the trainees and left the room.

28

TAYLOR HAD SPLASHED WATER ON HER FACE, Seth would bet. Her hair was wet where it framed her forehead, and there was a small, sooty smudge below the lashes of one eye. She was probably furious at herself for crying—maybe almost as angry as he was at himself for putting her in this situation. It had taken all his strength to resist pulling her into his arms when tears shone in her eyes and her voice began to quaver. *My life is moving on. . . ."* But if he suggested she bow out, he'd never hear the end of it. And now she was back, pretty chin lifted, and—

"Okay, now we'll switch the roles we'll be playing: survivors and crisis responders. Our next death notification scenario goes like this," Taylor said to her small group of trainees; they had split the class into three groups, and Seth was overseeing them all. He watched as she traced her finger down the high-lighted paragraphs in the California Crisis Care trainer's man-ual and began to read aloud.

"'Two crisis volunteers are sent to the home of Marjorie Jones, where she's preparing food for a large family gathering later that evening. The responders are there to notify Marjorie that her husband, John, has been killed while taking his new all-terrain vehicle out on a steep, curvy road . . .'" Taylor swal-lowed. "'In a remote area.'"

Seth flinched. Too much like Greg Cabot's accident.

"I'll be playing the part of . . . the surviving spouse," Taylor continued, a small halt in her voice. "Alec, you will be one of the responders and . . ."

"I'll be the other," Seth volunteered.

Taylor nodded, dredging up a smile that belied the new pallor in her cheeks. "Thanks, Seth."

She turned to their students. "You have your exhibit sheet 'Delivering the Notification.' We've already gone over how to make an initial introduction and the importance in moving the survivor to a room with a comfortable chair or sofa." She looked at the trainee. "Go ahead, Alec. I'm sitting and ready to listen."

The young trainee took a slow breath; Seth would bet he'd counted to seven. He felt a familiar rush of pride for these selfless volunteers.

"As I said at the door, Mrs. Jones, we're here at the request of the San Diego Police Department. Because . . ." Alec glanced down at his hands. "I'm sorry to have to tell you that your husband, John Jones, has been in a serious accident on his ATV. And is . . . gone."

"Gone?" Taylor leaned forward, clasping her hands. "Where—what do you mean?"

Alec grimaced, glanced at Seth.

"Mrs. Jones." Seth leaned forward in his chair, looking directly into Taylor's eyes. "Your husband was killed in that accident. He died."

"But . . ." Taylor pressed a hand to her chest. He wished to heaven that she were simply a good actress. "I can't believe this. I . . . don't know what to do."

Seth left his seat and knelt before Taylor's chair. "We're here to help you, Marjorie. We'll do everything we can to get you through this."

Taylor stared at him for an endless moment. He was relieved when she finally broke their gaze. And grateful, once again, that he hadn't been the one to tell her she'd become a widow on that night three years ago.

"Alec," Taylor said gently, turning to the student. "Do you understand your mistake?"

"I said *gone*," he acknowledged with a sigh. "I know better. Not *gone* or *passed away* . . ."

"Died. Killed. Dead," Taylor confirmed, closing her eyes for a split second. "You have to tell this wife that her husband's dead. Leave no room for doubt or—" Seth caught her barest wince—"hope. You can't let this woman latch on to the idea that her husband is still alive. Or that it's some kind of cruel mix-up, and . . . he's going to walk through our door at any minute."

"Our door."

"We do this with all the kindness we can muster," Seth added, taking his seat again. "We look the survivor directly in the eye, use the deceased's full name. Speak simply and directly. No euphemisms. And no matter how natural it feels, we don't say, 'I'm sorry' during that initial notification.'"

Alec nodded. "Because an emotional survivor might infer that the responder has some sort of responsibility for the death." He touched a fingertip to his worksheet.

"It's okay to convey sympathy later," Seth added, "but your initial duty is to deliver the notice of death as clearly and kindly as possible. As hard as it is, for the survivor and the responder, this process really is the first step on the journey toward acceptance and hope."

"For me . . ." Taylor's voice was soft and her eyes had a faraway look. "It was the hospital chaplain. I got word my husband had been hurt. I went to the ER expecting that it was bad. They escorted me to the quiet room. The doctor came in and the nurse was carrying a box of Kleenex." She shook her head, a sad quirk to her lips. "As a nurse, I'd done that a hundred times. I'm sure I heard what they were saying, but it wasn't until I saw Greg on that trauma gurney and the chaplain said, 'I'm so sorry your husband died' . . . It wasn't real until then. My body went numb. She put her arm around me . . . I'll never forget the sound of her voice."

———

"That's it?" Taylor asked, glancing back at the emptying classroom. "We're done?"

"Done," Seth confirmed, leaning a shoulder against the doorway. "Good class, great role-playing." His eyes met hers, that look that always speared Taylor's heart. It left her no room for false bravado—or deliberate fudging. "Thank you for doing this. I know it wasn't easy."

"Not so bad," Taylor managed. "I did want to help. This one last time."

"I guess I should be grateful you don't have that disclaimer printed on a banner: 'One last time, for the gimpy chaplain . . . for old time's sake.'" Seth's crooked smile only underscored a note of sadness in his dark eyes. "I don't want to lose you, Taylor."

Her heart cramped. "Don't put it that way."

"But it's true." Seth leaned forward very slightly, warming the space between them. It made Taylor remember the scent of his leather jacket and that much-needed motorcycle escape. He shook his head. "My flaw—bald honesty. The crisis team is what brought us together, and now that's done."

"You're the heart of this team, Seth. All I've been is a tiny part. It sort of . . . filled a hole in my life when I needed it most. I'm grateful for that." Taylor blinked against the threat of tears. "The team is growing. It's far from 'done.' And neither are you. I heard you've been offered the directorship."

"Uh . . . right." Something flickered across Seth's face that she couldn't read.

"What is it?" Taylor asked. "Is something wrong?"

"No." Seth's big shoulders rose in a halfhearted shrug. "Not wrong, I guess." He glanced toward the empty classroom for a moment. "Look, I leave in a few days. I still have a couple of meetings I need to attend. One later this evening. But I want to talk with you about some things, Taylor. Let me take you out to dinner again. Not chaplain-to-chaplain. Just you and me . . . us. You're off tomorrow evening, right?"

"I am but . . ." Taylor felt a pang of regret. She reminded herself of what she'd told that class not two hours ago. *"My life is moving on."*

"But?"

"Rob asked me out."

Seth shifted in the doorway. "You've been seeing him a lot lately."

"Yes." Taylor smiled, the woozy new warmth there again. "I have."

Moving on . . . old wounds done. New life, clean slate.

———

Dirty Girl.

Sloane lowered the soapy rag and read the words on her car's back window again. Her stomach shuddered. It could have been there for days; she wasn't known for her housekeeping, let alone her ability to keep a squeaky-clean car. There were probably six-year-old french fries under her front seat. The security guard at San Diego Hope, Duncan, had called her attention to the vandalism after her shift today, familiar kindness in his age-lined eyes offering her undeserved absolution. *"Hellion kids, Ms. Wilder. Don't take it personal, but thought you should know."*

"Dunk" had offered to wash it for her, wipe it away and make it right. He'd always treated Sloane that way, like he'd never imagine her in a short skirt, thigh-high boots, and too much eyeliner. Or hadn't seen her arrive twenty minutes late and hiding behind sunglasses to ease a hangover. He looked at Sloane like she was a lady, an angel of mercy—so much the way she'd always imagined her father would have. If she'd ever known him. It could have changed so many things. . . .

Sloane frowned, refusing to go down that pointless path again. The landlord had given her fifteen minutes to park behind the complex and said he'd send her a bill if she wasted enough water to make puddles. She'd get the Jetta clean and then run an ad on craigslist, try to find something else she could afford. Thanks to Paul, her credit rating was abysmal, so the interest rate on any car loan would stink. But if Sloane was forced to start over yet again, it had better begin by getting rid of this car. The apartment, the car—it was a toss-up as far as her safety went. The message on the window had shaken her. Sloane couldn't risk believing Duncan's reassurance about "kids." Not after those calls.

"Funny girl . . . you're still driving that heap-of-trash Jetta."

Between that and the message at work from her "brother," she had to accept the idea that there could be somebody who'd actually followed her from Sacramento. Or at least had connections to local muscle. She needed to do whatever was necessary to keep herself safe. To save her sorry life, for whatever that was worth.

Sloane slapped the sponge against the Jetta's window and scrubbed.

———

Taylor jerked awake, confused for a moment in darkness softened only by the seven-watt night-light she'd installed in a wall plug for—"Hooper?" She pushed the covers aside, her pulse ratcheting upward as she heard his doleful whine. "What's wrong?"

She switched on her bedside lamp and saw that he'd left his bed to lie in front of the bedroom's French doors. Stretched out, scarecrow thin, and nose fogging the glass. "Hooper? Whatcha doing over there, boy?"

The old dog turned his head toward her voice and the light from the lamp reflected off one of the cataracts in his eyes. White slice of waning moon. He turned to the glass door, watching for a moment, then lowered his head to the floor with a deep sigh.

Hooper dutifully followed Taylor to the front door, but

when he showed no interest in going outside, Taylor walked him back to the bedroom, shortening her barefoot steps to match his; he was so painfully slow. She helped him resettle on the lumpy pillow bed, then sat cross-legged on the white carpet beside him. There was a soft rattle in his breathing now and too much hair left on the bed's cover. An ache crowded Taylor's chest. How many years had he slept on this bed? The pillow cover was getting frayed and thin; there were some tears in it. Holes.

Taylor thought of what she'd said to Seth earlier, that the crisis team had *"filled a hole in my life when I needed it most."*

She watched as Hooper laid his head down at last to sleep. Then gently smoothed the worn material beneath his graying muzzle, making extra room for his breathing. Old dog, old bed . . . Tears stung Taylor's eyes at the truth: this was part of the fabric of her life, and there were still holes.

She stroked his head and bent low to kiss him. "Good night, Hooper."

29

SETH PUSHED FORWARD, squinting against the morning sun as he increased his stride over the wet sand. If his knee complained, too bad. The scars and arthritis pain, this blasted limp he'd lived with for nearly two decades were reminders of his past mistakes, and if he didn't run fast and hard right now, he'd make a new one by showing up on Taylor's doorstep. The thought of it had kept him awake for hours, imagining scenarios too much like what they'd done in the classroom yesterday. He'd show up at her door, guide her to a safe place to sit, and . . . what? Deliver some sort of love notification? Knowing that she was dating Rob Halston? After seeing the smile the man put on her face?

Seth's gut lurched, short-circuiting his forward momentum like a stun gun. He staggered a few steps and then stopped, sea foam lapping at his running shoes. He glared at the ocean, bit off a curse. He was glad he'd been smart enough to leave Lucy at Walt's place; she didn't deserve his mood today. The truth was, Seth had entertained a far more sinister scenario in those sleepless hours last night. Several ugly twists that involved showing up at the surgeon's house instead. Grabbing hold of his Italian silk tie, hoisting him off the ground, and telling him *exactly* what he thought of the man's plan to turn Taylor into a gorgeous figurehead for his glory-seeking, tax-deductible philanthropy and—

No. Seth snatched a handful of his T-shirt, mopped at the sweat burning his eyes. He took a slow breath, counting to seven the way he'd taught so many rookie crisis volunteers. He couldn't let these feelings turn into anything close to combat. He'd come too far to let his temper send him back two decades. And he'd made a promise to God. Releasing the breath, he closed his eyes for a moment. God had this; he had to trust in that even if he couldn't see how it was working right now. Even if so much of it was so hard to accept . . .

In three days he'd be back in Sacramento, doing what was necessary to take the reins of his father's business. Taylor would disappear from the roster of California Crisis Care and, essentially, from Seth's life. She'd wear that new dress to an event honoring Dr. Halston's many charitable contributions. She'd smile that smile . . . for him. At some point, Seth would probably see them smiling together on a family Christmas e-card. He glared at the ocean again, thought about changing his e-mail address. But when it came down to it—when the pluses and minuses were all tallied—Dr. Halston was what every woman considered "a catch." And Seth . . . he was a man who'd made mistakes and done jail time, someone who'd found his faith and his heart's passion in the process . . . which led him to becoming Taylor's friend. An honor he didn't regret. But realistically Seth was very likely a reminder of things she'd rather forget. In Taylor's mind—her heart too, maybe—he and the crisis team were inexorably linked. Part of her past, with no place in her future.

"I'm moving on with my life."

Seth took one last swipe at his face, then started to jog again; he set his jaw and picked up speed. God had a plan. He trusted that to the bottom of his soul. But he still had some time here—maybe they could work something out, together.

———

"I'm surprised that you got the time away from work. To come here and see me." Kasie met Daniel's eyes across the hospital cafeteria table. She hoped she imagined what she saw there but—

"I wanted to be sure that you'd be there tonight. I had to practically beg the counselor to reschedule us so late in the evening. She has a family. She makes that a priority."

And I don't? Daniel's words jabbed like a hemostat into an abscess. "I appreciate that, Daniel. I appreciate that you found her for us . . . that you care enough to do this." *Even if it feels like condemnation. And you don't even try to understand me.*

"I was hoping we could make it more like a date," he told her, something vulnerable in his tone that made Kasie remember the days when she first came to love him. When she believed she'd found her soul mate. She prayed it was still true. Daniel frowned. "But then you agreed to help at the Deep Blue Grill tonight after work."

"Because it's family," Kasie told him, not proud of the

defensiveness in her tone. "*Our* family . . . soon. They're really booked tonight, and they can't afford to hire extra help."

"I understand that. I love you for it, Kasie." Daniel reached across the table, grasping her hand. "You are generous. To a fault sometimes. I'm trying to accept that. But tonight this appointment has to be a priority. I need to see that from you. Our relationship can't be second to some community crisis or—"

"It won't. I hear you, Daniel. I'm not on call for the team." Tears stung Kasie's eyes. Why, dear God, *why* did she have to choose between the man she loved and what spoke to both her heart and her soul? Was he asking that now? "I'll help my family tonight, but I'll be there for our counseling appointment afterward. I promise."

He patted her hand. "I'll drive you to the restaurant and pick you up when you're finished."

"Thank you," Kasie told him, pushing down the uncomfortable feeling that Daniel's offer was less considerate and more . . . controlling. She squeezed his hand. "I appreciate that."

"This is an important night for us," Daniel reiterated, returning her grasp so firmly that the stone in her engagement ring bit into her skin. "I think it could change everything."

———

"Browsing," Sloane explained to the volunteer on duty, realizing it sounded far more T.J.Maxx than animal shelter. But she didn't want anyone bugging her about adopting. She'd called ahead to be sure that the girl she'd talked with before wasn't working today, and probably wouldn't have come at all if anybody had been able to identify Marty. Or assure her that he'd found a home. But no luck. Apparently they'd had a slew of new kittens come in and . . . *Oh, there you are, little pal.* Her heart did a squeeze it had never bothered with for a man . . . or maybe only one man.

"Here," Sloane whispered, glancing up and down the aisle as she pulled a small sandwich bag from her jacket pocket. "I cut it up really small. Chicken—organic, free range. No GMOs." She smiled as the little black fuzz ball wobbled toward the cage bars, sniffing the air and mewing. "The guy at Safeway looked at me like I was nuts. He's never seen me go through the line with anything healthier than cheese puffs. But you . . ." Sloane's throat tightened as the kitten's shiny gray eyes met hers. "You deserve only the very best."

She pinched a piece of meat between her fingers, offering it before his bigger cage mates could push him away. "Not too fast now. I wouldn't want to try a kitty Heimlich maneuver." She watched him eat, rerunning the idea that had come to her while she was washing the Jetta. If she asked the hospital security guard to keep the kitten until she found a new apartment, maybe—

Sloane's cell phone buzzed in her pocket. "Hang on, Marty."

She squinted at the phone number, not sure if it was one of the car dealerships. She'd left messages with several places about trading in the Jetta. And she'd blocked the number from the creep but . . .

"Yes?" Sloane waited, straining to hear a response over the shelter's blend of meows, grunts, and yapping. "Anybody there? . . . Fine, you had your chance, buddy. If you think any sicko heavy-breather calls are going to scare—"

"Wait, don't hang up, babe. It's Paul."

30

"How's San Diego?" Paul inquired casually, as if it hadn't been eight months since they'd spoken. And as if he'd never—

"Beautiful, amazing," Sloane spat, stomping out the doors of the animal shelter. She walked a few more yards, nerves jangling, then leaned against the cement block wall, close enough to smell bins full of excrement and—her stomach churned—something that smelled like burning fur. "It's God's paradise," she continued, bitterness sharpening her voice. "I'm hanging out at the beach and getting a fantastic tan." She gripped the phone hard enough to make its case pop loose. "That is, when I'm not working double shifts to keep creditors off my back and food in my stomach."

"Like I always said, you were smart to go into health care. Nurses can work anywhere."

Sloane's teeth ground together. What he'd always said, joked to their friends, was *"A nurse with a purse. A man can't go wrong there."* How could she have been such a fool?

"Write your own ticket, for sure," Paul continued over what sounded suspiciously like the bells, clinks, and snatches of jackpot jingles from slot machines. "I always said my girl was as smart as she was gorgeous."

"Why are you calling?"

"To see how you are, babe. It's been a while. Don't you want to know how I'm—?"

"What do you want?"

"I was thinking. About that ring I bought . . ."

"*I* bought." The pathetic truth made Sloane sick. She'd bought herself an engagement ring.

"I was paying on that bill too, right? A nice pile of cash, the way I remember it. So I thought maybe if you sold that ring, we could—"

"I can't believe this! You put me in debt, ruin my credit rating, *wreck* my life. Then disappear to who knows where. And you have the nerve to try to tap me for money?"

"Wreck your life?" His laugh was caustic. "You're the last one who should accuse someone of that. Seems like you had the skills there—deadly skills. Maybe I made some mistakes with money, but at least I didn't—"

"Don't." She swallowed against bile.

He clucked his tongue. Satisfied, no doubt, that he'd pried the edge of a scab.

"Don't call me anymore," Sloane managed. "I have nothing to tap. And I don't care what happens to you."

"Now see? That's where we're different," Paul told her, his voice gentling a little. "I do care. I always have. And that's the main reason I called. To tell you this: Be careful, babe. There's some bad guys out there. They know I have a soft spot for you, and I wouldn't put it past them to—"

Sloane punched the phone's Disconnect button. She closed her eyes, inhaling through her nose to try to control her shivers. Tears gathered, but she swiped them away. Paul knew exactly how to hurt her most.

"Maybe I made some mistakes with money, but at least I didn't—"

There was nothing she could do about that now. Nothing would make it right.

At least she knew that the threats were real. She'd sell the Jetta, find a new place to live. Maybe move up to LA . . . Sloane glanced toward the doors of the animal shelter and found a smile. There *was* something she could do right. Save Marty. She'd come back and adopt the kitten tomorrow and talk Dunk into keeping him for a little while.

But right now what she needed most was a stiff drink.

———

"No, I was . . ." Taylor glanced at her mascara brush and eye shadow, feeling a prod of guilt. Then walked away from her bathroom carrying her cell phone. Greg's mother in Sacramento. And Rob was due to arrive in twenty minutes. Which meant ten; he always set his reminder alarms at least ten minutes early. "You didn't interrupt anything, Eileen."

I'm not going to ask how you are—I know the answer. It's March 24.

"I wanted . . . to check on Hooper. The last time we talked, you said he was finishing those treatments."

"That's right." Taylor's guilt doubled. Had it been that long since she called this woman? "All finished with the chemo." She looked toward Hooper's bed. He'd left the room again. So restless, too weak. "He's hanging in there."

"What does the vet say?"

Taylor squeezed her eyes shut against an echo of her mother-in-law's voice the night of Greg's death. That awful moment when Taylor called from the UCD trauma room after seeing Greg's body and told Eileen Cabot her son was dead. *"What did the doctors say? Are you sure you heard it right?"*

"Dr. Wendy said to keep Hooper comfortable as long as I can. And I'm doing that, Eileen. I promise."

"I'm sure, dear. And . . . how are you?"

Taylor breathed slowly through her nose, trying not to think of that new shoe box in her closet. Sparkles . . . "I'm keeping myself comfortable too."

"Good. You are always in our prayers."

"Thank you."

"I was going through some old things and remembering—"

"Oh, dear, Eileen, I see one of the neighbors walking up to the porch," Taylor interrupted. "I should go. I promised I'd . . . help her with something," she added, hating herself.

"Of course. We love you, honey."

"Me too."

She disconnected, the untruths leaving a sad, bitter aftertaste. There was no one at the door—yet. Sparkles, lies. And Hooper was anything but comfortable. Taylor walked down the short hallway, looked in the living room, the kitchen, and . . . *there*. Her heart ached at the now-familiar sound: whimpering, scratching—the old dog's toenails against the door to the garage. She walked through the laundry and found him there. The same way she'd found him at the front door and in the living room with his nose pressed against the window . . . whimpering, whining, watching, pacing. Over and over the past two days, thousands of stiff and painful steps. Unsteady on his feet and fueled by far too few calories, but relentlessly driven. Day and night.

At first she'd thought Hooper needed to go out or that he'd heard something. She'd walked him. Bought and laid down some puppy training pads, just in case. Checked all the bushes for cats and done everything she could to distract, soothe, and reassure him. But the old dog continued to check the doors, watch the windows through those milky eyes, whine, scratch—and late last night, the truth had launched a direct hit to Taylor's heart: Hooper was looking for Greg. It was the exact way he'd behaved in the weeks after the accident. He hadn't done it since, not on any of the other anniversaries. But now—

"Taylor? Are you there? It's Rob."

Knocking, then the doorbell. She'd been deaf to anything but her dog's misery. "I'm here, coming!"

Taylor let Rob inside, grimacing as his shoes skidded on the puppy pad lying on the pale bisque tile flooring. "Oops. Sorry; let me get that."

"No problem." Rob's nose wrinkled. "The dog's losing control?"

"No." Taylor folded the pad and slipped it into the small foyer closet, giving herself a moment to collect herself. *The dog.*" She reminded herself of those tickets to Legoland; this man had a very good heart. "Just being cautious."

"Smart." His eyes skimmed over her with respectful appreciation. He obviously approved of the way she'd dressed for what was essentially their first date. "Especially with all this white carpeting and tile. My mother has an elderly poodle, and she uses these sort of rubber pants with pads."

"Not necessary," Taylor told him, sensing she was a nanosecond from sacrificing her Deep Blue Grill dinner for the sake of defending her dog's dignity. "Hooper isn't having any prob—" Taylor stopped short as Rob took a few steps down the hallway, peering toward the sounds of scratching and whining in the distance.

"What's that?"

"Hooper." Taylor gestured toward the living room. "Have a seat for a minute. I'll go get him settled, and we can leave. No problem."

Except that my poor sweet dog is waiting for my dead husband to come home.

31

"I'M HELPING WITH THE TRAINING SCENARIOS TONIGHT." Evan raised his coffee cup as Seth joined him at the Starbucks table. "Fair warning: I'll be running on pure caffeine."

Seth smiled at the sleepy-eyed new father. "Your z's being shanghaied by a certain seven-pounder?"

"Sleep? What's that? I don't think I remember sleep. But still . . . he's so amazing." Evan's expression could only be described as smitten. "Paige's mom is here for the week, so I said I'd help out with the trainees tonight, then take some call. I'm still on family leave from the day job, so this works out great."

"Lets you stretch your legs a bit."

"Exactly. And lets Mom and Grandma have some time too. Good all round." He met Seth's gaze. "You're on your way back to Sacramento?"

"Not for a couple of days yet. I'm officially finished with my part of the training. I'd planned to go over to Catalina Island but think I'll stay in the city after all. Put myself on backup call—maybe drop in on tonight's class."

"Seriously?" Evan stared at Seth over his coffee cup. "The classroom over Catalina Island?"

Seth managed a shrug. Better than telling the truth: he needed time to see Taylor before he flew out. "You're covering self-care for the crisis responder tonight? Avoiding secondary traumatization?"

"That's right."

Seth nodded. "Important subject."

Compassion fatigue. All first responders were at risk for it; it wasn't possible to work around trauma victims and survivors without feeling the effects of stress. Medical workers, firefighters, and law enforcement officers all dealt with it, whether they admitted it or not. Because the fact was that painful, grisly, and seemingly senseless incidents were daily reminders that tragedy could strike at any of them at any moment. Or any of the people they loved. Crisis volunteers witnessed and participated in the extremes of human experience, much of that involving death. Most considered the work a true calling and felt a deep sense of fulfillment in their interactions with survivors. "A blessing returned a hundredfold," a seventy-year-old retired librarian once told him. But a mixed blessing nevertheless.

Seth thought of one of the training exhibits, "The Rewards of Crisis Care":

No paycheck
Physical hardships
Potential danger
Long, unpredictable hours
Limited resources
Extreme, intense emotions
Sometimes ungrateful and even rude survivors, officers,
    coworkers

Welcome to my ministry. . . .
The potential impact of stress on volunteers—unmanaged secondary traumatization—was nothing to sneeze at either: deteriorating physical health, failing personal relationships . . . and premature termination of involvement in crisis care. Was that Taylor's reason for quitting? Cumulative stress? He'd been watching her so carefully from the beginning, but had he missed something?

"I figure, with this no-sleep look I've got going," Evan mused, "I'll be pretty convincing as a victim of secondary trauma. I get to play the stressed volunteer who's in denial. You know, the guy who has no clue he's a wreck. Flying high, feeling like a hero, indispensable, un . . . breakable."

Seth smiled as Evan covered a yawn. "You're going to need more coffee, Superman."

Evan laughed. "I'm still trying to get past you opting out of Catalina Island to be on call. I wonder what the esteemed chaplain to the chaplains would say about that." A good-natured tease warred with the fatigue in his voice. "Mr. Donovan would probably quote something from the training manual about setting limits. Like . . . 'If your family and friends say you're overcommitted, you probably are.'"

Seth shook his head. Overcommitted? No. This, tonight, wasn't nearly that altruistic. He simply needed a worthy distraction, something to keep his mind off the fact that the woman he loved was out with another guy.

———

"Small world," Kasie said, refilling the heavy, cobalt-blue water glasses. She gave Taylor a warm smile. The nurse, so pretty in street clothes, looked a little flustered. "How is the grilled Costa Rican swordfish?"

"It's . . . wonderful." Taylor glanced down at the barely nibbled fish served in a spendy splash of sherry, California dates, smoked bacon, and herbs. Forty-three dollars' worth— the doctor was out to impress. Daniel would have a stroke. "I didn't realize you'd be here tonight," Taylor told her.

"I come in when it's busy. Sort of on call—like with our crisis team." Kasie saw instantly that her attempted joke fell flat; Dr. Halston looked about as happy as Daniel at the concept. He went back to cutting an oyster into biopsy-size bits, something Kasie had never before witnessed. "Anyway, I'm just helping out the family."

"I'm sure they appreciate it," Taylor said. "I know we're blessed to have you in the ER."

"Absolutely," the doctor agreed, making eye contact with Kasie for the first time—here or in the ER. "And our compliments to the chef, please. Impeccable."

"Thank you. I'll pass it along," Kasie promised before excusing herself.

One of the waitresses caught her as she made her way toward the doors to the kitchen, remarking about the good-looking couple Kasie had conversed with.

"I work with Taylor in the ER. She's a nurse," Kasie explained, "and he's a plastic surgeon."

"Bingo." The waitress, probably Kasie's mother's age, sighed. "Good looks and magic hands. What I wouldn't give . . ." She shook her head. "More than a few of your hospital staff stopping by these days."

"Yes." Kasie glanced toward the bar in a room off the restaurant, concern making her brows pucker. "At least these two are behaving themselves."

Sloane Wilder sure wasn't.

———

Rob glanced at the food remaining on Taylor's plate. "There's probably not a thousand calories in that entire meal. Mostly protein." His lips tugged upward. "You're not cheating."

"I know." Taylor smiled back at him, wishing this awkwardness would go away. Or that Eileen hadn't called when she did. And that her dog wasn't behaving so strangely. "It's not that."

"You're worrying about Hooper."

"Yes," Taylor admitted with a dizzying rush of gratitude. She wasn't sure if it was more because Rob remembered her dog's name or because he'd been so intuitive, but it felt good. "He's been really restless these past few days. Not eating much, wandering from room to room and acting sort of vague. He doesn't see well, but it seems like more than that."

Rob's expression was kind. "Do you think he's having some mental deterioration?"

Taylor's throat tightened. "Dr. Wendy said that was likely."

"Dr. . . . ?"

"Our vet at Bayside Animal Hospital, Wendy Mack. She's

wonderful. The hospital's not even a mile from my house, and they have a clinic for after-hours emergencies. One of the techs lives a few blocks from me and helped get Hooper home the last time I had him there." Taylor sighed. "They've been nothing but kind."

Rob reached across the table, took her hand. "I'm sorry, Taylor. I hate how hard this is on you."

She was beyond grateful he'd said nothing more, hadn't used the word *inevitable* the way he had in the past. Rob really cared. He understood. It made Taylor feel safe enough to give words to what she'd been struggling with. "Dr. Wendy said to let her know if . . . when . . . I'm ready for the next step."

"Are you?"

Oh, God, please . . . "I told myself as long as he was comfortable, ate, and still wagged his tail, I'd wait," Taylor tried to explain. Tears welled. "When Hooper finally settled down last night, he licked my face. And he hasn't had any other seizures—I wouldn't want him to live like that. But I think, maybe . . . he'll be okay until next week. I'll make the decision then." *After the twenty-sixth . . . after that day is past. I couldn't bear it otherwise.*

"There's my girl," Rob said tenderly. A smile crinkled the edges of his eyes. "Until then, we have the nanny cam."

We.

"And maybe . . ." Rob's smile spread, making Taylor's stomach flutter a little. "One of those fresh fruit sorbets . . . with two spoons?"

"Yes," she said with a laugh. And a wonderful new sense that she might be saying that same thing more and more to this good man.

Sloane rattled the ice in her glass, shooting Kasie a sideways glance from the barstool. "Does nobody notice when a woman's drink is empty in this *waaaay*-too-small world? Be a good little tech and—"

"I'm not working in here," Kasie told her, pointing toward the food service side of the Grill. "I'm waitressing. I only came in to see if my brother-in-law needs me much longer. I have an appointment."

Sloane laughed. "I do too. With my friend Jack. And Coke." She raised her glass, laughing again at her cleverness. Then watched as Kasie indulged in that nervous little habit she had of twisting the diamond on her finger. "I guess you didn't buy that yourself."

"Buy what?"

"Your engagement ring."

Kasie's expression—rightly—called Sloane a fool.

Sloane smirked. "And I guess you're going to tell me that my question isn't appro*ooo*priate." She wondered if she sounded as buzzed as she felt. "But hey, we're not at the hospital, kid. And there's a big stretch on 'appropriate' in a bar."

Kasie looked at her watch and then glanced around as if trying to find her relative.

"You're probably smart," Sloane told her, hoping her buzz wasn't heading toward weepiness. She'd started drinking too early—always risky for emotional land mines. "To make him buy that ring. And then hold out until he marries you. Corny maybe, but smart. Because I've done it the other way and—no, wait, I didn't even do that." She stared at Kasie, saw four eyes, two frowns. "I didn't do the wedding dress and the bridesmaids, the gift registry at Macy's, those awkward wedding night nerves . . . or the h*aaappp*ily ever after. Definitely not that. Nope." Sloane smacked her drink glass to her chest, spilling an ice cube into her lap. "Nurse with a purse, that's me." She laughed. "Nurse with a purse and a cat in a sack. Now *there's* your happily ever after. With a shot of Dr. Seuss." She waved the empty glass. "Speaking of shots, where's my—?"

"I think you should slow down with that stuff."

"Oh, honey, you're so wrong. I haven't had nearly enough." Sloane glanced toward the archway leading to the restaurant. Liquid courage—she had to get the dose exactly right. Then she'd go over there, interrupt that cozy little dinner, and drop a bomb on the grieving widow. Maybe it was time for a controlled detonation—safer that way. Maybe she'd waited long enough.

32

KASIE CHECKED HER WATCH. Daniel would arrive at the Grill in forty minutes to pick her up for their eight o'clock appointment with the couples' counselor. He'd already texted three times to remind her. She hadn't told her sister and brother-in-law about the appointment, going along with their good-natured teasing about Daniel being her "chauffeur." He obviously didn't trust Kasie to leave the restaurant in time to get to their appointment.

She glanced toward the bar. Sloane had wandered over to the restaurant ten minutes ago, looking for Taylor. Fortunately she and Dr. Halston had finished their dessert and coffee and left—hand in hand. That Sloane would go out of her way to talk with Taylor made no sense; there was no love lost between those two. Kasie couldn't think of a worse mood killer than having a meal interrupted by a half-snockered coworker . . . except being dragged to a couples' counseling appointment. She glanced at the clock once more, then saw the bartender walking her way.

"Kasie . . . That nurse in the bar is your friend?"

"Sort of. Yeah." Kasie knew where this was going. "Why?"

"Talk her into taking a cab, would you? She's not listening to me. I cut her off a while ago, but I don't have a good feeling about letting her drive herself home."

Great. There was actually something worse than being dragged to counseling. "I'll try."

When Kasie got to the bar, Sloane was gathering her things, weaving a little, and looking about as happy as . . . she looked most of the time. Kasie walked up as she was fishing around in her purse.

"Hey," she started when Sloane set the keys on the bar. "Heading home?"

Sloane raised her brows. "Is this a pickup line? No offense, but you're not even close to my type."

"The bartender thinks you need a cab."

"And I think he's off base. Do I look like I need a cab?" Sloane wobbled a little, her boot heel rolling over. She frowned, her expression like that of a kid caught in a lie.

"I'll pay for it," Kasie offered. "My treat."

"Remind me to do my next overtime shift on a tech's pay scale. Look, I live like eight miles from here. Right up the coast. I could walk it. I'm fine to drive."

"I can't let you." Kasie swiped her keys off the bar.

"You *what*?" Sloane's eyes narrowed in the way that always prompted Kasie to find an excuse to leave the trauma room.

Except they weren't there now. And Sloane needed help, like it or not.

"Fine," she said finally. "I'll call a cab. Just give me my keys."

"I don't trust you. I'll give the keys to the cab driver. He'll return them to you when you get home."

"I need my car. I have to work in the morning. I'll drive slow. It's eight miles. Give me my keys."

Kasie glanced at her watch, her stomach knotting. It would be tight but . . . "I'll drive you home. My fiancé was picking me up here. I'll call and have him go to your place instead." Sloane's eyes were menacing slits. Kasie prayed for strength. "Look, if you take off in your car, I'll have to call the police. I'm not having it on my conscience if you get smashed all over the road."

"If . . ." Sloane closed her eyes. Her face paled.

"Are you going to throw up?"

"No." Sloane hefted her purse over her shoulder, tossing Kasie a withering look. "I'm going to be prisoner in my own car. I hope you know how to drive."

"Count on it."

"The only thing I'll be counting is the miles until you're out of my hair."

Kasie phoned Daniel while Sloane went to the ladies' room, gave him the apartment complex address, and tried to explain the situation. He wasn't happy.

"Why does it always have to be you? You don't even like her."

Kasie shook her head, trying not to judge his heart in that last remark. "She needs some help. I can do that for her."

"You're supposed to be doing something for *me* . . . us."

"It's practically the same distance to pick me up—a few

minutes closer really," she added. "Meet me there, and we'll go on to the appointment. My friend will be safe. It's the right thing to do, Daniel."

There was a prolonged silence, and Kasie thought she'd lost the connection. "Daniel?"

"If you do this and we miss the appointment . . . If you choose this over us and it ends bad . . . I don't know, Kasie. I don't know where we go from there."

Her stomach plunged. *Please, Lord . . .*

"Kasie? Did you hear me?"

"I'll meet you in front of the apartment."

"Make yourself at home," Taylor called out from the kitchen, still smiling. Rob had greeted Hooper by name and even risked hairs on his tailored slacks to give her dog a good petting. He'd made no comment when they found Hooper in the laundry room staring at the front loader as if it were a window. He simply stroked the old dog, offering what comfort he could for his sad litany of whining. Nothing could have endeared Rob to Taylor more. "I'll fix the coffee and bring it to the living room."

"I can help," he offered. "I wanted to try to get Hooper settled on his bed. It, uh . . . looks like his favorite spot."

"It is." Taylor chuckled, imagining the ratty cushion in this fastidious surgeon's hands. He was doing it because he truly cared for her and because what was important to her was also important to him. These were all good signs for sure. *Thank you, Lord.* Her first-date nerves were rapidly disappearing. "I'm fine in here. No worries. Find some music, maybe?"

Taylor added the almond milk creamer to her tray, reached

for the stevia sweetener she'd remembered to buy that afternoon, and caught sight of her cell phone on the counter. There was an alert for a call that had come in earlier; she'd muted the phone during dinner.

She prayed it wasn't her mother-in-law again or her mother. It wouldn't be Seth since he knew she was out with Rob. He was too good of a friend to interrupt. Unless there was some kind of problem . . . Taylor glanced toward the living room, heard Rob switching through music selections, and decided it wouldn't be bad date etiquette to check for messages. As if she even remembered any date etiquette . . .

A voice mail . . . from Sloane?

Taylor listened, confused at the slurred message. She tapped Replay to listen again and try to make out the words.

"It's me . . . Sloane. *Sometiiimes* known as 'Dirty Girl.'" A laugh that sounded more like a groan. "Looks like you had fun tonight . . . Like somebody who's figured out how to forget. Oh, *maaaan*, that's the trick—teach me how, wouldya? 'Cause I'm not doing that so well. But then I guess we've already proved I don't do *anything* as well as you." Another laugh-groan. "You gotta show me how to *cloooose* my eyes and not see it over and over . . ." There was something that sounded like a muffled curse. Maybe even a sob. "Hey, forget I called, okay? You enjoy your evening, Cabot. . . . Hope you get lucky."

Taylor tapped the Disconnect button and stared at the phone, sickened and no less confused. She'd made out the words, but it didn't help her understand the message. Sloane was drunk; that much was obvious. It could have been a misdial, except that Sloane had used Taylor's name at the end. And by the way she'd said, *"Looks like you had fun,"* she'd obviously been at the Deep Blue Grill. Rob had seen Sloane in the bar there before. That much made sense. But the rest of it was no more than gibberish from a very troubled woman. Taylor had no idea what she should or could do about that.

She set her phone down and picked up the spoons and napkins for the coffee, still thinking about the message. Sloane's last jab about hoping Taylor got lucky was meant to be crude. But the truth was, she *was* having a good time. And intended to continue.

Taylor lifted the tray and carried it carefully toward the living room, where she heard strains of classical music. *Rachmaninoff?* She shook her head, chuckling at the irony. Sad movie, happiest day in a long while. Despite anything Sloane Wilder might imply, Taylor was making big strides in the right direction. She'd worked hard to get to this point; luck had nothing to do with it.

33

"YOU DRIVE LIKE AN OLD WOMAN," Sloane complained, almost wishing she'd left that half-empty packet of mustard on the driver's seat when she cleaned the car. She liked the thought of the do-gooder tech with condiment smudges on her holy armor. "I seem to remember that you promised you'd never play savior with me."

"You told me to never come 'peddling hope.'"

"Great. An old woman with a photographic memory." Sloane grimaced against a wave of nausea as Kasie changed lanes on the curving coastal highway. If this kept up, mustard stains would pale in comparison. "Why do you keep doing that?"

"What?" Kasie squinted at the rearview mirror and then at the darkened lanes ahead, two in each direction.

"You're jerking us back and forth like a bumper car ride."

"I'm sorry. That guy behind us is following too close. I'm trying to move out of his way. But every time I move, he moves." She squinted again. "He has his brights on too. It's bothering my eyes."

Sloane turned to look, head swimming with the movement, and saw what Kasie saw. "I'd say tap the brakes and scare him, but I think the idiot would end up in the backseat and—" Sloane's torso pitched forward, hard, against the shoulder belt. "What the . . . ?"

"He hit us," Kasie gasped, incredulous. "I seriously can't believe this. His bumper actually—"

"Move over. Get in the right lane." Sloane twisted to look again. The last thing she needed was to have a road rage nutcase depreciate this car any more. The headlights looked like they were mounted on the Jetta's trunk. "Let him by."

"I *have* been—didn't you hear me?" The tech's voice had gone shrill and shaky.

"Speed up then," Sloane barked, tired of this game. "Get to the next exit and pull—" Her seat belt bit into her again, momentum whipping her forward and then backward as the car was struck a second time. "Floor it, Beckett—forget the stupid turn signal. Move over and hit the gas!"

Kasie merged into the right lane, hunching over the wheel; her gaze darted between the road ahead and the rearview mirror. She pressed the accelerator, closing the space between herself and the commercial truck ahead of them. "He's backed off. Oh, thank you, God. That guy must have serious problems."

"Don't you even think of going all do-gooder fix-it." Sloane pulled her cell phone from her purse. "That maniac's biggest problem is the 911 call I'm about to—"

"Oh no . . . *no*," Kasie wailed, cranking the wheel again. "He's speeding up, trying to squeeze between those two cars and—"

There was a screech of shearing metal, blasting car horns . . . Brake lights, headlights. Sloane watched in horror as a car behind them swerved sharply in defense, crossed the median, and crashed head-on into another vehicle. "Did you see—?"

"He's still coming!" Kasie jerked the wheel right toward the gravel shoulder.

"Don't!" Sloane yelled. "We're too close to the—"

Sloane hurtled sideways against Kasie, then hard the other way, her shoulder and then her head smashing against the passenger window. "Stop . . . *stop!*"

"Oh, please . . . God . . . help."

Sloane grabbed the dashboard, bracing herself as the Jetta fishtailed, tires spinning in gravel with the brakes' futile attempt to halt their careening course. She gritted her teeth, heart roaring in her ears, as Kasie fought for control, praying and then screaming.

"*Noooo!* We're going over!"

There was a surreal instant of weightlessness—like being in the front seat on a Magic Mountain roller coaster—when the Jetta dropped over the edge of the highway, followed immediately by a bone-shaking series of impacts as the car bounced, slid, rolled, and flipped end over end in the darkness. Then finally stopped.

Sloane's screams dissolved to grunts, then a strangling gargle. Tasting blood, she tried desperately, upside down, to move against the seat belt that dangled her like a spider's prey. She sucked in a breath that tasted of gasoline. There was pain. So much pain. "Kasie . . ."

"I'm here. . . . Oh, God, please help me . . . do this." Kasie grunted. "I think I can get out. Go for help."

"I can't move. Pinned." Sloane tried to find the seat belt buckle, but her hands shook uncontrollably. "Glass everywhere. I think it's in my eye. Blood—can't see. My belly . . ."

"Don't move. I've got this, Sloane. It's going to be all—"

Sloane retched, closed her eyes, and succumbed to blackness.

34

"YES," SETH TOLD the elderly couple again, "both your son,
Grayson Pilner, and his passenger, Mark Fielding, were
killed in a highway accident tonight." His heart ached at their
stricken expressions—especially the mother, who had a portable oxygen concentrator tucked beside her on the sofa. Late-
stage emphysema, like Seth's father. "A head-on collision at
freeway speeds. It was necessary for the firefighters to cut
your son and his friend free from the wreckage. The car had
been in flames. There were no signs of life in your son or his
passenger. The paramedics pronounced them both dead at
the scene."

"But . . . our boy was a very careful driver. I taught him
myself." The victim's father, one hand resting on his dog, a
quaking Yorkie who seemed in tune with his humans' suffering,

stared between Seth and his fellow volunteer. Evan tonight. "How could this have happened?"

"We don't know the details, Mr. Pilner," Evan explained. "The highway patrol will investigate. Witnesses reported that a car crossed over the median and struck Grayson's sedan head-on. There were several vehicles involved."

Five vehicles. The two fatalities they'd just sadly voiced, and a total of seven more accident victims with a wide range of injuries. Three had gone to San Diego Hope; Seth was headed there next. One victim had been airlifted to UC San Diego's trauma center with head injuries. He prayed that a hospital chaplain wouldn't be doing a death notification there. "We're here now," he assured these parents, "to do anything we can to help you both. Any way we can."

The little Yorkie whined and burrowed his nose under his master's arm.

"Our pastor is away at a conference this week," the man explained, his eyes shiny with unshed tears.

"This gentleman said he's a chaplain, dear," his wife said, reaching over to grasp her husband's hand. A puff from her oxygen concentrator supported the words. Her eyes met Seth's. "Will you pray with us?"

Seth's throat tightened. "Yes, ma'am."

———

"You'll love the other board members," Rob promised, his eyes lit with obvious passion as he spoke of his commitment to the children's medical care ministry. "You'll recognize a number of them from their TV and film work," he added, something in his smile saying he'd dangled those enticing names many times before. Especially when donor checkbooks were involved. "But it's these children who are the real stars, Taylor. We're doing it for them."

"I love that," Taylor told him honestly. Though she was more than a little nervous that his palm had somehow moved to cradle her cheek. A touch not her husband's—*why am I thinking that?* Her stomach fluttered. "There's no better feeling than to put yourself out there for someone who's desperate for hope."

Rob's thumb stroked Taylor's cheek. "And I love that you get that too. Your intelligence, that beautifully giving heart . . . You'd be a wonderful asset to our team. I can hardly wait to introduce you." His expression was a perfect blend of modesty and well-deserved pride. "The gala will be hectic and filled with too many obligations." Rob lowered his hand, but his gaze still held hers. "But you'll have a chance to meet my family. My sister's excited you'll be sharing her suite. And the next day, aside from some interviews at breakfast, we'll have San Francisco all to ourselves. Just the two of us. No set time to end our day, no airport lines—" he chuckled—"or need to take off our shoes. One of the perks of traveling by private jet. No fuss, no worries."

Except for Hooper. Taylor glanced to where he slept, his graying chin sagging over the edge of the old fleece bed. She'd committed to spending roughly twenty-four hours away. A nanny cam wouldn't help ensure Hooper's safety; things had changed too much. He really shouldn't be left alone. Aimee would be back in a few days. She'd already agreed to check on Hooper, but if she could stay here overnight, it wouldn't be necessary to board him at the vet clinic. . . .

"Sound good?" Rob asked, capturing Taylor's attention again. "Our San Francisco getaway?"

"Yes. Great." She tore her gaze from her dog, smiling as Rob took her hand.

"I'm proud of you, you know."

"Me? Why?" Taylor's skin warmed as Rob inched closer on the couch, the motion seeming to match a flourish of piano in the background music. She'd have giggled if her nerves weren't fraying like too-taut bowstrings. Only Rob Halston could manage such choreographic perfection.

He swept a tendril of hair gently away from Taylor's face. "I'm proud of you for so bravely going on with your life. Taking charge of things after such a painful loss. I know how hard that is—I've been there."

His divorce. Again. She wanted to say it wasn't the same, but right now all Taylor could think of was . . . *He's going to kiss me.* She wasn't sure she remembered how. Three years clueless . . . Her pulse began to skitter like a fifteen-year-old's; she didn't know if it was from anticipation or panic or—

Whee-oooo, whee-oooo! Her phone wailed in the siren ringtone assigned to the ER.

"It's the hospital," Taylor explained, glancing toward her phone on the coffee table. She was breathless, embarrassed by the heat that had flooded into her face. And still trembly. "I'm sorry, Rob. But the ER wouldn't call unless it was something important."

"It could as easily have been my phone. I'm on call for my group tonight."

"Thanks. Really . . ." Taylor grabbed her cell, stood, and walked a few steps away, not sure if a sudden wooziness was from regret or relief. She traced a finger across the screen, accepting the call. "Taylor Cabot."

She paced, pressing a hand to her chest as she listened

to what the unit secretary relayed. She said a quick, silent prayer and then paced a few more steps. "Of course, I understand. But I'm not sure if I can do that," she said finally, glancing toward where Rob sat on the couch. "I . . . I'll call you back."

"Something happened?" Rob asked, rising from the couch.

"A multi-casualty incident on the freeway," Taylor reported, her mind whirling. "San Diego Hope got several ambulances. The ER is short staffed and the charge nurse asked the secretary to put out some calls for help. This secretary's new, so she doesn't know everyone or all the details but . . ." She grimaced.

"But what?" Rob asked, touching her shoulder.

"One of the trauma victims is an employee—ER staff. The secretary didn't have a name, but I can imagine how hard that is on everyone."

"Did they ask you to come in?"

"Yes. For an hour or two," Taylor explained, her emotions warring one against the other. "Until they get things under control. But I don't know . . ."

"Hey." Rob squeezed her shoulder. "Don't worry about disappointing me. That's another plus in our relationship: no apologies when duty calls. It comes with the territory."

"Right," Taylor said, feeling a jab of guilt. Rob had *not* been her first concern. "And . . ." She hoped her voice sounded casual. "With the way Hooper's been behaving, I'm not sure about leaving—"

"No problem," Rob interrupted, grasping both of her shoulders now. He smiled at Taylor. "I'll stay with the old boy. I'll wait right here until you get back. I can use the time to work on my acceptance speech. And I'll make some notes to help you get started with that time management program we've talked about." His smile spread. "I'll have your schedule figured out by the time you get back. Go; do what you need to do."

Tears sprang to Taylor's eyes. "Seriously? You'd dog-sit for me?"

"I'd do *anything* for you." Rob's voice lowered to a husky whisper. "Haven't you figured that out yet?"

Taylor tried to find words. "I . . ."

"Should go change your clothes," Rob finished for her. "I'll phone the ER and let them know you're on your way."

"Okay," Taylor managed, her knees weak with gratitude. "Tell them I'll be leaving here in five minutes."

It took her three. When she walked back into the living room dressed in scrubs, stethoscope, and hospital ID, Rob was already in the garage with the car and garage doors open and ready.

"All set," he told her as she stopped beside him. "The ER's expecting you." He reached out, touched Taylor's cheek. "Their gain, my loss. Hooper and I will hold down the fort."

"Thank you, Rob . . . so much." Taylor stepped closer to give him a grateful hug. His arms moved around her. She drew back a little to smile at him. "I can't tell you how much this—"

Rob's unexpected kiss stopped Taylor's words. And took her, ready or not, one step further toward her goal of moving on.

35

"THIS GAUZE . . . I need it off. Take it off. I can't see. . . ."
Sloane moaned against the oxygen mask, dizzy and nauseated
from the intravenous morphine. It had done nothing to ease
the pain in her left eye, ice-pick sharp and stabbing mercilessly at her brain. Her upper belly was bloated, tense, and
throbbed with a deep and relentless ache that made it harder
and harder to fill her lungs. The rescue collar around her
neck made things worse. If only she could sit up a little more.
"Take these bandages off. And the collar. *Please.*" She shivered, gagged against the pressure of the gastric tube snaking
through her nostril. "I've got to see . . . and sit up. Raise my
head higher. I can't breathe."

"I'm sorry, Sloane. Can't do it." The nurse's deep voice

sounded close; he must have been leaning over the gurney. He smelled of old coffee and fresh cinnamon Tic Tacs. "Your oxygen saturation's stable. But we can't raise your head any higher because your pressure *isn't*. Four liters of IV fluids and your BP still won't budge past 80 systolic—your heart's doing drumrolls to make up for it."

Blunt trauma . . . my belly.

"There's a bruise the size of San Bernardino County on your abdomen," he continued, raising his voice above the sound of groaning in the distance. Another trauma patient? "I don't have to tell you it's not a good thing. I'm hanging a unit of blood right now. The FAST scan showed hemoperitoneum— blood in your belly. As soon as I get the green light, you're off to OR." His hand connected with Sloane's forearm in an encouraging pat. "Doug's got your back; don't worry."

Right, Doug. The nurse they'd snagged from the ICU when catastrophe shoved short staffing into the proverbial fan. San Diego Hope . . . *my own ER.* On the wrong side of the stethoscope. Sloane still couldn't believe it. Or any part of this nightmare.

"The bandages have to stay over both eyes," Doug added over the insistent beeping of monitors. "There are deep lacerations to your left orbit, brow, and lids, and maybe some embedded glass in your eye," he explained. "Any movement is risky to your eyesight. The on-call ophthalmologist will be in the OR. You're going to have a fleet of surgeons."

The groans in the distance became agitated wails. Female . . . *Who is that?*

"You'll be in good hands in surgery, Sloane," Doug added, patting her arm again. "How's that belly pain now? Can you give me another number on the ten scale?"

"Fifteen," Sloane said through gritted teeth. "Seven if I weren't all trussed up and trapped in the dark like . . ." The ice pick stabbed her brain. And then her heart stalled as she remembered. "Like some doomed kitten in a grocery bag." *Marty . . .*

There was a waft of cinnamon-coffee as Doug chuckled. He finished rewrapping the blood pressure cuff on her arm. "I'm marking your belly pain as a seven. If you're giving me animal metaphors, it means that last dose of morphine is kicking in. Kitty cats are a happy sign."

"Don't bet on it, Doug."

Sloane shivered as the hazy fragments tumbled over in her mind. Blinding headlights, the sound of car horns and scraping metal, the horrible sensation of falling as her car left the road, bone-jolting impacts, again and again . . . Then Kasie, crawling out through the windshield to get help. *She did that . . . didn't she?*

"Doug. You still there?"

"Yes, ma'am."

"Tell me . . ." Sloane clenched her jaw to keep her teeth from chattering. She tried to turn her head toward the doorway, but the stiff collar stopped her. "That patient I keep hearing . . . that woman crying out. Is it Kasie?"

"Someone else from the accident?"

"Kasie Beckett. She works here too."

"Sorry. I don't know too many folks in ER. But no, your friend's not here. We have two other victims, an older woman and a teenager. Nobody named Kasie. And right now we need to concentrate on you." His words were underscored by an ominous shrill of monitor alarms. "I still don't like that blood pressure."

Kasie got out. I saw it. . . .

"I'm hanging a second unit of blood, Sloane."

"Okay." She battled another wave of nausea, tried to get a full breath and failed. She was wringing wet with perspiration, cold despite the warm blankets, and way too hungry for air. All foreboding signs of shock.

"They say Sloane's car went over the embankment," Taylor said, glancing away from Seth and toward the doors to the emergency department. "I can't imagine how terrifying that would feel."

"From what I understand, she doesn't remember too much of the accident," Seth said, trying to reassure her. Taylor hadn't been in the trauma rooms yet; he'd caught her in the corridor outside. She'd already heard a few details from the clinical coordinator and seemed less surprised at Sloane's identity than Seth had been to see Taylor arrive at the ER. On her evening off . . . when she had a date with Halston. "I know one of the investigating officers," he explained. "He said Sloane's memory is pretty hazy. From a concussion and . . . possibly some other impairment." *Like alcohol.*

Taylor's expression gave no clue if she'd heard anything regarding the blood test results. But Seth's California Highway Patrol friend hadn't minced words: Sloane Wilder's breath reeked of alcohol. He'd felt certain the lab results would verify it.

"Fire had to use the Jaws of Life to cut Sloane from her car," Seth continued. "She was wedged in there pretty bad. Upside down. The car roof was crushed in on one side."

Taylor grimaced. "How many victims total in the incident?"

"Nine. Two fatalities, seven injured. One was airlifted to UC San Diego's trauma center with severe head trauma. A young woman."

Taylor pressed her hand to her chest. "Oh, dear Lord . . ."

Taylor's raw compassion for this stranger touched Seth's heart. Yet another reason he loved her.

He sighed. "Evan and I delivered a death notification to the parents of one of the fatalities. I'm here now to support the families of the victims who were brought here. And the San Diego Hope staff, since one of their own is a patient too." He touched Taylor's arm. "Will you be all right? Treating Sloane?"

"Fine." Taylor's expression mirrored a mix of emotions. "We're teammates—maybe reluctantly. Not close friends, but of course I care about what happens to her. We've agreed on a truce. Over differences I honestly can't even define."

Seth thought of the strange exchange he'd had with Sloane that day in the chapel. He couldn't define that, either.

"Anyway," Taylor continued, "if that's my assignment, I can handle being Sloane's nurse." Her brows pinched. "From what I've heard, it's serious, Seth. Things don't look good. As a nurse, she probably realizes that. It must feel like her car's going over a cliff again." She glanced toward the ER doors. "Well, I should—"

"Sir, you can't be in here!" a guard called down the corridor. "C'mon back. Let me see what I can do to help."

"No!"

Seth and Taylor turned toward the commotion. A young man jogged their way, his expression distraught and determined; he'd managed to slip past the security doors. Intent, apparently, on getting into the ER.

"Easy there, sir," Seth said, stepping in front of Taylor and nudging her safely behind. "What's going on?"

"Please . . . ," the young man huffed, coming to a stop beside them. "No one will tell me anything. I have to find her. Please."

"Okay. Easy now." Seth nodded at the guard, saw him step discreetly aside. "Let me try to help you. I'm Seth. And you're . . ."

"Daniel. But that doesn't matter now. I need to find her."

"I hear you, Daniel." Seth kept his voice calm. Nothing in the man's expression spoke of threat. Only fear. "Who are you trying to find?"

"My fiancée. I was supposed to meet her, but she didn't show up. Isn't answering her cell. And then I heard about that bad highway pileup."

"You think she was involved in the accident?" Taylor asked, coming alongside Seth.

"I don't know—maybe. I asked at the desk, but they won't give out names." The young man ran his fingers through his hair. "I only know she was on that road at that exact time. She wasn't supposed to be but . . ." He closed his eyes. "I guess this woman at the Grill was too drunk to drive, so Kasie took her keys away and offered to—"

"Wait . . ." Taylor gasped, gripping Seth's arm. "You're looking for Kasie Beckett?"

"That's right." Daniel stared at them. "Didn't I say that? Kasie works *here*. In the ER. And she volunteers with that crisis team. I keep telling her it's not her job to fix everything, but she . . ." His gaze moved to the ER doors. "The news reports said they were bringing accident victims here. I've been praying she's not one of them. But can you find out if she's here or . . . ?"

"Yes," Seth assured him. "I can do that. We'll find out together."

Daniel tried to speak, then simply nodded.

"I'm going to take Daniel down to the chapel, where it's quieter, so we can make some calls," Seth said, turning to look at Taylor. His heart tugged at the look on her face that said exactly what he was thinking: *That head injury patient. Don't let it be Kasie.*

"Okay," Taylor said.

"The clerk has my cell number if anyone needs me," Seth added. "I'll be back here as soon as I can. Promise."

He clapped a gentle hand on Daniel's shoulder. "This way. Let's find your fiancée." He led the way, remembering Kasie's offer to help with the training scenarios. How she'd said, half apologizing, *"I haven't even done a death notification yet."*

Seth thought of the news he and Evan had carried to the Pilner family tonight and prayed he wouldn't be doing that same thing with Kasie's fiancé.

36

"PEDDLE IT . . . somewhere else . . . Cabot," Sloane groaned, apparently having recognized Taylor's voice in the room even before she approached the gurney. "I need a surgeon, not a crisis chaplain."

"I got called in. As a nurse," Taylor explained, distressed, even after hearing Doug's grim report, at how bad this woman looked. Heavy bandaging around her eyes, skin deathly pale with an ominous sheen of perspiration, and lips gray-tinged despite the oxygen. "Doug probably told you that we're infusing packed cells." Her eyes skimmed the nearly empty plastic transfusion bag hanging over the gurney. And the monitors. Blood pressure had only risen to 88 systolic. Her heart rate had come down some but—"The OR said they'd be coming for you in five minutes."

"Coming . . . for me." Sloane's pale lips attempted her signature smirk. "You make that sound like the grim reaper."

step *by* step

Taylor's thoughts rushed immediately to Kasie. Where was she? Then guilt jabbed; she was here for Sloane. Gallows humor or not, this woman had to be terrified. "I only meant to reassure you that we're getting this under control. You're going to be okay, Sloane."

"Sure. I've got tubes . . . coming out of everywhere. My belly's full of blood . . . and . . ." Sloane's lips twitched again. "I ruined your date."

Don't.

Taylor gripped the gurney rail, grateful for the bandage over Sloane's eyes. The remark not only brought back the confusing phone message she'd gotten earlier, but it might well validate Daniel's fears. Taylor knew something Seth didn't: Sloane must have been at the Grill. Her blood alcohol report had come back at .09, more than legally drunk. If Kasie had seen her in that condition, she would have certainly offered help. It would be unlike her not to.

"Airlifted to UC San Diego's trauma center with severe head trauma. A young woman."

Sloane Wilder might have ruined far more than a dinner date.

―――――

"Kasie, can you hear me? Squeeze my hand, hon, like you did before." The voice, feminine and kind—distant, odd, like someone who'd inhaled balloon helium as a party gag—blended with a strangely familiar mix of electronic beeping.

Where am I? What happened?

"Nothing. No movement on that left side," the voice said, maybe talking with someone else now. It was hard to tell.

"Medics said she was ambulatory on scene. Trying to help. It took them a while to get her assessed. She was completely lucid when she arrived here. She's looking more and more like an epidural hemorrhage."

"Kasie," someone else said, more of a buzz than a voice. "I need to check your right side too. Can you grip my hand? Squeeze my fingers. . . ."

"The effects of the intubation drugs should be gone by now," the feminine voice said. "The paralytic for sure. Even with lingering sedation, she should be able to follow commands. But she's only responding to pain. Still appropriately, thank goodness. But you can't pay me enough to hurt her again to test it. She's one of us, part of an ER team. A tech at San Diego Hope."

The hospital. Work? Was that where she was? Her head hurt so bad . . . too hard to think.

Kasie drew in a breath and heard a whooshing sound, air pushing into her lungs through a tube . . . in her mouth, down her throat? Something smelled sour like vomit. Was she on a bed? Or . . . *in the car? Oh, Lord . . . the cliff.* Kasie sucked in a stuttering breath, struggled to shove her tongue against the plastic in her throat. Heard a faster beeping sound. No, felt it . . . inside her head. Beeping, pounding—

"Heart rate's up. And CT gave us the go-ahead to take her down for the scan."

"Kasie." The woman's voice came close again. "Yes, that's it. Open your eyes. Good girl."

Kasie blinked, cringed against the lights. Too bright. Was this a dream? Everything was fuzzy . . . inside a searing glare. Her head. Like a firecracker in a Halloween pumpkin. Was somebody talking? She couldn't hear. Or see now. She was dizzy. And something was buzzing inside the pumpkin and—

"Seizure! Get the doctor. I'm grabbing the lorazepam."

Kasie was floating . . . could see now, even without her eyes. Clearly. So very clearly. Her father in his police uniform—so handsome, alive. He was reaching out to her, his eyes full of love. And pride . . . *You're proud of me, Daddy?*

"We'll start her with a loading dose of Dilantin," someone said. "I'd bet money she's going from the CT scanner to the OR. At least for placement of an ICP bolt to monitor her intracranial pressure. Maybe a craniectomy . . . could go either way. The neurosurgery resident is on his way down from upstairs." There was a sound like a deep sigh. "Already lost two out on that highway tonight. Tragic accident."

Accident?

Kasie fought the floating, forcing herself to think. *Highway. Accident.* Images swirled in her throbbing head. The headlights in the rearview mirror. The burnt-rubber smell of brakes . . . the cliff. Sloane Wilder screaming . . . Daniel waiting . . .

"She's twitching again. Let's get more lorazepam onboard."

"Right here."

"Good. And . . . ." The deep voice dropped lower. "Has anyone called the chaplain?"

A chaplain?

Kasie struggled against the returning rush of dizziness, tried to blot out the firecrackers igniting in her head. The surreal irony exploded first.

A chaplain. *For me.*

Please, God. Don't let it end like this.

37

"About a five . . . and a half," Sloane answered, realizing what an irritant she'd been all these years asking patients to rate their pain. A traumatic epiphany: pain should be expressed with adjectives. Or expletives. This one in her belly hurt like—

"I'm getting things packed up," Taylor said. "The OR team will be here in a couple of minutes to run you down there."

"Make sure you fasten my seat belt. We don't want an encore." Sloane tossed a grim smile in the general direction of Taylor's voice; they'd refused to take off the bandages and the nurse disappeared and reappeared like an apparition. "I guess my Jetta's totaled."

"Your car?" She swore she could hear Taylor's body stiffen.

"I shouldn't ask? I'm getting pretty tired of no one telling me anything."

There were footfalls, coming back to the gurney. If Sloane were the type to bet, she'd put money on the hunch that something else was bugging Cabot besides getting called in to work.

"I don't think now is the time to worry about something like that," Taylor said in a decidedly terse whisper. "Cars can be replaced."

"Easy for you to say." Sloane shifted her hips on the gurney, prompting a debilitating wave of pain. She barely stifled a groan.

"I'm going to give you some more pain medication," Taylor told her. The merciful offer did nothing to diffuse the awkward tension in the air. "You look uncomfortable."

Not as uncomfortable as you sound. . . .

In mere seconds, Sloane was floating on a wave of chemical relief.

"Excuse me," Taylor said, her voice softer now; it was a toss-up whether that was genuine kindness or a narcotic-induced perception. Frankly, Sloane didn't care. "I need to step out for a minute."

"Sure. I'm not going anywhere."

Taylor's footfalls receded into the distance, an apparition again. In hushed conversation with someone else. A man . . . familiar, maybe . . . Sloane didn't have the strength to mull it over.

She closed her eyes, let the medication wash over her. She knew that it didn't actually stop the pain; it simply made her brain not care. She smiled despite a convicting tug at her heart. Hadn't her whole life been like that? Soul-racking pain and a conscious choice to blot it out—numb herself and carry on—regardless of the personal toll? No matter how she was judged, how much loneliness she had to bear. What Taylor Cabot thought didn't matter.

―――――――

"I wish it weren't true," Seth told Taylor, also wishing there had been a way to spare her. But she'd have heard it from someone anyway. "Daniel got a call from Kasie's mother before I could start contacting other hospitals. She and her husband are driving down from Long Beach."

"She's in surgery now?" Taylor asked, glancing at her watch.

"That's what I was told by the ER. They expect it could take several hours." He shook his head. "I'm still trying to get my mind around the fact that it was Kasie and Sloane in that car. When Daniel explained about what happened at the Grill, it made more sense but . . ."

Taylor's brows drew together. "She called me from there—left a message."

"Kasie?"

"Sloane. She was obviously intoxicated, and what she said didn't make any sense at all. It was . . . strange."

And ugly, Seth would guess from the discomfort in Taylor's expression.

"Daniel's parents arrived shortly after I talked with the ER," Seth explained. "Evan's already at the trauma center, so he'll be able to wait with them. At least until I get there and Kasie's mom and stepdad arrive." He said another silent prayer that he wouldn't be giving them bad news. "I talked with my CHP friend and he told me that Kasie crawled out of the car and up the embankment. She managed to flag down help for Sloane. I don't get that. If she had a bad head injury . . ."

"An epidural bleed can present that way," Taylor explained. "A brief loss of consciousness followed by normal behavior, even though the hematoma is developing." Sudden tears welled in her eyes. "And Kasie is like that. Helping, always."

"She is. And she can count on us to pray for her." Seth touched Taylor's shoulder. "You going to be okay?"

Taylor nodded, wiped at a tear. "I won't be here much longer. After I get Sloane to the OR, I'll go home." She glanced toward the trauma room. "Looks like the crew's ready to move her now."

———

Taylor told Seth good-bye and returned to the bedside. She helped the techs get their patient ready to move by securing the IV pumps, monitoring equipment, portable oxygen, and—

"I told her not to crank that wheel," Sloane mumbled, trying to shift her head on the pillow. "Beckett drives like . . . an old lady."

"Hold still." Taylor's jaw tensed. "They're here to take you to the OR."

"I told her . . . don't try any of that savior stuff on me," Sloane continued, her voice thickened by the drugs and a dry mouth. "But no. She's got to be the hero. Drove us off a cliff. This whole thing is her fault and—"

"Stop it," Taylor hissed, teeth clenched. She bent low over the gurney, grateful the techs had stepped away. "Don't say another word. Not a single selfish syllable." She hated that she was trembling, hated so much more what she was feeling. "Kasie wouldn't have been driving your car if you weren't drunk. Don't bother to deny it. I've seen the tox report. And

I've seen you walk into this department late and hungover too many times to count. None of this would have happened if you'd been responsible enough to find yourself a twelve-step program."

Sloane lifted a Kleenex, wiped at her mouth. "Yeah, well . . . guess that figures. I'm two pints of blood in, about to lose my spleen, and the little tech walks away like a hero."

"Kasie's *not* walking." Taylor gripped the side rail of the gurney to keep her hand from balling into a fist. Tears rose. "She's at the trauma center in critical condition with an epidural bleed. After doing everything she could to save your ungrateful skin."

Oh, Lord, what am I doing? Please, stop me . . .

"I'm sorry, Sloane," Taylor apologized, horrified at herself. "I shouldn't have said that. I don't have any right to—"

"Blame me?" Sloane's voice was halting, made more so by the quiver of her chin. "Why wouldn't I expect that?" She drew in a breath, nostrils flaring around the oxygen prongs. If her eyes had been visible, Taylor would have been the target of an icy stare. "I'm sure that's what you and Chaplain Donovan were discussing out there a minute ago. That was him, right? Bad-mouthing me?"

Taylor felt sick. "No, Sloane. Really. No one's said anything like that."

"Right. And let me guess." Sloane's pale tongue swept over her lips as if to test the bitterness of her words. "You talked about Greg, too."

What?

"How that accident was also my fault. Three years ago . . . out on that road. He's dead and you blame me."

Taylor glanced at the monitors, certain oxygen deprivation

was playing a role in this crazy talk. But the saturation percentage was fine. "I don't understand."

"Greg was at my house. With me."

Taylor's legs threatened to give out. "You're lying."

"He'd been there before—too many times to count."

Taylor's mouth went dry, her head thudding. "I don't . . . believe you."

"Ask Seth Donovan."

38

"I'm glad you're able to be there," Seth told Evan. He leaned back in the chapel chair, switched the cell phone to his other ear. "Though I don't like pulling you away from that little boy of yours."

"We'll get reacquainted at the 2 a.m. feeding." Evan sighed. "There hasn't been any word about Kasie from the OR. I've been sitting tight with Daniel and the parents. How's it going there?"

"Two of the patients are headed for discharge from the ER," Seth reported. A senior-age woman who'd suffered multiple lacerations and a teenage boy with a fractured nose and dental injuries; Seth had no doubt he'd already posted trauma selfies on his social networks. "Sloane Wilder went to surgery a few minutes ago. No family here. I've been checking in with the staff to see how they're handling their own stress. They seem okay so far." He wasn't sure how truthful that statement was; there had been tears in Taylor's eyes when he told her about Kasie. "Did you hear anything more about the accident investigation?"

"Only what I've caught on my news app. More than one witness is convinced that someone deliberately caused the accident. Pushed that one car over the median and forced Kasie off the road. One of them insisted they saw the car riding the Jetta's back bumper, even smashing into it a few times."

Seth frowned. "They ID that driver?"

"No. There's a description of the car—several conflicting ones—but no one's come up with a pic or license plate. At least not yet."

"Road rage?" Seth asked, thinking not for the first time what pathetic fools humans could be. Himself included. "Somebody just lost it?"

"That's the common thought. But I don't think Kasie was able to confirm anything about that bumper tag. And from what I hear, Sloane Wilder was in no shape to do that either."

"No." Shock from blood loss and alcohol intoxication— Sloane's ability to think coherently had to be about nil. "Maybe she'll be able to shed some light on things later. Kasie too," he added quickly. *Please, Lord . . .*

"Are you going to head this way?" Evan asked, raising his voice over what sounded like sirens in the background.

"I'll be there in thirty minutes or so. I want to check in with Taylor before I leave. She's had it pretty rough tonight."

———

Taylor paused outside the chapel, opened the nanny cam app on her phone, and scanned the live feed again. Nothing.

Hooper's bed, empty. There was no sign of him or Rob anywhere. Couch, hallway, fireplace, breakfast bar . . . as far as the camera would allow her view. Odd. Lately, by 9 p.m., the old retriever was stuck like Velcro to that threadbare cushion. She'd thought about texting Rob but didn't want it to appear she was checking up on him. He'd been so kind tonight. Still, Taylor hoped Hooper wasn't moving window to window—to washing machine—and whining again.

Looking for Greg.

Taylor tensed against the disturbing anger that had replaced her earlier shock. Crisis team dropout or not, she'd had to do some combat breathing to put that trauma room exchange back into perspective. Sloane Wilder had always looked for ways to hurt her. Their truce was a joke. Combine that inexplicable but ongoing malice with alcohol, pain medication, and traumatic stress, and it wasn't surprising that Sloane would lash out in the cruelest way possible. At the worst-ever time. She'd hit her mark. And to try to drag Seth into it was beyond despicable.

But Taylor was at fault too. She'd let her reaction to Kasie's situation get the better of her. Let it get in the way of her duty as a nurse . . . even in the way of her compassion. She was deeply ashamed. She'd pray for Sloane's full recovery the same way she'd pray for Kasie's. It was right and the only way to find peace in this turmoil. Today was March 24 and she was so close to completing her Survival List. She couldn't lose control now. Taylor took one more glance at her empty-stage nanny cam and walked into the chapel.

Her heart tugged at the sight of Seth. Rumpled a bit more than usual, sitting there poring over his hand-scribbled scraps of paper—spread across his lap and adjacent chairs. Making notes, plans for how best to help hurting people. There wasn't anyone more genuinely transparent than this good man.

"Hi," he said, noticing her. "Sorry; I was . . ."

"I know." Taylor smiled at him, watching as he gathered up his papers to make room for her on a chair. "Any word on Kasie?" she asked, settling beside him.

"Not really. I spoke with Evan at the trauma center. She's still in surgery. No update yet." There was worry in his dark eyes despite his calm voice. "This brain injury. I'm not sure I want to know, but . . . what's the usual prognosis?"

"It depends on a lot of factors." Taylor sighed. "This kind of bleeding is from an artery, so it happens more quickly than in other brain injuries. A collection of blood between the skull and the brain, putting pressure on it. Like I said before, sometimes the patient is lucid, 'normal' for a period of time. Until the increasing pressure on the brain causes symptoms: headache, nausea, rapid lapse into unconsciousness. And . . ." She winced, imagining Kasie. "There's often partial paralysis and loss of sight on the side opposite the bleed. But Kasie's young and healthy, strong." Taylor nodded, not sure if she was trying to convince Seth or herself. "The fact that she was lucid initially is a good sign. And thank heaven she was taken to surgery so quickly. All of that is in her favor. There can be good outcomes in cases like that."

"And how is Sloane?"

"She . . ." Taylor glanced away, rocked by a rush of emotion.

"What?" Seth touched her shoulder, concern in his voice. "Taylor, what is it? Did she die?"

"No." Taylor met his gaze again, tears threatening. She was sickened by a sudden thought: Would Sloane's death be harder to handle than her vicious lies? "She made it to surgery. The transfusions stabilized her some."

"Good." Seth was quiet for a moment as Taylor blinked back tears. "But there's something you're not saying. I see it."

"I . . . let her get to me. I should know better—be better."

"But?"

"Sloane knows how to push my buttons. She was low on blood, high on alcohol, loaded with morphine . . . and mean as a cornered animal." Taylor's gaze dropped to her lap; she rubbed her hands together, tried to control her breathing. "She's a liar. I should've walked away and had another nurse take over."

"Taylor." Seth turned her face so she had to meet his gaze. "What did she say?"

"She . . ." Taylor shivered, angry tears spilling over. "She said Greg was with her the night he was killed. She said it wasn't the first time. She . . . implied that they were having an affair and—" a fierce wave of nausea tried to choke her—"she even had the gall to say that *you* knew about it."

"I . . ." There was sudden pain in Seth's eyes. And something far worse.

"Oh no." Taylor's throat closed. She stared at him, read it in his expression. The blood swept away from her brain. She dropped a hand to the adjacent chair to steady herself, scattering Seth's scratch-paper notes to the chapel floor. "It's . . . *true?*"

"Taylor. Not exactly. I only knew—"

"Don't!" she screamed, anger propelling her to her feet like a swarm of wasps. "I see it on your face. You *knew* this awful thing. You knew it all along."

"Wait, please." Seth scrambled to his feet, stepped toward her. "Taylor, listen to me. It's not that simple."

"Simple?" Taylor's voice hit a pitch she didn't recognize. "You mean the truth? You mean it was too complicated all those times I poured out my heart to you? All those *years* I tried so hard to understand what had happened that night?" She narrowed her eyes, hating him like she'd never hated anyone before. "I *asked* you, Seth. I asked you back then and . . ." The sudden realization made her teeth clench so tightly that she bit her tongue and tasted blood. "I asked you again only last week, after I found out about Greg's appointment with you. You said you didn't know what it was about. You said you didn't know why he was on that road."

"Please." Seth stepped close, tried to grasp her hand. "Let me—"

"Don't touch me. And don't lie to me anymore. You are—" a sob tore free—"*worse* than she is. Pretending to be my friend. Pretending to care about me. Letting me suffer with all that confusion. You couldn't have been more cruel. Self-righteous, arrogant . . . hiding behind that chaplain's uniform." Taylor glared at him, tears spilling down her cheeks. "You lied, Seth, and you *used* me. You dangled me like some pathetic . . . widow puppet . . . a resource." She gritted her teeth. "You even had me playing the grieving spouse for the death notification class."

"No, Taylor . . ."

"I don't ever want to see you again," she said, snatching her purse off the chair.

"Okay, wait . . . I hear you. But . . ." He was pleading now. "Let me find someone else for you to talk with. Don't get in your car like this and—"

"And what?" A laugh, half sob, escaped Taylor's lips. "Drive my car over a cliff? Thank you for your kind concern, Chaplain Donovan, but it's a little too late."

Taylor had made it as far as the ER corridor when her phone rang in her pocket. An incoming call with the tone she'd assigned to . . . the vet clinic?

"Yes?" Taylor leaned against the corridor wall, confusion piggybacking on her already-tumbling emotions. "This is Taylor Cabot."

"Ah, Taylor. Wendy Mack here. I'm taking call at the emergency clinic tonight."

"Oh, you're so good to check in," Taylor said, her throat aching with fresh tears. Finally something kind and decent in these sorry few hours. "But Hooper's doing all right today. Not any worse, anyway . . ."

There was a moment of silence. "I see. So you didn't know he's here?"

Taylor's breath caught. "No. I . . . don't understand. What do you mean?"

"You friend Dr. Halston brought Hooper in. He apparently had another seizure. It resolved by the time he arrived but . . ."

"But what?"

"It's the reason I called. Your friend requested we euthanize Hooper. He said he had permission to act on your behalf. It didn't smell right. And we can't do that legally, so—"

"Don't do anything. I'll be right there."

39

"I TALKED DANIEL and Kasie's parents into going out for something to eat," Evan explained as Seth took the seat opposite him in the trauma center's neurosurgery waiting room. "One of the surgeons came to say it's going well. Kasie will be in the operating room for at least another hour. She said they are optimistic that the bleeding was caught early enough. But that only time will tell."

Time. It was something Seth didn't have if he wanted to convince Taylor to hear him out. Time and credibility. His gut twisted. He'd made a huge mistake.

He met Evan's gaze. "I'll hold on to that encouraging news about Kasie."

"Right. You look rough, Seth," Evan added, kindness in his voice.

"It's been a rough day."

"Amen to that. When are you headed back to Sacramento?"

"Three days from now. If that's the twenty-seventh." Seth smiled grimly. "I'm losing track of my calendar."

"I know the feeling." Evan stretched out his legs and peered across at Seth. "I probably shouldn't ask, but is it true you're going to take over as director of California Crisis Care?"

"Self-righteous, arrogant . . . hiding behind that chaplain's uniform."

"Doesn't look that way," Seth told him, avoiding the discussion surrounding his difficult decision—he didn't have the stomach for that right now. He couldn't help wondering if Taylor had actually nailed it. Maybe he'd taken on this work for all the wrong reasons. "Good to be asked but . . ."

"Sure." Evan nodded. "I won't pry. Just wanted to say that we—all of us—were pulling for you. But having you on the team, even here in San Diego only a couple of times a year, is great. We count on that."

Seth's throat tightened.

"Oh, did you hear about that car? The one from the freeway?" Evan asked.

"The road rage idiot?"

"Yeah. Someone did grab a phone pic of the car. And the license plate. Stolen. So now they aren't sure whether it was road rage, a joyride gone wrong, or . . . both."

Seth shook his head, remembering Taylor's face as she railed against him in the chapel. No joy there—lots of rage. He prayed she'd found some measure of comfort.

"He's not sedated?" Taylor asked, her fingers continuing their gentle circuit from Hooper's forehead to his ear and back. She glanced at his thin chest as he lay on the exam table, saw the slow rise and fall of his ribs. "No Valium like last time?"

"It wasn't necessary." Dr. Wendy's brown eyes were kind behind her glasses. "There hasn't been any seizure activity since his arrival."

Taylor struggled to keep her voice clinical. "Do you think he really had one?"

The vet's eyes widened only a fraction; she understood the implication. "Our boy's had them before, Taylor. He's in deteriorating health."

"None of which gives Rob the right to do this."

"No, it doesn't. And that's why I called you." The vet's expression couldn't have been more caring. "I'm sorry this happened. If it helps at all, Dr. Halston seemed genuinely concerned about Hooper's suffering. And yours."

"Thank you. But it doesn't help. Not at all." Taylor's throat ached so badly she could barely speak. But she had to ask. "Will Hooper wake up?"

"I don't know. The symptoms you've described are all signs of brain involvement. He's frail and his blood chemistry is undoubtedly out of balance. . . . I didn't think you'd want to put him through more blood draws or invasive procedures."

"No." Taylor's heart squeezed. "Is he suffering now?"

"I don't believe so. But we can't know about tomorrow."

"I only need tonight," Taylor whispered. "I want to take Hooper home. We need that time." She looked up at the doctor through welling tears. "Would that be okay?"

"Yes." Dr. Wendy stroked Hooper's head, then gave Taylor's hand a pat. "I'll give him a sedative. And I'll send you home with some extra. In case . . ." Her voice cracked. "Give our boy some love and comfort tonight, Taylor. And we'll talk more tomorrow."

"Okay." Taylor wiped at her eyes, glanced toward the door. "I saw Rob's car. He's still here?"

"In my office."

He was inspecting the wall display of framed certificates when Taylor walked in. He turned as she was closing the door behind her. "Taylor . . ."

"I'm surprised you waited," she said, praying she could get through this without losing her grip altogether. She was batting 0 for 2 right now. "I thought you'd be gone."

"I wanted to explain," Rob told her, his voice as controlled as if he were trying to describe a watering sequence for lawn sprinklers. Or the time management program he was designing to improve her life.

Taylor's body tensed. "How *does* one explain away killing someone's dog?"

"That's not fair."

"And I can't believe you just said that."

"We talked about it tonight at dinner," Rob said, walking toward her. His manner was practical, unemotional. But gentle. "You told me you'd spoken to Dr. Mack and made a tentative plan."

"Which gave you the right to make the decision for me?"

"Taylor . . ." Rob stopped in front of her. "I was only trying to spare you."

Taylor never swore, but oh, how she wanted to now. "You were *sparing* yourself, Rob. What was this, a way to assure that our trip to San Francisco wasn't going to be derailed by my awkwardly dying dog? Was that the plan—kill him first, no worries?" Her face flooded with heat; she'd begun to tremble. "You wanted to control Hooper's death for your convenience."

He stared at her. "How can you accuse me of that?"

"How can *you* pretend to know what I'm feeling or what I need? You have *no* idea. And no right to compare my pain to yours. Or tell me how to get through it. A divorce isn't a death. Hooper isn't a fish." Taylor didn't care that tears streamed down her face. "He's *Greg's* dog. And there's no way I'll let *anyone* take him from me."

"I appreciate your being here, more than I can say," Kasie's mother, Trisha, told Seth. She glanced across the small surgery waiting room to where her husband and Daniel stared, unseeing most likely, at the wall-mounted TV. "And that Evan drove Daniel over here from San Diego Hope. The poor boy sounded so completely undone on the phone—my heart broke having to relay the news we'd heard." She reached up, attempted to secure some strands of hair that had escaped her tidy ponytail—dark as Kasie's. "He was so upset about their last conversation. They were on their way to a counseling appointment. They've had some troubles recently, I'm afraid."

Seth offered a small nod; he suspected the "troubles" had everything to do with Kasie's crisis work. He should have followed up more on that situation. What good was a chaplain to the chaplains if he'd let that slip? He thought of what Taylor had said about her insisting on driving Sloane home: *"Kasie is like that. Helping, always."*

"She loves her volunteer work," Trisha continued. "I've

never seen Kasie so dedicated to something. The day she was called to that awful murder scene, we talked for close to two hours on the phone. She was really wound up. And upset, I think, that Daniel couldn't understand why it had been so important to her. But much more than that, Kasie was grateful you were there with her. That she could learn from you."

Seth's throat tightened. "It goes both ways. Your daughter's a good reminder of what it takes to do this work. She has the heart for it."

"Yes . . ." Trisha smiled despite the sheen of tears. "Kasie's father was much the same way. Very giving. Always going that extra step to help. He was a police officer."

"She told me that." *Killed off duty, doing a good turn.*

"They were inseparable." She brushed at her eye. "I have a photo of Kasie when she was maybe six. Wearing her daddy's uniform shirt and dress hat—so big it covered her whole forehead." Trisha shook her head. "She'd found my eye pencil, drawn a mustache over her upper lip . . . She insisted that I get a photo of her saluting."

Seth thought of his father's photos behind the counter at Donovan's Uniforms.

"She told me," Kasie's mother continued, "that she knew her father would approve of what she's doing as a volunteer. Making him proud has always been so important to her."

"She said something like that to me, too."

Trisha hugged her arms around herself. "Of course, the truth is the same as I've always told her. Her father would be proud of her no matter what Kasie chooses to do with her life. As long as it really makes her happy . . . deep down." Her eyes met Seth's. "Isn't that every parent's wish for his child?"

"Yes. I'm sure—"

"Doctor's coming!" Daniel reported from the doorway. "Headed this way."

Kasie's mother joined her husband, and Seth tried not to interpret the surgeon's expression as he strode through the doorway. He prayed he'd be calling Taylor with good news. Then amended the thought. Regardless of the news, Seth was probably the last person on earth she'd want to hear from right now.

———

Her heart was breaking all over again, coming apart like a wound sutured by an incompetent medical staffer. No, *she* was incompetent. A complete fool to think a new life was a check mark or two away. This, today, was unbearable. *I can't do this. Not again.*

"Oh . . . please." A tear dropped from Taylor's chin onto Hooper's shoulder. He didn't even twitch, hadn't moved a muscle since she got him home. There was no guarantee he'd ever do that again or even keep breathing through the night. She stared up at the ceiling, her pain honed by what had become relentless waves of anger. "Why are you doing this, God? You know how hard I've been working. You know what I want. I told you so many times. I *need* to get my life back. I can't do this. I won't . . . survive." Taylor groaned at her choice of word. In twenty-four hours, she'd be at the threshold of March 26, and it felt like she'd been sucked back into the abyss of three years ago. There was no survival.

She stroked Hooper's ear, her heart aching at the coolness of his skin beneath the fur. His body shutting down. She wasn't ready for this . . . couldn't do it. She smoothed the fabric beneath his nose, wishing beyond reason that it would ease the deepening rattle in his chest. Taylor and Dr. Wendy had carried him carefully into the house from the car, using her white bed comforter as a sort of transport stretcher. It was the same comforter Taylor had used to take him to the clinic after the first seizure. The night she'd been modeling her evening gown in the bedroom mirror and imagining herself at the gala, stepping into a new life.

With Rob.

She pulled her trembling fingers back from Hooper's ear before the anger tightened them into a fist. Rob had kissed her. And then tried to have her dog put to sleep. Was there anything more unimaginably cruel and horrible?

Yes.

Taylor cast her gaze toward the whitewashed ceiling again as the trembling threatened to overtake her. Greg . . . cheated. With Sloane Wilder. Nothing could be more horrible. Nothing could possibly hurt more. She sucked in a breath, desperate to quell the lurch of her stomach as the words repeated without mercy.

"Greg was at my house. With me. . . . Too many times to count."

Her husband. With that woman. How could God let it happen?

All those times Greg was gone . . . he'd been with her.

Those months Taylor was aching to start a family, he was—

"No!"

She scrambled to her knees and reached over Hooper to snatch the jewelry box from the glass table. She hurled it at the fireplace and watched its contents scatter: her wedding rings, the love poem . . . things she'd held so dear, so sacred. Almost as sacred as . . . Her gaze moved to the Bible, lying alone on the table. Anger and tears welled at the same time, paralyzing her. Stopping her from . . . What was she going to do? Rip out pages of Scripture like Ava Sandison shredded that funeral brochure?

"'*Anger lives in sorrow's house.*'"

Donovan quoting Lucado.

Taylor sat back down, hunched forward, holding her face in her hands. She choked on a sob. "Seth . . . knew. All this time." He'd kept the truth from her, watched her struggle and suffer as she tried to understand what had happened. She'd asked him and . . . *he lied.* He'd betrayed her as much as Greg had. Her mentor, friend . . . her sounding board. Seth had been the one person she could turn to. And now that was over too.

Taylor glanced toward the table again, pristine glass encasing that small, flawless beach of white sand. And the single shell, peaceful and protected. The way she'd longed to feel. The sight of that perfect space had brought her comfort. Now even that felt like a lie. There was no comfort, no peace . . . no hope?

She slid the Bible across the glass and into her lap. Felt the weight of it, the well-worn leather cover under her fingers. The tide of anger receded, but the pain only got worse. She'd always believed in God's promise of hope, but it seemed it wasn't meant for her. All those steps toward moving on with her life, the Survival List, her new dress, those sparkly shoes. *A second chance at love* . . . It had all been a pathetic fairy tale. And she was being punished for wanting it so much. Her faith in her husband had been destroyed, she'd sent Seth away, and now . . . *I'm losing Hooper too.* How could God let this happen?

"Please," Taylor prayed, gripping her Bible and feeling far

too much like the pilot's wife fighting to control that plum-meting plane. "I can't do this without you, God. I need you. Please help me."

"I'm on call for my group," Halston explained after catch-ing Seth in the corridor outside the surgery waiting room. Something about the doctor looked off. Like, despite the *GQ* grooming and reflex smile, his spirit had taken a serious whup-ping. "Mastectomy patient with complications."

"Sorry to hear that," Seth told him, figuring that accounted for his manner. Maybe the guy had more heart than Seth gave him credit for.

"You're here because of the accident?"

"Yeah." Seth decided against mentioning Kasie; it could be several more hours before they had an update from the NSICU. Besides, Halston had probably heard about Kasie from Taylor. Seth tried not to imagine what else she might have told him. "Long day."

"It has been." There it was again, that look in the man's eyes. Halston cleared his throat. "Have you talked with Taylor?"

"Not in the last couple of hours." *And maybe never again.*

"Not about her dog?" Halston looked like he was going to be sick.

"No. Something happened?"

"You could say that." The doctor grimaced slightly. "I was watching him for Taylor when she got called in for the acci-dent. The dog had another seizure while she was gone. His condition was terminal—we'd talked about that a few hours earlier, at dinner. So I . . ."

"What?" Seth asked, getting a very bad feeling. "What did you do?"

"I took him to that after-hours clinic. I asked them to put him out of his misery."

"You . . . *what*?"

"Put him down—euthanize him."

"Without asking her?" Seth's gut twisted; he couldn't believe his ears. "You killed Hooper?"

"I was only trying to spare her—" Halston backed into the corridor wall, palms raised, as Seth stepped toward him.

"You heartless—" Seth bit back the curse, battling the instinct to grab the man by the throat. He leaned close, his temples throbbing with fury. "Now you tell me why I should spare *you*."

"Easy . . . c'mon, Donovan. You don't want to do this."

"More than anything I can imagine."

"Okay. I hear you," Halston said, beginning to perspire. "And I get that I was wrong. Taylor had a lot to say about it when she showed up at the clinic. After the vet called her."

"She came there?"

"Yes. They couldn't do . . . what I'd asked without her permission. Hooper's in bad shape, but he's still alive." Halston's breath escaped as Seth took a half step backward. "She basically told me where to go. Then took the dog home."

Seth's legs weakened with relief.

"I don't expect you to believe me," Halston continued, trying to assume his usual attitude of control, "but I really was trying to help Taylor. I wanted her misery to end too."

"I hope you don't expect me to say thanks."

"No." Halston's eyes met Seth's. "I'm telling you this because I care about Taylor. She's the finest woman I've ever met. Her heart's going to break when that old dog dies. I think she needs a chaplain tonight. A good friend. I think Taylor needs *you*, Donovan."

Seth was on her porch in fifteen minutes, telling himself she'd probably banish him to the same perdition she'd wished on Halston. But he had to try. He rapped lightly on her door.

"Seth. Why . . . ?"

"I had to come." His chest constricted at the sight of her. Fragile, distracted, hair mussed, and eyes swollen from crying. She looked every sad inch a trauma victim. "I heard about Hooper."

Taylor closed her eyes for a moment, leaning on the door handle as if her legs might give way.

"I want to keep you company," Seth told her, feeling too much like a chaplain delivering a death notice. "That's all."

She stared at him for an endless moment.

He held his breath. *Please, Lord . . .*

"There will be rules," Taylor said, lifting her chin a little. Seth nodded.

"No talk about Greg. Or God."

"Okay."

Her chin quivered. "This is about Hooper."

And you . . . sweet Taylor. This is about you, too.

40

"TOMATO SOUP." Seth set the steaming mug and small plate on the glass-topped table. Taylor perched on the edge of the couch, keeping her vigil over Hooper as he slept. Or sank deeper into a coma; from what she'd relayed, it could very well be the case. "With crackers and cheese. Though, if you ask me, that's a stretch when it's quinoa crisps and goat cheese. What ever happened to cows . . . and Ritz?"

Taylor tried to smile, but somehow it made her look even more tragic. An abandoned waif in an old sweatshirt, yoga pants, and panda slippers. "Thank you," she said. "I forgot about food."

"No problem."

Seth wasn't surprised. Taylor had been thinking only of

Hooper's needs; one look around this usually tidy room proved it. Water and food dishes, a dozen dog toys and a half-chewed shoe, all pulled close to a nest she'd fashioned by covering the old dog bed with some kind of fluffy bedspread. White, of course. Or had been; it was dirty now with splotches of soggy kibble, dog drool, and oil stains from when Taylor and the good-hearted veterinarian slid their patient through the garage to the house. Seth's throat tightened. *Life is messy . . . love, too.*

There was also evidence that Taylor had been consumed with something more. Anger played a role here as well. Seth had pretended not to notice the small velvet jewelry box upside down on the fireplace hearth or the two wedding rings lying far enough away to strongly hint she'd chucked the box across the room. He could only imagine her pain: a scab ripped from a healing wound with such cruelty. She'd assigned a huge part of that hurt to him—maybe rightly so. Yet somehow Seth was still here, and he'd do whatever it took to help her get through this. By Taylor's rules: No Greg. No God. No doing or saying anything that might get him tossed out like that jewelry box.

Sacred silence. Ministry of presence. We've got this, Lord.

"Not bad," he said around a mouthful of the no-cheddar-no-Ritz snack. He set his mug of soup on the table, next to hers. "I could learn to like this stuff." He pointed to a dozen or so photos spread across Taylor's lap. "What have you got there?"

"Nothing." She shrugged. "Old photos of Hooper. Goofy puppy shots. Nostalgia, I guess. You know, the standard silly stories with every photo. The kind of thing Aimee would totally get—except she's on vacation."

"I can be Aimee," he said, wanting to cringe the moment the corny words left his lips.

"You?" She laughed, a sound Seth had missed like a grieved loss. Her green eyes swept over him, making his pulse hike in a way it definitely shouldn't. "You could never pass for Aimee."

"But I'm here." Seth smiled at her. "And I have my own goofy puppy, remember?"

"'Lucy, I'm home,'" Taylor mimicked. "How could I forget?"

"Then lay it on me. Eat your soup and tell me everything I should know about Hooper Cabot. I'm listening. . . ."

———

Am I dead?

No. Death wouldn't hurt like this. *Unless I'm already in hell. Figures . . .*

Sloane tried to swallow what felt like splinters of broken glass packed in gravel. The tube in her nose made her queasy with its sick slurping noises. And her belly . . . *so much pain.* She groaned and opened her eyes, blinking against bluish fluorescent light. "Where . . . ?"

"You're in the SICU, Sloane." A middle-aged nurse leaned close, a small plastic angel attached to the stethoscope around her neck. "About five hours ago now, you had an exploratory laparotomy. And a splenectomy. You lost a lot of blood; we're still pumping it back in. Do you remember the car accident?"

"Acc—" Sloane swallowed, wincing against the pain in her throat. Then reached up, trying to move something obscuring the vision in her left eye.

"Oops, don't touch." The nurse pulled her arm back down. "You've had some extensive suturing around that left eye.

You'll have a plastic surgery consult. But for now the gauze needs to stay put."

"Oh." Sloane tried to sweep her tongue over her lips. "So . . . dry."

"Here." The nurse raised a mouth swab. "Let's get your lips moistened. Your throat's going to be sore from the ET tube, and we can't start ice chips yet, but this will help."

Sloane sucked at the sponge, managed a better swallow. Then a hoarse whisper. "Thanks. A . . . tequila shot would be better but . . ."

The nurse's lips twitched. "Do you remember being in the ER?"

"I . . ." Sloane squinted, struggling to sort through what felt like a bad dream. No, that wasn't even close: a nightmare spawning the worst hangover in all of history. "Yes. The ambulance, then . . ." She shook her head and oxygen prongs bit into her nostrils. "Cabot?"

"Taylor Cabot. Yes, she was called in. I think she helped get you to the OR."

Sloane closed her eyes, snatches of it coming back now. Taylor in the ER, leaning over her bed.

"Don't say another word. Not a single selfish syllable. . . . Kasie wouldn't have been driving your car if you weren't drunk."

"Oh no . . ." Sloane stared up at the SICU nurse, nausea swirling despite the greedy tube in her nose. "Beckett . . . Kasie? Is she—?"

"She's at the trauma center. Out of surgery. I haven't had a chance to get another update."

"She was driving," Sloane rasped, trying to make sense of a sudden barrage of images. Kasie holding her keys. Headlights in the rearview mirror . . . Taylor's face. Upset, angry, and—

"That's right," the nurse said, pushing a button on an IV pump. "They haven't sorted out the details yet. Or caught the driver responsible. I shouldn't speculate, but it sounded like some lunatic. There were five cars involved in the pileup. Two on-scene fatalities. Even with all this . . ." The nurse glanced at the equipment and back down at Sloane. "I'd be counting my blessings."

"Right." Sloane closed her eyes; rolling them would hurt too much. The nurse with the cutesy angel stethoscope would never understand that someone like Sloane was always last in line when blessings got passed out. Or in the wrong line altogether. That kind of mercy was saved for pious people like Taylor and Seth Dono—

"Greg was at my house. With me."

"You're lying. . . . I don't . . . believe you."

"Ask Seth Donovan."

Sloane retched, gagged up bitter bile. "Oh . . . no . . ."

"Easy there. I'll get you something for the nausea and irrigate that tube. You'll feel better in a few minutes. You're going to be fine."

It wasn't true; she wouldn't feel better. She wasn't going to be fine. Sloane was going straight to hell. No, that would be far too easy; there would be a vicious bout of d.t.'s first. Suitable embarrassment and humiliation. She wanted to laugh, but it would hurt too much and might spew vomit all over this night nurse. No one deserved that. But the truth couldn't be more obvious. What happened tonight was no accident; it was a clear case of judgment and justice. Sloane was being punished, and it came as no surprise. She'd seen it coming for a long time now. Almost three years. Three years on—

"What day is it?" Sloane felt woozy as the medication hit her veins.

"Early morning, Friday."

"No, I meant . . ." Sloane hesitated. Swore she caught the scent of singed hair. "What's the date?"

"March 25."

Sloane closed her eyes, seeing the black kitten's sweet face. Tomorrow would mark three years since the night Greg Cabot died. And it would see the end of Marty's too-short life. A pain stabbed deep in her core that had nothing to do with the loss of a spleen. A tear trickled behind the bandage covering her eye. There were no blessings.

"Oh," the nurse said, adjusting her pillow. "Your brother called."

41

TAYLOR HAD FALLEN ASLEEP sitting cross-legged beside Hooper's nest, the soft hairbrush still resting against his ear.

Like it or not, Seth had to agree with Halston: *"She's the finest woman I've ever met."* Taylor had the best heart of anyone Seth had ever known. Courageous, kind, honest . . . stubbornly loyal. It was after 2 a.m., and she'd spent the last hour gently brushing her dog. And smoothing the once-white comforter . . . watching him breathe. Now and then, she'd lean low with her lips against his ear and whisper something. She was keeping a vigil over her much-loved friend. It was killing Seth to see her like this, knowing something he'd done had added to her pain.

"Oh . . . ugh," Taylor murmured, sweeping a hand over her

shiny tangle of hair. She glanced around the room, saw him there. "I must have dozed for a minute."

Twenty minutes, thank heaven. He'd been debating the wisdom of picking her up and carrying her to bed. "Maybe for a minute."

"I'm good now." She rested her hand on Hooper's chest, releasing a breath. "He's hanging in there. No muscle twitches."

"He looks peaceful," Seth offered. Praying—silently, not breaking her rules—the very same for Taylor. *Please bring her peace.*

"You lit the fireplace," she said, barely besting a yawn. "Nice."

He'd lit the half-dozen thick white candles artfully arranged in her gas-log fireplace. San Diego was hardly the frozen north, and the house was comfortable, but he'd seen Taylor shiver a few times. He'd hoped the candles would provide at least an illusion of warmth, comfort. "I thought you might like it."

"I do." Her eyes met his. "It's late, Seth. You should go home."

"It's early. Barely starting tomorrow," he told her without missing a beat. "And I'm staying. As long as you're up with Hooper, I'll be right here."

"I . . ." Her voice choked. "I have to be here. I have to stay with him."

"I understand," Seth said, remembering his own vigil beside Camille's hospital bed. It occurred to him that maybe this time with Hooper was the good-bye she'd never had with Greg. "But I can spell you for a while. Let you sleep."

"No." Taylor sat up. She scrubbed her hands over her cheeks. "I think maybe if I splashed some water on my face and then jogged around the neighborhood for a few minutes,

I'd get my second wind." She lifted her arm and frowned at the plastic bracelet on her wrist. "I really need to log some steps."

Jog at 2 a.m.? Steps? Seth stopped himself from saying it aloud. The small gated community was well lit, and this rigid daily regimen—regardless of whether or not it was initially prompted by Halston—was obviously important to Taylor. Maybe even something that provided a measure of peace. How could he argue with that?

"Go," Seth told her. "I'll watch Hooper." He'd almost said, *"You can trust me,"* then remembered she'd done that with Halston and the man had trundled her dog off to a death sentence. Right now, because of what Sloane had revealed, Seth was equally suspect. More than anything in the world, he wanted to disprove that. "Get your steps. I'll be right here."

"Okay then, I will." Her gaze moved to Hooper again. "I won't be that long. I'll take my cell. . . ."

"I'll call if anything changes. Promise."

"I have the nanny cam."

"Right." His integrity . . . shot. At least she hadn't kicked him out.

Seth put on a fresh pot of coffee and then sat down on the floor beside Hooper. He'd started to tap in the phone number of the trauma center's NSICU when Taylor came back through the door.

"Why . . . ? What's wrong?" he asked, rising to his feet. Fear jabbed. Her expression was so—"What happened?"

"I couldn't make myself go." Taylor hugged her arms around herself. She looked down at Hooper, her eyes filling with tears. "Everything . . . I have left is here."

"Taylor . . ." Seth wasn't sure who moved first, but in a heartbeat he was holding her. Holding her up as she sagged into him, clinging and sobbing like she'd never stop. "Shhh," he murmured against her hair, cradling her head with his palm. "I've got you. . . . I'm here. We'll do this together."

Twenty minutes later, Seth decided Taylor's racking sobs were far easier to bear than this silence as she leaned against him on the couch. Eyes closed and one hand clutching a puppy photo in her lap, the other lying limp on Seth's leg like a bird shot from the sky. He hoped he was imagining it, but it almost sounded as if she and her dog were breathing in unison, his sad rattle and her soft, hiccuping sighs. Not a word, only a painful vacuum. She shivered again and Seth tightened his arm around her shoulders, hiking her a little closer.

"I could make you some hot chocolate," he whispered against her hair. "Or blow out those candles and start a real fire. If you're cold."

Taylor sighed. Said nothing.

He watched the candles, the only source of light in the room now, wondering if the remote control lying on the arm of the couch controlled the music system as well . . .

"How uncomfortable was it to sit there, even for a few minutes, and not fill that silence with something . . . anything?"

His question to the crisis team trainees. A bid for "sacred silence." He'd taught that same thing dozens of times, believed in its value absolutely. Why did it seem so impossible now? Why, when he cared so deeply about helping, did he feel so blasted helpless?

"Among the unique aspects of death notifications is that in this one instance, it is the crisis responder's actions that are the proximate cause of a survivor's trauma. We are their trauma."

Seth's heart stalled. The reason this was so hard was that he'd had a hand in Taylor's misery. Those sobs and that awful look on her face when she came back into the house weren't only for Hooper. It had to feel like she was losing her husband all over again. As if everything she'd believed about her marriage was a lie. Even if it was Sloane Wilder who'd said the words, the blame fell in large part upon—

"You . . ." Taylor lifted her head from Seth's shoulder and leaned away to look into his eyes. Her whisper was halting, raw. "You knew . . . about Greg?"

42

SHE DIDN'T WANT TO HEAR. She had to know. Even if . . .

"Tell me." Taylor made herself say it. She battled a wave of trembling, forced herself to take a measured breath. In, out. "You knew Greg was seeing . . . Sloane?"

"Not exactly." Seth grimaced as though he knew how ridiculous that sounded—like the old joke about being "a little bit pregnant." The remorse in his eyes was almost as painful as Sloane's revelation. It was clear he'd never wanted to have this conversation. "Greg told me he was doing something he shouldn't. I thought it had to do with the illegal gambling. But then he confided it involved a relationship with a woman."

"Sloane."

"No." Seth shook his head. "I mean, he never gave a name."

Could she believe him? She wanted to. But—"Sloane said, 'Ask Seth Donovan.' Like you knew."

"I don't get that." Seth scraped his fingers through his hair. "She said something crazy to me, too. About how she wasn't going to let me ruin her life again. I have no idea what she meant. As far as I know, I never even met Sloane until a few weeks ago."

"Wait . . ." Taylor's mind tumbled. "Could she have been lying? About the whole thing?"

"Why would she do that?" Seth's gentle expression said he'd seen the irrational hope in her eyes. "Why would Sloane tell you a lie?"

"Because everyone lies." Taylor braced herself for a rush of anger, but there was only an eddy of sadness. "Like Greg did in his phone message that awful night. Saying he wanted things to be better between us." She met Seth's gaze directly. "And you lied. I asked you why my husband was out on that road. You said you didn't know."

"I didn't." Seth hunched forward, his eyes not leaving hers. "It's true that Greg canceled our appointment. I suspected he wanted to talk about that relationship, but I didn't know for sure. I didn't know it was Sloane, and I definitely didn't know where this 'other woman' lived." There was sorrow in his expression when Taylor flinched at the ugly cliché. "What little Greg told me was confidential. I barely knew you back then. Then, a few weeks later, Greg was killed. It was more than a year before you and I started working together. We became friends, and I . . ." Seth swallowed. "I couldn't bring myself to hurt you further. I didn't see the point in that, Taylor."

"You don't know any details? How long he'd been seeing her or if Greg was planning to . . . ?" *Leave me? Oh, God . . .*

"No," Seth said quickly. "No details. Frankly, I was surprised he mentioned it to me at all. Like you said, it wasn't in his nature to open up like that. I only know that he seemed very troubled by the situation."

Taylor closed her eyes, trying to take it in. Wishing she didn't have to, wishing this—all of it, everything—had never happened. There were still so many unanswered questions, but the wreckage of her marriage was as undeniable as that Cessna crumpled on the beach.

She opened her eyes when Seth spoke again.

"I'm sorry," he said, his voice thick with emotion, "that you found out the way you did. I wish I could have done something to change all of it. Your friendship has meant more than I can say." The light from the fireplace candles reflected in Seth's dark eyes, created shadows across his face. His beard stubble had that russet cast too. "I would never willingly do anything to hurt you. Ever. Those things you said to me in the chapel after Sloane told you . . . I deserved that. And—"

"Seth, wait." Taylor reached for his hand to stop him.

"Please," he said, grasping her fingers gently. "Let me finish. I need to say this."

———

Seth took a slow breath, grateful for her hand in his and thankful beyond measure that she'd let him in the door last night. He'd be going home day after tomorrow. This needed to be said. "You were completely right to lay into me about holding back what I knew. I hedged my answers to your questions more times than I can count. I'm not proud of that, especially when I see how much pain this is causing you. It makes me sick that I'm a part of it. Maybe I have been self-righteous; maybe I do hide behind my chaplain uniform."

Taylor grimaced. "I shouldn't have said that. I was upset."

"You had every right to be. But you're dead wrong if you think I'm using you. Dangling you like a pathetic widow. I never planned for you to do death notifications in our classroom role-playing. I don't think of you as a grief 'resource.' There is *nothing* pathetic about you, Taylor. You're strong and intelligent . . . caring and beautiful, inside and out." Somehow he'd reached up to rest his palm against her cheek. It was still damp with tears. "You're the bravest woman I've ever known. I see how hard you're trying to make a new life for yourself."

"I am." Taylor's eyes glistened with fresh tears. "Today it feels like I'm doing that without a map. No . . . today I'm slogging backward through mud. No map, no flashlight, no clue." She laid her hand over his. Seth's heart stalled. "But now you're here. I can't tell you how grateful I am for that, Seth. Thank you."

Before he could speak, Taylor leaned forward and touched her lips to his cheek, then wound her arms around his neck. She sighed. Seth slid his arms around her, holding her . . . holding his breath, then breathing her in. It felt as if an ache he'd borne for far too long was easing away, replaced by something comforting and real. He didn't want it to end.

"Thank you," she said again, leaning away enough to look at him. The candlelight flickered over her face. "I don't know what I'd have done without—"

"You're very welcome," Seth whispered, taking her face in his hands. He pressed a gentle kiss against her forehead, then touched his lips to her cheek before leaning back a little, his thumb caressing her skin. She blinked at him, lips parted. He could hear his heartbeat in his ears. "I care for you . . . so much, Taylor. More than . . ."

He couldn't be certain if she inched closer or he bent down, but somehow their lips met. Lightly, warm against warm, soft . . . tender. He was vaguely aware of her fingertips moving against the nape of his neck, her barest intake of breath . . . and then the incredible feel of her lips as she responded to him. Sweet and so beautifully alive.

"Seth . . . ," Taylor whispered, pulling away. Even in the pale light, her cheeks looked flushed, pupils wide. "I shouldn't have . . ."

"It was me," he offered, wanting the closeness back despite his stab at chivalry. Needing her beyond reason. "I did that." He took hold of her hand, prayed she wouldn't draw back from that small connection too.

"I'm so confused," Taylor whispered, still holding his hand. Her fingers were shaking. She glanced away. "And tired."

"Of course," Seth agreed. Was he that insensitive? "I understand. I should never have—"

"*Grr-oomph . . . errrr . . .*"

Seth glanced toward the floor. Heard the strange sound repeat. Taylor tensed.

"It's Hooper," he confirmed, seeing movement. "He's trying to get up."

"No." Taylor slid from the couch to her knees. "It's another seizure. Grab the medication."

43

"DR. WENDY IS A BLESSING FROM GOD," Taylor said, breaking her rules again. She'd told Seth in no uncertain terms that they wouldn't be discussing Greg or God. And now she'd delivered both her taboos on a platter. The rules were apparently suspended in these wee hours. That kiss certainly proved it. "Having her at the emergency clinic is such a relief."

"She didn't think you need to bring Hooper in?" Seth asked, glancing down at the slumbering retriever.

"No. He's okay for now. She'll stop by on her way home, around seven thirty. We'll decide what to do next then." *Our last good-bye, Hooper—can I do that?*

"He looks comfortable."

Taylor nodded, grateful beyond words that Seth really

noticed. His caring was transparent on his handsome, sleepy face. She loved him for that. And for calling the trauma center to get an updated report on Kasie: still under sedation, but stable vital signs.

"It was a half dose of Valium," Taylor explained, "because the seizure was localized and had already ended." Not only had it ended, but Hooper had had a sweet moment of consciousness, responding to Taylor's soothing words with a few thumps of his tail. *Thank you, God.* "Dr. Wendy said the medication would hold him until morning."

"Not long now," Seth noted, glancing toward the windows. Dawn was only a few hours away. The kindness in his eyes warmed her heart. "How's that hot chocolate?"

"Good." She smiled, noticing a faint chocolate smudge on his lips. Her stomach fluttered. Confusion, cocoa, and—"I can't believe you found marshmallows. I thought I'd purged my kitchen."

"In the freezer, behind the Girl Scout cookies. I'm learning your secrets."

"You are." She blinked against the threat of more tears.

"What is it?" Seth set his cup down.

"I . . ." Fatigue was tearing at her defenses as recklessly as that plane slicing through a thousand fanciful kites. "I sort of made a Survival List." Taylor shook her head. "No. Not sort of. It's formatted with bullet points, check boxes, and a due date."

"Halston's idea."

"No. Mine." Taylor waited for the familiar sense of accomplishment, but it eluded her. "I gave myself three years to pull my life together. I've been getting it done. The move to San Diego, my job in ER, finding a good vet for Hooper." Taylor prodded a mini marshmallow with her fingertip. "Ditching the junk food and getting into shape."

Seth regarded her fitness bracelet. "Counting your steps."

"Exactly."

She thought of the last item on that list: *Fall in love again*. It had been a foolish thought in the first place and now, though she'd been kissed by two men in twenty-four hours, it only seemed more impossible. Clearly, after Greg, she had no clue about—

"I don't know . . . ," Seth said, his brows drawing together. "And granted, this is coming from a guy who still scribbles notes with pencil and paper, but I don't need to keep track like that. I run until I'm tired or until this bum knee reminds me I'm no superman. I guess I've dealt with grief that same way too." Despite his offhand shrug, there was certainty in his expression. "After Camille, my heart felt like so much ground meat, and there wasn't any way around it. I prayed and I hurt. I hurt and I prayed."

Taylor's throat tightened.

"I met with a grief-sharing group for a while too—it helped a lot. I finally learned to accept that my healing, my new relationships . . . and my future would move forward according to God's timing, not mine," Seth continued. "Not to say I'm not an active participant. There's personal responsibility, absolutely. But from what I've seen, if we get caught up in planning our lives meticulously, point by point, then it's like control *becomes* our god. We reach for control, when what we really want . . . is peace." He looked down at his hot chocolate for a moment, then met her gaze again. "I guess what I'm trying to say is that I'm not worried about counting the steps. If I'm going in the right direction, if I'm on the right path, I'll feel that certainty in my soul."

————

Seth blew out the candles and glanced toward the windows. Still dark for another hour or so. But at least . . . He turned to look at Taylor on the couch. She'd finally fallen asleep. He'd covered her with his jacket and she lay with one hand curled, childlike, against her cheek—knees tucked up, only one slipper remaining in place. He thought of what she'd said about her Survival List and how all that had happened made her feel like she was *"slogging backward through mud."* He understood that feeling. And wished he could do so much more to help her through it. The journey wasn't over yet.

Seth's gaze moved to the accumulation of clutter atop the small table. Soup mugs, hot chocolate mugs, his coffee cup, crumpled napkins, and a single soggy miniature marshmallow glued by cocoa to the glass surface. Taylor's perfect white beach topped by the messy and unexpected flotsam of life. Somehow, despite the pain, it seemed like a step in the right direction.

He lifted her Bible from the tabletop and settled on the floor beside Hooper's bed to wait for dawn.

————

Where . . . ? What?

Taylor lifted her head, groaning softly; her neck was sore. She blinked at the pale light, saw that it was coming from the living room windows. She'd fallen asleep on the couch.

An ache spread across her chest as it all came back. Kasie, Sloane, Greg, Rob, Hooper, and . . . *Seth.*

She lifted herself on one elbow and peered down at the floor. Seth was stretched out on the carpet, her Bible open beside him. He was lying next to Hooper's bed, with one big palm resting against the dog's back. As if to offer reassurance or to make sure that Hooper was still—

Taylor's heart turned over. *God, please . . .*

She slipped from the couch to kneel at Hooper's head, held her breath, and touched his ear. Soft . . . cold.

No . . . The ache in her chest rose to her throat.

She bent low, listening for a breath she knew wasn't there. Then stroked her dog's ear, his face, and drew her thumb gently across his closed eye. She gazed toward the window through a lens of tears. Dawn's pale light filtered through the window, the pane smudged from Hooper's nose, his restless vigil these last few days. Window after window, room by room, watching and waiting. It was over. Hooper was finally at peace.

If only Taylor could find that comfort.

44

"I DON'T WANT TO LEAVE YOU," Seth said, desperate to ease the stricken look on Taylor's face. He glanced over the breakfast bar toward where Hooper still lay, the white comforter tucked up to his shoulders. The sound of Taylor's soft crying had awakened him. And shredded his heart. "When will the vet be here?"

"Less than ten minutes." She peered at him over her coffee cup, her eyes filled with sadness. "Kasie's family wants you there when they talk with the doctors—you need to go, Chaplain." Her small smile made his heart ache all over again. "And then you have to check on Lucy and get some sleep."

She was writing a survival list for him.

"Besides . . ." Taylor's teeth scraped across her lower lip. "I want to sit with Hooper for a while. You know."

Seth nodded. They both knew, too well.

"Thank you," Taylor said, setting her cup down next to the coffeemaker. "For being here. For everything."

He hated that it sounded like good-bye. "I don't leave for Sacramento until day after tomorrow—evening flight."

"Aimee will be back that night."

"Good," he said, despite the fact that it wasn't what he wanted to hear.

Taylor was walking to the door. He had no choice but to follow.

"Call me about Kasie?" she asked as he stepped onto the porch.

"I will."

He stood there after Taylor disappeared into the house, glad she hadn't noticed she was still wearing his jacket. It would be an excuse to call her . . . come back, meet her somewhere. Anywhere. Seth thought of what he'd told Taylor in the hours before dawn. That if things were right, he'd feel it in his soul. And he did, more than ever now.

I love you.

———

"I only know what I heard on the radio when I was driving into work," the traveler nurse told Sloane, frowning as she manually cycled the blood pressure machine again. The last two readings hadn't been good. "They found the car that was terrorizing y'all on the highway," she explained, the Alabama accent stretching her words. "Abandoned. And torched. No way to ID the driver. 'Course with the car being stolen, it makes it so much harder. And it's not like they can ask Kasie if she's recalled any more details. Poor little thing. I can't count the times she's offered to help me."

"She's . . ." Sloane sucked in a breath, light-headed again. "Still in a coma?"

"Far as I hear. You know the privacy rules. We only get secondhand information." The nurse adjusted the rate on an IV pump; the rapidly infusing fluid felt like ice water in Sloane's forearm. She shivered. "I'll get you a warm blanket, hon. And I'm going to tell that detective outside she's going to have to wait to talk with you."

"Detective?" Sloane grimaced against a wave of pain in her belly; something didn't feel right in there. "Why a detective?"

"About the accident. Probably to see if you can provide a clue why someone would be following your car."

"I see you're still driving that heap-of-trash Jetta." . . . Dirty Girl.

Sloane's teeth chattered as the nurse pulled a warm blanket over her chest and shoulders.

"But no detectives until after we get things stabilized here," the nurse promised. "Doctor's ordered another blood draw, and looks like we're getting an ultrasound of your belly. That pain still there?"

"Yes," Sloane whispered, understanding the implication. These were signs of internal bleeding, from the surgical site or from something they hadn't found before. Both bad. "Can I get some more medication?"

"Sure." The nurse laid her hand on Sloane's shoulder. Her eyes were kind. "Should I call someone for you? I know you said you don't have any family here. But maybe a pastor or a good friend?"

"No pastor." Sloane closed her eyes, heard the ominous alarm as the blood pressure cuff deflated. "No good friends. But there's someone I should talk to."

"I'm stepping back inside to use your bathroom," the vet said, meeting Taylor's eyes across the open tailgate of her SUV. Hooper lay inside, still on the old camouflage pillow and white comforter. Dr. Wendy had backed her car into the garage to provide privacy and to avoid the eyes of neighborhood children. The school bus would be by soon. "It will give you a minute more," she added.

"Thanks."

Taylor hiked herself onto the tailgate and only on the last boost realized she was barefoot. She had no idea what she'd done with her slippers. Seth would know. She was still wearing his jacket. Her throat tightened. She'd been so awful to him at the hospital and still he'd come to be with her. Stayed all night. Lying on the floor beside Hooper.

Somewhere in the distance she heard a familiar bark. The schnauzer, Heidi.

"Sweet boy . . . ," Taylor said, running her fingers gently over her dog's head. She bent low and whispered the familiar words as best she could around the lump in her throat.

"Good night, Hooper."

Tears slid down her face. *Good-bye, Greg.*

An hour later, she'd rinsed the dirty cups, scraped a marshmallow off her coffee table, and collected Hooper's toys and food bowls in a grocery sack. She put her wedding rings and Greg's poem back in the jeweler's box, resisting the urge to read the poem one last time. She'd find as little comfort there as she would listening to the voice mail he'd left, telling her they should drop everything and go to Paris. Nothing made sense anymore. Tomorrow was the twenty-sixth, and instead of celebrating her survival, Taylor was further from hope than ever before. She'd finally lost everything.

For some reason she thought of that crisis team training scenario she'd done with Seth. The death notification. And how she'd corrected the trainee when he'd told a survivor that her loved one was "gone." Taylor had explained the importance of using the more concrete words. *Dead, died, killed.* It was correct, of course. More humane, because it avoided painful confusion and groundless hope that the victim was still alive. But . . .

She hunched forward on the white couch and let her gaze drift back to Hooper's noseprint on the window. *Gone.* The word held no confusion for her. So many things she'd counted on and loved were gone. All the steps she'd so carefully taken had simply led her here. To this too-quiet, too-white place where she was alone. Taylor's heart cramped so mercilessly she thought she'd collapse. She drew in a breath, counted . . .

"Please, God. I need to know I haven't lost you, too. I can't do this by myself. Show me the way. I'm really listening now. . . ."

A few minutes later, Taylor picked up her phone and tapped Aimee's name in her contacts. Her cousin answered on the second ring.

"I was going to call you today," her cousin said, "and see how—"

"Hooper died. And . . . I can't tell you the rest over the phone. I need you, Aimee."

"I'll be there. First flight I can get out of Florida."

"Thank you," Taylor told her, voice choking. "I love you."

"Ditto. I'm calling the airline the minute I get off the phone."

Taylor hugged Seth's worn-soft canvas jacket around her, curled up on the couch, and closed her eyes. Her phone rang less than ten minutes later; Aimee was fast to the rescue, bless her. But—Taylor checked the caller ID—it wasn't her cousin. It was a San Diego Hope number. It was her day off, but maybe they were understaffed and calling to offer overtime . . .

"Yes?" she said, telling herself she was in no shape to report for work, regardless. She'd taken tomorrow off too, to celebrate her survival. Now she needed it for her sanity. "This is Taylor Cabot."

"Meghan Porter in the SICU," the caller said, her accent more than hinting that she was one of the traveling staff from a Southern state. "I'm the RN caring for Sloane Wilder."

"Okay . . ." Taylor's brows scrunched. *What on earth?*

"She's asked to see you." The insistent sound of monitor alarms rose in the background. "If you're coming, it should be soon. She's not looking good. They're talking about taking her back to surgery within the hour."

45

"I LIKE THE LIGHT in here better than in the other waiting rooms. Good for sewing. Better coffeemaker, too." Ruthie Marks rested her embroidery hoop on the patchwork fabric lying across her lap. "You're here as a visitor today?"

"I'm . . . waiting to see a friend," Taylor said, thinking that it was her luck the chatty grief ambassador was also sitting in the SICU waiting room. She'd lied; Sloane Wilder was the antithesis of a friend. She was the woman who'd seduced Taylor's husband. Nothing could be uglier. She should never have agreed to come. That Ruthie was here was proof of that. She forced herself to smile. "You're visiting someone who's had surgery too?"

"My boyfriend."

Taylor's jaw sagged. "Your . . . ?"

"I know." Ruthie shook her head, but there was a gleam in her eyes. "At my age, that is such an awkward term. I haven't figured out anything better. Allen's had gallbladder surgery. That's why I'm here."

Taylor was stunned. She glanced discreetly at the woman's blouse; the chain with the wedding rings was gone. How had she missed that?

"We're both members of the Solace Share group. Allen's wife passed in 2005. She was an avid gardener. Even won ribbons at the Coronado Flower Show. Allen taught himself how to propagate her African violets from leaf cuttings. He's so proud of his 'babies.' I can't tell you how many little plastic pots he's brought to the meetings over the years. I don't think anyone's gone home without one. I have fourteen." The love in the volunteer's expression was palpable. "Now Allen's teaching me to do the cuttings too. Snip off a leaf, put the cut edge into the soil, cover it with a plastic bag, and make sure it has water and light. Then wait. It's a long wait. But all of a sudden there they are." Ruthie smiled. "New leaves, new little plant—a brand-new life. It's sort of a miracle, really."

Taylor's throat tightened.

"Anyway," the woman continued with a small chuckle, "it only took Allen and me a decade or so to fall in love. I guess we'd both doubted something like that would ever happen. We'd worried early on, like everyone does, how we'd manage alone. Who would walk the dog, feed the cat . . . bring us broth and crackers if we got sick."

Taylor thought of Seth setting the mugs of tomato soup on her glass table.

"Maybe we were slow learners." Ruthie smiled. "But it's like we tell folks at the gatherings: everyone's path is different. And it's not like you get rid of the sorrow altogether. It's more like . . ." Her finger moved over a line of embroidery. "It's like you put it in a special place in your heart. So you can remember the good times and all the love you had for them and for the life they lived. Then you use it to help other people on their journeys. That's the real bless—"

"Ruthie Marks?" a nurse's aide said, appearing in the doorway.

"Yes, that's me." Ruthie began tucking her fabric into a tote bag.

"Good." The aide smiled at her. "We have a very nice gentleman in the recovery room who is eager to see his girlfriend."

Ruthie had barely waved good-bye when Taylor's phone buzzed with a text from the SICU saying Sloane could have a visitor. She walked to the doors of the unit, touched a fingertip to the security keypad, then hesitated. Her stomach knotted and a hundred warning bells clanged in her head. She was a fool to be here, a glutton for punishment. Taylor peered down the hallway, telling herself to retrace her steps to the elevator and on to the parking lot. Go home; be spared this one last cruelty . . .

And then she tapped the keypad, took a deep breath, and walked through the doors.

———

"What do you mean?" Seth asked, shifting the cell phone to glance at Daniel, sitting slumped and sullen in the NSICU waiting room. He gritted his teeth as the young man repeatedly bashed the toe of his shoe against the leg of the chair next to him. Kasie's fiancé was having issues. Seth rephrased his question to the attorney. "The Modesto store manager can't handle it?"

The man didn't bother to conceal his sarcasm. "That deal you let fall through is looking better all the time, right?"

Keep your cool, Seth. . . .

"I'm trying to assess the situation at the store, Randall. You said no employees were hurt and there was no property damage other than a cracked display case. Just tell me what I'm missing here." Seth fought to keep his irritation at bay despite a headache pounding his temples. No sleep, too much on his mind. "I've got a flight out tomorrow night. It's not like we haven't dealt with shoplifters in that store before."

"Not like this one. It's threatening to become a media circus. I'm surprised you haven't gotten calls already."

Seth had ignored them. The only person he wanted to hear from right now was Taylor. And she wasn't returning her messages either.

———

Taylor thought she'd braced herself, but it hadn't been nearly enough. Sloane looked awful. Worse than that. Right this minute, she was the very definition of that dark medical euphemism for a desperately ill patient: "circling the drain." Sickly sallow, air hungry, lips blanched—all signs of shock from blood loss. Her burgundy-black hair clung to her perspiring forehead, and the whites of her eyes showed through her half-closed lids. Those wounds around her left eye . . . Taylor winced. There were dozens of sutures, as black against her pale skin as her lashes. Even with follow-up cosmetic surgery—

"You're here," Sloane rasped, opening her eyes. She seemed

to read Taylor's expression and reached up to gingerly touch the sutured lacerations. "Right. No more . . . beauty pageants." She failed at her smirk. "Going to have to hang up my tiara."

Taylor wanted to say something reassuring but knew Sloane would call her on the lie. And scars were the least of her worries now. "I heard you're going back to surgery."

"So they tell me."

Taylor cleared her throat, letting her gaze follow the transfusion tubing from the drip chamber down the line to where it met the IV catheter taped to Sloane's pale forearm. Red and white, like drops of blood on the snow in that old Grimm's fairy tale. She made herself look into Sloane's eyes. "They need to get you to the OR fast. I'm really surprised they allowed a visitor at all."

"C'mon, Cabot." Sloane's tongue slid across her lower lip. "You're not a 'visitor.' You never planned to come here. I'm sure you were disappointed I didn't die on the table the first go-round."

Taylor's stomach lurched; she told herself it wasn't true.

"You're here because you know I have something to say. And . . ." Sloane grimaced against a wave of pain. Her blue eyes captured Taylor's. "They let you in . . . because it might be the last thing I ever say."

"Sloane . . ."

"So sit down."

46

"SIT," SLOANE REPEATED. "Please . . ." She glanced toward the monitor as an alarm alerted for another low blood pressure reading. "They said I could have five minutes. So sit down and listen, okay?"

"Okay," Taylor agreed, dread crowding in. "But I'll stand."

"Right." Sloane shook her head. "Got to have it your way."

"I'm listening."

"It's about what I told you in the ER. About Greg."

Taylor had known that, but hearing this woman say her husband's name, knowing . . . She wanted to be angry, but all she felt was sick.

"It was true," Sloane said. "Greg was with me that night. Because I begged him to come. I told him . . ." She frowned as a second alarm began to shrill. "I swear, if that nurse comes over here, I'm going to—"

"Got it." Taylor pressed the Reset button. Sloane should be resting, not doing this. Her condition was critical; the alarms underscored that. It was the perfect excuse to turn around and—"Go on," Taylor heard herself say. The thumping of her heart replaced the silenced alarm. "Finish what you wanted to say."

"It all started because of that mess at the fire department. Paul was mixed up in it, in a bad way—a dangerous way. Greg needed it all gone."

"Because he wanted to be promoted."

Sloane nodded. "It's complicated, but my ex managed to put a tap on Greg for money. Then turned it into a sort of extortion deal. Paul . . . isn't a good guy. You could say that'd been a pattern for me. Until Greg."

Taylor's stomach twisted.

"He was the most decent guy I've ever known. The only one, maybe. Greg saw the mess I was in . . . the mess I *am*—" Sloane's smile was grim—"and wanted to help. I didn't trust that. Not at first. He was a man, and I figured the only thing he wanted was . . ." Her voice choked. "But I was wrong. He mostly wanted someone to listen."

What?

"News flash, Cabot: I didn't sleep with your husband. Which doesn't mean I didn't want to. Maybe that's exactly what I had in mind that night." Sloane closed her eyes. "No *maybe* about it. It was my plan."

Taylor breathed in. Counted to seven.

"Greg had an appointment with Donovan that morning," Sloane continued. "He'd told me he was feeling bad about where things were heading between us. Hadn't even done the deed and was already tearing himself up over it. Over us . . . and not making captain."

And over me pressuring him for a baby?

"He called later that afternoon and said we couldn't see each other anymore," Sloane explained. "Just like that. No meeting for coffee, no phone calls . . . no more contact, period. Donovan's doing, I'm sure."

Except Greg didn't keep that appointment.

"I couldn't handle it. I texted him a few times and he didn't answer. Then later that evening, after I'd had a few drinks . . ." Sloane's pale fingers stroked her throat.

"You called him," Taylor whispered. Sloane Wilder had been the "buddy" who needed Greg's help with an entertainment system. If she let her mind go there, she'd throw up.

"I told him only a coward would end things over the phone," Sloane recounted. "I told him I deserved better. And . . . if he didn't come, I might do something desperate. I think I even said my death would be on his conscience for the rest of his life. My death. His life." She groaned. "Your God sure ran with that one."

Taylor closed her eyes.

"He was at my place for maybe thirty minutes. Long enough to call my bluff, apologize again, and make sure I was safe. Greg the Boy Scout. Always." Sloane tried to smile, but it did nothing to ease the sadness in her eyes. "Maybe twenty minutes after he drove off, I climbed into the Jetta to go to the 7-Eleven. I was out of wine. It's not that far, country road the whole way. Even if I weaved a little across the road, not much chance of a cop spotting me. It wasn't like I'd never done that before."

But Kasie wasn't going to let it happen again. And now . . .

"I rounded a corner and had to hit my brakes," Sloane continued, "because the lanes were blocked by fire trucks and patrol cars. I saw Greg's truck parked off the road. There were paramedics kneeling on the asphalt, doing CPR. On Greg."

Oh, dear God . . .

"I saw it all," Sloane whispered, her eyes shiny with tears. "I saw the woman Greg stopped to help. And I saw the woman who hit him, too. I tried to get to him, but the police held me back. I sat down in the gravel . . . and I watched the ambulance pull away. I kept thinking it couldn't be happening. It wasn't right. Not Greg. Not the one man who'd ever been good to me. And . . ." Sloane pressed her knuckles against her mouth, failing to quiet her sob. Tears streamed from her eyes and over the dark lines of sutures. "Greg would never have been out there if—"

"I'm sorry to interrupt," a nurse told them, arriving at the bedside. "The OR will be calling for you in a few minutes, Ms. Wilder." She glanced between Sloane and Taylor, concern in her expression. "I wish I could give you longer, but I can't."

"That's okay. I . . . understand," Taylor managed. Her voice was quavering. "The important thing is to get her bleeding stopped. So I'll—"

"No." Sloane pushed herself up on her elbows, the small exertion hiking her heart rate enough to set off another alarm. "We need two more minutes. Two minutes won't make any difference in where I'm headed. Make the devil wait." She murmured thanks as the nurse stepped away, then sagged back onto the pillow and sucked in a few shallow breaths. The alarm subsided.

"Sloane . . ." Taylor leaned over the bed rail, a new emotion surfacing. Against all odds she'd begun to ache with sorrow for this troubled woman. "That's enough. Let them take you to surgery."

"After I tell you one more thing."

"There's nothing more I need to know."

"There is. I don't want to die without telling you."

Taylor's heart wedged into her throat. *Please, God, have mercy. On both of us.*

"No matter how I felt," Sloane said, "and how much I wanted it to be different, Greg loved you. You. Not me. It was the last thing he said to me that night. He said he could never be with me because he was still in love with his wife. He said you meant everything to him and he was going to do whatever it took to make you believe that. Make his marriage work. He was on his way home . . . to *you*."

Taylor's tears spilled over.

The phone message. *"I'm coming home . . ."*

"I'm sorry," Sloane whispered. "And I'm sorry about Kasie, too. I hope she makes it. If she does . . . tell her that there was no way to save someone like me. But tell her I said maybe there's some hope left for this sorry world . . . with people like her in it." Her pale lips quirked. "And like you, Cabot. Even as uptight as you are. Greg was right about you. You're good and decent too."

Taylor's throat ached so badly she could barely speak. "I know you didn't have to tell me what Greg said. But I'm grateful. I don't know what to say to you or how—"

"Go." Sloane's lids fluttered; perspiration dotted her upper lip. "Get out of here, Cabot. I've got a date with a scalpel."

"Give me your hand."

"What . . . ? Why?"

"Shut your mouth and give me your hand." Taylor reached over the rail and grasped it. Sloane's fingers were cold as death.

Please, Lord . . . help me with this.

"I'm going to pray with you," Taylor told her.

"Great—when I don't have the strength to fight it."

"Good." Placing her other hand on Sloane's, Taylor leaned over the rail. "Because first we're going to pray. And then I'm going to walk alongside you to the surgery doors. And try, with everything I have left . . . to forgive you."

47

I WANT YOU TO KNOW how much comfort your kind concern and your prayers have meant to me these past three years. . . .

Taylor read what she'd typed so far in response to the young woman Greg had tried to help that tragic night. She'd be writing something similar to the teacher who'd accidentally hit him, responding to that annual card with a handwritten note. She'd already asked Rob to meet her for coffee today so she could apologize. Even if he hadn't done it well, he'd been trying to spare her an agonizing decision.

She glanced across the room and saw the morning sun lighting Hooper's smudge. Not exactly standard window art, but far too precious for Windex; she'd decided to leave it there until time erased it. Like the sea eventually made rocks into sand. And the way God was transforming Taylor's confusing anger into a peace she'd never imagined. Even with those checklists and carefully logged steps and . . . Taylor shook her head, still so amazed at all that had happened in just twenty-four hours. It was poignant evidence that God had crafted his own survival plan for her; she'd been a fool to ever doubt that.

"We reach for control, when what we really want . . . is peace."
Seth. He'd nailed it, of course.

Taylor wrapped her arms around herself, the bulky-soft warmth of Seth's old jacket feeling almost like a hug. She nestled her cheek against the corduroy collar and smiled; it smelled like him. She'd reached for the jacket first thing this morning, a familiar comfort in a world where too many things had changed. Taylor was so very grateful that Seth Donovan *hadn't*.

But was that true?

She rubbed her palms over the fabric, remembering that moment between them, very different from anything they'd shared before. That kiss . . . so unexpected. That it still stirred her was unexpected too. He'd been quick to accept responsibility, though Taylor felt fairly sure she'd made the first move. She'd been honest when she drew back, saying she was confused and tired. All of that was true. The same way it was true that Seth had been there as a friend, to offer her comfort. Nothing more . . . right?

"You're strong and intelligent . . . caring and beautiful, inside and out."

Seth had been trying to reassure her. A wonderful blessing, but nothing more. There was no point in continuing to go over

It in her head. Her heart. No reason for this foolish flutter in her stomach or—

Her doorbell rang: Aimee.

———

"Hate to see you leaving early," Walt said, smiling as Lucy tried her eager best to nudge awake his own Labrador, asleep on the rug of the garage apartment. He watched Seth wedge a sweater into his suitcase. "Cindy asked me just this morning about having a little dinner tonight. Maybe inviting Taylor, too."

Seth's chest constricted. "Tell Cindy I appreciate it but . . ."

"You have to respond to a merchant crisis."

"Right. Wouldn't you think a thief might figure a uniform store would have Tasers?" He groaned, reaching for the package of antacids he'd purchased that morning. "And is it too much to expect that my employees think before they do something that stupid?"

"Sorry . . ." Walt tried to squelch a laugh. "We saw the news coverage. That perp should get an Emmy. You think he'll really sue?"

"Will that ocean out there keep pounding the shore?"

Images rose in Seth's mind: Taylor jogging alongside him, her eyes in the light from the beach fire pit . . . and her face in candlelight as he bent low to kiss her. He turned his attention back to packing. "Got to accept that some things are beyond our control."

"Then again . . . a lot of things work out fine," the older man said, meeting his gaze. "You'll stop by the house before you leave for the airport?"

"Sure. I've still got a few hours before my flight."

Not two minutes after he saw Walt out—and waylaid Lucy

from following—Seth's cell phone rang. His pulse quickened at the caller ID. Taylor, at last. They'd been playing phone tag since yesterday morning.

"Hey," she said, something in her voice he couldn't quite identify. "I got your message. The update on Kasie. So hopeful. But . . . you're flying out early?"

"Yeah. Problems at the Modesto store. Looks like I need to be there." Seth touched the packet of antacids; he'd better stock up. "How are *you* doing?"

"Okay. Better than okay. You're not going to believe this, but I talked with Sloane again."

"When?"

"Yesterday. She asked for me. They were taking her back for emergency surgery, and she said she needed to tell me some things. I think she thought she wasn't going to survive."

Seth thought of Taylor's own survival plan. "And?"

"She did all right. They had to tie off a bleeding vessel, but she's stable now. And . . . I told her I forgive her, Seth. It's more of a work in progress at this point, but I'm going to try my best."

His breath snagged. "Wow."

"I can't even explain how much better I feel. About everything. You were so right. God's planning the steps. He's got this. It's like you said: I was reaching for control when, all the time and all these years, what I really wanted was peace."

Warmth spread through Seth's chest. *Thank you, Lord.*

"And it's like something that Ruthie Marks said too," Taylor continued, a small lilt in her voice. "The grief never really goes away. But I can put it in a special place in my heart, the same way I put my wedding rings back in the jewelry box. I can remember the good things . . . and I can use all that love, and the loss too, to help other people. Like I did yesterday with Sloane. And the way we help as crisis volunteers. You, me. The team. I see that now."

The team.

"Right . . ." Seth tried to swallow around the ache in his throat. It seemed she was coming back. "It all sounds good, Taylor. Really good. I want to hear more." His pulse hiked. "There's something I want to say too. My flight leaves in a couple hours. But I can come over there now."

"Aimee's here," Taylor sighed. "Which would be fine, but I need to leave in a few minutes. There's something I have to do today—it won't wait." It sounded like she chuckled. "I promise it's not an official checklist. But I'm on a sort of roll after Sloane. I have to make things right. I'm meeting Rob at—"

"No problem." Seth snatched up the antacids, ripped open the plastic wrap. "Do what you need to do."

"I could come to the airport," Taylor offered. "If I get everything taken care of in time, I could meet you there. I'll call, regardless—I promise. I wish you didn't have to leave."

And I wish . . . for so much more.

"Give me your flight information," Taylor insisted.

He did that, reciting the time and flight number while chewing the first of two antacids. Taylor wouldn't show. She'd meet Rob Halston for whatever they'd planned . . . and then step right into her shiny new future.

48

"WHAT DO YOU MEAN?" Taylor asked, spooning mini marshmallows into a cup of hot cocoa. She'd pulled the bag from the
freezer this morning and couldn't seem to stop eating them.
"How do I seem different?" She handed a second mug to her
cousin and walked toward the living room. "You mean because
I'm stuffing my face with sugar?"

"There's that." Aimee laughed, following her. "And that
you're wearing a three-sizes-too-big jacket, which I have seen
you sneak a sniff at least twice now."

Taylor's face warmed.

"And then there's that blush," her cousin added. "I'd say
your Sacramento chaplain is the difference."

"He's a friend, Aimee." Taylor sat on the couch, making

room for her cousin. "Maybe the best friend I've ever had."
Her throat tightened. "Seth's been through a lot of the same
things I have." And far more. She thought of his brush with
violence and the resulting consequences. Then his mother's
death, followed by his father's. "He understands. Cares."

"I care for you . . . so much, Taylor."

"It's like he's always been there," Taylor continued, "from
way back. After Greg died. And all the time I was in training
for the crisis team. He'd sort of watch out for me during callouts, make sure I was okay emotionally. And . . ." She smiled.
"Take me out for chocolate cake and sweet potato fries."

Aimee raised her thumb. "Bonus points for the good
chaplain."

"Seth tried to protect me from all that with Greg . . . and
Sloane. I see that now. But I gave him such a bad time when
I found out. I accused him of lying and said some really awful
things."

"But he still showed up here for you and Hooper."

"Yes." Taylor snuggled her cheek against the collar of Seth's
jacket. "Made me soup, cocoa . . . talked me through it all."

Held me while I cried, kissed me . . .

"So . . . may I ask a question?" Aimee's brows rose.

"What, I haven't already bared my soul?"

"It's just . . . I'm trying to picture this guy who belongs to
that big old jacket. I mean, I've seen Dr. Halston. I'm guessing
there aren't two like that." Aimee wrinkled her nose. "So I'm
getting this image . . . Beauty and the Beast?"

"Beast?" Taylor laughed, setting her cup down before
she spilled. "No. Seth is . . ." Her skin warmed again as she
remembered him in that blue shirt at the tapas restaurant,
jogging shirtless down the beach, his crooked smile and those

dark-chocolate eyes . . . "He's beyond amazing. Looks and heart."

"Ah . . ." Aimee's expression, freckles and all, seemed far wiser than her tender years. "And will you wear this amazing man's jacket when you have coffee with the mere mortal plastic surgeon?"

Taylor frowned. "What are you getting at?"

"You said you're not working from a checklist anymore. That's cool. I love that you're feeling so good about doing what's right, for Sloane—" Aimee glanced at the stationery supplies on the breakfast bar—"and for those women from Greg's accident. Plus that fun little errand of mercy we ran this morning." She smiled. "I see that it's all giving you some peace. Like it's making what's always been such a tough day more of a blessing."

"It is." *Thank you, God.*

"But what about *you*, Taylor? What are you doing that's right for you?"

Taylor waited; her cousin was headed somewhere with this.

"Because . . ." Aimee set her cocoa cup down. "From everything you just told me and from that look on your face the whole time, I think there couldn't be anything more right than you and Seth Donovan. So it makes no sense to be on your way to meet another guy for coffee when the man you're falling in love with is about to climb on board an—"

"Love?" Taylor's stomach dropped.

"That's right. I don't think hospital dietary staff is supposed to diagnose, but it sure seems like you have all the symptoms. Hey, sweetie . . ." She reached out, took hold of Taylor's hand. "Don't cry."

"I'm not. . . . Oops, I guess I am." Taylor swiped at her eyes.

Then smiled at her cousin through a prism of tears, certain she must look like a crazy woman. Maybe she *was* a crazy woman. "If that's true, even the teeniest bit possible, then I should . . ." She shook her head, ridiculously giddy and profoundly confused. "I don't know what to do!"

"Hold on." Aimee bit back a laugh. "First, take a breath. Slow breath—good. Now I think you should call Dr. Halston and say something came up."

"Right." Taylor nodded. Her hands were shaking. "And then . . . Oh, my gosh, Seth's flight! If I'm going to make it to the airport to catch him before he boards, I should—"

"Call him. Tell him you're on your way. Then get yourself together. Run a brush through your hair, throw on some of that lip gloss, and—" Aimee touched Taylor's face. "Never mind. Go exactly the way you are. I don't think you've ever looked more beautiful."

"But . . ." Taylor's mind tumbled. "What if Seth doesn't feel the same way? What if I'm wrong? What if—?"

"The only way to find out is to put one foot in front of the other and head through that door." Aimee chuckled. "But change out of those panda bear slippers. It's too hard to dash through an airport like that."

"Okay. Right—shoes." Taylor laughed, despite a rush of jitters. "What would I ever do without you?"

"You'll never have to find out."

Aimee stayed long enough to hear Taylor leave a message for Rob, then gave her a fierce hug and was out the door. Three minutes later, Taylor's thoughts were still tumbling. That she'd ever been a compulsive list maker seemed impossible now. Bullet points were as incomprehensible as hieroglyphics. But she knew she had to do exactly what Aimee suggested. It felt completely right, a sureness Taylor hadn't experienced in such a long time.

"If I'm going in the right direction, if I'm on the right path, I'll feel that certainty in my soul."

Seth's words describing exactly what Taylor was feeling. *Today, March 26.* It was beyond staggering. She'd prayed and plotted, counting mere survival as success. When all the time God had such an incredible plan. Taylor snatched her phone off the breakfast bar. The plan was awesome, the hope dizzying, but if she didn't get cracking and call Seth, find her shoes, and—

Taylor's phone rang. *Aimee?* She'd barely left.

"Where are you?" Taylor chided. "In my driveway?"

"Just turned around in the cul-de-sac. Stopped across the street."

"Well, you don't need to check up on me. I'm *doing* it," Taylor promised, carrying the phone toward the bedroom. "I'm going to call Seth. Then find my shoes, grab my purse, get in my car, and—"

"Forget it."

"What?" Taylor stopped in the hallway. "What do you mean?"

"No need to go jogging through the airport." There was a definite grin in Aimee's voice. "I see a big red puppy on your lawn. With an *amazing*-looking man."

49

"I COULD LEAVE HER in the crate," Seth began as Lucy wriggled and danced on the porch, eager to get closer to Taylor. He knew that feeling far too well. She looked so beautiful standing there with that look of surprise on her face. Wearing his jacket . . . "But she'd probably howl and drive your neighbors crazy," he added, aching to pull Taylor into his arms. "So maybe you could come out? Walk around the cul-de-sac? I won't stay more than a few minutes."

"Your flight was delayed?"

"Canceled. I canceled the flight." He tried to read her expression, feeling like he was leaping from a plane without a parachute. At this point, he didn't care. "I needed to see you, Taylor. I know you said you were going out, so I won't stay long but—"

"It's okay." She crouched down to rub Lucy's ears, laughing as the pup licked at her face. Taylor looked up at Seth, and something in her eyes made his breath catch. "I'm glad you're here."

His throat closed.

"Come in," she told him, straightening up again. Lucy strained against the leash, whining. "Both of you."

"Her manners aren't much better than mine. Your house is so clean and white."

"Chaplain Donovan," Taylor insisted, stepping back through the doorway, "if you and Lucy don't come inside right now, I'm going to be the one howling and disturbing the neighbors."

He smiled. "Yes, ma'am."

———

"Who's this Marty?"

Sloane opened her eyes, realizing she must have dozed off again. The narcotics were a mercy and a threat. They eased the pain but loosened her tongue far too much. She could barely distinguish between what she dreamed, thought to herself, or rambled on about aloud. Not good when talking with a detective. She met the fiftysomething woman's gaze, willing the drug's haziness to dissipate. "What did you just ask?"

"About Marty." The detective's smile was kind. Probably well rehearsed. "You were asking about him . . . or her? A couple of times now."

"Yeah." Sloane winced. "It's nothing—nobody. A pink elephant, maybe." A ripple of sadness ruined her attempt at a smirk. *Today is the twenty-sixth. . . .*

"I know you're tired," the detective said. "I only have a few more questions. Routine. As I explained before, you're not in any trouble."

Sloane almost laughed at the ridiculous assurance. She was responsible for Greg Cabot's death, Kasie's traumatic brain injury, and—

"The accident resulted in two fatalities," the woman continued, confirming Sloane's culpability as effectively as a gavel thump, "and multiple serious injuries. Including yours, of course. It's important we apprehend the person responsible. The driver who forced you off the highway."

"The car was found . . . burned. I heard that."

"That's correct. But it was a stolen vehicle. Several witnesses reported that your car was targeted by that driver. Struck from the rear more than once."

"I don't really remember," Sloane lied. She wondered if Kasie would remember. If she woke up. Sloane took a breath to dispel a wave of nausea.

"And you have no reason to believe anyone might have been trying to harm you personally? You've had no threats?"

"No."

Only phone calls from her nonexistent brother. Sloane battled a shiver, remembering her ex's warning that those men might come after her to put pressure on him.

"You spent some time at the Deep Blue Grill that evening," the detective said. "In the bar. That evening and other times too."

It was a statement, not a question. The implication was there regardless of the detective's professional manner: *You're that kind of woman.*

"Security camera footage from the vicinity shows the stolen vehicle," the detective continued. "Is it possible you had contact with the driver during your time at the Grill? Maybe struck up a conversation or . . . ?"

Bile rose in Sloane's throat. Could he have followed her there?

"Miss Wilder?"

"No. I . . ." Sloane fought an urge to tell the detective everything. Get it off her chest the same way she'd come clean with Taylor. But it wasn't the same. She'd told Taylor the truth about Greg because . . . it was the right thing to do. Resenting her, blaming Donovan all these years had done nothing to ease Sloane's pain or stop those awful memories. It was like protecting herself with a flak vest of barbed wire. It kept anyone from getting too close, but every movement, every breath, bit into her skin . . . *and my soul?*

"You didn't have a dispute with another bar patron?" the detective pressed. "Maybe someone trying to force unwanted attention—"

"No," Sloane said, forcefully enough to cause a stab of pain in her throat, still raw from the endotracheal tube. "I don't remember anything like that. And look . . . I'm tired. I don't want to talk anymore."

"Of course." The detective pulled a card from her notebook and set it on the tray table. "If you think of anything that might be helpful, please give me a call."

"Sure."

"Thank you." The concern in the woman's eyes seemed genuine, less like a cop and more like a mother. "I hope you feel better. And that things work out . . . with Marty, too."

"Right."

Sloane glanced away before the departing detective could see her tears. Things would not work out for Marty, but at least today would end the cruelty that had marked his young life.

One more item added to the long list of awful things Sloane had caused with hers. Greg, Kasie, those freeway fatalities . . . and now Marty.

"None of this would have happened if you'd been responsible enough to find yourself a twelve-step program."

Taylor's words in the ER after Sloane had stupidly, stubbornly blamed Kasie for taking the Jetta over the cliff. Taylor had been furious . . . and right. So right. It was too late for Greg—an ache spread across Sloane's chest—and the others. There was no way she could rescue Marty now. But she hadn't died on the OR table; she was going to walk out of this hospital. Which meant she could walk into an AA meeting. As many meetings as it took to get clean. It wouldn't change everything; Sloane wasn't enough of a fool to believe that. At least if she got sober, there was less of a chance that her bad choices would take anyone else down with her. She wouldn't be hooking up with a "Higher Power," but she'd be cheating the devil. It was a fair trade.

"First we're going to pray. And then I'm going to walk alongside you to the surgery doors. And try, with everything I have left . . . to forgive you."

Sloane closed her eyes. Taylor had done that. Forgiven her. The memory was dim—their walk to the surgery doors, Taylor's whisper. The effects of shock and the narcotics had left it all hazy, but they'd talked back and forth for a minute or so. Something about God and grace . . . She couldn't remember much. Except the profound sense of comfort and peace she'd felt at a moment she needed it most. For that, Sloane would always be grateful.

A tear slid down her cheek.

Good-bye, Marty . . .

50

"SHE'S FINE," Taylor insisted, watching as Lucy made another circuit around the living room, all glossy red against the white decor and happily poking her nose into every nook and hollow. "Probably smells Hooper. He was a few months younger than Lucy when I met Greg." She thought of how she'd banned the mention of Greg and God the last time Seth crossed her threshold. It seemed a lifetime ago. So many things had changed.

Thank you, Lord. And please see me through this now.

"I think . . . ," she said, turning to Seth, beside her on the couch. "I think I suspected Greg had been seeing someone else. I wanted to know . . . and I didn't. I wanted to put it aside, but I couldn't. It was like I had this slow simmer of anger. At God, too."

Seth stayed quiet, his very presence a gift.

"'Anger lives in sorrow's house,'" she said softly. "You quoted Max Lucado. At the pilot's funeral, after Ava went ballistic over those programs. I couldn't see it in myself."

"We never do."

"So I dumped it on Rob, on you and Sloane . . . while I hung on to Hooper because I was sure he was all I had left."

"Far from it, Taylor." The look in Seth's eyes made her heart ache.

"I know that now. Finding out that Greg's relationship with Sloane was a sort of emotional affair—I guess that's what people call it—maybe that helps a little. But I think forgiving him, her . . . and forgiving *myself* for all these stubborn, angry years helps far more. I'd worked so hard at forgetting, and it didn't seem fair that I had to forgive, too. But it gives me so much peace, Seth. It makes it finally feel right to move on."

He held her gaze. "I can't tell you how good it makes me feel to hear that."

"So . . ." Taylor's heart hummed in her ears. "Tell me why you canceled your flight."

———

Seth inhaled slowly; how could he explain it all?

"There was some sort of an emergency at one of the stores?" Taylor prompted.

"Right. Part-time salesclerk—full-time superhero—decided to zap a shoplifter with a Taser." Seth saw Taylor's brows rise. "Yep. And now the 'victim' plans to sue Donovan's."

"But that's . . ." Taylor shook her head. "So it fell on you to handle it."

"Yes. Or I figured it did. Until I got ready to turn Lucy over to air cargo and there was a glitch in the paperwork. It gave me time to think. I remembered something Kasie said to me about how hard she'd worked at trying to make her father proud. He was an LA police officer, killed off duty."

Taylor winced.

"Yeah. She hoped that her work with the crisis team would be something he'd approve of. Kasie's mother said her father would have been proud of anything Kasie did—he loved her that much. Walt said something very similar to me about his kids. When we were talking about my decision to take over the uniform stores full-time and stop working with California Crisis Care."

"What? But the directorship . . ."

"I know," Seth said, anticipating the surprise in her expression. "We'd had an offer to buy the business, but I turned it down because I thought my father expected me to stay on and run it. Probably because I thought I'd disappointed him by not becoming a police officer. Which I probably only pursued to make him proud in the first place." Seth shook his head. "Trust me, God knows how to use an air cargo glitch. Cosmic truths were hitting like a meteor shower."

"And?"

"I thought . . . if I had children, what would I want for them? If they felt a real calling and had a chance to do something that satisfied their souls, wouldn't that be what made me proud?" Seth's throat tightened a little. "Wouldn't that be exactly what I prayed for?"

Taylor's hand covered his.

"So I told air cargo to give me back my dog, called the lawyer, and told him to tell the buyer I've changed my mind;

I want to sell the business. And then . . . I thought about you, Taylor."

"Me?"

"Yes." He turned his hand over, grasped hers gently. "All that pressure I was putting on you about the crisis team. You were right; the training class was only part of the reason I came to San Diego. I'd seen your name disappearing from the call schedule and told myself I was going to find out why— convince you to come back. It's true that I believe you're a natural chaplain and a great fit with the team. But I think I put pressure on you because of my own indecision about quitting. I wanted you to stay on if I couldn't. But mostly, I think . . ." Seth held Taylor's gaze as his heart climbed toward his throat. "I came here because I was afraid I was losing you."

She watched his eyes, stayed silent.

"When I saw you, the changes you'd made, how hard you were working to move on with your life, and what's going on with Halston, I—"

"It's not."

"What?"

"Nothing's going on with Rob." Taylor's expression was thoughtful. "In case you didn't notice, I'm here with you."

"Only because I canceled my flight and showed up on your doorstep with my crazy red puppy." Seth glanced around for her. "Uh-oh, where—?"

"Don't worry about Lucy." Taylor gave his hand a squeeze. "Why are you here? I need to know."

Lord . . . talk to me like I'm standing in air cargo.

"I wanted to say this before," Seth began. "After that night on the beach when we talked by the fire. And that first time you invited me here to your place. Then the other night, when we were sitting up with Hooper." He watched her eyes. "I had so many things I wanted to say to you, Taylor. But the timing didn't feel right because you had so much going on. I thought we'd have one more day. Then I got the call about the business. And you said you were meeting Halston and—"

"I canceled," she added, taking Seth totally by surprise. Hope teased his heart. "And I was about to leave for the airport . . . to find *you*."

51

"YOU WERE . . . coming to me?" Seth's deep voice caught. He'd never looked so handsome. Taylor knew he was going to ask—"Why?"

"I needed to see you," she began, feeling once again like she'd taken over the controls of a careening plane. No, this could be good. It *was* good. Hopeful, like a kite lifted high. God had this. "I didn't want to lose you, either, Seth. After all that happened and how much better I'm feeling . . . I can see how much you're a part of that. The best part."

Taylor's heart was beating her senseless, but the beautiful kindness in Seth's eyes encouraged her on. He'd taken both her hands in his; she was trembling. "I was coming to the airport to tell you how much you mean to me. How much I care.

In a way I never understood before . . . or maybe I started to, the other night when we kissed. But . . ." Taylor frowned, frustrated with herself. "I'm not saying this right. But I was coming to the airport to see if there was a chance that you might feel—"

"I'm in love with you."

Her breath caught. "I think that's what I was going to say."

"You . . . think?" Seth's lips curved into his dear, crooked smile. "You think you love me?" He touched her activity bracelet. "According to specific parameters, factors . . . a series of steps in an equation?"

"No." Taylor pressed her shaky hand over her heart. "According to this. Right in here. And . . ." Seth drew her hand back and tenderly kissed her fingertips, causing her senses to swirl. "You're so . . . impossible," she managed to say. "I'm trying to tell you I love you and you're teasing me."

"Nope." Seth's expression grew serious. "Crisis management. I'm trying to keep this forty-year-old heart from exploding. It's not working." He cradled Taylor's face in his hand. "Say it again. Please."

"I love you." Taylor blinked at him through a happy blur of tears. She'd never seen anything more clearly. "I love you, Seth. So much. And—"

Seth's kiss stopped her words. Then tried to take her breath away.

His mouth moved over hers tenderly at first, then more thoroughly as she wrapped her arms around him, responding with a passion both remembered and wonderfully new. His solid warmth, his eagerness were comforting and exciting all at once. She felt treasured, beautifully alive, and . . . Taylor giggled, almost a purr, as Seth nibbled at her neck, hiked her closer against him, and then pressed kisses on her cheek, her nose, her chin, before finding her lips again. Her skin tingled, pulse skittering.

"*Yip, yip—woof! Yyyyowwww!*"

"What . . . ?" Taylor asked, leaning away.

"*Aaagh.*" Seth groaned. "Lucy . . ." He glanced toward the hallway. "I'd better go see what—"

"*Yyooooow! Pfft! Woof!*"

"Oh, boy. I forgot." Taylor turned to watch as Lucy bounded into the room, chased closely by—

"What's that?" Seth blurted, staring.

"That—" Taylor laughed as Lucy yipped again and the tiny black fur ball crow-hopped sideways, his back arched and eyes wide—"is Marty."

———

"Kasie, hold on to my fingers . . . just a little. I'm right here."

She drew in a breath and felt the triggered whoosh of air from the ventilator fill her lungs, then swallowed against the plastic tube in her throat. So sore, but not as sore as her head . . . *Ugh, it hurts.* It was all so confusing. Darkness, beeps, awful smells, and garbled voices.

"Squeeze me back, Kasie. Right here. Feel me touching you?"

She tried to swallow again. Then battled the fog and darkness, swimming up through murky water, toward the surface of—

"Kasie! Oh, dear God, thank you! Can you see me, sweetheart?"

She blinked, squinted against the light. Tried to fix her eyes on . . . Kasie made a futile attempt to speak. Then grabbed tightly on to the warm, familiar fingers as the image came into focus. Tears slid down her face.

Mom . . .

———

"They took Kasie off the ventilator," Seth reported, slipping the cell phone back into his pocket. He smiled at Taylor, sitting in the sand beside him. Once she'd explained how she'd rescued the kitten for Sloane, she'd insisted on loading Lucy into the car and driving to the Ocean Beach boardwalk. Seth would rather have stayed put, kissing Taylor a thousand times more, but he'd said sure, a run might be good. Except what Taylor really had in mind was—"How's that ice cream?"

"Great . . . perfect." She grinned at him, a frosty dollop of pink on her chin. "*So* worth waiting for."

Seth's heart squeezed. He couldn't have said it better.

"That's wonderful about Kasie," Taylor said, feeding a piece of the waffle cone to his mooching dog. "Is there a rehab plan?"

"Her mother's making arrangements to move her home to LA as soon as she gets the okay."

"And Daniel?"

"I don't know." Seth gazed out at the sea. "He's not sure he wants to be part of that." What he'd actually told Seth was that he wasn't sure if he wanted to be involved at all anymore. He couldn't get past the idea that it was Kasie's fault she was in the situation she was, that if she'd only listened to him, it wouldn't have gotten so out of control. "I'm hoping he sees the bigger picture in time," he added. "That the plan isn't all in our hands."

Taylor's gaze held his, the waning sun picking out those copper flecks in her eyes. "You're so wise."

He smiled. "You mean old."

She laughed around her last mouthful of cone. "I meant that you've been spot-on about so many things. Like when you told me you don't need to count steps to know you're going in the right direction."

Seth reached out to capture a wisp of hair the breeze tossed across her eyes. Then stroked her cheek. "You remember that?"

"I couldn't stop turning it over in my head. How you said the future would move forward according to God's timing, not ours. And how sometimes our need for control can become our god if we let it. How we reach for that . . ."

"When all we really want is peace."

"Yes." Her lips curved into the smile that sent his heart jogging. "And ice cream. Now I have that, too."

"There's a lot more where that came from," Seth told her. "Come here, you."

He reached for her, nudging Lucy back. Then hugged Taylor tightly and kissed her, savoring a sweetness that was better than strawberry ice cream. A promise of something he'd prayed for and—

Taylor leaned away. She was smiling but . . . were those tears in her eyes?

"Is something wrong?"

"No." She kissed him lightly and gazed into his eyes. "It's perfect. I just . . ." She shook her head, an incredulous look on her face. "That crazy list I made. There was something on it, one last thing that I thought was impossible, but now . . ."

"What?" Seth asked, knowing he'd spend the rest of his life loving this incredible woman. Doing everything possible to make her happy. "What was on your list?"

"You," she said, resting her palm against his face. "I didn't know it. But God did. He gave me . . . you."

Seth folded Taylor into his arms again, close enough to feel her heart beating along with his as they gazed out at the sea. Lucy stirred beside them and Seth saw what she saw: a couple of kids eagerly launching kites into the sky. SpongeBob and Superman. He smiled. It felt full circle somehow, except that this time it was happiness and not crisis on the horizon. This time it felt like they were walking into a hope-filled future. Step by step.

EPILOGUE

"You look absolutely beautiful," Taylor said, handing her cousin a ribbon-wrapped bouquet—an autumn mix, each flower carefully chosen for its bold, vibrant color. Petals as yellow as the coastal sun, a deep burnished copper, rich burgundy, along with a staggering array of purples. Not a single prim, classic, "must-have" stephanotis or dewy-chaste white rosebud in the mix. It was a bouquet as beautiful as a sunset, as joyful and celebratory as the gift of forever love. Aimee's softly understated gown, her sweet beauty were the perfect complements to that floral extravagance. Taylor loved it. She loved everything about today.

"And maybe a teeny bit nervous, too?" Taylor observed as

her cousin's glittering engagement ring trembled in the chapel's overhead lighting. "Though it's not as if wedding prep hasn't been on your mind 24-7 these days. . . ."

"You're right. But this, right now . . ." Aimee peeked through the stone archway at the assembled guests. She turned back to Taylor, her green eyes lighting. "I think I'm more excited than nervous, really. It's almost like I looked up *happily ever after* and found a photo of exactly this. So wonderful." She reached for Taylor's hand, her eyes brimming with sudden tears. "Of course, you know that."

"I do." Taylor shifted her own bouquet to give Aimee a warm hug. This day was exactly as it should be. A celebration of love and God's grace. What could be more perfect?

"I think we'll be ready to roll in a few minutes now," Aimee said, glancing toward the archway again. "The guests are all seated. The little boys look so cute in those bow ties. I think half of San Diego Hope is there. Aren't you going to peek?"

"No." Taylor shook her head, a wavy tendril from her upswept hair brushing the modest sweep of her gown's neckline. There was no need to peek. She could imagine it all. Their parents, grandparents . . . siblings, a handful of cousins, Lucas looking so handsome in his dark suit, and . . . Taylor's heart hitched. And Seth was—

"Showtime, Cousin," Aimee prompted as the beaming father of the bride walked toward them. He winked at the maid of honor, then captured his daughter's gaze with love and pride in his expression. Strains of music rose in the distance, stirring an unexpected flutter of butterflies in Taylor's stomach—choreography to the tune of happily ever after. Dear, sweet Aimee was wrong—*wonderful* didn't begin to describe this amazing day.

"Ready?"

Taylor smiled. "Absolutely. Let's do this."

———

Sloane tapped the screen of her laptop, watching the Facebook page update as each photo followed the next. Kasie Beckett was posting from her cell phone right now, real time. That she could manage such physical dexterity meant her rehab was going well. Such a huge relief . . .

The wedding photos continued to upload: The stunning redheaded cousins in simple but elegant gowns and wide smiles—"radiant," people would probably say—and those little boys, clowning and mugging for the camera. Old folks dancing—grandparents, probably. A few other people looked vaguely familiar, from Sacramento maybe. A slightly out-of-focus close-up of the bridal bouquet appeared, followed by a silly shot of the bride's and maid of honor's glittery sandals and matching pedicures. . . . Then there was the best man, raising his glass in a toast. Followed by several photos of the sunset over the ocean. Classic San Diego. It seemed so far away now.

Sloane sighed. *It is so far away.*

She shifted on the lumpy, leased couch, felt Marty's rumbling purr as he resettled on her lap. Then watched the screen, seeing more photos appear. More guests. Faces from San Diego Hope—a few she hadn't expected: Ava Sandison, the woman who'd lost her husband in the plane crash all those months ago. And that library cart volunteer, Ruth something . . .

Sloane's throat tightened as another grouping of photos posted. The bride and groom, holding each other. Kissing . . . smiling and gazing into each other's eyes.

Taylor and Seth . . . They'd accomplished it. Love and a second chance.

It was rare. And despite those things Taylor had said about God's mercy and grace, it was too hard to believe Sloane could ever have all that. She reached up, touched her fingertips to the still-pink scars on her face. No . . . happiness was too far a stretch for someone like her. Right now, she would have to settle for what she had here. A new address, new car, new phone number, new job, and . . . Sloane smiled at the sleeping kitten, his black paws kneading the leg of her jeans. "You," she said aloud. "I have you, Marty. We have each other. That's something."

She glanced at the time on the laptop screen. The AA meeting started in forty minutes. She'd get her six-month chip tonight. That was something too. It wasn't bouquets, wedding gowns, and fancy pedicures, but it was a step in a better direction. One day at a time.

———

"A duffel bag?" Taylor teased as Seth pulled the worn Army rucksack from his overly decorated car; the crisis team had loaded it up with *Just Married* soap lettering, a string of plastic soda bottles, metallic streamers, and dozens of balloons—the backseat was filled to overflowing with them. It was a miracle they hadn't been cited by a traffic cop, though most of the officers would probably have yelped their sirens in congratulations and then escorted them the rest of the way.

"I don't know," Taylor continued, laughing as a couple of balloons bounced from the car and took off down the cul-de-sac. The glow from the streetlight illuminated her face and her hair, fallen into loose curls after dancing in the sand. She had never looked as beautiful. "Couldn't you find more glamorous luggage for your wedding night, Mr. Donovan?"

Seth laughed. "In case you hadn't noticed, glamour isn't high on my priority list."

"I'm not sure about that. From where I'm standing . . ." The look in Taylor's eyes made Seth's skin shiver as she reached up to give his silk tie a playful tug. "James Bond himself never looked so good in a tux."

"Well . . ." He smiled, patting the battered Army bag. "You'll be wishing I always traveled this light when we're unpacking the U-Haul tomorrow."

After they'd finalized the purchase option on her house, they'd combined some of their belongings, things Seth couldn't keep with him at Walt's place. And Taylor had insisted he help her choose new paint for the interior walls: *Living, breathing color. I'm finished with all that lonely white.* He had no doubt their future together would be filled with color and far from lonely. And that their home would be alive with laughter and the joyful noise of children. Redheads probably.

"You can't fool me," Taylor said, her gown rustling as she snuggled close against him in the darkness. "You probably have crisis team call schedules in that duffel bag too."

"Maybe." He smiled, breathing in the scent of her hair and wondering why on earth he was hanging around in the driveway like a smitten teenager when they could be—

Taylor rose on her toes and kissed Seth's chin. "You can inform the amazing new director of California Crisis Care that his wife has other plans tonight."

"He respects that." Seth chuckled and pulled her closer. "Besides . . ." He patted the bag. "I also have travel brochures in here. We have a honeymoon to plan. We'll need to talk about that." He bent down to give his wife a lingering kiss. "Maybe sometime tomorrow. Or late the next day . . ."

"No rush. Plenty of time for talking," Taylor purred, melting against him. She wound her arms around his neck, tilting her face up for another kiss, and—

"Congratulations!" a neighbor called out from across the street. "All good wishes, you two lovebirds!"

"Thank you," they said, laughing. Apparently there was nothing subtle about newlyweds making out on the driveway—in the direct path of a balloon tidal wave. Married . . . *my wife*—it still stunned Seth. It didn't seem possible that only six months ago he'd walked up this same driveway to sit a vigil with Taylor and her beloved dog. A man with a limp and a past, a woman yearning for peace and a future. Friends first—friends always. But once they'd accepted their growing feelings, it seemed pointless to wait any longer. They wanted to start building a life together as soon as possible. There were no doubts it was God's plan unfolding.

"Let's get inside before we draw a crowd," Seth suggested, taking Taylor's hand.

"Good idea."

He set his duffel on the porch, pulled his set of keys from his pocket, unlocked the door, and—

"Oh no, you're *not* . . ." Taylor giggled as he began scooping her up in his arms.

"Try to stop me," Seth told her, dealing with yards of rustling fabric and loving the feel of her breath against his neck. He nudged the door open with his foot, stepped across the threshold, began to kiss his bride again . . . and heard a crescendo of frantic and eager barking from the direction of the back patio doors.

They looked at each other and laughed, then shouted it out together:

"Lucy . . . we're home!"

1

"YOUR RELATION TO THE INMATE?"

Sloane Ferrell's stomach tensed. "He's my stepfather," she confirmed, lips brushing her cell phone in a whisper. "It was . . . manslaughter."

She glanced past a grouping of palm trees toward the peach stucco entrance to Los Angeles Hope hospital's emergency department. Would she ever stop peering over her shoulder—watching her back? This past year it had felt as necessary as breathing and was the biggest part of why she'd left San Diego. New zip code, new living space, new job . . . a paper trail painstakingly shredded. She'd done all that, and thankfully, the last few months had been uneventful. Right now, Sloane was simply concerned that a fellow ER nurse would join her at any moment. She'd said something about taking their break together. This return call from California State Prison couldn't have come at a more awkward—

"We don't have you listed," the office assistant announced. Her tone was as friendly as the slam of a cell door. "It had to be arranged in advance and approved."

"I did that—and I was," Sloane insisted over the distant whine-hum of saws; preliminary work had begun on the new hospital wing. "I was promised a chance to speak at the parole hearing. My name *has* to be on the list. Could you check again?"

"Hang on."

Sloane closed her eyes and let the late September sun warm her face, a light breeze sifting strands of her dark hair. She pretended the construction sounds were ocean waves, imagining salt-laden moisture on her skin and the keening calls of gulls. She missed San Diego, even if it had started out as a place to escape to—and ended up as one more place to run from. Her fingertips found the still-pink scars around her left eye, from the accident that could have killed her. The short time in San Diego had changed her life, but how that would play out remained to be seen. Nothing was guaranteed. Especially not for someone like Sloane. Life had taught her that in strokes as bold as freeway graffiti. But right now all that mattered was—

"Nope," the woman reported. "I've checked twice. Nobody by the name of Ferrell on the list."

Sloane blinked. "It's . . . Wilder."

"You said Ferrell."

I did? Sloane bit back a groan. "It's Ferrell now. When I filled out the paperwork, it was Wilder." New zip code . . .

new name. "I'm sorry; I forgot. But I'm sure you'll find me under that name. Wilder. *W-i-l-d*—"

"Sloane!"

She turned, saw her friend waving.

Harper Tatum strode forward, long hair tossed by the breeze and stethoscope swinging against her watermelon-red scrub top. A Los Angeles native—an "Angeleno"—she was honey blonde, long limbed, and as effervescent as a shaken can of soda. Nothing at all like Sloane. This nurse's smile appeared in a TV commercial for whitening toothpaste, and she'd recently been signed as a foot model for a local day spa's magazine ad. *"Grasping fame, tooth and nail,"* Harper liked to joke. She was a sharp, skilled nurse every hour of every shift, and a model and aspiring actress every off-duty moment—until her student loans were paid in full.

Sloane returned Harper's wave and then hurried to wrap things up with the woman on the phone. "Got to go. It's Wilder, Sloane Wilder. Find me."

Find me? She almost choked on the irony.

"Hey," she said as Harper took a seat across from her at the visitors' table.

"Hey yourself, pal."

Sloane smiled. It was hard not to like this nurse—one of the few things she didn't have to overthink or completely fabricate. Not even six months ago, she'd have shot the gregarious coworker a back-off look but . . . "They let you out."

"Finally." Harper pointed at Sloane's phone on the red-tile table. "I interrupted you. Anybody date-worthy?" She arched a brow.

"No such luck." Sloane feigned a casual shrug, reminding herself that real friends were too much of a risk. She couldn't imagine telling Harper she'd changed her name to avoid the dangerous consequences of her last serious relationship. Or that the only "date" she cared about was a parole board hearing at the state prison.

"Nothing like the soul-soothing ambience of power tools," Harper pronounced over the staccato whap-thwack of a pneumatic nail gun. "Though I do like the contrast: men in hard hats, steel-toed boots, and layers of sawdust making it happen, while—" she nodded toward the ER doors behind them—"our man in a sports jacket and khakis hustles to get it all funded."

Sloane saw what Harper did: Micah Prescott, the new assistant director of the hospital's marketing and public relations department. He was early thirties, probably, with a lean build, sandy hair, sunglasses, and an undoubtedly practiced smile. An ad man with a well-appointed office a safe distance from stat pages and messy trauma, who preferred cash procurement over lifesaving. It was the kind of career that required finesse, charm, and an aptitude for creative spin. Unfortunately, Sloane knew the type far too well. Micah Prescott was the kind of person she tried avoid at all costs.

Harper watched as the marketing man was joined by two young men with cameras slung over their shoulders. "It's still five months until the official launch of the Face of Hope campaign, but Micah's already stirring things up and getting interest from the media. Of course, he's no rookie when it comes to publicity. With his connections and all."

Apparently the extended Prescott family was involved in the music industry—Christian recording artists and performers. Enormously popular, Harper had said more than once. Not surprisingly, Sloane had never heard of them. She only knew that she didn't like the intrusive scrutiny this marketing campaign brought with it—a "star search" for an employee who best personified the spirit of the hospital's mission. The campaign kickoff had coincided with the groundbreaking for the new wing, an event headlined by a megastar film couple, an impressive sampling from the roster of the Los Angeles Lakers, and even the diminutive widow of a much-beloved former president. The event immediately spawned rallies with staff, endless surveys, and photo shoots. There were days it felt more like a casting call than a workplace. Sloane avoided all of it as best she could. This past year had taught her that a low profile meant safety.

"Imagine it: your face on a billboard," Harper said, sweeping her hand in an arc as if the palm trees had been magically replaced by those old spotlights at movie premieres. "The Face of Hope. Looking down on the freeway. The 405 or the 101—both maybe. Thousands and thousands of people seeing it every day, for hours at a time, LA traffic being what it is. And smog willing." Her brows puckered. "You don't look too thrilled by the idea."

"I'll pass," Sloane told her, feeling a prickle of panic. Ridiculous—it would never happen. Besides, she'd changed her name, and there had been no threatening calls in months. If she got caught in the background of some publicity photo, no one would notice. "Anyway, I'm still on probationary status. You're a far more likely candidate. You're comfortable in front of a camera and—"

"And you are drop-dead gorgeous, my friend." Harper wrinkled her nose. "I probably shouldn't say 'drop dead,' considering our line of work. But I'm not kidding. The last woman to claim eyes like that was Liz Taylor. And even if you do your best to hide your light under a bushel, it's there. Not just looks.

The real deal." Harper's expression turned best-friend kind. "I see how you are with the patients. Especially our lost souls, people with nobody and nothing—and bad choices up to their eyeballs. Most of us draw straws to avoid dealing with them. But it's like you champion those people, Sloane. And you're not afraid to butt heads with management or stretch some policies to do that."

"Butt heads?" Sloane grimaced. "Did I mention probation?"

Harper laughed. "I don't think there's going to be a problem. I'm on the performance review committee."

Sloane hoped her smile wasn't as weak as it felt. This nurse was intent on making her into a Mother Teresa, when nothing could be further from the truth. What was altruistic about simply recognizing her own kind? Poor choices? How many had she made in her thirty-two years—how many more would tempt her? Someone like Harper would never understand. And right now Sloane's priority was simple: be there, Wilder or Ferrell, to make herself heard at Bob Bullard's parole hearing. Nothing felt more important. Until then, she needed to travel under the radar. Close relationships, friendships or otherwise, fit nowhere in that plan.

"We should get together away from the hospital sometime," Harper suggested, glancing toward the parking lot as a car with a noisy muffler screeched to the curb. "A movie, maybe. Or out to eat. I've heard good things about The Misfit in Santa Monica. They start happy hour at like noon. Five-dollar lunch specials, and it's all done sort of vintage French 'literary' décor, with card catalogs, shelves of old books, and those tall, tin ceilings." Her toothpaste smile gleamed. "You even get a free chocolate chip–sea salt cookie along with the bill for your cocktails and—"

"I don't drink," Sloane said in a rush, hating that it sounded rude.

"I don't either, really. I just thought . . ."

"My evenings are pretty booked. Because . . ." Sloane hesitated. Lying used to be much easier. "I'm taking some classes."

"No problem—good for you." Harper looked toward what sounded like a disturbance at the curb. That same car. "What's going on over there?"

"I can't tell for sure." Sloane stared, thinking it must be an argument—a man's voice rose above the background construction noises. A young woman wearing a black cap over pink hair opened the car's passenger door and attempted to slide out, but . . . Sloane stood, getting a bad feeling about the situation.

"Do they need help?" Harper asked, craning her neck to see. "It looks like that man is—"

"No!" the young woman shrieked, struggling to stand as the driver leaned across the passenger seat and gave her arm a savage yank. She dropped to one knee on the cement curb and pulled back, beginning to sob. The man grabbed a handful of her T-shirt, jerking her backward. She screamed again. "Stop! Let me go!"

Harper gasped, rising to her feet.

The car rolled forward, half-dragging the girl. "Help me!"

"Call 911!" Sloane ordered, then bolted for the parking lot.

ACKNOWLEDGMENTS

HEARTFELT APPRECIATION TO:

Literary agent Natasha Kern—you are such a blessing.

The awesome Tyndale House publishing team, especially Shaina Turner and editors Jan Stob, Sarah Mason Rische, and Erin Smith—you make my stories shine.

Fellow author and critique partner Nancy Herriman—you're the best.

My invaluable resources:

Chaplain Mindi Russell, executive director of Law Enforcement Chaplaincy of Sacramento, and David Vincent, director of US Crisis Care—I can't thank you enough for your help and inspiration.

The San Diego Police Department—your kind welcome to your beautiful city was most appreciated.

Sarah Peer, foster mom to countless rescue kittens—your help with Marty was priceless.

Daughter-in-law and veterinarian Wendy MacKinnon—your compassionate direction regarding Hooper meant so much.

Any inaccuracies, or changes to accommodate fictional portrayals, are mine alone.

Finally, to my wonderful family, especially my husband, Andy—I couldn't do this without your loving support.

And with deep appreciation to my readers—it is my great joy to bring you stories of hope. Thank you for your encouragement.

ABOUT THE AUTHOR

CANDACE CALVERT is a former ER nurse and author of the Mercy Hospital series—*Critical Care*, *Disaster Status*, and *Code Triage*—the Grace Medical series—*Trauma Plan*, *Rescue Team*, and *Life Support*—and the Crisis Team series—*By Your Side* and *Step by Step*. Her medical dramas offer readers a chance to "scrub in" on the exciting world of emergency medicine. Wife, mother, and very proud grandmother, Candace makes her home in northern California. Visit her website at www.candacecalvert.com.

More from
Candace Calvert

RESCUE TEAM

TRAUMA PLAN

LIFE SUPPORT

THE GRACE MEDICAL SERIES

Critical Care

Disaster Status

Code Triage

THE MERCY HOSPITAL SERIES